ALISON G. BAILEY

ISBN: 1482772973
ISBN-13: 978-1482772975

Interior book design by Angela McLaurin, Fictional Formats

Edited by Maria DeSouza

Cover design by Robin Harper, Wicked By Design

Photographer: Lorie Rebecca
Lorierebecca@yahoo.com
www.lorierebecca.com

Cover Model: Mackenzie Marie

Dedication

To my mom, Helen, and the memory of my dad, Dreher.
Thank you for giving me the strength of character,
the ability to hope, and the invaluable gift of humor.

Acknowledgements

I sat at the computer alone and wrote Present Perfect, but this book is far from a solo project. There were so many wonderful people that had a hand in bringing this book to life.

To Jef Bailey: Thank you for your complete support. You were patient while I freaked out over missing files, notes, and doubts. You were my eyes when mine were too tired and blurry to see and you helped me put things in perspective when I was overwhelmed. I appreciate you more than you know.

To Buster and Jack: It would be remiss of me if I didn't thank my two silent writing partners, my dogs. Yes, you read correctly. I'm thanking my dogs. They were by my side day and night listening to me talk, laugh, cry, and curse. Only two things drove them into the other room to hide, the sound of thunder and the sound of me dropping the F-bomb over and over again.

To Kelley Forsberg, my sister: Thank you for the love, support, and encouragement not only with this book, but throughout my life. We will always share a special bond. I wouldn't be here today without you.

To my *Perfect* betas: Each of you overwhelmed me with your passion and commitment. You made me a better writer during this process.

Beth Hyams (You will always be Beth Anne to me. I remembered the 'e'.): You've been with me through everything in my life- the good, the bad, and the ridiculous. I cherish our friendship so much. It means everything to me, having you by my side throughout this journey. I love you.

Stacy Bailey Darnell (aka Princess): I would need to write a thousand more books to thank you as much as you deserve and it still wouldn't be enough. Your support, guidance, humor, and friendship mean the world to me. Present Perfect was already a success before it was even released because through the process of creating it I got to know you better. Love ya, P!

Lisa Harley (aka HS): This is all your fault. You inspired me, guided me, kicked my butt when I needed it, and created my Cade. You have my undying love and respect.

Kristina Amit: How many messages have passed between us? A gazillion? Your insights had me rethink some things and it made them better. I hope you like how Noah wears his baseball cap now.

Ana Zaun: You need to teach a class, Indie Author 101. I can't thank you enough for all the help and support you gave me with the overall process of self-publishing. You are my Mr. (um... Ms) Miyagi. (I was able to write this without using 'there' once.)

Kim Shackleford (aka Duchess): My Carolina girl sistah. I loved your notes to me. Sorry I made you cry but also thrilled. Avery is getting a fantastic mom.

Jamie Zishka: You were the first beta to give me feedback. I was excited and nervous to open that first email, but elated and touched by your response.

Nicki DeStasi: Your feedback made me smile and laugh because your words leapt off the pages with excitement. I can't tell you how many times I read your note when I was having a bad day and needed encouragement.

Susan Miskelly: Thank you for making me look and think of things from a different perspective. It helped more than you know.

To Maria DeSouza and Editing Divas: Maria, you are one of the kindest and most generous people I've met. From the first time we spoke, I felt as if I had known you for years. Your edits and feedback were invaluable and made Present Perfect a better book.

To Robin Harper and Wicked by Design: I adore my cover. I didn't know what I wanted, but I knew what I didn't want. Somehow you read my mind and then blew my mind with your design. Thank you for being patient and going above and beyond for me.

To Angela McLaurin and Fictional Formats: Thank you for not taking out a restraining order against me. I don't usually have stalker tendencies, but I wanted the best formatter and you are the best. Your work is amazing.

To my Smurfettes: Beth Hyams, Stacy Bailey Darnell, Lisa Harley, Kristina Amit, Jamie Zishka, Nicki DeStasi, Kim Shackleford, Daisy Esquenazi, Sandra Cortez, America Matthews, Alexis Durbin, Stephanie Loftin, Dawn Costiera, Jennifer Diaz, Jennifer Mirabelli, Christine Mateo, Leslie Cox, Marilyn Medina, Melanie Smith, Tabitha Willbanks, Tina Bell, and Tamron Davis. -

You ladies rock!! I'm so appreciative of all you did to help spread the word about Present Perfect.

To The Writer's Block Group: The support, information, and encouragement you have shown me has helped push me forward to achieve my goals.

To Kindle Buddies: The first reading group I ever joined on Facebook was Kindle Buddies. I've met and become friends with a lot of great people through KB. I want to thank them for introducing me to so many wonderful books and authors that have touched my life and made it richer. Thank you, Crysti Perry, for starting the group and taking such good care of all of us.

To the Bloggers: An enormous THANK YOU to all of you. When I first started this journey I couldn't quite figure out why people would spend hours and hours blogging, especially if they weren't getting paid. As I got to know the blogging community, I *"got"* it. The love, dedication, commitment, and passion you show for books and authors is incredibly admirable. Thank you for all you do to support authors, especially indie authors. Your time and support is greatly appreciated.

To the readers: Thank you! I'm honored that you picked Present Perfect to read. The mark of a great book, to me, is one that makes you feel, think, and maybe look at life a little differently. I hope this book does that for you. Enjoy!

PROLOGUE

IF THERE'S NO SUCH THING AS PERFECT

THEN WHY DOES THE WORD EXIST?

"Amanda, you need to sit still and be good like Emily."

"Amanda, you need to let Emily help you with your homework. She made the honor roll again."

"Wow, you and Emily are sisters? *She's* so pretty."

"Amanda, when are your boobs going to get as big as Emily's?"

I love Emily. She has always been a great older sister. She let me hang out with her and her friends, *sometimes*. In fact, a few times she even took the blame for me. She's as beautiful on the inside as she is on the outside. It's not her fault that she was born first and stole my thunder. It's not her fault that she's been perfect at everything. I wanted to be perfect, too. I just couldn't seem to get there.

But I could tolerate living under the shadow of perfect Emily, because even though she had everything going for her, there was one thing she didn't have: Noah Stewart. I had him.

Noah had always been my best friend, my partner in crime, my protector, my soul mate, the love of my life. My everything. I may not have gotten all the beauty, intelligence or talent, but I got Noah Stewart, the one "perfect" thing I could claim as mine and I wouldn't trade him for anything in the world.

Entry 1

I've been unsure about many things in my life except that I have always loved him. Every single minute of every single day that I have been on this earth, my heart has belonged to him. It has never been a question, never a doubt. My love has taken on many forms, but it had always been a constant.

There are experts on love who will tell you how to get it, keep it, and get over it. We're led to believe love is complicated. It's not the love that's complicated. It's all the crap that we attach to it that makes it difficult. If you're smart, you'll realize this before it's too late and simplify.

Amanda Stewart

Noah Stewart

Noah and Amanda Stewart ♡

I was born on March 23, 1990 at 10:57 pm in Charleston, South Carolina at Saint Francis Hospital. Noah was born on March 23, 1990 at 10:58 pm right down the hall from me. Other than the one minute that separated our births, Noah and I have always been together. We shared all of our firsts: first teeth, first smile, and first words. We started crawling at the same time and even took our first steps together.

When Noah's mom returned to work, my mom, being a stay-at-home mom, offered to take care of him during the day. Mom figured two babies were just as easy to take care of as one. Usually, that isn't true. Two babies means double the diapers, double the feedings, double the screaming, and double the headaches. But not with Noah and me. As long as we were together, we were happy babies.

He and I had become an extension of each other. My mom said we developed our own language, like twins. To the untrained ear, the noises we made sounded like a bunch of gibberish, but Noah and I understood exactly what the other was saying. Noah could read me like no one else could. He knew my thoughts, my moods, and my feelings, just like I knew his.

Halloween 1996

Even at the age of six, I knew I would look hideous in it. The moms of all my friends were wholeheartedly embracing the conveniences of modern day America, like store-bought Halloween costumes. But my mom decided it would be wonderful for me and

Emily to have homemade costumes. I blame Martha Stewart one hundred percent for causing my mother's temporary insanity. Mom didn't have a crafty or artistic bone in her entire body.

Emily wanted to be a princess. She had been taking ballet lessons since the age of five, so she had all the elements for a decent princess costume.

Mom grabbed a couple of Emily's light pink tutus and hot glued one on top of the other for the bottom of the gown. The top was made of one of Emily's hot pink leotards. Mom drizzled hot glue all over the fabric, and then, threw handfuls of glitter at it. She topped off her creation with a tiara made of foil and multicolored marbles for the royal jewels. Emily's costume didn't look too bad. If you throw enough glitter on something, people get distracted by the dazzle and don't notice the ugly.

I, on the other hand, wanted to be a cowgirl. A cowgirl costume was the easiest costume to put together. All that was needed was a pair of jeans, a plaid shirt, a vest, a pair of boots, and a hat. Ta-da, cowgirl! No hot glue or glitter required. I had everything I needed, except the most important item.

Mom and I were at Target when I saw it. It was made of bright red felt, the brim was trimmed in white, and the word '*cowgirl*' was stitched across the front. It was the most beautiful thing I had ever seen. My heart started to flutter.

I grabbed the hat and ran up to my mom beaming with excitement. "Mom, look at it. Isn't it the most perfect cowgirl hat you've ever seen?"

"It's a very nice hat, Amanda. Now go put it back. We've got more shopping to do," she said while pushing the shopping cart down the aisle.

The smile dropped off my face. I ran up behind her, clutching the hat against my chest. "But Mom, I need it."

"For what, sweetie?"

"Um … for my Halloween costume," I said with a smirk, and an eye roll.

"I'm making your costume this year, Amanda. You know that." I followed behind her as she continued down the aisle, paying more attention to the items she was placing in the cart than me.

"I want to be a cowgirl. It's the easiest costume to make. I already have everything except the hat. I need this hat, Mom," I pleaded.

She glanced over her shoulder at me and asked, "Why do you want to be a cowgirl?"

"Because cowgirls are cool," I said.

As if this wasn't the most obvious thing in the world.

"Noah's going to be a cool knight. I want to be a cool cowgirl and I *will be* if I have *this hat*. Please, Mom."

She stopped and squatted down in front of me, bringing us eye-to-eye, and said, "Sweetie, you *are* going to be the coolest kid trick or treating this year."

"So I can get the hat?" I felt the smile slowly crawl back across my face. I waited with great anticipation to hear the word, "*yes*" float past her lips.

"No. Guess what you're going to be for Halloween?" She smiled at me with her stormy blue grey eyes filled with excitement. Standing, she started looking through the shopping cart. When she turned back around she was holding the biggest bag of bright yellow feathers I had ever seen. I looked up at her, my face twisted in confusion. "You're going to be Tweety Bird! Isn't that going to be fun?"

I was stunned. "I don't want to be Tweety Bird. I want to be a cool cowgirl. Why can't I be a cowgirl?" I whined.

"Because I already have all the things I need to make Tweety," she said, tossing the big bag of feathers back in the cart.

"We could just put that stuff back, and you could get me this cool cowgirl hat."

"Amanda, you're going to be Tweety Bird this year. Stop arguing with me. You need to try and be more like your sister. She never gives me any trouble. You can be a cowgirl next year. Now, go put the hat back."

With my shoulders slumped and my head lowered in defeat, I dragged my feet slowly as I made my way down the aisle to put the perfect cowgirl hat back on the shelf. "I don't want to be stupid Tweety. I want to be a cowgirl. It's my costume," I grumbled.

"Amanda, hurry up! We need to get going."

My mom was so obsessed with making the Tweety costume I had started to wonder if she thought I looked like a jaundiced bubble head with puffy cheeks and lips.

I was standing in our family room dressed in a skin tight pale yellow leotard that Mom made me put on over shorts and a t-shirt. She walked into the room weighted down with an armful of supplies and dumped them out on to the floor beside me. "Whew! Ok, let's get the show on the road," she said, rubbing her palms together. I couldn't believe how excited she was about this stupid bird costume.

She began setting out her supplies, as I gasped for air, and said, "Mom?"

"Hmmm …?"

"This leotard's too tight. I can't breathe." I gulped in as much oxygen as the vacuum packed garment would allow.

"It has to be a little tight, Amanda. Otherwise the feathers will weight it down and make it sag. You don't want to be a sagging Tweety do you?"

"I don't want to be Tweety at all," I muttered.

"Enough of that. I don't know why you're being so difficult. Your sister didn't complain about her costume."

"That's because she gets to be a fairy princess like she wants to be."

"Let's get started."

Mom pulled a few more things out of her tote bag, and then, walked over to the wall to plug in her hot glue gun. When she turned back around, the glue gun was pointed directly at me.

My eyebrows immediately shot up, I could feel my eyeballs pop right out of their sockets as beads of sweat trickled down my neck. My voice was shaky when I asked, "You're not going to shoot me with hot glue, are you? I promise I won't say anything bad about Tweety ever again."

"Oh Amanda, you're so dramatic. I'm not going to drip hot glue on you. I need to figure out where to place the feathers while you're wearing the leotard."

She pulled out a huge roll of duct tape, started ripping off small pieces, and rolled them up. She then stuck them all over me. Taking handfuls of the bright yellow feathers, she began to shove them against my body. I tipped over a couple of times when she got a little over enthusiastic.

After she helped me out of the torture chamber, I watched as she removed sections of feathers from the leotard, drizzled hot glue, and plastered them back on. Sighing deeply, I turned away, and went to my room. I couldn't bear to watch any longer.

Halloween morning I walked into the family room and found Mom bent down picking up a pile of feathers that had fallen off my costume. This had become a daily ritual that made me smile and gave me hope. If the feathers didn't stick, there'd be no chick. Maybe my cowgirl dreams would come true after all.

Clearing my throat, I said, "Mom, would it be okay if I didn't wear my Tweety costume to school? I don't want to get it messed up before tonight."

She placed the armful of feathers on the coffee table, stood up quickly, and turned in my direction, trying to hide the pile of feathers behind her. She didn't want to admit the fact that Tweety had a serious molting problem. She hesitated for a moment, running her hand behind her neck a couple of times as she glanced back at the pile of feathers.

"Sure, that would be fine. It will give me time to spruce it up a little before tonight. How about you go to school as a cowgirl. You mentioned about being a cowgirl, right?"

Only about one thousand times.

When the time had come to get ready for trick or treating, Mom had secured all the feathers back on the leotard. My cowgirl dreams had been dashed.

The rest of the Tweety costume consisted of an old pair of fuzzy bedroom slippers, spray painted gold for my feet. A few extra feathers were left over, so Mom decided Tweety needed a headband. Then she brought out this sizable jar of greasy neon yellow makeup. It looked like something she had from the 1980's, when apparently, it was cool to smear your child with toxins. The last bit of humiliation to be added was a handful of glitter that she poured over me, coating my head, arms, and chest. I looked like the love child of Big Bird and Liberace.

The time had come. I tried to delay going outside for as long as possible, waiting for the sun to disappear completely from the sky. I figured darkness would be my friend. It was a warm night, so Emily and I didn't need to wear our jackets. I was willing to risk a high grade-fever in order to hide this yellow-glitter- incrusted nightmare that I was wearing, but Mom wouldn't hear of it.

Emily and I always trick or treated together. It was her job to hold my hand, ring the doorbell, and say trick or treat. All I had to do was collect my candy. This year, since she was 10 years old, Emily wanted to go with her friends. Mom made, what I felt was, a very poor parental choice when she allowed Emily to go with them instead of staying with me and continuing this sacred family tradition. Didn't she think of me at all? Didn't she understand that I would suffer a severe candy deficit, without Emily by my side?

We were standing at the bottom of the Dean's driveway, I swallowed hard as I watched my sister walk away with her friends to another neighbor's house.

Mom must have sensed my fear because she drew me in close to her side and whispered, "You can do this, Amanda. You're a big girl now. There's nothing to be afraid of. Your sister was five when she started going up to the doors by herself. I'll be right here." She let go of my hand and took a step away from me.

I continued to stand there, frozen. I felt abandoned. I hated it. I was terrified of a monster opening one of the doors. Sure, I had never seen a monster in our neighborhood, but there was a first time for everything.

As much as I wanted to, I couldn't seem to move my fuzzy gold feet. I felt my face getting warm as butterflies took over my stomach. I was too scared to move. My eyes began to sting from the tears that were building up. Although, they could've been caused by the poisonous substance that was smeared across my face.

I took in a deep breath as I looked down, trying to find courage, when I noticed a small pile of yellow feathers that had collected at my feet. My eyes followed the trail all the way back to my house. The street was covered with so many feathers, it looked like the yellow brick road. When I glanced up I couldn't believe my eyes. Walking towards me was Andrea Morgan dressed in a full Dorothy costume with her little dog too.

I looked over my shoulder at my mom, then up at the Dean's front door, then back at my mom.

"Go on, Amanda. Don't be a baby," Mom said.

Tears began to trickle down my face. I needed to make a decision. Time was of the essence. I needed to suck it up, walk up to that door, and get some candy before the rest of my feathers flew off, leaving me naked as a Tweety bird.

I looked back up at the Dean's house. I saw my friends walking down the driveway, with their bags overflowing with deliciousness. Deliciousness that I wouldn't be getting if I didn't get a move on.

Then I saw him, my knight in plastic armor, with his light blue eyes peeking out from under his hood along with just a little bit of his dark brown hair.

He was coming down the driveway, by himself, and headed straight toward me. His bag was loaded with candy.

When he reached me, he took the sleeve of his shirt and wiped my tears away. "Don't cry."

"I'm not getting any candy tonight. My feathers are falling off, and I'm going to be naked in the street." I was sobbing so hard that my words came out like hiccups. We both glanced behind me. "See all the feathers?"

"Open your bag up." Noah started filling it with handfuls of candy from his bag.

"Noah, you don't have to give me all your candy."

"I'm not giving you all of it. I'm giving you half." He smiled at me and I knew everything was going to be alright.

After we made the candy transfer, he grabbed my hand and started pulling me towards the Stevenson's driveway. I jerked my hand out of his and stopped. "What are you doing?"

"I'm going to take you trick or treating and show you there's nothing to be scared of," he said.

I looked up at Noah and gazed into his trusting eyes. I reached out my hand timidly and he led me to the next house.

Noah walked me up to the front door and rang the doorbell. My heart started beating faster and my palms got sweaty. The door slowly opened and Mrs. Stevenson stepped out, dressed like a big fat cat. She made me laugh. Noah dropped my hand long enough for me to hold my bag open and for him to wipe his palm off on his costume. Mrs. Stevenson gave me *two* sour apple Blow Pops because of my bravery that night.

Mom trailed behind us, grinning, as we went to a few more houses. With my bag filled with candy, Noah and I walked hand-in-hand down the last driveway. Stopping at the bottom, I turned and gave him a kiss on the cheek.

"Thank you, Noah."

He smiled. "I'll always take care of you and make sure you have candy, Tweet."

It was the first time he called me by the nickname that would stick with me forever. And despite my total disgust with the Tweety Bird costume, I didn't mind being called Tweet at all by Noah. In fact, I loved it.

ENTRY 2

THE UNPREDICTABILITY OF LIFE SUCKS.
ONE MINUTE YOU'RE RIDING HIGH WITH THE WIND WHIPPING THROUGH YOUR HAIR AND THE NEXT MINUTE YOU'RE FLAT ON YOUR ASS WITH A FACE FULL OF GRAVEL.

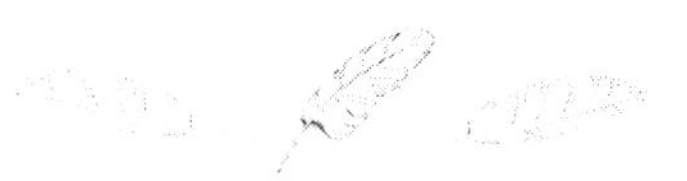

I had always had a passion for cycling. From the very first moment I sat on my red tricycle I knew bike riding was for me. I got my first big girl bike for my eighth birthday. It was the most amazing bike ever made. Most of my girlfriends had pink bikes, but mine was yellow. I had recovered completely from the Tweety trauma, and yellow was now my favorite color. *Go figure.*

My bike was beautiful and different. The tassels on the handlebars were made of white, yellow and silver threads with glitter. The wicker basket was white and silver. The white banana seat had silver specks that looked as if they lit up when the sun hit them. The spokes of the front tire were adorned with white and silver beads, and the spokes of the back tire had a noise maker that sounded like a motorcycle. Yeah, I was a badass on a yellow and silver bike.

It had been two weeks since I ditched the training wheels. Noah and I couldn't wait to get home each day, finish our homework, and take to the road. I was allowed to go as far as the Porter's house, which was three houses away from mine, but Noah was allowed to ride all around our neighborhood.

He had been riding his Schwinn red and black BMX for over a year now and he was awesome on it. Not only could he do forward and backward wheelies, he could do the Bunny Hop, the one hander, and jump a couple of trashcans. Noah was so cool. I wasn't cool—as proven by the fact that I was 8 years old and had only been riding my bike sans training wheels for two weeks.

I had been satisfied with riding to the Porter's house, but after two weeks, the temptation to go further was eating me alive. I begged Mom daily for permission to ride around the block to Noah's house but she kept telling me no.

I knew Noah was getting tired of riding up and down the same small portion of street I was confined to. He didn't complain, but he and I never needed words to pass between us to know what the other was thinking.

"Tweet, don't worry about it. Really. I can still practice my tricks. Your mom will let you ride to my house soon. You're riding really good now."

Soon, but not soon enough to suit me. I had an itch that needed to be scratched.

I rode up beside him keeping my voice low. "Let's do it."

"Do what?" He asked confused.

"Let's take these babies for a spin around the block to your house."

"I don't think that's such a good idea. Your mom will be mad and we'll get in trouble."

"She'll never know. We'll only go one time and then, come right back. Pleeease, Noah. You said I was riding really good."

He looked away then back at me and said, "We'll ride to my house then back, but that's it." I nodded excitedly, agreeing with anything that came out of his mouth. "One time. I mean it, Tweet. Promise me."

"I promise," I said, crossing my heart at the same time.

We made sure my mom wasn't peering out of any windows. Then we started to ride. It felt the same way it had for the past two weeks, until we went past the Porter's house. The excitement started to build. I was really doing this.

Adrenalin pumped through my veins as my heart pounded against my chest. Noah stayed ahead of me, making sure the road was clear. We rounded the corner. The wind was whipping through my hair. It felt amazing, like I was flying.

Noah rode up alongside me cheering. "You're doing fantastic. Tweet! We're almost to my house."

He rode off, returning to his position in front. It made me so happy to know Noah was proud of me, there was no better feeling in the world. Then it happened.

I don't know what I did, but all of a sudden the handlebars

shook, and I lost control of the bike. In a split second, I was face down on the road. My legs twisted around the bike. Noah must have glanced back and saw that I was no longer behind him.

I heard him yelling, "Tweet!"

He rode over to me as fast as he could, jumped off his bike, and let it fall to the ground. The palm of my hands started to burn, and I could feel the blood dripping down my left leg.

I heard Noah's panicked voice. "Hold on, Tweet. I'm here. Can you move?"

He pulled the bike slowly away from my knotted legs and tossed it to the side. He knelt beside me and helped me sit up. Tears and sobs started coming out of me. My hands felt like they were on fire. I held them up as Noah blew on them, trying to cool them off. My left cheek was red and covered with dirt and gravel. Taking the bottom of his shirt, he wiped as much of it off as he could. My left knee was the biggest casualty. The skin was completely scraped off and hanging to the side. The knee was covered in bright red flesh with blood oozing from it. When I looked at it, I started to cry harder. Noah wrapped his arm around my shoulders, trying to calm me down.

Pulling me into a hug, he whispered, "I'm so sorry, Tweet. I should have stayed with you. I'm going to take care of you. I promise. Can you walk?"

He helped me try to stand. I put my weight on the left knee, pain shot through me like a knife, and my knee gave out.

It was hard getting the words out through my sobs. "I can't walk. It hurts too much."

Needing to get out of the street, Noah helped me as I limped to a neighbor's front yard and sat on the grass.

"Will you be okay here while I go get your mom?"

I shook my head rapidly. "No, no, no, you can't tell my mom. Please, Noah. She'll take my bike away and ground me forever." I held my breath, waiting anxiously while he made his decision.

The next thing I knew, I felt his left arm under my knees, his right arm against my back as he scooped me up off the ground. "Grab around my neck."

I did as he said. I rested my head on his shoulder as Noah carried me down the street. "I'm not too heavy for you to carry me?" I asked. I was still a lot smaller than Noah, but I had grown a little taller over the past year.

"You're light as a feather," he said, smiling at me.

"Where are we going?"

"To my house, we have a first aid kit."

Noah's parents were out back doing yard work, so we were able to sneak into his room, unnoticed. He gently sat me down on his bed and left to get the first aid kit.

As I sat waiting for Noah to return a million thoughts ran across my mind about how my mom was going to punish me if she or my dad found out. The sound of the bedroom door opening distracted me from my thoughts of impending doom. Noah closed the door quietly and sat down on the bed in front of me. He stared down at my knee. When he looked up, his eyes appeared watery. He leaned in and draped his arms around my shoulders as mine found their way around his waist.

"Thank you, Noah," I whispered.

"For what?" He said into my hair.

"For taking care of me."

Wiping his eyes, he sat back on the bed, and began to gently clean my face with an antiseptic wipe. As the alcohol hit my raw skin, I winced in pain. I saw Noah cringe each time he started to wipe my face.

"I promise, I won't let anything bad happen to you again, Tweet"

I gave him a small smile. He opened another wipe and cleaned my hands and knee, trying hard not to hurt me.

Once he finished, my face and hands didn't look bad at all. A lot of the redness and burning had gone away. My knee was the worse injury. Noah gently applied antiseptic ointment and a large Band-Aid. I stayed in his room while he left to put the first aid kit back. It felt like a lot of time had passed before he returned. Finally, the door opened and I breathed a sigh of relief. "Where've you been? You were gone for like an hour."

Shaking his head he smirked at me. "I was gone for like twenty minutes. I had to go get our bikes. Then my mom stopped me in the kitchen when I was getting this for you." He had a huge piece of chocolate cake with a fork sticking out of it. He handed it to me. "She wanted to know what I was up to."

"What did you tell her?" I said with a mouth full of cake and frosting.

"That you were here. Then she wanted to know if you were staying for supper. My dad's grilling hamburgers."

"I need to call my mom and let her know that I'm over here and ask if I can stay." I could feel tears sitting behind my eyes. I was scared Mom would know something was wrong the minute she heard my voice.

"You don't need to call her. Mom said she would check to make sure it was alright if you stayed."

I let out another deep sigh. This bought me a little more time for my knee to feel better and for the redness to go away from my hands and face.

I noticed Noah staring at me while I ate the cake. I held the fork out to him. "You want some?"

"Nah, you need it more than I do."

I pushed it closer in his direction. "Have some," I insisted.

Grabbing the fork, he took a big bite while I held the plate for him. We passed the fork back and forth until the cake was gone.

After setting the plate down, Noah laid back on the bed, lacing his fingers behind his head. "Feeling better?"

"Yes. Much better," I told him.

"Good. I figured that would help."

"What?"

"The chocolate cake."

"Yeah, why's that?" I asked with curiosity.

Noah smiled. "Cause chocolate cake takes the hurt away and makes everything better."

Entry 3

YOUR WORLD CAN CHANGE IN AN INSTANT

WHEN YOU SEE SOMEONE THROUGH ANOTHER'S EYES.

We were at the final baseball game of the season. Noah was the star player for the city league, the Tigers. It was his last year playing for them. We were starting our freshmen year in high school in a few months and Noah was a great baseball player, so there was no doubt he'd make the high school team.

The extent of my baseball knowledge was practically nonexistent. I had been coming to these games forever so you would've thought I'd have retained some information through osmosis at least. I wasn't the sporty one of the family, Emily was. She had been playing basketball since she was 10 years old and started running track her freshman year in high school. She'd won trophies for both sports. Surprise, surprise. Really, the only reason I came was to support and cheer for my best friend.

Noah started playing T-ball when he was 4 years old and quickly fell in love with all things baseball. Even though I never understood the game, there wasn't a better way to spend a Saturday than watching Noah out there on the field. Baseball made him happy and excited. It was worth sitting through a game I didn't understand to see how much joy it brought him.

I decided to invite Beth Sanders, a potential new friend of mine, to the game. Her family had moved in next door to us about three weeks ago. She was still in her friendship trial period. So far, she had done pretty well, but I hadn't introduced her to Noah yet.

She was exotic looking with her deep tan, long jet black hair, and emerald green eyes. She had really sharp facial features, her nose, cheekbones, and jaw were all well-defined, unlike mine. My face was round and my cheeks were chubby, at least I thought so. Beth was taller and thinner than me, with legs that went on for miles. She was fun to hang out with, a little boy crazy, but certainly not on the road to becoming Queen of Whoreville.

"Wow, I'm going to love living here. This place is crawling with hotties," Beth said, as we carried our food up the bleachers to our seats "Who is that?!"

I turned towards the field. "Who?"

"The batter, Stewart."

"That's my Noah."

"*Your* Noah? I thought you just had an older sister and your last name was Kelly."

"Not brother, best friend," I said.

"Your best friend?" She scrunched up her face confused. "You can't have a guy as your best friend."

"Why not?"

"It's unnatural. Weird," she said, her lips pursed into a straight line.

It was hard for me to think that there was something unnatural or weird about my friendship with Noah. Everything with us had always felt like the most natural thing in the world.

Beth continued to ramble on. "… and you especially can't have a guy who looks like *that* as your best friend."

"A guy who looks like that? What are you talking about?"

"Don't tell me you haven't noticed how scorching hot he is?"

"I never thought about it."

She huffed. "I don't believe you," she paused for a moment. "Are you a lesbian?"

"No!"

"I'm just asking because a lesbian is the only type of female, who wouldn't think Noah was hot."

"I don't know if you and I are going to be friends," I deadpanned.

She smiled at me. "Oh, come on. Look at him. His body is insane."

"I think *you're* insane."

"He's a perfect triangle. Broad shoulders, thin waist, amazing ass."

"I'm beginning to think *you're* an amazing ass." I was getting more than a little annoyed at the way she was talking about Noah.

"I haven't even gotten to his arms and legs." She was almost panting.

I held my hand up, hoping to stop her diarrhea of the mouth. "How do you know him?" She asked, breathlessly.

"We grew up together. There hasn't been a day in my life that I haven't been with him. Our families even take vacations together."

"Where does he live?" Beth was becoming too inquisitive about Noah.

I narrowed my eyes at her, not answering.

"Does he live in our neighborhood?" I remained silent. "Oh! My! God! He lives in our neighborhood. Why haven't you introduced us? You've been holding out on me. You *have* to introduce us."

Once she started talking about Noah, her words came out at such a rapid fire speed that I could barely keep up. She was talking so fast and excitedly, I had the urge to punch her in the neck just to slow her down.

"Yeah. I'll be doing that real soon," I said sarcastically, rolling my eyes.

I didn't know Beth well enough to make a judgment call, but she appeared to be in need of some sort of medication.

"Come on, Amanda. I need to see if his front is as amazing as his back."

I looked at her in annoyance, shaking my head.

For the remainder of the game, Beth sat there ogling not only Noah, but every guy she deemed hot, which was the majority of the team. She even thought Coach Sawyer was hot, and he was old. He had to be at least forty.

The game was almost over. It was Noah's turn at bat. The score was tied. If he scored with this run, the Tigers would be city league champs for the first time.

The crowd grew quiet. The pitcher took a few seconds and then, threw a fast ball straight at Noah. The sound of the bat connecting with the ball was so loud that it sounded like a cannon had just fired. Noah dropped the bat and took off running faster than I'd ever seen him run before. He rounded first, then second, then third. He slid feet first into home plate. When the ump yelled, "SAFE!!" my Noah became a city league legend, leading his Tigers to their first championship. The crowd went crazy, jumping up and cheering.

I stood and looked on the field, watching as Noah's teammates ran over, picked him up, and placed him on their shoulders. They started to chant, "STE-WART! STE-WART! STE-WART!" as they turned him towards the excited crowd.

Beth gasped. "Oh yeah. His front is definitely as amazing as his back."

I shot a piercing glance in her direction.

The cheers got louder and the crowd began to chant, "STE-WART!" Noah looked up into the bleachers. His eyes locked with mine. He had the biggest smile across his face, matching mine. He took off his baseball cap and waved it in the air, looking at me the entire time. He was the only one I saw out there on that field, and he looked at me like I was the only one he saw in the bleachers. Warmth coursed through my body as I stared at him. He really was nice to look at.

I was overwhelmed with pride and joy for him. Beth was wrong. There's nothing unnatural or weird about the connection Noah and I shared.

We descended the bleachers and walked toward the field where Noah was standing. A large crowd had already gathered around him, shaking his hand or slapping his back in congratulations. I stood off to the side with Beth. I wanted to watch him enjoy his moment. After several minutes, the crowd began to thin. Noah looked past a few people and spotted me. He shook a few more hands, but never took his eyes off mine.

When he reached me, his arms immediately wrapped around my waist, and he lifted me off the ground. He spun me around a couple of times, causing me to squeal.

"Can you believe it, Tweet? League champs!" Excitement ricocheted off of him.

I felt a shiver radiate through me when my body slid down his as he placed me back on the ground. I swallowed hard as I steadied myself.

"I know. Congratulations! You did it! I'm so proud of you."

He took his cap off and placed it on my head. It was soaked with his sweat, but I didn't care. I beamed up at him for a few seconds before I was startled by the clearing of a throat.

"Oh, Noah, this is Beth. She just moved …" I trailed off.

I wasn't sure why I didn't tell him she lived in our neighborhood. I wasn't trying to keep it a secret. Besides, Beth would tell him where she lived eventually. I just felt very protective of him all of a sudden. I didn't like the way she looked at him or talked about him. Beth would have to find her own Noah. This one was taken, and he was mine.

Entry 4

A friend is someone who knows the song in your heart and can sing it back to you when you have forgotten the words.–Author Unknown

(Damn, I wish I'd written that.)

"What do you think?" Noah asked, as we sat at the picnic table in the neighborhood park. This had become *our spot.* It was the end of summer vacation. This time next week, we'd officially be high school freshmen. I wanted to enjoy every minute of tonight because once school started, time spent here would be limited.

Summers in Charleston were brutal with the high heat and humidity. Tonight, there was a slight breeze so it wasn't as hot as it had been. The crickets were singing in the trees all around us and I could hear an occasional ripple of water from the pond when the ducks paddled by.

Noah was sitting very close to me. We were both wearing

shorts and the feel of our bare thighs touching was something new and exciting. I noticed just before the summer, he had started being more affectionate with me. Noah had always been sweet, but recently he hugged me more, held my hand more, and sat closer to me. I liked it. A lot. My body tingled every time he was this close.

We were sharing his set of ear buds listening to music. Both of us were huge music fans; alternative, indie, punk, rock, etc. The music of our favorite band, Lifehouse, was pulsating through the ear buds.

"They're awesome," I said, swaying side to side, my eyes closed, letting the music flow through me. "The entire CD is brilliant. The song '*Everything*' is my favorite."

"Mine too. It reminds me of you," he said.

I quickly glanced at him, not sure if I heard what I thought I heard. I looked down and closed my eyes again. When the song ended, I looked over at Noah and caught him staring at me with a slight smile across his face.

"What are you smiling at?" I asked.

"You, I like watching you listen to music. You get so lost in it."

Our eyes locked as I sucked in my lower lip, running my teeth over it. I felt a warm blush start to creep across my cheeks. I smiled at him, as I handed back the ear bud.

"Do you think they'll go on tour soon?"

Noah shrugged. "Maybe."

"If they come to town we have got to see them. I bet they're unbelievable in concert."

Suddenly, he hopped off the table and stood in front of me. Reaching into the back pocket of his cargo shorts, he produced two tickets, and held them up in front of me. He tried to contain it, but the grin on his face was getting bigger and more adorable each second.

"Performing Arts Center, three weeks, you and me, Tweet," he said excitedly.

It took a second for me to register what he had just said. This would be the first concert either of us had been to. It was hard to contain my excitement.

"You're kidding?!"

"Nope."

I jumped up and flew into his arms, causing him to stumble backwards, and fall to the ground with me landing on top, straddling him. We were out of breath and laughing.

"Noah Stewart, you are the bestest best friend a girl could have."

"I am pretty awesome, aren't I?" He shot a flirtatious smirk up at me and my insides melted.

"Yes you are," I said in a low voice.

We laid there, so close our noses were almost touching as our eyes locked on one another again. Noah had the most amazing eyes. They were light blue and so bright, it looked as if they were lit from the back.

I wish I had eyes like that. Mine were a weird color. Mom always said they were teal. What kind of color is teal? I can guarantee the teal is the least used crayon in the Crayola big box.

I realized I should have probably gotten off of Noah immediately, but I didn't. He seemed perfectly fine with me staying put, straddling him. My palms pressed against his chest and I could tell how toned and solid his body was. Playing baseball since we were little kids had been very, *very* good to him. I could also feel how excited he was. I had never felt anything like that before pressed against me. Surprisingly, I wasn't scared. It felt right.

My gaze fell to his mouth. When I saw his tongue dart out slightly and run across his lower lip, a warm sensation took over my body. The butterflies in my stomach were doing cartwheels. Our breathing had gone from shallow and quick, to deep and slow. I wasn't exactly sure what was going on. Noah was my best friend. I had always been excited when I saw him and wanted to spend all of my time with him, but what I was feeling was more than what I had experienced before.

Noah's gaze dropped down to my lips, slowly moved up my face, and back to my eyes. Raising his hand, he tucked some of my hair that had fallen against the side of his face, behind my ear. My cheek and the shell of my ear tingled as the tips of his fingers skimmed across them.

"You were extremely sure of yourself, getting those tickets without asking me first. What if I didn't want to go with you?" I said, teasing him. My voice was so quiet, it almost sounded like a whisper.

"Impossible. I know my girl too well," he said, smiling up at me. I loved it when he called me his girl. He cleared his throat and then said, "I guess we better get up."

"Oh. Yeah. Sorry about that." A rosy blush took over my cheeks.

I rolled off of Noah's body and sat up next to him. He didn't stand immediately. I guess he needed a little time to calm down, so did I.

When he stood, he held his hands out to me, and helped me off the ground. Once I was on my feet, he pulled me in close against his chest, and said, "That was fun. What would you do for tickets to see Green Day in concert?" He had a smirk on his face.

The combination of our bodies pressed together, his bright blue eyes, and that smirk, had my head spinning, and my body experiencing sensations that I wasn't use to.

I wasn't sure if it was my raging hormones or Beth drooling over Noah, constantly, but I had started looking at him differently. I didn't like the way she looked at him or talked about his body parts. These new feelings were confusing to me. I knew when I was with him, I felt excited, happy, and safe. When we weren't together I felt like a part of me was missing.

Since we shared all of our firsts together, I guess it was only natural that my first crush would be on Noah. Even though his body responded when I was on top of him, I knew teenage boys got like that for no reason at all. It was just the hormones flooding into his penis that caused it to react that way. Noah saw me as a friend, not a girlfriend.

Besides, I knew I wasn't the right girl for him. There was nothing special about me. I was average height like my mom, not tall like Emily. My features were okay. I had been told I was cute. Probably because of my round face and puffy cheeks. Relatives always wanted to pinch my cheeks at family gatherings which I never understood. Pinching cheeks might be fun for the pincher, but not for the pinchie. I wanted Emily's slender face and high cheekbones. My figure was slightly curvy, not athletic like my sister's. A few months ago my boobs decided to make an appearance all of a sudden. They had been developing slowly and steadily. Then one day, ta-dah, I had ta-tas. They weren't huge, they weren't small, and they were average. My shoulder length hair was dark brown, like Emily's, but not silky and shiny like her hair always was. My skin was pale, unlike the year round golden tan of my sister's complexion. And then there were my freaky teal colored eyes that caused a lot of stares to be directed my way.

Noah deserved perfect because he was, and I was as far from perfect as you could get. Plus, we were best friends and I never wanted that to change.

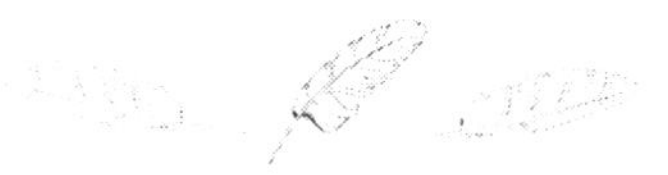

The first week of high school was a blur. I was intimidated by the new classes and new teachers, but after the first day jitters were gone, things seemed to fall into place. I had two classes with Noah, three with Beth, and we all shared the same lunch period. High school life was going pretty well until, The Interloper invaded.

It was almost the end of lunch. Noah was sitting beside me studying notes for his next class. Across the table from us sat Beth, who was rambling on about every cute guy that walked by when she wasn't stealing glances at Noah. I don't think this girl ever shut up about anything, especially guys.

Every school has their version of *her*. Our version had just walked into the cafeteria. The Interloper was a walking cliché'. She was tall, blonde, blue eyed, very curvy, and to my surprise, headed straight to our table. Her eyes immediately zeroed in on Noah. A big Cheshire cat smile slowly crept across her overly glossy lips. I instinctively knew she was trouble and we would be mortal enemies.

She was well aware of what her assets were and displayed them shamelessly. Her shirt and jeans were tight and low. Her heels and boobs were high. As she walked, every part of her body bounced.

I read an article in Cosmo one time that said guys like girls with bouncy parts. The Interloper was extremely bouncy. No part of my body bounced. There were a few parts that jiggled. I've never read an article about guys liking jigglers. I glanced over at Noah and wondered if he liked bouncers or jigglers.

I continued to watch as her hair, boobs, and ass bounced their way across the cafeteria. The closer she got to our table, the tighter the knot in my stomach twisted. I felt like there was a vise clamped around my lower intestines. As she sauntered up, I felt an icy chill run up my spine.

"Yay, I found ya'll!" She said.

"Hey, Brittani, I saved you a seat," Beth said, pulling out the chair next to her for The Interloper to sit.

What the shizzle?! Had Beth lost her mind?

The Interloper, or TI for short, slid into the chair next to Beth, and positioned herself directly in front of Noah. She stared at him, trying to get his attention. When that didn't work she cleared her throat loudly, hoping he would look up at her. Noah finally did look up from his notes, surprised that someone was sitting in front of him, staring.

She extended her hand, palm down, like she expected him to kiss it. "I'm Brittani Monroe."

She introduced herself as if she were making an earth shattering announcement. Her southern drawl was so thick and sweet I felt my teeth rotting with each word.

A confused Noah took her hand by the fingers and shook it. "Um … hey. I'm Noah Stewart."

He looked over at me with eyebrows raised, like he was checking to make sure he'd done what he was supposed to do. Pursing my lips, I returned his look, without uttering a word.

I started drumming the fingers of my right hand on the table while chewing my left thumbnail. This chick was unbelievable. She hadn't acknowledged me at all, and hadn't looked at or said another word to Beth since sitting down.

"It's *very* nice to meet you, Noah. I'm so glad Beth asked me to join you for lunch." Noah kept glancing back and forth between me and TI.

I stopped drumming, and chewing long enough to shoot Beth my DEFCON 1 evil eye. I could tell she got the message from the look of fear that crossed her face.

"Um … Brittani, this is my friend Amanda." Beth's voice was shaky.

TI never took her eyes off Noah. Her voice was flat when she finally acknowledged my existence. "Hey."

She shifted her position forward and propped her boobs up on the table revealing the Grand Canyon of cleavage. "What 'cha studying, Noah?"

She squirmed a little in her seat squishing her boobs together even more. Noah's eyes landed right where she wanted them to. The Grand Canyon must have had hypnotic power because Noah couldn't seem to tear his eyes away from it.

Unable to tolerate the sightseeing trip any longer, I elbowed him in the ribs. "Ouch! What was that for?" He said, rubbing his side.

"You mentioned that you needed to get to class early." I smiled innocently at him.

"Yeah, I guess I better go." He closed his notebook and shoved it into his backpack.

TI tilted her head to the side, gave him her best pouty face, and whined, "I don't want you to go yet. I'll miss you too much."

Unbelievable.

Noah stammered, "Yeah, well … um … maybe later." He stood. "I'll see you in Algebra, Tweet." I gave him a slight smile. "See you later, Beth and um …"

"Brittani!" She squeaked, biting her lower lip.

Backing away from the table, Noah hesitated, and then said, "Um … yeah … Brittani."

Both girls twisted in their chairs and watched as Noah walk away, staying in that position until he was out of sight.

TI sighed deeply as she turned back around. "He's all kinds of yummy, isn't he?"

Beth nodded in full agreement, "Yeah, all kinds." I shot her another DEFCON 1. "What? Come on, Amanda. You can't tell me you haven't noticed how hot he is."

"He's my best friend. I don't think of him that way."

I lied. I do think of him that way. A lot lately. In fact, he has made a few appearances in my dreams. I got goose bumps every time he came within 10 feet of me or I heard the sound of his voice. A few days ago, I saw him mowing the grass in his backyard. He was shirtless, sweaty, and his shorts were hanging low. From the pounding in my chest and the lightheadedness, I thought I was having a heart attack.

TI picked up a napkin and started fanning herself. "That's not something you think about. That's something you feel, all over."

"Yeah, all over," Beth said, in a dreamy voice.

I sat there silently listening to these two rattle off all of Noah's attributes. A burning sensation starting in my stomach traveled up to my chest. My entire body started to tighten up the more they talked about my Noah.

"He's exceptionally hot. He's far and above any of the guys around here. He could pass for a junior. I mean, look at most of the guys around here our age. They're covered in pimples, scrawny, and uncoordinated. Arms and legs flying all over the place," TI said, waving her arms in the air. "I can tell Noah's body is rock hard. The muscles in his arms are A-MAZ-ING."

I've had those muscles around me. They are amazing.

"He's a baseball player," Beth chimed in.

"That explains it."

"His tan and that dark brown hair are a sexy as hell combination," Beth giggled. "I want to run my fingers through it. It looks so soft."

I'd felt that hair across my cheek when Noah hugged me. It was very soft and smelled like oranges.

"Oh god! Beth. Did you see his ass?"

"Um ... Yeah. It's perfect."

"His ass is mouthwatering." Resting her chin in her hand TI looked away daydreaming, no doubt about Noah's ass. "I'm going to crawl all over his body."

"Like a fungus?" I asked, popping the last of the cheese puffs I had for lunch into my mouth.

She sneered at me. "Ha-ha. I'll be crawling all over Noah before the semester is up. I guarantee it. Unless you have dibs on him, Beth. I won't go after a boy if a friend of mine has dibs on him."

"I don't have dibs on him." Beth glanced over at me,

annoyance written all over her face.

"Good."

"What about me?" I asked.

"What about you?" TI narrowed her eyes at me. A smug smile plastered across her face.

"Maybe I have dibs on him."

"You just said you didn't think of him that way. It wouldn't matter even if you did."

"What's that supposed to mean?" I asked. She and Beth exchanged a knowing glance.

"Noah's pretty much out of your league, don't you think?"

"Brittani, don't," Beth begged.

"She asked." TI turned her attention back on me. "I don't know you at all, but it's pretty obvious there's nothing much to you. You're not ugly, but you're not very attractive either. You really should try to fix yourself up."

"Brittani, stop it." I could tell Beth was getting mad.

"I'm doing her a favor. I mean, look at her- brown *blah* hair, pale skin, and her eyes are weird. They're kind of freaking me out. Dull and boring. Maybe if she got some highlights and some sun that might help, but it's only going to help her so much. It's not a miracle worker."

She was talking about me like I wasn't there.

"On the hotness scale, Noah is a solid ten. He needs to hook up with at least an eight or nine, if not another ten. If I'm being honest, which I always am, you are barely a two, and that's being generous."

"Alright, that's enough. Come one Amanda, we need to get to English."

I watched as Beth and TI got up and grabbed their things. I just sat there, frozen. I knew I wasn't anything special and not good enough for Noah. What shocked me was that a girl, who only met me ten minutes ago, knew it too. My eyes started to water.

I would not cry in the middle of the cafeteria.

I jumped up, quickly grabbed my things, and hurriedly walked out. I headed straight to the bathroom, getting there right before the tears started.

Entry 5

When my mother gets a thought in her head, it's there for life. It's cemented in place, never to be removed. I've recently realized that I am one step closer to turning into my mother, because I can't get the thoughts of dreamy light blue eyes, soft dark brown hair, and amazing muscular arms out of my head.

Noah and I were at his house, hanging out in his room, listening to music. After the conversation with Beth and Brittani earlier today, it's been hard to look directly at him without thinking about his perfect ass. Thank god he was sitting at his desk right now, concealing it. For added protection, I opted to lie on my back on the bed. My feet rested on the headboard. My eyes aimed straight up at the ceiling.

I heard the wheels of Noah's chair roll in my direction across the hardwood floor. The noise stopped and the music got low.

Shutting my eyes tight, I swallowed hard. My body heat shot up at the same time I felt tremors ripple through my stomach. My head began to spin.

I continued tapping my foot in the air to the rhythm of the music, pretending that, that was my focus. Did he want to talk? Am I going to have to gaze into his dreamy light blue eyes and look at his perfect ass?

Damn Beth and Brittani. I have *got* to get these thoughts out of my head. Focus, Amanda.

Aunt Agnes in a bathing suit. Aunt Agnes in a bathing suit. Aunt Agnes in a bathing suit. Noah in a bathing suit that hung low on his hips, right above his perfect ass. Shit.

I heard him clear his throat. "Tweet," he said, the sound of his voice causing my pulse to rev up.

"Yep."

"You know that girl who sat at lunch with us today, Brittani Monroe?"

"Yep."

"What do you think about her?"

"She's a slut with a stripper name."

The sound of him chuckling made me smile. "Tell me how you really feel. Don't hold back."

Lowering my legs, I swung them over the side of the bed, and faced him, trying hard not to make any eye contact. I leaned back on my arms, propping myself up. My gaze stayed downward.

Trying to sound very nonchalant, I said, "Why are you asking me about her?"

"She asked me out."

I shot straight up. "On a date?!" I couldn't hide the shock in my voice.

"Yeah, I guess."

"That's crazy talk!" My expression was pinched. Jealousy oozed out of every pore of my skin.

"What's so crazy about it?" He asked.

Glancing up, I saw a little smile appear across his face. I wasn't positive, but it seemed as if Noah was enjoying my reaction. The bastard.

"Um … well, number one, we're only fourteen and not allowed to date until we're sixteen. Number two..."

"I can date now."

Folding my arms across my chest, I narrowed my eyes at him. "You're kidding?"

"My parents said it was okay."

I was desperately trying to think of other reasons for him not to go out with the slut/stripper, the slipper. My list of pet names for her was growing by leaps and bounds.

"How are you going to get to the date? You don't even have your driver's permit yet. I'm pretty sure your handlebars aren't wide enough for her to sit on. I mean, have you seen the ass on that girl?"

"I've noticed her ass," he said, smirking at me.

I did not like his choice of words. *Seeing* her ass and *noticing* her ass were completely different.

"She asked if I wanted to go bowling. Her dad's going to drop us off."

"So you're going to go through with this?"

"I guess. Why not? She seems nice enough, and she's kind of pretty."

Pretty? Pfft! Had he been smoking crack? She had big tits, a big ass, and was willing to let any guy crawl all over them.

Looking down, I began picking at an imaginary piece of lint on my jeans, "Well, do what you want. It's your life to ruin."

"It's just bowling, Tweet," he said, the smile evident in his voice. He was having fun.

Tilting my head back and towards one shoulder, my eyes focused on the ceiling, I said, "Yeah. Well, first it's bowling, then it's a movie, and then you'll get married, buy a house, and have little slutty stripper kids. But, if that's what makes you happy, who am I to stand in your way."

Several seconds passed before Noah said anything. "Can I ask you something else?"

"Shoot," I said.

He hesitated for a moment. "Have you ever kissed a guy?"

"I've kissed my dad and my granddad."

He shook his head. "I don't mean relatives. I mean a guy. Have you ever had a *real* kiss from a guy?"

"You know the answer to that is no." My voice was weak. I tucked my chin to my chest, looked down at the floor, and nervously shuffled my feet back and forth.

"We'll, I've heard from a reliable source that Brittani has kissed a guy, a few of them, in fact."

"That doesn't surprise me." We sat in silence for another moment, and then a thought crossed my mind. "OH MY GOD!!! Are you going out with her so you can *get some*?"

Noah bolted up in his chair. "What?! Get some what?!"

"Brittani, lovin'." I glared at him. The muscles in my neck and shoulders stiffened.

"No! I'm going because … I don't know … She asked me. Besides, you know how much I love the fries at the bowling alley. If you don't want me to go, I won't go. Just say so."

This was it. I needed to make a decision. I could hold on to him for a little while longer, and hope that eventually my feelings would change, or I could let him go. Maybe if I saw him with another girl, it would help knock some sense into me, even if it was with the *slipper.*

I looked away from him when I said, "Go." I paused. "It's just … I don't think she's the right girl for you."

"Oh, I'm positive *she's* not the right girl for me."

My eyes immediately shot to his. I had butterflies in my stomach. He looked incredibly sweet sitting there in his worn jeans, t-shirt, and Red Sox baseball cap. He was wearing it backwards and a little bit of his hair was sticking out through the opening, just above the adjustable strap. He really was 'all kinds of yummy', I wanted to jump up and wrap my arms around him.

Noah ran his hand over the back of his neck. "The thing is … is … um … You know I haven't kissed a girl yet. I'm not saying it's going to happen, but what if she kisses me, and I don't do it right? Word would get out and I might as well go be a priest, because no girl would want to go out with me."

I took a big gulp of air thinking what it would be like to have Noah kiss me. I must have zoned out because the next thing I heard was him saying, "Earth to Tweet."

"Sorry. Um … Don't worry about it. You'll do fine."

He leaned forward, resting his elbows on his knees, which brought him closer to me.

"You know what would help me?"

"What?"

"If I could practice," he said, anxiously.

He held my gaze for several seconds until it dawned on me what he was thinking. "With me?"

"Yeah."

I shook my head. "No, I don't think that's a good idea."

"It's a great idea. We'll practice on each other, so we won't embarrass ourselves in front of anybody." His eyes sparkled with excitement over this ridiculously stupid idea.

"I don't have anyone who wants to kiss me in the near future," I admitted, you could hear the embarrassment in my voice.

"I wouldn't be so sure about that."

I glanced up at him and watched as his grin grew wider. He slipped out of his chair and down on one knee, begging, "Think of it as preparing for your future. Please, Tweet. I need you."

I sat there for what felt like a lifetime. Did I really want to do this? I didn't want Noah to go out with Brittani in the first place. I sure as hell didn't want him to kiss *her*, but I sure as hell wanted him to kiss *me*, and I wanted to kiss *him*. He was my best friend and he needed me. I would be doing this for him. Plus, maybe all I needed to do was kiss him one time, get it out of my system, and everything would go back to normal.

I looked into his beautiful eyes and said, "Okay."

"Seriously?" He asked.

"Yes."

Noah lunged forward tackling me on to the bed. He started tickling me, mercilessly. I was laughing so hard I couldn't catch my breath.

"Tweet, you're the bestest best friend a guy could have. You're awesome, incredible, fantastic …"

I continued to laugh and gasp for air as the tickling intensified. "Stop tickling me! I told you I'd help. I won't let you look the fool."

He kept up the torture.

"Promise?"

Laughing with tears in my eyes, I said, "Yes."

"Say it!"

The tickling eased up and when my vision cleared, I looked up at Noah hovering over me. With each heavy breath, our chests pushed against one another's. He was holding himself up with his hands, which were on either side of my head. Our legs were tangled together. We laid there for several seconds just staring at each other before I realized I hadn't answered him.

"Promise," I whispered.

"This is becoming a habit."

I scrunched my eyebrows in confusion. "What is?"

"You and me on top of each other." He had a devilish twinkle in his eye as the edges of his mouth began to curl up.

His lips were so close. I wondered what they tasted like. I bet they tasted like cherries. Noah looked like he would taste like cherries. His lips started to move toward my neck. Shiver after shiver ran through my body. Was he going to kiss my neck? I swallowed hard and froze when I felt the tip of his nose graze just below my ear.

"Wow. You smell really good," he whispered. His warm breath flowing over my cheek and neck caused me to shudder.

"I had a sour apple Blow Pop before I came over." I heard him chuckle.

My breaths were coming out in short spurts and my eyes hadn't blinked in the past five minutes. I was completely mesmerized.

Moving away from my neck, he smiled down at me, and said in a low voice, "Thanks for helping me, Tweet."

"You're welcome." I was so overwhelmed with what had just happened, my voice was almost inaudible.

Noah matched my gaze, and then asked, "You know what they say, don't you?" I shook my head. "Practice makes perfect. We may need to practice a lot. I'm kind of a slow learner." He waggled his eyebrows and smirked.

I took in a huge gulp of air. "Do you want to start now?" My voice was so high pitched, it sounded like a dog's squeak toy.

He dipped down closer to me before pushing away, and vaulting off the bed.

"Can't right now. I got a dentist appointment. Mom will be picking me up soon."

I rose up on my elbows, still feeling quite dazed. "Oh … okay."

I slid both my hands into Noah's outstretched ones. He pulled me off the bed, and into his chest, gently pinning my arms behind my back.

Looking down at me, smiling, he said in a commanding tone, "Tonight. Seven o'clock. Our spot."

"Okay, I'll see you then," I said, breathlessly.

Taking a couple of steps back, he took his Red Sox cap off, ran his fingers through his hair a couple of times, turned his cap around, and put it back on. We never took our eyes off of each other.

Noah's Adam's apple bob up and down a couple of times as he swallowed hard, and said, "Thanks again, Tweet, for helping me out. I'll see you tonight, okay."

"Okay … yeah … tonight … see you then."

I watched as he walked out the room, letting out a deep sigh once his perfect ass had disappeared from view. I needed to get a hold of myself and get Noah out of my system. I won't risk losing my best friend just because of a stupid girly crush.

The adrenalin was pumping so fast through me after leaving Noah's house I needed to keep moving, so I hopped on my bike, and went for a long ride. Whenever I had a problem or just needed to clear my head, cycling was my therapy. I loved the solitude, the freedom, and the control I felt when I was out for a ride.

When I got home I showered and dressed quickly in my pale green maxi dress and sandals. I put my hair up in a high ponytail and threw on a pair of small silver hoop earrings. I wasn't trying to dress special, I told myself.

I still felt a lot of nervous energy. There was no point in eating supper because I might throw it up. My stomach was in a constant state of flip-flopping.

As I walked into the park, I saw Noah standing at our spot. His back was to me. I could tell he heard me approach, my steps crunching on the gravel that surrounded the picnic area. When he turned around and saw me, his eyes looked as if they had doubled in size and it looked like his mouth was forming the word, "*Wow.*". I shyly smiled at him. He looked perfect in his baggy black shorts that hit him just below the knee, showing off his tan muscular calves. His broad chest was covered in a white Nike t-shirt. He had on his black and white Nike shoes, and as usual, his Red Sox cap, turned around backwards.

As he stepped away from the table I couldn't believe my eyes. Dinner for two had been setup; a red and white checkered tablecloth, paper plates, sodas, and napkins had all been placed on our table, at our spot. In the middle of the table sat a candle in a red glass holder, just like at the pizza place. Noah's iPod was playing "You And Me" by Lifehouse.

He was standing with one arm behind his back. As he approached, he brought his arm around, and handed me the most beautiful bouquet of wildflowers I had ever seen. No one had ever given me flowers before.

"These are for you," he said, smiling at me.

I took the flowers, brought them up to my nose, and inhaled their sweet scent.

Noah stood rocking back and forth on his heels with both hands in his pockets. He was nervous and adorable. "You look really pretty, Tweet."

My face began to heat up. "Thanks. What is all this?" I was completely overwhelmed that he went to all this trouble for me.

"I wanted to thank you for helping me out. I know it's a lot to ask."

I smiled even though I could feel tears forming behind my eyes. I wanted so much for this to be a real date and not just one friend helping out another. A feeling of sadness overtook me as I reminded myself that this was just Noah's sweet way of thanking me and knowing that tomorrow night another girl would be having a real date with him.

Lightening the mood, he walked over to my side, nudging my arm with his elbow. "Stop standing there being such a girl," he teased. "It's just our regular old table. Sit down."

"Thank you, Noah. This is … it's …" For the first time in my life I was at a loss for words.

Sitting across from each other at the table, we stayed quiet, looking at each other, and listening to the music. It wasn't awkward at all. It felt comfortable and natural.

"Can I ask you something?" I said, breaking the silence.

"You can ask me anything, Tweet."

"Do you think it's weird for us to be best friends?"

"What do you mean weird?"

Shrugging my shoulders, I said, "Beth thinks it's weird."

He reached across the table, took hold of my hand and laced our fingers together.

"It doesn't feel weird to me. When I'm with you everything feels perfect. I can't picture anyone else being my best friend and I don't want to."

Looking down at our joined hands, my pulse quickened. I had to keep reminding myself that this was not a date, I was not his girlfriend, and would never be.

I cleared my throat and whispered, "I feel the same way."

A tear rolled down my cheek as I let out a deep sigh. I tried to wipe it away before Noah noticed it, but I wasn't fast enough.

He brought my hand up to his lips and placed a soft kiss on the palm of it, never taking his eyes off me. "Don't cry, Tweet."

There was something in the tone of his voice and the look in his eyes that made me think he wanted to tell me something, but didn't know how to say it. Noah knew me better than anyone else and could read my thoughts and feelings. No doubt he could tell I was getting all girly and mushy over the dinner, the music, the flowers, and him. He was trying to figure out a way of letting me know that this was just a thank you and not a date, without hurting my feelings.

The sound of a car horn saved Noah from the awkwardness of letting me down and me from any embarrassment. Raising his free hand and pointing his index finger in the air, he said, "I believe our dinner has arrived."

We had pizza for dinner and breath mints for dessert. Noah thought of everything. Now it was time to practice.

We were both nervous. Noah hit the table a few times like he was playing the drums. He looked like he was trying to decide on something. He stopped drumming and looked at me.

"I guess standing would be the best way to do this," he said. I nodded my agreement.

We stood, he walked over to me, landing a couple of feet away, directly in front of me. He rolled his shoulders, forwards and backwards a couple of times, stretched his neck from side to side, and then shook his arms out. It looked like he was gearing up to run a track meet. He bent down, rubbing his palms over his shorts a couple of times while exhaling a few deep breaths. Standing back up, he announced, "Ok, here it comes."

"I don't think it's a good idea to slap a warning label on it."

"I'm not going to say that tomorrow." I gave him double

thumbs up.

"Sorry. I thought that might have been one of your moves."

Noah moved in closer to me, leaving very little space between us. Looking into his eyes I could see that the nervousness had somehow already disappeared and had been replaced by a look of excitement. We stared at each other. My heart was beating so loud I was sure he could hear it. Tingles shot through my body. They started at my core and exploded in every direction until I was completely consumed by them.

I felt Noah's hands cup my face just before his thumb lightly stroked my right cheek, causing a shiver. He smiled down at me when he felt how my body responded to his touch. My breathing had become shallow and I was burning up. If it weren't for the beautiful boy standing in front of me, I would have thought I was coming down with the flu.

Light blue eyes gazed at me with intensity; I was completely mesmerized by them. It was as if he were trying to memorize every part of my face. Noah's gaze lingered on my lips for a while then moved back up to my eyes. His thumb made its way towards my mouth and gently, he ran it over my lips a couple of times before returning to my cheek.

We both started breathing faster. I swear I could hear the blood pumping through my veins. Parts of my body that I didn't know existed were vibrating.

Slowly his lips moved closer to mine. Our song, *Everything,* filled the air. When our lips met it felt like fireworks were exploding in me.

At first, his lips were gentle and lightly touched mine. I felt the tug of my bottom lip as he sucked on it slightly. I nearly fainted. My hands reached out grabbing his arms to steady myself. Then I felt the tip of his tongue between my lips waiting for me to make the decision. I willingly parted them. Our tongues met, lightly stroking each other at first.

I had heard about French kissing and thought it sounded disgusting. It wasn't disgusting *at all.*

Noah tasted so good. He didn't taste like cherries. He tasted like peppermint. Our tongues started to move faster with more eagerness. I had never felt anything this amazing in my life before.

A slight moan escaped from me as our movements began to slow. Noah pulled away a little bit, our lips still touching. I thought I heard him whisper, "You're perfect." I was so discombobulated, that he may not have said a thing.

We stood there, eyes closed, foreheads resting against each other while trying to catch our breath. Noah ran his hands down the length of my arms, clasping our hands together. All sense of time, space, and others disappeared.

After our breathing finally calmed down we opened our eyes, but our foreheads stayed together. Noah glanced at me and whispered, "Wow."

"Man," I said, breathlessly. Are you sure you haven't done this before because you have some pretty awesome moves. Where'd you get moves like that?" I asked.

"Wal-Mart." A sly grin crept across his face.

The corners of my mouth slowly started moving up to form a smile. "How long did it take you to think that one up?"

"It just came to me actually. I thought it was pretty good."

After cleaning up, Noah walked me home in comfortable silence. When we reached my front door we hesitated. It felt strange, like neither one of us knew how to end the night. We were still friends even though that kiss was definitely more than friendly. My feelings were rapidly becoming stronger. I needed to force myself to get past this. He was my best friend and I wasn't going to do anything to jeopardize that. I had to keep telling myself that nothing could ever happen between us. Besides, he didn't think of me that way even though that kiss was amazing. Teenage boys would kiss almost any girl, they were so horny.

Finally, I broke the silence. "Well, goodnight. It sure was fun practicing with you. Brittani is a lucky girl." My face immediately contorted and I regretted the words that came out of my mouth.

"Don't bring her up, not now." He looked back and forth from my lips to my eyes. "Thanks for tonight."

He glanced away for a second, and then looked back at me as a sweet smile spread across his face. "Goodnight, Tweet."

"Goodnight Noah."

As I watched him back away and walk down the front steps, tears started to collect in my eyes. I suddenly had this empty feeling. I didn't want him to leave. I didn't want these feelings. They were going to ruin everything.

Noah suddenly stopped at the bottom of the steps. "Tweet." His voice was low and raspy.

"Yeah?" I tried to keep my voice steady.

"Tonight was amaz …," he paused. "You're amazing."

"Noah …" I trailed off as I choked back a sob.

"I wish you believed it," he said.

He left without saying another word.

Standing alone, watching him walk away, the only thought running through my mind was, *I wished I believed it too, so I could be your girlfriend.*

I was at my locker the Monday morning after my kiss with Noah. I hadn't seen or talked to him since our practice on Friday night. His date with The Interloper was Saturday night. I had to work on a paper all day Sunday, so there really was no time to get together.

Plus, I wasn't all that interested in finding out how his date went. That's a lie. I was a little interested. That's a lie too. I was completely consumed by thoughts of his date the entire weekend. I was too afraid of what I would hear, so I avoided him. If I didn't see or hear about it then I could pretend it didn't happen.

I startled when he came up behind me and whispered in my ear. "Mornin, Tweet."

"Good morning."

"I've missed you. I called you all weekend. I saw your mom yesterday. She said you were busy working on a paper." He leaned his shoulder against the lockers.

"English," I said.

Just then one of Noah's teammates, Brad Johnson, walked up, slapped Noah on the back, and said, "Hey Stewart, heard you had a great time this weekend. I just got out of class with Brit. She couldn't stop singing your praises, dude. Way to go." As Brad walked off, Noah turned to me and shrugged.

Two other teammates, Jeremy and Spencer, came up. Spencer playfully grabbed the back of Noah's neck, and said, "Heard you had a hot date this weekend. How about that, just a freshman and already a player." Noah looked back at me as the guys walked off.

Innocently, I asked, "Your big date was *this* past weekend?"

"Don't do that."

"Do what?"

"Play dumb. You're no good at it, Tweet."

"Well, it sounds like your first date was a success," I said with just a tad bit of snarkiness in my voice.

"I would say my first date was perfect."

I started shoving books around in my locker, not looking at him. I knew I was being ridiculous. I knew he had the date with *her* Saturday. As I banged things around, I could feel him smiling at me. The bastard.

"Uh ... you about done beating up that innocent locker, Rocky?"

"Congratulations! I'm glad your first date was ... "

"Perfect." He was enjoying himself at my expense.

"Perfect," I repeated, sounding pissed off. "Oh, did I tell you that I joined the school newspaper? You know, maybe I could write an article about having the perfect date and interview you and your perfect date since your date was so perfect." My words got snippier the longer my sentence ran on.

"Do you have any idea how adorable you are right now?" I narrowed my eyes at him. "Those guys are talking about my second date."

"You've already had a second date?"

"Saturday night."

"Saturday night?" My anger and confusion were about to go through the roof. "I thought Saturday night was your first date."

"Friday night was my first date."

I scrunched up my eyebrows, not understanding what he was talking about. "But you were with me all Friday night."

He leaned in so close our noses were almost touching. His voice was low. "You didn't think I wanted Brittani to be my first date and kiss, did you? I've shared all my firsts with you." His eyes scanned my face as a shy smile played across his full lips.

Maintaining eye contact, he pushed off of the lockers, turned and then sauntered down the hall without saying another word, leaving me dazed, confused, and breathless. That had to be the sweetest, and hottest, thing any guy has ever said to any girl.

Entry 6

He had the power to fill me with 1000 lifetimes of happiness. He also had the power to bring me to my knees. Most people would jump at the chance for that much happiness, but not me. The more happiness you have, the more devastating the fall is, and there is always a fall, a crash, or a collision. With all-consuming, earth shattering happiness, there are always casualties, it's unavoidable.

No, I'll maintain my subpar happiness. I've had a taste of what it feels like when the fall starts. Just a taste, and it almost destroyed me.

I might not experience 1000 lifetimes of happiness, but I won't be shattered into a million pieces that I can't put back together.

(Note to self: Eating king size Hershey bar and drinking Diet Pepsi @11:25 pm, not a good idea. Hope what I just wrote makes sense tomorrow when I come down from my sucrose and caffeine (sucraffiene)

OVERDOSE. CHECK TO SEE IF SUCRAFFIENE IS AN ACTUAL WORD. ONCE VETTED, START TO USE IT, SO IT WILL BEGIN TO INFILTRATE INTO SOCIETY. MAN, I AM WIRED BEYOND BELIEF.)

Academically, my freshman year had been okay. I ended up with a B+ average. As usual, I missed my goal, but collected another ribbon for participation. Yay for me. I'm nothing if not tenacious, though, and it was a new school year. I needed to achieve that perfect A status like Emily always did. I was determined as a sophomore to finally get that trophy.

The feelings I had towards Noah kept growing stronger. I got butterflies every time I saw him walk towards me, away from me, beside me. The closer he got, the more intense they became. I daydreamed about him constantly; during class, in my room, in the car, when I ate. Basically, he was on my mind every minute of every day. I felt warm and tingly when I thought about something he said to me or when he touched me. I got goose bumps every time I thought about our first kiss, and I thought about it often.

Mom caught me several times in a Noah-induced haze. One morning over breakfast, she and Dad actually staged an intervention. She even had a handful of *'Just Say No'* pamphlets from the 1980s. I think they were from her own personal stash when she was a teen.

At first, I thought I was just going through a passing phase, just an innocent crush. I had always loved Noah. It was something that came naturally, without thinking, like breathing. I figured when we started hugging more and holding hands, it was just a natural progression of our friendship. Then I noticed how it made me feel and apparently these feelings weren't going anywhere anytime soon. I thought we were both just raging with hormones, it was a biological thing, and eventually it would go away. Well, I'm an idiot because just the opposite happened.

As our freshman year progressed, more and more girls sought Noah out, and their shameless flirting drove me insane. Noah was nice to them like he was to everyone, but I never saw him flirt back.

Brittani was the most persistent. She shamelessly flirted with him every chance she got but he always brush it off. Then one day, while Noah and I were at our lockers, Brittani came up, as usual, and flirted with Noah, as usual. But this time I noticed it made him uncomfortable. He looked at me with sadness and regret in his eyes before rushing me away from her. It didn't take me long to realize that something had happened between them that Noah didn't want me to know about. I never asked. I just kept living in the world of make believe where no one would ever come between me and my knight.

It was a beautiful day outside, so Beth and I decided to forgo the cafeteria and spend our lunch period in the courtyard area at school.

"Are you going to the dance?" She asked, as we were finishing up our lunch.

"What dance?"

"The TWIRP dance."

"What's that?"

"The Woman Is Required to Pay. Girls have to ask boys to go."

"Then that would be a big fat nooo," I said.

"You ought to go."

"Why? I can't dance."

"It will be tons of fun."

"I highly doubt that. Besides I don't have anyone to go with."

I balled up my empty bag of chips and tossed it in the direction of the trashcan, missing it by a foot and a half. I walked towards the crumpled bag, scooped it up, made another attempt at a basket, and missed again. How the hell did Emily score so many points during a basketball game with the basket hanging in the air, and I couldn't toss a piece of garbage in a giant trashcan from a foot away. I made two more attempts before giving up.

"Screw it," I said, walking back and sitting down on the bench.

"*You* have to ask a boy, silly."

"Don't do that again."

"What?" Beth asked.

"Call me silly. Eccentric is fine. Quirky I like. Just not silly. I don't like silly."

"God, you're weird sometimes."

"Weird is acceptable as well."

We had a few more minutes left during lunch period, so I decided to work on my color a little bit. Leaning back on the bench, I closed my eyes, and tilted my head up, letting the sun warm my face. I hadn't been brave enough to get highlights in my hair, like *Bitchani* had suggested, but I had gotten some sun over the summer, and was trying to maintain.

Beth and I sat there in silence. She had been acting kind of strange lately, but I chalked it up to that was just Beth. She acted weird at times, especially when she had a boy on the brain. I peeked out the corner of my eye and saw her biting her nails.

"I'm thinking about asking Noah," she said in a low breathy voice.

When I heard her words, the only body part that moved was my mouth when I asked, "Noah who, about what?"

"Noah Stewart, about going to the dance."

I sat completely still for a full minute, attempting to process what she just told me. I tried to hide any visible signs of my increasing irritation, but my jaw was clenched, and I could feel my nails digging into my thighs. The heat of anger and jealously surged inside me. Slowly I sat up and turned to face her. I put my best poker face on. I couldn't let on how I was feeling. I needed to stay calm when I explained to her how incredibly stupid she was for even thinking about asking Noah.

"That's ridiculous," I said.

"Why?" She asked, lowering her hand from her mouth.

"Because it just is. He's not going to go to a lame dance with you."

"Why not?"

"Well, number one, he hates *dancing*. Number two, if he were going with someone, it'd be with me. It would be the first dance either of us went to and we do all our firsts together. Number three, the two of you can't go out together without me."

"Why can't we?"

"Because I'm the glue," I said,

"The glue? What?" Her face was pinched together in confusion.

"The glue. Noah and I were friends first. Then you moved in and I became your friend first. I introduced you to Noah. Then you became friends with him."

Beth looked at me as if another head had sprouted from my neck. I slowed my speech down hoping my point would be clearer to her.

"I introduced you and Noah. You two wouldn't be friends if it hadn't been for me. *The glue.* I'm the common bond between the two of you. Noah and I can hang out together. You and I can hang out together. But you and Noah can't hang out without me." I placed my palm to my chest. "The glue. I'm the glue."

Beth stared at me for a minute, and then shook her head. She looked down at her wringing hands and took a deep breath. "I'vealreadyaskedNoahtogoandhesaidyes." She exhaled loudly.

"Excuse me?"

"I've already asked Noah to go and he said yes."

"How long have you and Noah been planning this little dance date?" I threw her a raised eyebrow, but kept my voice steady and calm.

"Not long," she hesitated. "A couple of days … or weeks … or maybe a month."

"A month!!" I leaned in closer to her.

Beth wouldn't make eye contact with me as she stammered through her words. "I needed at least a month. I had to get a new dress and shoes and …"

"Why didn't either of you tell me this? I should know about

these things."

"We weren't sure how you would react. You're a little weird when it comes to Noah."

"Weird? You know that's the second time you've referred to my friendship with him as weird," I said, annoyed.

"Maybe weird is the wrong word. Possessive. You're very possessive of Noah."

"That is *so* not true."

"You get crazy jealous when other girls come around him."

"I don't get jealous. I just don't think they're good enough for him."

"Amanda, do you like Noah?" She asked.

"That's a stupid question, of course, I like him. We're best friends."

"You know what I mean. Do you *like him*, like him?"

"Noah's my best friend and he means the world to me."

I wasn't about to tell Beth what my feelings were for Noah. I was confused about them myself. I realized I couldn't have him, but I didn't want anyone else to have him either. I knew it was stupid and unfair, but it was how I felt.

"Fine. I don't get you," she paused. "Why don't you ask a guy and come? It'll be fun." Picking up her backpack, she stood. "Look, I got to run to my locker before class. At least think about going to the dance."

I watched as Beth walked away and into the main building. I wasn't mad at her for wanting to go out with Noah. Every girl in this school wanted to. I was hurt and angry with Noah. I couldn't remember ever being angry with him before. I didn't understand why he hadn't said anything to me about this date. We told each other everything. What had changed?

Maybe I should go to this dance. It might help me to see them together on an actual date. I had no idea who to ask. I certainly didn't want to give a guy the wrong impression. I just needed a date for this dance that was all, nothing else. The dance was in a week, anyone would do at this point.

I looked around the courtyard hoping my '*date*' would magically appear. After seeing my prospects were slim to none, I sat, looking down as if the answer was written in the concrete.

Getting ready to head back to class, I picked up my backpack, glanced up, and there was my answer, sitting right across from me.

"Hey!" No response. "Hey!"

Vincent looked over each of his shoulders to see if anyone was behind him. "Are you speaking to me?" He asked.

Vincent Chamberlin was the smartest kid in the sophomore class, probably in the entire school actually. He was also a nerd and awkward as hell, but nice and harmless.

"Of course. Who else would I be speaking to?"

"Practically anyone besides me," he said.

"Do you have plans this Friday night?"

"Seriously?" He paused, looking up as if his social schedule was written in the clouds. "No."

"You want to go to this dance thing?"

"Are you asking me out on a date?"

"Technically."

"Well ... um ... let me think about this for a minute. No one has ever asked me this question before." He rested his chin between his thumb and index finger, running them up and down his jawline as he pondered my question. "You and I *have* known each other since kindergarten. Although, you haven't really spoken to me since then or even acknowledge my existence."

I couldn't help my eye roll. Vincent was actually going to make me work for this. "I'm shy, what can I say. Yes or no?"

"Yes. It would be an honor to escort you to the dance. What time shall I pick you up?"

"Do you know where I live?"

"I'm not sure," he said.

I stood. "I'll meet you at the dance. No sense in cluttering your mind with my address."

"Wouldn't you like to go out to dinner before the dance?"

"I'd love to, but I think I'll be so excited and nervous that if I ate before, I might spew all over you." Vincent's face scrunched up in disgust. Leaning towards him for emphasis, I continued, "You wouldn't want my spew dripping off of you, would you?"

He leaned away, shaking his head rapidly. "I'll meet you at the dance."

Masochist-someone who obtains pleasure from receiving punishment, aka Amanda Marie Kelly. I wasn't even a good masochist, because no pleasure would be received from what I was about to do.

I couldn't concentrate for the rest of the day on anything except the impending Noah and Beth date. I needed and wanted to know why Noah kept it a secret from me and I would find out after school today.

I signed up to work on the school paper again this year. I loved writing. I planned on majoring in journalism in college but was undecided about what area I wanted to focus on; television, newspapers, or the internet. Maybe I'd even write a book someday. All I knew was I wanted to write.

Noah had been asked to play on the varsity baseball team this year. It was pretty unheard of that a sophomore would be playing for the varsity team. The school paper wanted an article written on him and had assigned it to me, obviously because we were friends, it certainly wasn't because of my baseball knowledge.

I thought it would be great to conduct the interview at the baseball field. Something magical happened to Noah when he was out there and I wanted to try and capture that with the article and accompanying picture.

Tony Hoffman was the school paper's photographer. We got the pictures out of the way first. Tony had Noah pose in a few baseball stances and sitting in the bleachers under the sign that bared the school name and mascot. When the pictures were done, Tony left, leaving me and Noah alone.

I went through the standard questions even though I already knew the answers. Like, how old were you when you started playing baseball? Which player influenced you the most? Then I moved on to the deeper questions.

"Okay, I only have one more questions then I'll set you free." I glanced away from my notes and smiled at him. "What made you first fall in love with the game?"

"My dad, he loves the game. He introduced me to it when I was 4 years old. That's when I watched my first game on TV, sitting next to him on the sofa with a liter of orange soda and two huge bags of chips on the coffee table." A slight smile played across his face. "I don't remember who was playing. It didn't matter. What mattered was I got to spend time with my dad sharing something that he loved.

The first couple of years I played t-ball and little league I liked playing the game, but the best part was always the time he and I spent together. No matter how busy he got at work, he would make it to every practice and game.

When I was six, he took me to my first pro game at Fenway Park. The Red Sox played the Minnesota Twins, 9-1, Sox. I was in awe of everything; the players, the stadium, the field, the stands, the dugout, the food, the parking lot," he chuckled. "My dad gave me one of the best days of my life."

As far as the game itself, I love everything about it; the teamwork, the way the bat feels in my hand, the sound of the ball hitting the leather glove, the smell of the grass, and concession stand food. I love looking up into the stands and seeing the fans and the most important people in my life."

Our eyes locked. The affection in his held me for several seconds. I wanted to crawl into his lap and hug him forever. Thank god I had brought a recorder to record his answers. There was so much reverence and love in his voice when he talked about his father, I had been too captivated to take notes.

Obviously caught up with emotion, he cleared his throat and said, "Sorry Tweet. I didn't mean to ramble on."

"You didn't ramble. You were perfect." I couldn't stop staring at him.

"So, any more questions?"

"No. I'm good. Thanks for doing this."

"No problem. I wouldn't miss spending time alone with my girl," he said, winking at me.

At that point, I didn't need to know why he kept the date a secret. It felt petty asking him about it after he had just given me that beautiful answer. I started to fidget, tapping my pen rapidly on my notebook.

"What's wrong, Tweet?"

The voice in my head kept repeating, get up and leave Amanda. NOW! Do not ask him about the dance, not now. DO NOT ASK!!!

"Why didn't you tell me you were going to the dance with Beth?"

Letting out a deep sigh, he rested his elbows on his knees. He took his baseball cap off and ran his hand through his hair as he swallowed hard a few times before starting to speak.

"You know what, forget I asked," I interrupted and began to quickly gather my stuff. Standing, I took one step in front of Noah before he grabbed my wrist.

"Don't run away from me. Sit back down." His voice was steady and raspy. I took a deep breath and sat beside him. We didn't look at each other. "I felt guilty. I know I'm getting ready to sound like a pussy, but I was disappointed that *you* didn't ask me."

"I didn't know you wanted to go."

"I don't give a shit about going to a dance. I wanted to go with you and I was hoping you would want to go with me, but you never said anything. When Beth asked I said yes for some reason. I wished I hadn't after it came out of my mouth. She seemed so excited and happy. I couldn't tell her I changed my mind."

"Why'd you feel guilty?"

"I don't know. It felt like I was cheating on you." He paused for a moment, as if he were struggling with what to say next. Looking over at me, he said, "Tweet, I've been having certain thoughts and feelings about you."

I sat in silence. My head was spinning. I wasn't prepared for this conversation. I could feel my throat starting to close up. The muscles in my neck and shoulders were tightening. I needed to get away from here. Noah's words were replaced by a whooshing sound in my ears as heart and pulse rates rose. Then I felt a warm hand touch mine and it brought me back. I turned my head to see a pair of light blue eyes that I could get lost in.

"I think about you all the time, Tweet," he said, lacing his fingers through mine.

"It's nice to be thought about." To date, that was one of the stupidest things I had ever said.

He smirked at me. "When you're around, I want to touch you, hold your hand, or put my arms around you. I want to kiss you again." He continued to hold my gaze, looking for some reaction on my face and in my eyes.

I swallowed a big gulp of air. I was ten seconds away from a full on panic attack. I could feel beads of sweat starting to form on my forehead and neck. My throat closed a little more and my muscles twisted even tighter. I didn't know what to say, so I did what I usually do. I ran.

"Um … Noah, I have to go."

Those beautiful eyes that were filled with caring a second earlier looked shocked, hurt, and pissed off. "You're leaving?!" He definitely sounded pissed.

"I need to go check and make sure Tony got enough pictures

and … um … Look, I'm sorry. I'll see you later. Thanks again for the interview." I had been clutching my backpack in one hand while Noah held the other. I got up and walked quickly away, pulling my hand free from his grip.

Entry 7

Honesty is not always the best policy when it hurts the person you care about the most and pushes them away.

I hung out in the journalism classroom for an hour before heading home. My hope was that Noah had already left school. I felt horrible running away from him like I did, especially since he had been so wonderful and sweet. He caught me off guard. I don't do well on the fly, not when it comes to important things. I just needed some time to clear my head and collect my thoughts.

Brenda, a senior student reporter, was nice enough to give me a ride home. I entered my house taking in the aroma of my mom's five star spaghetti sauce. Tossing my backpack on the kitchen counter, I found Mom hard at work frosting a chocolate cake.

"Hey. Mom," I said as I grabbed a bottle of water from the fridge. I walked over to where she was and leaned back against the counter. "What 'cha doing?"

"Well, sweetie, I'm spackling the walls," she said, throwing a quick smirk my way.

"People often ask me where I get my smart-assness from," I said.

"Do you let them know it's from your father's side of the family? You know they're all afflicted."

I noticed the table was set for six. There were only three of us in the house now that Emily was off at college.

"Why's the table set for six?"

"The Stewarts are having dinner with us tonight," she answered.

"Why?" The word felt thick in my throat.

"Because they have to eat, sweetie."

She handed me the chocolate covered spatula and moved the cake over to the table.

"All of them?" I asked, my mouth full of frosting.

"Last time I checked, they all ate food."

She was moving around the kitchen at warp speed, getting things ready for our dinner guests. She was a great mom, really, especially when she made extra frosting because she knew how much I loved it. However, there were those times, like right now, that it felt as if she and the universe were plotting against me.

As I sucked every last drop of frosting off the spatula, I could feel my nerves already starting to overtake my body at just the thought of seeing Noah later. I tossed the spatula in the sink, grabbed my things off the counter, and headed to my room. I heard my mom say, "Dinner will be in about two hours," just before I shut my bedroom door and tried to figure out how I was going to get through this dinner.

I had too much nervous energy, so I went for a quick bike ride around the neighborhood, completely avoiding Noah's street. Usually cycling cleared my head. Today I had so many thoughts and feelings running through me that I couldn't get a grasp on any of them.

When I got home, I showered and changed into my gray and white striped tank dress. I toweled dried my hair some and then let it air dry. I was sitting at my desk working on Noah's article that was due by the end of the week, when there was a knock on my door.

"Yeah?" I asked.

The door opened slightly. I didn't need to look up to know who it was. The butterflies that were whirling around in my stomach and the goose bumps across my skin told me who stood in my doorway.

Noah poked his head in. "Your mom wanted me to tell you dinner is in twenty."

"Thanks."

He stood in the doorway for a minute before stepping completely inside my room, closing the door behind him. He walked over to me, placed his hands on the back of my chair as he looked over my shoulder, and asked, "What are you working on?"

"Your article," I said, tilting my head back and looking straight up at him.

"Make me look good."

"There's no other way for you to look."

Where the hell did that come from, Amanda Marie Kelly?

When he's this close to me, I get flustered, and I can't always control what comes out of my mouth.

Smiling at me, Noah crossed the room and sat on the end of my bed, leaning back on his arms. I turned my chair to face him. I knew he wanted to talk, but I still didn't know what to say. My feelings were completely confusing to me. I needed him in my life. I knew I wasn't good enough for him, but I couldn't stand the thought of another girl having his attention. The pull I felt towards him kept getting stronger and with what he said to me earlier today, I wasn't sure if I could control these feelings much longer without acting on them. But, I knew acting on them would be the worst thing for our friendship. For now, I figured I would just wait to see if he brought it up. I would just have to wing it.

"Tweet, what was the deal today?"

"What deal are you referring to?"

"Don't do that. Now's not the time to play dumb."

"You seem to be under the impression that I *play* dumb."

"Why'd you run away from me today?"

"I really had to leave."

I was starting to feel anxious and when I feel anxious, I have to move. I walked over to my dresser and fumbled around until I found my brush. I pushed the bristles forcefully through my hair before piling it on top of my head, and pinning it securely. I could see in the mirror, Noah watching my every move.

"Why?" he asked.

"Because we we're having guests for dinner." I was trying to keep things light and breezy. By the look on his face I could tell Noah wasn't in the mood for light and breezy.

Siting up straight he began to shake his head. Huffing in frustration, he said, "Dammit Tweet, would you stop being such a smartass for one minute." I turned to face him. "You do this every time there's something serious to talk about."

"Do what?"

"Make jokes and then run away." He kept his voice low, but he was fuming.

He ran both his hands over his face a couple of times while waiting on my response.

"I'm sorry," I whispered.

"Please talk to me."

"I'm not sure what you want me to say."

"Then I'll start," his voice was soft as he continued. He stood and walked slowly towards me. "You're the first girl I've ever noticed and the last girl I'll *ever* notice. My first kiss was the greatest first kiss in the history of first kisses because it was with you. I can't stop thinking about you."

I took a step back, bumping into the dresser. He was standing right in front of me, his light blue eyes holding me captive. He placed his hands on the dresser, on either side of my hips, and leaned in close. My breathing accelerated. I felt his lips lightly brush across my temple. The shivers he caused were off the charts. His lips moved down to my ear, skimming lightly across my skin like a feather. The feel of his warm breath on my neck caused my head to spin. I had to lean back more on the dresser to support myself. Once his lips reached my ear, I heard in a whispered tone, "I want you to be more than my best friend. I want you to be my girlfriend. What do you want, Tweet?"

I knew this would happen. I'm weak. I snapped. I couldn't take it any longer, the months of dreaming about him day and night, the constant butterflies in my stomach caused by him. He was so close. His lips left a trail of heat wherever they touched, his words made me melt, his eyes where that beautiful shade of blue, and he smelled like sweet fresh oranges.

I had reached my breaking point when I breathlessly whispered, "I want you."

Noah pulled away slightly and tilted his head. As his lips moved in closer, my breathing became more erratic, and my heart was pounding against my chest wall. The new sensation between my legs was driving me insane.

His gaze traveled up and down my face, landing on my eyes. "God, you're beautiful," he whispered.

My eyes automatically fluttered closed. I felt the slightest touch of his lips on mine. My mind was whirling around as my body responded to him. Suddenly, a loud knock reverberated around the room startling us both. Noah jumped back, turning away from me. The quick movement caused me to fall forward slightly. We heard my dad yell, "Dinner!"

Noah glanced at me over his shoulder, a look of terror flashed across his face.

"Don't worry. He won't come in," I said.

My dad was famous for the knock and walk. He implemented it the day he came in the front door to find Professor Tampon, aka my mother, giving a 12-year-old Emily and two of her friends a lecture on the proper use of feminine hygiene products, with visual aids.

Steadying myself, I ran my hands down my dress, smoothing it out. I looked over at Noah. He still wasn't facing me. My eyes started at his broad shoulders and then traveled down his muscular back, to his hips, where his hands rested. His biceps strained slightly against the material of his shirt. I shook my head trying to clear it of thoughts of Noah's body.

I took one more quick look of his fantastic back side before clearing my throat, and asking, "Noah, are you coming?"

His chin was tucked into his chest as he held up his index finger, indicating he needed a few minutes before he would be able to join us. I felt it was best to leave him alone, so I went to dinner.

We were all sitting around the table eating by the time Noah joined us. He sat in the only empty seat left which happened to be next to me. Dad and Mr. Stewart talked about work while Mom and Mrs. Stewart shared the neighborhood gossip. I was trying to recover from the intense moment in my room earlier, which I would have been able to do if Noah hadn't been sitting right next to me. That was bad enough, but he kept finding subtle ways of touching me. What happened in my room was a mistake, even though it didn't go very far, it went far enough. I had to be strong and put a stop to things happening between us.

Noah put his arm around the back of my chair and reached across me for some bread, which brought his face so close to mine his lips were almost touching my cheek.

Keeping my voice low, I said, "I know what you're doing."

"I do too, I really like garlic bread."

"I could have passed it to you if you had asked."

"Yeah, I know, but my way I get to look down your dress." My eyes shot immediately to his. "Oh, by the way, your bra selection tonight … Excellent."

I slapped my hand to my chest trying to close the gap he had been peering down.

"Please tell me your panties match," he whispered, and then leaned back slightly, glancing down in the direction of my panties. When I looked at him, I was met with a wink and a smirk before he shoved a big piece of garlic bread in his mouth.

"Noah, congratulations," my dad said.

Just then I felt a hand on my knee and fingers creeping under the hem of my dress. My breath hitched and my eyes darted over to Noah. I'd be completely pissed at him if his hand didn't feel so incredible on my naked leg.

"Thank you, sir."

How he could remain so calm, cool, and collected in front of our parents while his hand rubbed over my knee was beyond me.

"It's pretty rare that a sophomore gets asked to join the varsity team. We're proud of you." My dad always thought of Noah like a son.

"His mom and I are extremely proud of him. He's a chip off the old block," Mr. Stewart added.

The dads laughed as if the comment was hilarious. Noah smiled at his dad while his hand began to move up my thigh. I slapped it away and inadvertently hit the table with a loud thud, causing it to shake.

"Amanda, are you okay?" Mom asked.

'Yes. I'm fine." Noah snorted as he tried to contain a laugh. "I was swatting a fly away."

My mom looked at me, slightly annoyed, but maintained her cheery voice, and said, "That's ridiculous. We don't have flies in this house."

"My bad," I said.

Noah's hand landed back on my knee. He squeezed slightly, causing a loud gasp to escape me. All four parental heads turned to look in my direction.

"Um … Mom would you please pass me the … um …"

Noah's hand was relentless. He would squeeze my knee then rub the inside of my thigh. It was impossible for me to think or form a coherent sentence.

"The stuff in the bottle, that you … um … pour on … um … lettuce?" My pitch grew higher and higher with each word.

"You mean *salad dressing*?" Mom said, sarcasm flowing from her words like a torrential rain. I nodded. "You already have some on your salad."

"I need more. Please give me more."

She looked at me like I didn't belong to her before passing me the dressing.

"How's Emily?" Mrs. Stewart asked while I doused my salad.

A prideful smile appeared across my mom's face. "She's wonderful. She's loving college."

"That's fantastic," Mrs. Stewart said.

"In fact, she joined the debate team. *She's* an *extremely* articulate young woman," Mom said as she glanced in my direction. If she had any clue what was taking place under her dinner table, she might cut me some slack.

I was so out of sorts, I dropped my fork just before loading it up with salad. "I'll get it, Tweet."

Noah's hand disappeared from my leg. I took the opportunity to take a drink of water trying to calm down. Noah scooted his chair back and then bent down to grab the fork.

"Dead horse!" Dad announced while holding up the empty wine bottle.

All of a sudden, I felt a pair of lips on the outer side of my thigh right above my knee. I almost did a full blown spit-take at the exact same time my dad asked, "Are we game for another?"

Noah sat back up and I had three sets of eyes glued to me. The Stewart's eyes held pity, for my parents, no doubt. My mom's eyes held regret that she didn't send me for those etiquette lessons when I was younger and my dad wasn't even paying attention to my faux pas. He was busy holding the wine bottle above his glass desperately trying to get the last drop of wine to drip out.

"I'll go get you another bottle of wine. I'm done eating, anyway," I said, as I wiped the spray of water from my face.

I quickly rose from the table and made my way to the kitchen to put my plate in the sink. Without stopping, I headed to the garage where we had an extra refrigerator that my parents used for their wine collection.

Standing in front of the open fridge, I realized I didn't know if they wanted red or white. I took a bottle of each to be on the safe side. I closed the fridge and turned around coming face-to-face with a beaming Noah. I took a step back. He placed his hands against the fridge on either side of my shoulders, caging me in. He really liked caging me in.

"What the hell do you think you're doing in there with all the touching and the kissing? You kissed my *thigh* under the table. The family dinner table, for god's sake."

"I couldn't resist. You're mighty tasty." He waggled his eyebrows and moved in closer.

Holy crap on a cracker, tingles were taking over my body.

"Leave me alone for the rest of the night." I tried to sound mad, but even I could hear the smile in my voice. It was hard to be mad at Noah, especially when what he was doing felt so amazing.

"Okay, I will." He dropped his arms and stepped back giving me room to get by.

"Thank you."

As I passed him going back toward the door I felt the hem of my dress rise up behind me. I quickly stepped to the side, out of his reach. "Dammit, Noah! Stop it! I can't defend myself with these bottles in my hands."

Holding his hands up in surrender, he said, "I thought you had a speck of something on your dress. I was just trying to help is all." I narrowed my eyes at him before heading back into the house.

I passed on dessert, even though chocolate cake was my all-time favorite. I excused myself from the table, saying I needed to work on a paper, and went back to my room away from the glaring eyes of parents and the roaming hands and lips of my best friend.

As I sat on my bed remembering how his hands and lips felt on my skin, I could feel the heat building up inside of me. What the hell is wrong with me? I'm was just sitting there thinking about him and getting all hot and bothered. The knock on my door brought me back to the here and now. "Yeah?" My voice sounded raspy.

The door cracked open and all I saw was a floating plate with a piece of chocolate cake on it. I smiled. Then I saw my favorite pair of light blue eyes.

"I brought you some dessert."

Noah stepped in and closed the door behind him, tapping it with his foot. He placed the cake down on my bedside table and sat across from me on the bed. He held up the fork, which was already loaded with chocolate frosting. I was still feeling the effects of dinner as I stared at my two favorite things in the entire world. I parted my lips letting out a slight sigh. We never took our eyes off of one another. He handed me the fork.

Bringing it to my mouth, I slowly slid the fork between my lips. The tip of his tongue darted out of his mouth and ran across his lower lip. He watched the movement of my lips as they curled around the fork. I heard him swallow hard as I slid the fork out of my mouth. He took it from me and as he reached over to place the fork back on the plate, his lips almost grazed my cheek.

He moved in closer and whispered, "You have a little frosting in the corner of your mouth."

I stayed still. My eyes were completely focused on him as he hovered for a few seconds no more than a half inch away from my mouth. The temperature of my body shot up a hundred degrees. What the hell was I doing? I needed to stop this. I was so weak and stupid for allowing this to happen. Besides, both our parents were at the other end of the house. Thoughts of losing Noah sprinted across my mind. Just the idea of him not being in my life was too much to take. Who would I share my dreams and fears with? How could I possibly feel safe without Noah in my life? I started to panic. I could feel my chest tightening. I felt dizzy and smothered. I leaned away from him.

He pulled back and stared at me. I didn't want to see the look in his eyes, but I forced myself to face him. He needed to understand how serious I was when I said these words.

"We can't do this. I can't be your girlfriend." He stared at me for a few more seconds before turning away, staying seated on the edge of the bed with his elbows on his knees, and his head down.

"Why?" he asked in a raspy voice.

"I'm afraid if something happened to cause it to end, then it might fuck things up so badly you wouldn't want to have anything to do with me after that."

"That's bullshit."

"No it's not. You remember Tyler Evans? He and Emily were close friends. Not as close as we are, but very close. They decided to cross that line and date. It lasted six months and ended badly. They couldn't even stay friends. Emily and I saw him at the mall over the summer and he was so ugly toward her. I can't have that happen with us."

"We're not them."

"I know, but Emily does everything perfectly. If she couldn't make it work, I sure as hell can't. I have to have you in my life. I won't cross that line with you. It's too risky and I won't chance it, not with us. I'm sorry about tonight. I never should have let things go that far."

"I'm not sorry about what happened between us in here. Except that you won't be with me."

"It's not that I don't want to. It's just that I don't want to mess up our friendship. Besides, you deserve better than me, Noah."

You deserve the best and as much as I want that the best to be me, I know I will only end up disappointing you. I feel like I'm always disappointing people and you're the last person on earth I want to disappoint.

"There isn't anyone better than you for me," he said, looking at me over his shoulder.

"These feelings will fade away and things will get back to normal. Our bodies are going through a lot of changes. Hormones are flying all over the place. We just need to control ourselves and ride it out." I was trying to hold back my tears. He sat up and turned to me, showing me how crushed he felt. It was impossible not to let a few tears escape. "I can't lose you, Noah."

"You'd never lose me, Tweet. I'll always be here if you need me." He raised his hand, bringing it to my face. The tips of his fingers grazed down my jaw to my chin.

I shook my head, leaning away from him slightly. "Please Noah, I can't," I whispered.

In one fluid movement, his hand dropped, he stood, and walked to the door. His hand grabbed the doorknob.

"I'll see you in the morning when Mom and I pick you up for school, right?" I asked, my voice caught in my throat.

He didn't turn around to look at me. "I don't need a ride tomorrow. Coach called a meeting for the team before classes. Travis is going to give me a ride."

When he didn't turn and look at me the nerves took over my body. My voice got shaky. "I'll see you at school then."

"Maybe. See ya around, Tweet."

When I heard the door click, I fell apart completely. The ache that had been in my stomach made its way through the rest of my body. I turned over and buried my face in a pillow to hide the sounds of my sobs. I couldn't keep my body from shaking. I was burning up inside and out. I had never felt pain this intense before. The sense of loss I had when Noah walked out of this room was all consuming. I kept telling myself that I would talk with him tomorrow. He's upset now, but once he's had a night to think it over, he'll realize I'm right. Why change something that has worked perfectly for us so far? And even though our relationship might get better for awhile, I was certain that I wasn't good enough to be with him forever. And I wanted Noah in my life, forever.

Entry 8

The two most devastating feelings in the world are failure and loneliness.

Failure, to a certain degree, is under you're control. In theory, if you work hard and give 100% you will achieve your goal. I think I work hard, but either I'm fooling myself or there is just an innate inadequacy gene woven through my DNA. Maybe I had a great, great, great, great, great grandparent, who was a total loser.

Loneliness, is worse than failure. Loneliness is controlled by others. But there's only one person in my life who influences whether or not I feel lonely. And being that vulnerable to a person is frightening.

I hadn't talked to Noah for three days. We had never gone that long without talking. In fact, we had never gone a day without talking or seeing each other. It was not for lack of trying on my part. I called several times, but he never picked up, the calls all went to voicemail. I saw him briefly at school. In class he was very distant, practically ignoring me. He'd say *hi* if we were near each other, but that was the extent of it. I spent a lot of time in the girl's bathroom, crying after each encounter I had with him. I couldn't concentrate on anything. After just one day of not having contact with him I almost went over to his house and made him talk to me. I thought I could put aside my insecurities. I thought I could step over the line and be his girlfriend. Then fear crept back over me. I didn't know how to keep it from dictating my actions. I didn't know how to overcome it.

Immediately after school each day, I found myself in the journalism classroom flipping through all the pictures of him that had been taken for the article I wrote. Then I would go and stalk him. I hung out at the boy's locker room, which garnered me some strange looks and a few phone numbers. He saw me a few times, but never acknowledged me. I was lost not having daily contact with him. I didn't know who I was without him. My words the other night hurt him, I knew that, I guess I didn't realize how much. He said he would be there if I needed him. I needed him now, but he wouldn't even look at me.

It was the day of the dance. I got home earlier than usual. Emily was home for the weekend to help me get ready and she told me to get home as soon as possible. She said we needed several hours to achieve my look. I wasn't sure how to take that. It usually didn't take me that long to get ready for anything. At this point, I didn't even want to go to the stupid dance, but I had asked Vincent. I couldn't bring myself to call and cancel.

I was laying on the bed in Emily's room while she rummaged through her closest for the perfect party dress for me. Thankfully, my sister was a pretty girl who went to a lot of dances and was similar in size to me. I was still shorter and a little curvier than Emily, but the difference wasn't as noticeable now like when we were younger. I couldn't have cared less about what I wore tonight. I heard her mumbling something while still in the closet. She stuck her head out when I didn't respond.

"Amanda, did you hear me?" she asked.

"Huh?"

"How do you feel about yellow?"

"As long as it doesn't have feathers glued to it, yellow is fine, Emily." My voice was flat.

She looked at me for a second and then started laughing. "Right, I had forgotten about Tweety. That was hilarious. We knew exactly where you were. All we had to do was follow the trail of feathers." I looked up glaring at her. "Too soon? Sorry. Okay, go take a shower, shampoo your hair, and shave everywhere."

I glanced at the clock on her nightstand. "I have two and a half hours before I have to be there," I whined.

"I know. You need to hurry up. We don't have a lot of time." She tugged my arms, pulled me to my feet, and pushed me out the door.

I did exactly what Emily told me to do even if it didn't make sense to me. My brain was so numb I didn't have the capacity to make any decisions right now. Noah was the only thought that played repeatedly in my head. I showered, shampooed, shaved, and returned to my sister's room.

The dress she picked out was hanging on the closet door. It was the one she wore the first time she ran for homecoming queen. She won, of course. The dress was a pale yellow strapless taffeta. The bodice fit me perfectly, hugging me in all the right places, giving me a curve or two. The skirt hit me right at the knee and was full and flowing with three dimensional flowers sporadically placed close to the hem. She had matched it with a pair of silver strappy sandals with almost 3 inch heels. I wasn't sure about the heels, but like everything else, I didn't care.

Emily had me put the dress on first before tackling hair and makeup. I was sitting at her vanity covered in a huge towel so nothing would get on the dress. There was an awful lot to do for a dance I didn't even want to attend.

"I think your hair would look awesome pinned up. Oh, and you can wear my diamond teardrop earrings that Mom and Dad gave me for my sweet sixteen," Emily said enthusiastically.

"Whatever you want to do is fine." My voice was monotone.

"For someone going to her first big dance, you don't seem very excited." I just shrugged my shoulders. "So what time is Noah picking you up?"

My chest tightened. I never told her who I was going with. I just told her I was going to the dance. "Noah's not picking me up."

"Why not?" she asked, eyeing me in the mirror while she brushed out my hair.

"Because I'm not going with him." She stopped brushing for a few seconds, a look of confusion crossed her face.

"Oh, sorry. I just assumed …"

"Well, you know what that does," I said.

"Why aren't you going with him?"

"Because I didn't ask him."

"Are we going to keep doing this or are you going to explain why you're not going to your first dance with Noah?"

"I just didn't ask him. Besides, he's not really happy with me right now." I shifted my gaze down to my lap, breaking it from Emily's. I was afraid if I said anymore I would start crying.

She stopped what she was doing and leaned against the vanity in front of me. "You want to tell me what happened?"

I couldn't speak. I was on the verge of breaking down now. If I opened my mouth to say one little word, I wouldn't be able to hold it together. I just shook my head. With the tips of her fingers, Emily tilted my head up to look at her. Tears were already swimming in my eyes.

"Talk to me, Manda. What happened?"

"I don't know what to tell you. I just know that he hasn't talked to me in three days. He doesn't answer his phone and he ignores me at school." I wiped a tear from my face. It was a good thing she hadn't done my makeup yet.

"There has to be a reason. That doesn't sound like Noah. You can tell me. I won't say anything."

I debated whether or not to open up to her. It wasn't that we weren't close, because we were, it was just embarrassing to admit the problem was me. I was a loser and a screw up. I had screwed up my friendship with Noah.

"Things are changing and I … um don't know what to do." My voice cracked and a few tears spilled.

A slight smile played across Emily's face. "It's hard when your best friend becomes a very cute boy, isn't it?" I didn't respond. She could see in my eyes that she was spot on. "Is there a girl that Noah likes?" I nodded. "Do you like her?"

"No, I don't. She's not good enough for him." I looked away from her. I wasn't exactly lying. It was just Emily didn't realize the girl we were talking about was me.

"Is that why he's mad?"

"Yeah," I whispered.

"Sweetie, I know it's hard and it doesn't feel right now like things will work out, but they will. You and Noah have something extremely special, you always have. Nothing will ever come between the two of you for any length of time."

"Thanks."

"Let's finish making you the hottest girl at the dance tonight." She hugged me and got right back to work.

This whole dance thing was already a nightmare and I hadn't even gotten out of the car. The minute we pulled into the parking lot, I felt like I was going to be sick. I was nervous about everything, the way I looked, socializing with Vincent, seeing Noah and Beth together, and just plain seeing Noah. I constantly tugged on the taffeta flowers that were stitched to my skirt during the ride over here. The cherry on top of my nerve sundae was the fact that I was sitting in the back of my parent's car. I wanted Emily to drive me here and pick me up, but my parents insisted. They said that since I was meeting Vincent here instead being picked up at our house, they wanted to come and see us together and take pictures. I agreed, after all, it was my first dance.

Dad parked and escorted me and Mom to the gym where the dance was being held. As we got closer, I saw a barrage of flashing lights as Vincent's parents took picture, after picture, after picture. He really wasn't a bad looking guy. Some would even say he was cute, in a nerdy sort of way. He had on a dark sports jacket, khaki pants, and a light blue button down shirt with a paisley bow tie. Not exactly GQ material, but it worked for him.

Vincent saw me walking towards him. I smiled as I saw his mouth drop open and his eyes blink a few times, like he was amazed at what he saw. I knew I probably wasn't, but I felt pretty for the first time in my life. Emily had done a fantastic job for what she had to work with, which wasn't much. Vincent and I stood there suffering as both sets of parents took what felt like a million pictures of us. Finally, we said our goodbyes to them and headed inside.

With every step I took towards the entrance, my stomach flip-flopped. The entrance to the gym actually looked nice, with an archway decorated with white roses and tiny white lights.

When we first entered, it was difficult to see anything before my eyes had time to adjust to the dim lighting. White columns were placed at each corner of the basketball court, strung with the same tiny white lights. Balloons in the school colors of white and navy blue had been tied everywhere. The DJ was setup at the farthest wall and a table with punch and snacks was set against the wall opposite of him.

I scanned the crowd looking for Noah and Beth. Neither one of them knew I was going to be there tonight. I wasn't sure I wanted them to see me. A ton of people were already here, so getting lost in the crowd would be easy. I just wanted a quick look at the two of them, anyway.

Vincent and I took a spot up against the wall behind a crowd of girls and boys who were too scared to ask each other to dance. My gaze went from the entrance to scanning the crowd and back again.

"Do you want to dance?" Vincent asked nervously.

"Do *you* want to dance?"

"Well, we are at a dance."

"Vinnie, let's not let the rules of society dictate our actions. I thought you were an independent thinker, man. That's the main reason I asked you to come tonight." He simply shrugged and leaned back against the wall.

I had been standing and scanning for at least 40 minutes and still no sign of Noah and Beth.

"I'm going to get some punch. Do you want any?" Vincent sounded blasé.

"What? Oh, no thanks. I'm good."

As Vincent walked away, he passed in front of me, blocking my view for a split second. When he moved I saw them. Noah and Beth had just walked in. I don't know if it was the altitude of the heels I was wearing, but when I saw Noah, my knees became weak and I got dizzy. I had to lean against the wall so I wouldn't fall.

Noah looked amazing. While most of the guys wore either a sport coat and khaki pants or just pants and a button down shirt, he had on a suit. It was black and paired with a light grey shirt and darker grey tie. Even in the dim light, his light blue eyes looked even brighter against the monochromatic colors of his suit. With the combination of those eyes, that dark brown hair, and dark suit, he exuded a smoldering sexiness.

As he and Beth walked further in, they were greeted by a few other couples. The girls ended up huddled together and the guys stood off to the side. I couldn't keep my eyes off of Noah. I was so focused on him that I was startled when Vincent walked up.

"Amanda … um … Sarah Grice just asked me to dance. I told her I needed to check with you first."

"Are you dumping me half way through our date?" I'm not going to lie, but I was a bit surprised at Vincent.

"No. I wouldn't do that. Listen, I know why you asked me to the dance. I heard you and Beth talking the other day at lunch." I felt bad that I was kind of using him. "It's okay. I'm glad I came with you instead of a real girl." My eyebrows furrowed as I huffed at him. "You know what I mean. Besides, everyone at school knows how you and Noah are."

"How are we?"

"I don't know. You guys seem like you're something."

"We're best friends. We grew up together. That's it."

He began fidgeting with the bottom of his jacket. "Look, this conversation is making me uncomfortable. I don't want Sarah to ask another guy to dance, so is it okay if I go now?"

"Yes."

"Thanks Amanda. You're a real pal." He patted my shoulder, turned, and disappeared into the crowd.

I directed my attention back to Noah and Beth, who were still in the same position, standing away from each other. Things were good. I was hidden and Beth and Noah were not dancing. The night was running pretty smooth and then I heard her.

"Hello Amanda. What on earth are you doing here?"

"Hello Brittani. It's a school function. I can't attend a school function?"

"You know you were supposed to bring a date."

"I brought a date."

"Who?" she snapped.

"Vincent Chamberlin."

She craned her neck over the crowd. "Yeah, where is he?"

I hesitated for a few seconds before saying, "He's dancing with Sarah Grice right now."

"Oh my god! You're pathetic! You can't even keep a nerd like him interested." I narrowed my eyes at her.

Out the corner of my eye I saw her remove something from her purse and palmed it so I couldn't see what it was. She raised her hand to her mouth and tilted her head back. She was drinking from a flask.

"You want some?" She held it up offering me a swig.

"You are just a walking afterschool special, aren't you?" I shook my head at her. "You better watch out. If you get caught, you'll be expelled."

She followed my gaze over to where Noah was standing. "He's perfect. You're never going to have him." I didn't respond. I hoped she would just slither away. "I feel a little sorry for you. You'll never know what it feels like to be pressed up against him, to have his lips and hands all over your body. He especially likes these." She pointed to her massive chest region. "He can't seem to keep his hands off of them and my ass mesmerizes …"

"Is there a point to you?" I abruptly asked.

"You think you're better than me, don't you?"

"I don't *think* I'm better."

"I can see why Noah said he would never hook up with you. He thinks you're a stuck up bitch. In fact, he told me and Beth, he's been trying to ditch you since the beginning of our freshman year. He just didn't know how to get rid of you. He didn't want to hurt your feelings, I guess. Now that you know, why don't you leave him alone? He and Beth look great together. They're perfect."

I could feel the tears prick my eyes. I didn't know if it was the alcohol making her an uber-bitch or it was just her natural state of being. She knew my weak spot and hit it dead on. I would not give her the satisfaction of thinking she had made me cry.

Pushing through the crowd, I walked quickly across the dance floor to the exit. I could hear her laughing the entire way.

Once outside the night air hit me in the face. I took a couple of deep breaths trying to calm myself. I needed to be alone. Around the corner of the building, there were steps that led up to the top floor of the gym, set back into an alcove, with a brick wall on either side, that would allow me some privacy until my parents came to pick me up. I walked up a few steps and sat down. When I knew I was safely tucked away out of sight, I covered my face with my hands and let the tears flow.

I hated that I let Brittani upset me that much. I knew it was more than likely she was lying, but she knew how to play on my insecurities. I felt like I was free falling and there was nothing for me to grab a hold of. Maybe he really *did* want me out of his life now. He's been ignoring me for days. He doesn't even answer his phone when I call. All I wanted was to keep our friendship the way it's always been. We just needed to step back a little. I never meant to push him away completely.

My parents were to pick me up in a half hour and I planned on staying put until then. I took a few more deep breaths, trying to stop the tears. When it felt like I was finally getting them under control, I heard footsteps approaching. I scooted up as close to the wall as I could, hoping they would just walk on by. It was completely dark on the steps, so no one could see me. The only light in the area was a small pool of light that spilled over from the outside of the music building. The footsteps got closer and closer, and then suddenly stopped. I held my breath.

"Tweet?"

I looked up and saw Noah's head peering around the wall, up the steps and right at me. I hadn't heard him say my name in three days. He hadn't really looked at me in three days. Maybe Brittani was telling the truth and Noah did want me out of his life now.

"Hey," I choked on the one word.

"Are you okay?" He stepped closer and stopped at the bottom of the steps. I couldn't let him see me with tears streaming down my cheeks. I stayed seated in the dark and tried to sound nonchalant.

"I'm fine. What'cha doing out here?" I wasn't successful at hiding the shakiness in my voice.

"I was about to ask you the same thing. I didn't know you were coming tonight."

"Yeah, well, it was kind of a last minute thing. How'd you know I was here?"

"I saw you cross the dance floor and I followed you. Plus, you seem to be molting again, Tweet." He smiled at me and held up two yellow taffeta flowers from my skirt that had fallen off. No doubt the two that I had abused the most on the ride over here. "Can I sit next to you?"

A sharp pain pierced my stomach as my chest began to tighten. I quickly wiped under my eyes and stood up, but stayed in place. "No, I'm getting ready to leave. My parents will be here soon."

"Why are you crying, Tweet?" His voice was warm and caring.

I had to think of something to tell him, so I lied. "Because my date dumped me half way through this stupid dance and ran off to dance with another girl."

"Point him out and I'll kick his ass. Any guy who would leave you is a douchebag."

"Well, I seem to have an overabundance of them right now." I cringed when that slipped out of my mouth. I didn't want to argue with Noah. I just wanted him back.

Chuckling, he asked, "Would you do me a favor?"

"Depends on what it is."

Noah extended his hand in my direction. "Dance with me?"

"I can't go back in there, Noah. My parents are expecting me outside, so..."

"We don't have to go inside," he paused. "Please, Tweet."

I couldn't see his face clearly, but his voice was cracking as if he were fighting back tears. I took a deep breath, squared my shoulders, and slowly walked down the stairs.

I took Noah's hand and he guided me down the last few steps.

We took a couple of steps back, landing us in the small pool of light. Noah slipped his other arm around my waist and pulled me in close. My breath hitched. I had chills from head to toe. He let go of my hand, palmed one side of my face and wiped my tears away with his thumb. Leaning his forehead against mine, he whispered, "You look beautiful. I like your hair up."

I looked down hoping he wouldn't notice my blood shot eyes. "There's no music," I said, softly.

Noah removed his hand from my face and wrapped his arm around my waist. My hands found their way behind his neck. Pressing his cheek to the side of my head, he placed his mouth right at my ear. We began to gently sway back and forth. In a low, barely audible voice, Noah started to sing '*Everything*'.

I shut my eyes tight. It was impossible for me to stop the tears from rolling down my face. I knew I had missed him over the past few days, but I didn't realize how much until right now in his arms, where I felt safe. My body started shaking. I was no longer able to control my sobs. I burrowed my face into his chest. Noah stopped singing and tightened his hug.

He whispered in my ear, "I'm sorry. I've missed you so much. I tried to stay away until the urge to touch you went away, but it's just gotten stronger."

"Noah …," was all I could choke out between sobs.

"You've always been my girl and always will be. No one will ever take me away from you, Tweet. You're my heart and soul and that's never going to change, no matter what you say."

There was no other place on earth I wanted to be except in Noah's arms, listening to his words. I was desperate to be with him. I was so in love with him that nothing else mattered. I barely survived three days without him. Maybe if I'm extremely careful and we take it super slow, we could be together. I could talk to Emily and find out what happened with her and Tyler, so it wouldn't happen to me and Noah. In a split second, I decided I was going to tell him I loved him and had to be with him.

I took in a deep breath, "Noah, I …" Abruptly my words were interrupted by the sound of Beth calling his name. It broke the spell that was over us and we both took a step back.

"There you are," Beth said as she rounded the corner. "Oh, hey Amanda. I didn't know you were coming tonight."

"It was a last minute thing." Noah and I never took our eyes off one another.

Beth looked back and forth between the two of us. "What are you guys doing out here, anyway?"

"I wasn't feeling well and needed some fresh air. Noah came out to check on me," I answered.

"Are you okay now?"

"Not really. My parents will be here any minute, though."

"Good." Beth grabbed Noah's arm and began to tug him away. "Come on."

Noah had his feet planted, never budging. His eyes were still glued to me. "Did you have something you wanted to tell me, Tweet?"

I looked into those beautiful bright eyes that held love, pain, and longing. I knew they matched mine perfectly. I'm a firm believer in the theory that everything happens for a reason.

This belief helped me answer his question. "No. I was done." I whispered. Disappointment and frustration crossed his face.

Beth tugged on his arm a little more forcefully. "We need to get back in there. We haven't even danced together yet." Surprise flashed in my eyes.

Before he let her pull him away, he gave me a slight smile. "Goodnight, Tweet," he called back over his shoulder as he was being led away.

"Goodnight, Noah," my voice was so soft it was almost a whisper. "You're my heart and soul, too."

Entry 9

Daily affirmations are ... What's the word? Oh yeah, BULLSHIT.

There are thousands and thousands of books trying to convince you how wonderful you are. The authors don't know you. How could they possibly affirm that you're good enough, just the way you are? There are a lot of pure unadulterated losers in the world. (Holla to my peeps!)

These books are filled with, a one size fits all prescription. Besides, I'm suspicious of people who say they love everyone for who they are. It smacks of cultism.

(Smacks is a funny word. Smacks ... smacks ... smacks ... Sounds like a kid eating. Oh great ... Now I'm hungry.)

Then the kumbaya authors say you can make up an affirmation that fits your personality and say this to yourself throughout the day. Even if I came up with my own positive affirmation, why would I listen to myself?

WHAT DO I KNOW? I'M A FREAKING LOSER. IF I COULD TALK MYSELF INTO FEELING BETTER ABOUT MYSELF, I WOULDN'T HAVE PURCHASED YOUR STUPID BOOKS.

(WONDER IF THERE'RE STILL CHEESE DOODLES IN THE PANTRY.)

Slowly, Noah and I started to hang out again. It was awkward at first, neither of us knowing exactly how to act. I wanted our old friendship back. Noah wanted to move our friendship forward into new territory. We were stuck in a weird limbo. I watched as girls flirted with him daily and eventually he started going on dates with random ones, nothing serious. I tried hard to pretend it wasn't happening by focusing on my grades and writing.

For the past two years I had taken extra classes during the summer to get ahead. Now, in my junior year, my schedule allowed me to have a free period at the end of the day. Sometimes I left early, but more often than not I stayed and went to study hall to finish homework or to the journalism classroom to finish up on any article I was working on. Somehow I had gotten rooked into a study group with Stacy and Kim from my American Government class. We met once a week during study hall, which they were required to attend.

I was at the table glancing over the chapters we were being tested on next week, when Tweedledee and Tweedledum came bopping in. They took their regular seats at our table. Neither one of them said a word to me at first. I glanced up. There was a look of sympathy across their faces. I didn't know these two very well, but they didn't strike me as very caring people. Stacy's nickname was princess, Kim's nickname was duchess, and from the way they acted, I think they had deluded themselves into believing they were actual royalty. They loved to spread gossip and stir up trouble.

Stacey, tilted her head slightly to the side, giving me a weak smile, she sighed deeply. "Things will get better you know."

She exchanged a knowing glance with Kim who nodded in agreement. They turned their attention back on to me. Kim, who was sitting directly across from me, reached her hand across the table, touching the top of mine. "I realize we don't know each other very well, but we want you to know, you're not alone."

"That's right. We're here to listen whenever you need us to. In fact, we can exchange numbers so you can get in touch with one of us at all times." Stacey offered up another deep sigh and tilt of the head.

I felt like I had entered the Twilight Zone. I was completely baffled, but curious. I looked back and forth between them a few times before I asked, "What are you two talking about?"

Again, they gave each other a knowing glance. When they turned back to me, they tilted their heads in the opposite direction from each other. Kim leaned in closer to the table and loudly whispered, "We heard about Noah and Beth."

As soon as the bell rang I bolted from the classroom. I walked quickly with purpose down the hall towards the lockers. My nails were digging into my palm due to the tight grip I had on the strap of my backpack. I felt the heat rising inside me from the anger and betrayal I was experiencing over what I had just heard moments ago. Beth was facing her locker when I walked up. I stood there in silence, waiting for her to turn around. She was startled when she saw me.

"God, Amanda! You scared the shit out of me."

"You and Noah are dating?" It came out as an accusation.

Beth looked around, making sure no one was close enough to hear. Biting her lip and fidgeting with her purse strap, she said quietly, "Um … yeah … kind of."

"When the fuck did this happen?" I bit out. My anger was palpable.

"Do you really want to talk about this right now? Right here?"

I looked up and down the hall. Students had all but disappeared, leaving Beth and me alone. I crossed my arms in front of me and stood firm. "Answer my question. When. Did. This. Happen?" I said slowly through gritted teeth, clipping each word.

"Um … Well … Let's see. I'm not really sure," she stumbled over her words, trying to buy time.

"Quit stalling." I was getting more and more impatient. Narrowing my eyes, my voice strained, I asked, "When?"

"A little while ago."

"How long is a *little* while?"

Looking down, she began twisting the ring on her right hand. She did that whenever she was nervous. She hesitated for a few moments before answering. "About a month."

My body stiffened. The air completely pushed out of my lungs. "Both of you have been lying to me for a month?" I already knew the answer was yes. I just needed to hear her admit it.

"We never lied to you, Amanda." She looked everywhere except at me.

"You kept it from me. I've been around the two of you and never noticed anything different."

"I wanted to tell to you when it first started, but Noah said no." Her eyes narrowed slightly as her lips pursed into a straight line.

With each piece of information that dribbled out of her mouth, I felt my body stiffen more. My voice had become robotic. It was as if my entire self was shutting down physically, mentally, and emotionally. But, I couldn't seem to stop my mouth from asking questions that I knew the answers would destroy me.

"You want to know how I found out? Stacey and Kim told me. They gave me their sympathy and now want to be BFFs. Apparently everyone knew about this, except me."

"They saw us at the movies a couple of days ago. I guess they figured something was up." She still wouldn't make eye contact with me as she went from twisting her ring to fidgeting with the strap on her purse.

"How would they figure that out?" I asked.

"Because I was holding Noah's hand."

I could feel the vibrations start to take over my body. I didn't have much time left before I crumbled. I hadn't processed the fact that Beth and Noah were together yet, let alone that they would have physical contact.

"There are a hundred guys at this school. You could have had any one of them. Why did it have to be Noah?"

"You know I've always liked him. He's sweet, fun, popular..."

"AND MINE!" I yelled. That was the first crack in my already fragile foundation.

"You need to calm down," she paused for a moment. Squaring her shoulders, she looked me directly in the eye now. "Look Amanda. I know you and Noah had this *bond* or whatever when you were kids, but..."

"*Have*," I interrupted.

"What?"

"We *have* a bond. It's not past tense," I insisted.

"Yeah. Well, it was cute when we were kids, but we're not kids anymore. I've never understood this thing between the two of you, anyway. But, did you really think he was going to hold off on dating anyone forever? Noah's one of the hottest guys at this school. I don't know a girl here that doesn't want to hook up with him. I don't mean to sound harsh. You're my friend and I love you, but it's time to grow up."

I hated it, but I knew she was right. I had convinced myself that Noah would always be mine. I knew he had been on dates with a few girls. I didn't like it, but I dealt with it because he never seriously dated anyone. It never crossed my mind that he would.

"I know," I whispered.

Inhaling and exhaling a deep breath, Beth said, "I think I'm in love with him, Amanda."

That was crack number two in my foundation. I continued to stare in her direction. I wasn't really looking at her. I wasn't looking at anything. My mind was numb. I had information overload. I couldn't listen to anymore. I saw her mouth moving and heard sound come out of it, but it was muffled. It felt like I was under water. She just kept moving her mouth, never waiting on any reply from me. She reached out and touched my arm breaking me from my daze.

"I might as well go ahead and tell you everything. You know, pull the band aid off quick. I'm staying over at his house tonight." She saw the look of confusion on my face. "His parents are out of town for the weekend."

"I know. They're going with my parents. They take this trip every year together."

She looked around nervously. Leaning closer to me, she whispered, "I'm going to have sex with him tonight."

That was crack number three of my foundation. Beth was completely clueless how her words were affecting me. She kept rambling on as I stood there, immobile. This was the most surreal experience I had ever had. Beth. Noah. Sex. Love. It played on a continuous loop in my head.

"I've been dying to tell you. I thought you could help me out. I wanted to surprise him and cook dinner tonight." I still had no idea why she kept talking. "I figured you'd know what his favorite foods are. Amanda, are you okay? Your eyes look weird."

I had been hurt and jealous, but somewhere between her saying, "I'm going to have sex with him and tell me his favorite food", I got pissed. Good 'ol fashion pull your hair, spit in your face pissed. "I'm not going to help you have sex with Noah."

"I'm just asking you to tell me his favorite foods."

"You've dated for a month. You've never eaten together?" The sarcasm flowed from my mouth. I started to get the feeling back in my body as the adrenalin surged through me. I had been clutching the strap of my backpack the entire time so tight my knuckles were completely white. My heart was pounding so hard and fast, I thought it was going to break through my chest. I narrowed my eyes at Beth. She could tell there had been a shift in me.

"I know your pissed that we didn't tell you, but don't tell me you're pissed off because Noah and I are together?" She looked away, huffed, and rolled her eyes. "You're a piece of work, you know that. You don't want him, but you don't want anyone else to have him either. I've asked you more than once if you liked Noah, and you've always said, just as a friend. Well, I like him more than just a friend. I want him to be my first and he's going to be. If you wanted him as your boyfriend you should have done something a long time ago. You blew it. You missed your chance with Noah and now he's mine. We're together, so deal with it."

"I'm not even sure you *are* together. Noah tells me everything. He's never mentioned you once."

Heat started to course through me. I felt my chin start to quiver while the tears were building up at the edge of my eyes. My hands started to shake. I knew my time was up. I couldn't stand there any longer and listen to Beth talk about Noah and her.

She glared at me with a smug look. "Oh, I assure you, we *are* together. I've had the sore lips to prove it, so if you …"

Those were the last words before the final tremor shot through me, shaking my foundation, causing me to crumple completely. I turned on my heels cutting her off abruptly. I had to get away as fast as I could before the tears started to spill out and cover my cheeks.

I forcefully swung open the school door and headed straight to my car. The velocity from the time I left Beth to the time I got home and in my room was so hypersonic it was like one continuous motion. I didn't stop moving until I flopped on to my bed.

Wiping the tears away with the back of my sleeve, I tried to steady my breathing. I hadn't noticed how out of breath I was until I was still.

I should have kept moving, because once I stopped my mind went into overdrive.

I was losing Noah. Our friendship wasn't enough for him anymore. I wasn't enough for him anymore. I knew this would happen someday. I just didn't think it would be today, and I sure as hell didn't think it would be with Beth. I felt betrayed, angry, and tossed aside. I didn't answer Beth when she asked if I was pissed because they lied or because they were together. Truth is I got over being lied to three seconds after I heard her say she loved him.

I didn't want them to be together. I wasn't ready. I knew I couldn't have him, but I didn't want anyone else to have him either, not yet. I know that's irrational, but logical thinking was not part of my life right now. I can't lose him. He's the only thing that's all mine.

ENTRY 10

SEX IS A GAME CHANGER,

EVEN WHEN YOU'RE NOT THE ONE HAVING IT.

I bolted up and looked at the clock. It was only 5 pm. People don't have sex at 5 o'clock in the evening. That's dinner time. They wait until it's good and dark. I knew that was stupid and not true, but it calmed me somewhat knowing I had time to shut down Beth's sex dinner.

I hurried out of bed and ran to the bathroom. I washed my face free of the tear streaks, put some mascara on, a little lip gloss, and I was out the back door in a flash. I walked to the fence that separated our backyard from the Stewart's where I could see Noah through the window. He was pacing back and forth, talking on his cellphone. There was a strange look on his face that I couldn't read. He ran his free hand through his hair a couple of times as he looked out the window at nothing in particular. He didn't notice me staring at him, he was too focused on his phone call.

I jumped the fence and ran up to the Stewart's back door. It was unlocked as usual, so I let myself in as usual. Noah was standing in the family room, talking. "Alright. I will. I know." He sounded irritated at whomever was on the other end of the phone. My guess was Beth. He looked at me, flashed a quick smile in my direction. "I need to go." He ended the call without saying goodbye.

"Hey Tweet." He tried to sound cheerful.

"Hey, hey, hey." I tried to match his cheerful sound.

"Everything okay?" he asked.

"Yep." I popped the *p* when I said it. I was waiting for him to bring up the subject.

I walked over to behind the sofa and leaned back on it. "What'cha want to do tonight? Since both our parents our gone for the weekend, the world is our oyster. We can hang out the whole time." I took my cellphone out of my pocket and scrolled through my numbers. "Pepperoni with extra cheese good for you?"

"What?" It looked as if my question startled him.

"On our pizza. Pepperoni and extra cheese?"

"Yeah. That's fine."

I pressed the number and brought the phone to my ear.

Noah rubbed the back of his neck a few times before interrupting my call. "Um … Tweet … I kind of have plans tonight."

"What kind of plans?" I asked innocently, as I put my phone away.

There was a pause that felt like it lasted a year and a half. Noah was standing a few feet away from me, arms crossed over his chest, looking down at a spot on the floor.

"I sort of have a date," he said in a low voice.

"A date? With who?"

He looked at me through his long dark lashes. A smirk played across his face. "Don't do that."

"Do what?"

"Play dumb. You're no good at it. Besides, I just got off the phone with Beth."

"Did ya now? Are you referring to your *girlfriend*, Beth?" I tried not to sound sarcastic, but I wasn't very successful.

"I'm sorry. I've been meaning to talk to you about it," he said, sheepishly.

"So talk."

Noah motioned for me to sit on the sofa. I shook my head. I didn't want to sit and relax. I wanted to stay standing in case running was in my near future. We both stayed in our spots.

"I don't know where to start," he said.

"How about where you lied to me."

"I've never lied to you."

"Lie of omission! That's just as bad."

He shook his head, "Look, I know you're upset."

"GENIUS!" I threw my arms up in the air.

"Would you please shut your mouth and listen for five seconds. It's not a big deal."

"What's not a big deal?"

"This thing with Beth. It's...," he ran his hand up and down his face in frustration. "No matter what I say, I'm going to sound like the biggest dick in the world. I already know that, so keep your smartass comments to yourself," he paused. "This thing with Beth is just convenient."

My eyebrows and the pitch of my voice both shot up when I said, "Convenient?"

"Yeah. We've known each other for a long time. I knew she wanted something to happen between us."

Just hearing those words coming out of his mouth made my stomach churn. "Why was I kept in the dark about this?"

"I didn't want you to know."

"Why?"

He chuckled and shook his head. "The same reason why I never want you to know when I go out with a girl. Because I feel like I'm cheating on you, which is fucking ridiculous because we're not even together in the first place," he said, as he let out a frustrated growl.

"Why her?"

"Because I didn't have to work for it."

"She thinks she's in love with you, you know."

Noah closed his eyes and tilted his head back towards the ceiling. As he straightened his neck, he looked at me. The pain and longing in his eyes made me ache.

"I'll handle things with Beth," he sighed heavily. "I don't love her. You know that, right?" It sounded like he was pleading with me to believe him.

"What are you going to say to her?" I asked.

"I guess I'll let her know I don't feel the same way about her. That I never meant to lead her on. I'm not looking for anything permanent. If she's okay with that, we can continue on."

"What do you mean *continue on*?"

Noah let out another growl. He had one hand on the wall

bracing himself while the other hand rested on his hip. "I have needs," he said quietly.

"Needs? What kind of needs?"

"The kind a young man has." Confusion plastered across my face. He looked over at me and waited a moment for it to register before becoming impatient. "I need to get laid."

"You *need* to get laid?" My tone was condescending.

"I do."

"You're saying if she's okay with your terms then you'll fuck her?"

"Yes." He was grinding his teeth as his jaw began to twitch. I could see the anger change the stance of his body.

At that moment I became a complete mute. I didn't know what to say. A thousand words ran through my head, but only one made its way out of my mouth. "Don't."

"Don't what?" he asked.

"Don't have sex with Beth. Don't date Beth."

We stood, facing each other, staring, neither one of us wanting to be the first to blink. It looked like a western standoff.

"I don't even know why we're having this conversation." He was getting angrier. "What difference does it make to you? You made your choice. You and I are just friends." He spit venom with his last sentence.

"*Just* friends? Don't say it like that," I whispered.

"We don't have to ask each other's permission on who we can date." He sounded cold, emotionless.

My throat was beginning to burn from trying to hold my sobs in. I swallowed hard a couple of times, feeling the tears pooling in my eyes. He was slipping away from me a little more. Noah watched as my body reacted to his words. I don't know why I kept goading him. I should have just left right then.

"You're planning on doing more than having a date night with her," I said.

He turned his back to me, ran both hands across his face, and through his hair. He dropped his hands to his side as they fisted. Suddenly he rammed one fist into the wall in front of him and yelled. "GOD DAMMIT!!!!"

I startled. His outburst started my tears. Turning back toward me, his eyes pierced mine. Speaking slowly in a low voice through gritted teeth, he said, "Yes, I plan to fuck her, screw her, bang her, be balls deep in …"

"SHUT UP!!" My sobs were coming at a rapid pace now. I could barely get my words out. "PLEASE DON'T DO IT, NOAH! PLEASE!"

"WHY NOT?!"

"BECAUSE YOU'RE MINE!" I screamed at him through my sobs.

My eyes were so blurry from my tears I didn't see him cross the room toward me. The next thing I knew I felt the wall against my back. Noah's mouth was at my ear.

"Then why don't you fucking take me and stop this bullshit you keep putting us through? You're going to tell me you're okay with my hands running up and down her body? Touching her ass and tits. You're okay with my tongue licking every inch of her? You're okay knowing that while you're over in your bed, I'll be over here sliding into her, when we both know it should be you?"

My body began to convulse. The pain from hearing him say those words overpowered me. Tiny piece by tiny piece I shattered until I was completely broken. He stepped back allowing me to drift down the wall to the floor. I don't know how long I stayed that way. Noah had left the room, not saying another word to me, and never came back.

As I sat sobbing rage began to build inside me. I slammed by back against the wall out of frustration. Why can't I just stop being so fucking afraid and insecure? I'm pushing him away more and more and he's hit a breaking point. I have no right to keep him from living his life. I should have stayed away. Let him be with whomever he wants.

I pulled myself together enough to get up off the floor. My body was sore from the ordeal and my legs felt weak, but stable. My hand trembled slightly as I placed it on the doorknob. I hesitated for a moment, and thought about going to look for him, but there was nothing left to say.

They say the human body is made up of seventy percent water. Today I have expelled sixty-nine point nine percent through tears and snot. Sobbing uncontrollably is not a very pretty or lady like thing to do.

The only thought I had in my head was, "What the fuck just happened?"

I had been lying in my bed for almost an hour and I still couldn't wrap my head around what took place at Noah's house. I had never seen him that angry or heartbroken. He never talked to me that way before, but I couldn't blame him for being so angry with me. I knew I had no right telling him who he could date. I just couldn't bare the thought of someone else having that part of him.

My thoughts began to drift, wondering what Noah and Beth were doing right now. Did he already tell her that he doesn't love her? Did she take it well or did she slap him in the face and storm out? I wondered if she was over there cooking dinner for him. Was she standing at the stove, stirring some putrid concoction she made up while he watched her stir? Has he walked up behind her, placing his hands on her hips, then sliding them up and around to her stomach, wrapping his strong arms around her waist, pushing her back against him, so she could feel how excited he was to have her *cooking* for him? I had to stop torturing myself.

I reached over and grabbed my ear buds off the nightstand, crammed them into my ears, and connected them to my cellphone. The D-Bags blasted through my head. Kellan's voice always soothed me. I closed my eyes and tried to concentrate on the lyrics.

I was barely conscious when I realized the music wasn't blasting through my ear buds and my bed felt slightly sunken in, as if someone were sitting on the side of it. I wasn't alarmed. I knew who was sitting beside me without even looking. My eyes peeked open slightly and I saw Noah watching me. His eyes were glistening with tears and his expression was slack with sadness. I stayed still and shut my eyes.

"I know you're not sleeping," Noah whispered, as he cleared his throat, his voice sounding deflated.

I opened my eyes and looked up at his beautiful sad face.

"How long have you been here?" I choked out.

"I don't know, not long."

"What are you doing here?" I whispered.

The one thing Noah and I couldn't stand was to be angry at each other. We had only been mad at each other a couple of times, but nothing had come close to what happened tonight. I knew we would eventually fix things between us.

I sat up, coming face-to-face with him. We stared at each other for a moment. I broke our silence. "What about Beth?" I asked cautiously.

"She's not coming over. We're done."

"Why?"

"I told her there was someone else."

I let out a deep sigh. I knew he could tell by the look in my eyes how relieved I was.

"Come on, it's cake time," he said, a slight smile forming across his face. He tilted his chin toward my nightstand where a paper plate with a huge piece of chocolate cake wrapped in plastic wrap, and a fork sat. "Let's go to the park."

I wasn't sure why he wanted to go all the way to our spot. There was no one else at home, so we could talk without anyone barging in on us.

He stood up and held out his hand to me, helping me up off the bed. Without saying a word, his arms were around me, holding me tight against his broad chest. My hands rested on his muscular upper arms. Our faces were an inch apart. We were looking at each other with hypnotic intensity. It made me uncomfortable, I felt completely vulnerable, but I couldn't blink or look away. Slowly Noah lowered his head towards mine. Our foreheads touched.

His eyes were closed when he whispered in a low gravelly voice. "I'm so sorry. I never should have said any of that stuff to you. Please, don't be mad at me, Tweet."

My hands slowly moved up his biceps, over his shoulders, finally landing behind his neck. He bent down slightly, allowing both of us the ability to nuzzle into each other's neck. I held on to him as tight as possible and whispered in his ear, "I'm so sorry, Noah, for everything. I don't know how to change and make things better." I wanted desperately to change for him. But how does a person completely change the only identity they've ever known?

I felt his arms tighten around me as he buried his face deeper into my neck, his lips resting against my skin.

We stood there holding each other for a long while, neither one of us wanting to break free. Finally, Noah pulled his head away and said, "I think it's time for cake."

He picked up the cake, grabbed my hand, and we headed out.

Once at the park, we didn't go to our spot. Instead, Noah headed to the playground area. We sat in two swings that were side by side. I watched in silence as he unwrapped the cake and then handed me the fork. I stabbed the part covered in the most frosting, of course, and put the fork in my mouth then pulled it out slowly as I made a slight moan, my teeth and lips tightened around it. I wanted to make sure I got every bit of frosting, but was distracted by Noah staring at my mouth. Once the fork left my lips, I tilted my head back and looked up at the stars.

"Your mom buys the best cakes," I said, holding the fork out between us indicating it was his turn.

He took a large gulp of air. "You really know how to eat cake."

We sat there in silence, passing the fork between us until the cake was gone. As Noah was throwing our trash away, I thought about how this wasn't as awkward as I thought it was going to be. We'll go home, wake up tomorrow and all will be right with the world. Everything will be back to normal.

As he approached, I stood thinking we were headed home. Noah stopped a couple of feet from me. He looked so somber. His voice was barely a whisper when he said, "We need to talk, Tweet." My stomach immediately dropped to the center of the earth. I wanted to run back home to my room and hide under the covers.

We sat back down on the swings, but Noah made no attempt to initiate the conversation. I had a sinking feeling I was about to lose the most important person in my life. The silence was suffocating me. I could feel my throat begin to close and it became harder to breath. I decided to speak first before I passed out. "Why are we sitting over here?"

"I didn't want to talk at your house or our spot."

"Why?"

He took a deep breath. "Since you left my house, all I can see when I walk into the family room is you sitting on the floor, screaming and crying," he said.

"I don't understand."

"I don't want you to have the same pain as I do whenever you're in your room or at our spot." Just when I thought I had no more tears to shed, I felt them forming. "I don't think it's a good idea for us to be around each other for a while," his voice cracked.

I felt all the oxygen rush out of my lungs and my head began to throb. I knew the argument earlier was the worst we had ever had, but I didn't think he'd want to get rid of me. My eyes felt like they were the size of saucers. My tears were getting harder and harder to hold back. I needed clarification. Maybe he meant something entirely different than what I heard. I mean, even though we have a strong connection, we are of the opposite sex. Men and women misinterpret each other all the time.

For the second time today, a thousand responses flew across my mind in a nanosecond, but only one word escaped my lips. "Why?"

Noah's deep gaze focused on me, with tears glossing over his eyes. He hesitated before clearing his throat. His voice was so low and husky I had a hard time hearing him. "I think you know why."

"I think I do too, but I'd like to hear it from you, just in case I'm wrong."

Fear and apprehension crossed his face before speaking. "Tweet, I don't know," he paused. "This thing is confusing."

"What thing?"

He pointed back and forth between us. "This thing between us. It's so different."

"Different good or different bad?" I kept asking questions I already knew the answer to, desperately trying to prolong our time together. I knew exactly what was happening. I was losing my soul mate because I was so fucked up in the head and I didn't know how to change it.

"Different confusing. I know you've always been down on yourself. I know you think you're doing what's best for me. I hate that you think so little of yourself and I hate that you don't think we belong together. I've tried to be around you and stay in the friend zone. I've tried so fucking hard." Tears were flowing freely down both our faces. "I can't be around you right now. It hurts too much, because I am so completely and desperately in love you, Tweet."

Tell him how much you love him, Amanda. Stop being such a fuck up and say it. He loves you and wants you. You're losing him. What is wrong with you? Stop sitting here and say something.

"There hasn't been a day in my life that I haven't loved you. I wish you would just let me love you," he said.

He brought his hand up to my face and stroked it gently. Bringing our foreheads to rest together, he whispered. "You will always be the most important thing in my life. I'll always be there for you no matter what or who. I have no past without you and I can't imagine a future that doesn't include you. I just need some time to figure out how I can have you *in* my life without having you *be* my life."

Closing my eyes, I tried to compose myself. I was barely able to speak. I opened them and gazed at Noah. I brought my right hand up to his face, caressing from his cheek to his jaw. "I'm so sorry."

Walking back to my house, our hands gripped each other's as if we were holding on for dear life. We stood on my front porch holding each other for a long time. I wasn't going to be the one to let go first.

Noah whispered in my ear, "I need to go or I won't, and I have to do this."

"I know," I choked out through my sobs.

He took a step back. Our faces were drenched in tears and our chests were heavy from our sobs. The look in his eyes reflected so much … love, desperation, and the ache of losing the love of your life.

He stared at me for a few long seconds. "Goodbye Tweet."

"Goodbye Noah."

He watched me as he walked backwards down the steps, drawing out our time together as much as possible. He lingered at the bottom for a moment as we continued to take each other in.

My lips barely moved when I whispered, "I love you." For a split second, I thought he heard me, but then he turned away, and was gone.

I hated myself. The very thing I was trying to avoid happened. I lost Noah. I tried so hard to control the situation and keep our relationship unchanged that I didn't notice him slipping through my fingers until it was too late. Noah's happiness was the most important thing to me and although he wasn't happy now, I knew that in the long run he would be. It's amazing how in just a few hours my entire world came crashing down around me, and I just stood there watching it happen.

Entry 11

I think I might be a freak. At almost 18 years old, I have kissed one boy, one time. The only boy I have ever fantasized about is Noah, although, Zac Efron has made an appearance now and again. Yep, he's a pretty, pretty, pretty boy. His eyes are insane. His hair is so shiny.

Zac and Amanda Efron. OH MY GOD!!! That sounds awesome!!

What was the point of this entry? Oh yeah, am I a freak because I haven't had sex yet? A lot of girls at school have already had sex. I've had guys ask me out, but I always come up with some excuse not to go. I'm not sure what I'm waiting for, it' just sex. It's not a big deal. That's a lie. It is a big deal, at least to me. I guess, ever since I found out what sex was, I always pictured Noah being my first, which is stupid because we're not going there. I need to bite the bullet and at least go on a date.

I wonder if Zac Efron ever comes to SC. This entry sucks. Eh, I'm done. I got Zac brain.

Four months have passed since Noah and I had the "*breakup*" talk. I saw him at school, but we didn't interact much. We stopped eating lunch together and he started sitting at a table with the baseball team. We were also thrown together a few times when our families got together, and somehow I got through it.

Beth hadn't spoken to me since that day at her locker and from the eighteen page letter she wrote me, front and back, it appeared that the friendship was unsalvageable. I was sad that she and I were no longer friends, but losing her didn't affect me as much as not having Noah around. He and I were still technically friends. It just didn't feel like we were right now.

The three of us, who once spent the majority of our time together, had all gone our separate ways. The summer made it a little easier to avoid each other. Beth's family went to Paris for their summer vacation. We were entering our senior year, and Noah and I kept busy visiting different college campuses, separately, of course, and he went off to baseball camp for the month of July.

For the first time in my life, I felt completely alone. I had my family, but it wasn't the same. My *averageness* blossomed whenever I was around my sister for long periods of time. I could handle going to the movies or out to eat fairly well. Going to the beach was another story. Emily looked perfect in a bikini, surprise, surprise. I had no problem going places by myself, but it helped to get my mind off Noah if I went with someone. Since Beth was out of the picture, Emily was the chosen one. My sister tried to get me to open up to her about what was bothering me, but what was I supposed to say?

Um … Emily, ever since I can remember, I've felt extremely inadequate in all aspects of my life: looks, personality, and intelligence. Because of the hold my insecurities have on me, I can't give myself to the one person I want to, my best friend. I tried to control the relationship and keep it the same, so we'd remain friends. I ended up losing him anyway. I'm an idiot. Oh, did I mention that a lot of this is due to you being so perfect?

I didn't hate my sister for being perfect and beautiful. She deserved all the love and attention she got. I just wished I had been born first and had gotten her life. Maybe if I had, I would be with Noah right now.

Being away from him didn't lessen my need or want for him. If anything, those feelings intensified. I missed everything about him-his smile, his voice, his hugs, the ways he made me laugh. The time we spent at our spot talking about anything and everything. The irony is that I spent so much time and energy trying to keep things the same between us, so I wouldn't lose him, and it backfired. Instead of keeping him by my side, I pushed him away completely. I desperately needed my best friend now, to help me through this, but I couldn't have him. He said he needed time and that's what I was giving him. I owed him that.

I finally came to the realization that I had to try to move past this. I didn't want to let my senior year evaporate before my eyes and not enjoy it. I needed to spread my wings. Have new experiences with new people.

Brad Johnson had moved here during our freshman year and he

was a mighty fine specimen. His hair was dirty-blonde and he obviously paid a lot of attention to it. It was cut close on the sides. The top was a little longer and worked into a tousled chunky style. His eyes were sapphire blue. They were very pretty, but not beautiful like Noah's. Brad was at least six feet tall, same as Noah. He was on the baseball team, so he had a great body and he knew how to dress. His clothes always showed off his toned chest and abs. I didn't know if his abs sported a six pack like Noah's, but I could tell his chest wasn't as broad. His arms were muscular, but not overly so, and his hands were large. I figured that might be one reason he was a good baseball player.

Brad and I were not friends, or for that matter, acquaintances. Except for an occasional "Hi," we never spoke to each other. But even though I didn't know him personally, his reputation left a lot to be desired. Word was that he was a spoiled rich brat who lied and cheated his way through life, as well as girls.

But I made a pact with myself to abstain from listening to gossip. After all, I was a mature high school senior. Gossip was for the immature. Besides, I had endured years of rumors about Noah and me that were false. Plus, there had been rumors off and on about Noah and Brittani that I knew for a fact were not true. I was going to keep an open mind about Brad, and not let others influence me. Everyone deserves a chance.

Brad and I had a couple of classes together. During the second week of school, I caught him looking at me during class. He also started showing up around my locker a couple of times a day. He would say "hi" and smile, but that was it. After two weeks of this stalker behavior, I decided to take matters into my own hands.

It was the end of the day and I was at my locker. Out of the corner of my eye, I saw him. He was standing about three yards away when I turned to him and smiled. "Didn't your mother teach you it's impolite to stare?" I said, with a bit of snark in my voice.

"I wasn't staring. I was admiring." As he sauntered over to me, a devilish smile slowly crept across his face. He came to a stop about a foot away.

"Wow, that's quite a line."

"It's not a line." He crossed his heart, trying to look sincere, "Scouts honor."

"Scouts … .um … fast, what troop were you in?" I asked, challenging him.

"Troop 543. My dad was our troop leader."

I smiled and shook my head. "Why have you been stalking me?"

He leaned one shoulder against the lockers and smirked. He took his time saying each word, smiling bigger with each reason he listed. "Cause you're pretty. And smart. And funny. And pretty."

"You said pretty twice."

"Well, it bears repeating."

I couldn't help my eye roll. "Well, you got the funny part right." His smile turned up to full megawatt status. I felt a quiet gasp leave me. First impression, he was a bit of a douchebag, but a sexy as hell douchebag.

He moved in a little closer and with conviction said, "Jeremy Pratt's parents are letting him have a party at their beach house this

Saturday," the look in his sapphire eyes intensified. "What time should I pick you up?"

"We've gone to school together for over three years. Why are you asking me out now all of a sudden?" I was a little suspicious.

"Honestly? I never asked before because I thought you and Stewart had something going on."

"Noah and I are best friends," I said.

"I'm sorry to hear that."

"Why?"

"Because I wasted three years not asking you out … so … are you going to keep me waiting even longer or do we have a date?" And there it was again, as if on cue, that megawatt smile.

"What changed? I'm still friends with Noah."

"Really? You two haven't looked too friendly with each other. Are you sure he's still friends with you?" I didn't respond. I hated to admit he might have a point. "So Beautiful, what time should I get you Saturday?"

"You are quite the charmer," I paused for a moment considering my answer. "Eight o'clock. It should be fun."

"Oh, I guarantee it *will* be fun. I always aim to please." He pushed off from the lockers and stood. "Let's grab your stuff, so I can walk you to your car."

"Anyone ever tell you how bossy you are?"

He leaned in very close to me. If he had been less attractive, I might have considered it too close.

"I'm not bossy. I know what I want and I don't like to waste time." He winked.

Now I understood what Noah said, about feeling like he was cheating on me when he went on dates with other girls. I felt like I was doing something wrong. As if I was betraying Noah just by talking to Brad. I wanted to grab my stuff and run, but I stood my ground. This was me spreading my wings and trying new things. I gathered my books and placed them in my backpack. As soon as I turned around, Brad grabbed it before walking me to my car.

I unlocked the passenger door and motioned for him to toss my bag in. He followed me as I walked around to the driver's side. Opening the door, I leaned in slightly, and slung my purse over the seat.

Turning back around, I found myself nose-to-nose with Brad. He was standing between me and the open car door, his left hand rested on the upper doorframe, propping himself up. We were so close, I could feel his warm breath wash over my lips. His voice was low. "I'm *really* glad you want me …," he paused for a split second as his eyes moved down to my lips and then back to my eyes, causing me to swallow hard, "… to take you to the party."

I cleared my throat and nervously answered, "Me too."

"You know what?" he asked.

"What?" I whispered.

He focused on my mouth as he sucked on his lower lip, dragging his perfect white teeth over it. "Saturday is going to be the start of an awesome senior year."

I froze in place. I couldn't take my gaze off those sapphire eyes. Butterflies were taking over my stomach. Brad knocked me off balance with his confidence. There was an air of mystery and danger about him and I was curious.

"Yeah … well … thanks for the … um … the invite and the walk," I finally said, stumbling over my words. He smiled and glanced from my eyes to my lips and back again. I took in another gulp of air and said, "I better be going."

"You're extremely cute, you know."

Holy hell, he was hot. I had to get away from this guy. I was becoming increasingly unnerved every second I spent with him. Laughing nervously, I said, "Yeah … well … I am just the cute one in the family. My sister's the pretty one. Um … do you know my sister?" My voice hit a pitch that only dogs could hear. He just shook his head and smiled. "Her name is Emily. Emily Kelly. Of course, she has the same name as me, we're sisters. Not that we're both named Emily. We have the same last name. That's why we're sisters cause of our last name. I mean, that's not why really. There are a lot of people with the last name Kelly that I'm not related to. It's a fairly common name. We have the same parents. That's why we're related …," I began to trail off.

The voice in my head kept screaming, SHUT UP, AMANDA MARIE KELLY!!

"Yeah, incredibly cute," he said with a smirk.

He pushed off the car and stepped to the side, allowing me some breathing space. After closing the door and fumbling with my keys, I summoned the courage to glance up. Brad was still standing beside my car with his hands in his pockets, watching me with a kissable smile across his face.

Kissable smile?! What the hell is wrong with me?

Finally, I got the damn key in the ignition, started the car, and peeled out of the parking lot. When I got far enough away and my nerves had calmed, the ability to think clearly returned. I didn't know how that boy got me so unhinged, so quickly. Even though the Brad encounter was overwhelming, I was proud of myself for agreeing to go to the party with him. I needed to do this. I had to do this. It's time to put on my big girl panties and see what the world had to offer.

Entry 12

No matter how hard you try to move on, sometimes forces beyond your control won't let you

That night, I was in my room trying to study but I was having a hard time concentrating on my chemistry homework. My thoughts drifted from Noah to Brad. Spending the night thinking about Noah was nothing new. I had been doing that for what felt like forever. Thinking about Brad, on the other hand, was something completely different.

I couldn't figure out what it was about him that captured my thoughts so quickly and aggressively. I had seen the guy around school for three years and not once gave him a second thought. I never considered myself one of those girls who got giddy and flustered over a good looking and charming boy's attention. Our verbal sparring match at my locker was fun. Then he got very close to me and I became a babbling idiot.

I only allowed myself to daydream about Brad briefly before

focusing my thoughts back on Noah. I knew it was silly and made no sense, Noah was barely in my life, and it had been like that for the past four months, but I felt guilty for just thinking about Brad.

A tapping on my bedroom window caught my attention. I had been so focused on Noah and Brad that I thought I was hearing things. I went back to studying. I heard it again, but this time it was more forceful. It wasn't my imagination. I walked over, took a deep breath, and opened the window. The most exquisite pair of light blue eyes gazed up at me, accompanied by a dazzling smile that reached them. The butterflies started to appear in my stomach and my palms were getting moist. It had been a long time since I had been this close to him and it was intoxicating.

"Hey, Tweet," Noah said in a raspy voice.

God, I missed hearing my nickname flow over his lips, those incredibly soft full lips. I shook my head, trying to get my thoughts back to the present.

"Hey," I whispered.

"Can we talk?"

"Sure. What do you want to talk about?"

"Not here, at our spot."

I almost flew out the window, I was so excited. He wanted to spend time with me, alone, at our spot. I couldn't have cared less why he wanted to talk. It had to be good news. He was smiling. Maybe he had enough time and we could be together again. Right now, the only thing that mattered to me was Noah and me going to our spot to be alone.

We walked in silence the entire way. Noah seemed a little uncomfortable. If I were being honest, I was on edge too. It felt strange, but I figured it was because we hadn't been alone like this in a long time. Once we arrived, Noah extended his hand helping me climb up on the far end of the table. He didn't join me. Instead, he leaned back on the edge beside me, with his legs crossed at the ankles, and his arms crossed over his chest.

We stayed like that for several minutes, before Noah cleared his throat and asked, "How have things been going?" He was looking down at the ground instead of me.

My gaze joined his on the same spot as I answered, "Pretty good. How are things going with you?"

"Ok. Coach thinks we have a pretty good chance at the championship this year."

"Really? That's fantastic." I didn't give a shit about the baseball team right now.

"Yeah. We'll probably make the playoffs at least." Out the corner of my eye, I saw him glance over at me and give me a quick smile. "How are your classes so far?"

"Good. How about yours?"

"Good," he said.

I couldn't believe we were actually engaging in small talk. The weather should be next on the list. I hated that the time apart had created awkwardness between us. I was getting anxious, impatient, and I had had enough.

"Noah, why did you ask me here tonight?" My voice was low and filled with hesitancy.

His eyes stayed focused on the ground as he whispered, "I miss you."

At that very moment, I heard a choir of angels start to sing, *hallelujah*. I desperately wanted to jump up, throw my arms around him, and never let go, but I didn't.

"I've missed you, too," I said, trying to contain my excitement.

"It hurts being away from you. I think about you all the time."

"What do you think about?" It came out of my mouth more flirtatious than I intended.

Noah pushed off the table and moved directly in front of me. He took a few moments studying my face, like he hadn't seen it in years. He cleared his throat and answered. "I think about how lonely I am without you. How boring my day is without you. How much I miss hearing your voice and your laugh. How much I miss listening to music and eating cake with you." We smiled shyly at each other. His gaze lifted, looking directly into my eyes. "I miss taking care of you," he hesitated for a moment. "I miss my best friend and I want her back in my life." His words glued every piece of my shattered heart back together.

Noah looked as lost and alone as I felt. I was speechless. I had dreamed about this day since the night of the talk. I hated being separated from him. I wanted my best friend back. I didn't want to be lonely anymore.

He placed his hands on either side of me on the edge of the table, bringing his forehead to rest on mine, "So Tweet, will you be my best friend again? I promise I will stay in the F-zone."

He couldn't tell, but inside I was jumping up and down, clapping, and doing cartwheels.

Sighing I said, "I never stopped being your best friend." The hottest smile I had ever seen formed across that beautiful face that I had ached to see for so long.

He tilted his head slightly to one side and brushed his lips gently across my cheek. When he pulled back, he was smirking at me and said, "Hi bestie. Glad you're back where you belong." I beamed with joy. I was glad to be back, too.

Noah sat next to me on the table. I could feel the electricity between us when our shoulders and arms brushed against each other. He picked up my hand and laced our fingers together. Bringing it to his lips, he placed a soft kiss on the back of it. My face started to hurt, I was grinning so big. I'm not positive, but I think I actually giggled like an idiot. I felt his thumb begin to gentle stroke my wrist. That was permitted in the friend zone. Friends occasionally held hands and stroked one another … right?

Releasing a long deep sigh, he said, "Tweet, there's something else I need to talk to you about."

"Shoot."

He turned slightly toward me. His expression was serious and determined. "Is it true that Brad Johnson asked you to Jeremy's party?"

"How did you find out so fast? It's only been a few hours since he asked me." It will never cease to amaze me, the speed at which high school gossip travels. I don't even remember seeing anyone at school while Brad and I were together. Although, I was a bit flustered at the time.

"It doesn't matter how I found out. What matters is that I found out just in time. You're not going on a date with him, Tweet."

I glared at him in disbelief as I jerked my hand from his. "Hold on now. Is this why you suddenly wanted me back in your life, so you could dictate who I could and could not go on a date with?"

"No!"

"Because, for your information, I haven't been on one single date unless you count Vincent Chamberlain in tenth grade, which I do not since he dumped me in the middle of the damn date for Sarah Grice."

"He's a Smurffucker and you're not going out with him Saturday or any other time," he said loudly.

My expression tightened as I continued to glare at him. My body began to heat up with anger. I jumped off the table and step away from it. I turned on my heels to face him. My hands firmly planted on my hips.

"Who the hell do you think you are? For four months, I was close to being completely ignored by you. You know what I had to watch while I kept my mouth shut? Bitchanni sniffing around you first thing in the morning at your locker. Then there's Amy, and Paige, and Tiffany. Anyone else? Oh yes, let's not forget what started the four month sabbatical, the day you planned on fucking Beth," I yelled. I thought for a second I might hyperventilate, I was breathing so fast.

"That's different." He was standing directly in front of me now. The veins in his neck strained as he spoke through clenched teeth.

"How so?"

"It just is. Look, it's my job to take care of you and look out for you."

"Noah, it's just one date. The party is only a few days away. I've already accepted his invitation. I'd feel bad if I canceled on him now. It would be rude."

Noah scrunched up his eyebrows. "Accepted his invitation? What the hell do you think you're going to, some debutante cotillion bullshit?" Sarcasm was dripping from his voice.

"I know *exactly* where I'm going. Jeremy's party! Saturday night! With Brad!" I shouted, as I brushed passed him.

"I can't figure out why he even asked you." His words stopped me in my tracks. I turned back to let him see how hurtful what he said was to me.

"Thanks a lot." I'm not sure what came over me. I stepped toward Noah and shoved hard against his chest. "That was a shitty thing for you to say to me." I turned and started walking away.

He ran up to me, grabbed my elbow, and spun me around to face him. "Tweet. I'm sorry. That didn't come out right. You know what I meant."

I shrugged out of his grasp, taking a few steps back from him. I felt tears building, but I was determined to hold them back. "It came out just fine. I know *exactly* what you meant. No one like Brad could ever want to go out with anyone like me, unless he had an ulterior motive."

"Dammit! That asshole is nowhere near good enough to even be talking to you." He started walking towards me. I held my hand up, letting him know not to come any closer.

"It's fine. I've had the exact same question playing repeatedly in my head since he asked me out. It just hurts like hell when your best friend wonders the same thing."

"I told you I didn't mean it that way." His jaw was clenched so tight, I swear I could hear his teeth grinding together.

"I need to go," I said. Noah took one step toward me. "Noah, don't." I turned on my heels and started walking as fast as I could out of the park.

"Where are you going?" he yelled.

"Home!"

"You're not walking home by yourself at night!"

"Yes I am!" I just kept walking, never turning back to look at him.

He followed a few steps behind me, in silence, the entire way home. As the house got closer, my steps got faster, until I ran up the steps on to the porch. I took the key out of my pocket and slipped it into the lock. I could feel Noah's eyes on me, as he remained at the bottom of the steps.

Clearing his throat, he said, "Aren't you going to say goodnight?"

I kept my eyes glued to the front door and choked out, "Goodnight, Noah."

"Goodnight, Tweet." I could hear the anguish in his voice.

I started to twist the key to unlock the door, when I saw Noah's arms come up on either side of me, his palms flat against the doorframe. His lips were at my ear.

As I felt his warm breath across my neck, shivers ran to every part of my body. I wanted to lean my head back on his shoulder and have him hold me like that all night. His mouth was so close, that when he talked, his lips lightly brushed against the shell of my ear. He whispered, "Please, don't be mad at me. I just want to protect you."

"I'm not mad. I'm scared," I said breathless.

"Of what?"

"That we're not going to be able to go back to the way we were. You've been back in my life for an hour and it already feels like we're crossing that line. I just got you back. I don't want to lose you."

"I promised you I'd stay in the friend zone and I will. But the line has already been crossed, Tweet. I wish you'd step over it with me."

I started to feel lightheaded and my knees were shaky. I inadvertently leaned back against his chest, trying to keep myself upright. He pushed off from the doorframe and wrapped his arms around my waist. Placing a soft kiss behind my ear, he said, "I'll see you tomorrow." He kissed the top of my head, dropped his arms, and stepped back. I heard his footsteps as he walked away.

I stood on my front porch playing tonight over in my head—

his arms around me, his whispers in my ear, the way his chest felt against my back. My head began to hurt thinking about our argument earlier. I had just spent four months without him in my life. I wasn't going to do anything to jeopardize our friendship and risk losing him again, no matter how much I wanted him. Going out with Brad will be good for both of us.

How quickly life can change direction. Earlier today, I felt like I was finally taking steps to move on. Now I find myself right back at square one.

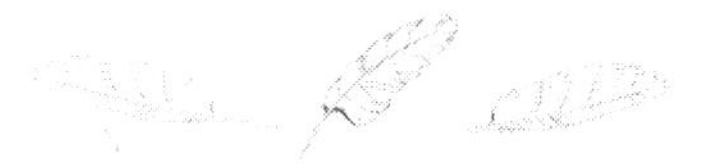

Friday afternoon finally arrived. The past few days had been weird to say the least. I hadn't talked to Noah since the other night, but I saw him everywhere. When Brad and I came out of our class together, Noah was there. When Brad and I were at my locker, Noah was there. When Brad and I were at lunch, Noah was just a few tables away. He never stopped watching us. I wanted to ignore him and be angry, but I couldn't. I liked him watching me. It made me feel safe and cared for.

I was about to get in my car to leave school that afternoon, when I heard yelling coming from the direction of the boy's locker room. I wasn't able to make out who the voices belonged to or what they were yelling. I knew the baseball team was training today. Brad had told me he had to be there right after school, so he wouldn't be waiting at my locker for me. I started to ignore the yelling and get in my car. Then I heard someone yell, "STEWART, GET OFF OF HIM!"

I threw my backpack in the car and ran towards the locker

room. Rounding the corner, I saw Noah pushing Brad up against the brick wall. His jaw was clenched, the veins in his neck were popping out, and the muscles in his arms were strained and bulging against his t-shirt, I thought the sleeves were going to shred. Two other players tried to pull him off Brad, but they weren't strong enough.

Holding a fistful of Brad's shirt, Noah jerked him forward off the wall, and then slammed Brad back hard. He got right in Brad's face and spoke through gritted teeth, "You're going to break the goddamn date and leave her alone."

I couldn't tell if Brad was scared, angry, or both. He wasn't fighting back.

He looked Noah in the eye and in a strained voice said, "What Amanda does is none of your business, Stewart. She's a big girl. She can go out with whoever she wants and she *wants* me." He gave Noah a smug smile. The boy's got balls, I'll give him that.

Noah pushed Brad into the wall again and said, "She's always my business, asshole. If you touch her, I will fuck up that pretty face of yours."

One of the other players, Spencer, said, "Stewart, come on. If Coach catches you, you're off the team."

Noah froze in position, sneering at Brad. After several more tense seconds, he released Brad from the death grip and backed away. He turned and saw me. My eyes connected with his. I couldn't believe what I had just seen. I was speechless. He broke our connection, turned and disappeared into the locker room, without saying a word. The other guys eventually followed.

I walked over to Brad who was leaning on the wall, bent over, his hands resting on his knees. I placed my hand on his shoulder and asked, "Are you alright?" He glanced at me and nodded his head. "Brad, I'm so sorry. I'll talk to him. I don't know what got into him."

He straightened. "Are you sure there's nothing going on between you two?"

"Noah is very protective of me." I lied. Sort of. Noah had always been protective of me, but this was more than that. It was jealousy and possessiveness. I should know because I felt the same way every time a girl even looked at Noah. "I *will* talk to him," I promised Brad.

Brad pushed himself off the wall and turned towards me. He took three steps, putting him directly in front of me. His head lowered, so that our eyes were in line with one another's. There was so little space between us, our lips were almost touching.

"Talk to him, because I *do* plan on touching you. A lot. If you let me." He leaned in closer and gently brushed his lips over mine. When he pulled away my breath hitched. He had sucked his lower lip into his mouth and was slowly grazing it with his teeth as he released it. This was the same move that got me all disoriented at my car the first day he approached me.

He took a couple of steps back, never breaking eye contact with me, then turned and walked away. I watched as the door to the locker room closed before slowly letting out the breath that had been trapped in my lungs since he touched me. Staying put, I tried to compose myself from what I believe to have been a swoon. Man, that boy was sex on a stick, deep fried.

Entry 13

GETTING OVER SOMEONE DOESN'T HAPPEN
BY GETTING UNDER SOMEONE. IT JUST REMINDS
YOU WHAT YOU SHOULD HAVE HELD ONTO.

Brad and I were on our way to the party at Folly Beach, aka The Edge of America. Noah and I grew up at this beach. Since it was only twenty minutes from our houses we spent as much time as possible there during the summer. It was a funky small beach community. Where the old and new collided. Center Street is filled with brightly colored locally owned bars, restaurants and standard tourist shops. The homes are as diverse as the inhabitants. There are the upscale McMansions for the McMillionairs, And beachside shacks for the old leathered skin hippies.

Of course the Pratts lived in an obnoxious beachfront McMansion. We pulled up into their driveway and went inside. I immediately felt overwhelmed. People were everywhere. Couples in the corners of the living room were making out, couples dancing were making out, and couples on the stairs were making out. It was like the John Hughes version of Caligula. It seemed like most, if not all, of the senior class was here. The music was incredibly loud and I felt the pulsating base vibrate through my body. The room was dotted with red cups, indicating that the alcohol had already started flowing.

Brad kept me close by his side as we walked through the maze of bodies. His hand never left the small of my back. I was wearing my cropped faded jeans and sleeveless light purple shirt, the hem of which skimmed the top of my jeans. Brad's fingers slid under my shirt and grazed my lower back. His touch sent a slight shiver through me. He always looked very good, but he looked extremely hot tonight. He wore dark tan cargo shorts and a sapphire blue button down shirt with his sleeves rolled up to his elbow. The color matched his eyes perfectly. He smelled good too, like cinnamon. Teenage boys don't usually have an appealing fragrance. The only boy I ever knew who always smelled wonderful was Noah. He smelled citrusy, like an orange.

Several people stopped Brad to talk. He would give them a quick, "Hey," and then direct his attention right back to me. We made our way to the kitchen. Wine, tequila, vodka, and rum filled the countertops along with various mixers. There was a sliding glass door that led out to a huge deck where a couple of kegs sat. Chips seemed to be on the menu for the night, just chips. All different kinds—potato, corn, pita, tortilla. You name the chip, it was there.

Once in the kitchen, we were greeted by our host, Jeremy. "Hey BroJo! Glad you finally made it, man. Now the serious partying can begin," Jeremy said as he high fived Brad. I was pretty positive that our host had already sampled the liquid refreshments.

"Pratt, you know Amanda?" Brad asked.

"Yeah, yeah, yeah! You're Stewart's girl." I felt Brad's hand stiffen against my back. "Glad you could make it." Glancing down at where Brad's hand rested, Jeremy leaned in and whispered loudly, "Better watch out dude. You don't want NoStew to catch you touching *his* girl, not after what happened yesterday. I've never seen him that pissed off before."

"She's not his girl." Brad looked down at me and I gave him a small smile.

Knots began forming in the pit of my stomach. "Where is Noah?" I asked Jeremy.

Raising his hands, he began to wave them above his head, as he slurred, "Somewhere..." He lost his balance and stumbled back against the counter. Slapping Brad on the back he said, "You guys make yourselves at home. Mi casa es su casa. Eat, drink, be merry, and all that shit."

As Jeremy disappeared, I scanned the room to see if I spotted Noah. Concern was written all over my face when I looked at Brad. "Me being here with you was a bad idea. I didn't have a chance to talk with Noah about yesterday."

Leaning down to me, Brad's lips gently brushed my ear as he whispered, "Being with you is never a bad idea. There's a ton of people here. We probably won't even see him. Just relax. I'll take good care of you." He placed a light kiss just below my ear. "What's your pleasure? As far as something to drink, that is. I can take care of your other pleasures later." He winked.

I made no attempt at hiding my eye roll as I shook my head and said, "Unbelievable."

Brad's megawatt smile appeared. "Beautiful, you have no idea."

I wasn't really a drinker. I had had wine before, but that was about the extent of my alcohol intake. Plus, with the strange effect Brad seemed to have on me, I thought it best to keep a clear head tonight.

Looking up, I shyly smiled, "A diet soda is fine. Thanks."

"Diet soda, it is. I'll be right back." He kissed me softly on the cheek before he left. Yep, he was definitely a swooner.

Within minutes Brad returned carrying two red cups, both filled with soda. I was surprised that he wasn't drinking something more potent. I asked curiously, "You're not drinking the hard stuff?"

"Maybe later. I want to be completely alert while I get to know you." Taking my elbow, he guided me to the sliding glass doors. "Let's go out on the deck. It's less crowded."

It was a beautiful night. The sky was so clear the stars looked like tiny bright white Christmas lights twinkling. I could even make out the Morris Island Lighthouse in the distance. There was a warm breeze coming off the ocean and the sound of the waves crashing against the rocks was soothing my nerves. We walked over to the railing of the deck facing the ocean. While I enjoyed the sea breeze and watched the waves, Brad watched me. I could feel my cheeks getting warm. His staring was making me feel a little uneasy.

I turned toward him, trying to sound playful and asked, "What is it with you and staring?"

"I told you before, I'm admiring. Why do you have such a hard time with guys looking at you?"

I was in full blown red face now. "Well, first of all, I've never had *guys* look at me. Second, I'm not exactly the type of girl that gets stared at, at least not for the good reasons."

He leaned down closer to me so we would be eye to eye. In a low voice he said, "You have no idea how hot you are. Do you?"

"Are you sure all you have in that cup is soda?"

Brad shook his head and smiled. "You're awesome. I'm so glad you said yes."

He gently pressed his lips to mine. My eyes automatically fluttered shut. A surge of electricity zipped through my entire body. He nipped at my bottom lip and then I felt his tongue glide over them. His lips were so soft and tasted like soda. Our lips moved slowly against each other's, and then the tip of his tongue slipped between mine. I parted them slightly for him and his tongue slid into my mouth. Every movement he made was so slow, deliberate, and hot as hell. He wasn't in a hurry to get through this kiss and neither was I.

Suddenly, Brad jerked away from me. I heard people shouting. My eyes shot open. I was so disoriented from the kiss, I didn't immediately comprehend what was happening. Once my eyes focused, I saw Noah dragging Brad down the steps to the beach. Several people followed. By the time I got to the bottom, I heard flesh hit flesh.

"I FUCKING WARNED YOU ABOUT TOUCHING HER!" Noah screamed as he slammed his fist into Brad's side.

Unlike yesterday, Brad fought back. He shoved Noah, and then brought his fist around connecting to the left side of Noah's jaw. Noah stumbled back a few steps and shook it off. He came at Brad with full force, tackling him to the ground. Noah's attack was relentless, punching Brad over and over again in rapid fire.

I ran up screaming, "NOAH, STOP IT! YOU'RE GOING TO KILL HIM!" Tears were streaming down my face.

Finally, Jeremy and two other guys went over and pulled Noah off Brad.

Walking over and kneeling at Brad's side, I tried to help him sit up. "Oh god! Are you ok? We need to get you to the ER."

He shook his head at me and whispered, "I'll be ok. Just give me a sec." He was gasping for air.

Looking up, my eyes pleaded with Noah to calm down. His chest was rapidly pumping as his breaths came fast and heavy. His jaw was clenched tight and his hands were still formed into fists. He didn't make any move towards Brad, though. His eyes shot daggers right through me. I thought he was furious yesterday, but that was nothing compared to the rage coming off his body now. He had never directed this type of anger towards me before.

Sneering at me, he asked, "Is this what you want? Some mother fucking son of a bitch who just wants to get into your pants?"

I didn't know how to respond. I was completely embarrassed and Noah was to blame. I just looked at him with tears in my eyes. I didn't understand what was going on. I knew he hated the idea of me going out with Brad. But it was just one date. Noah was acting like I was going to marry the guy and be doomed to a life of hell. Without saying another word, he turned and bulldozed his way up the steps and into the house.

Jeremy, trying to get the party back on track said, "Now it's a party! Okay folks, nothing more to see here. Move along." The crowd started to break up and head back into the house.

I helped Brad up. "Are you sure you're okay?"

"Yeah. I'm fine," he grunted.

He put his arm around my shoulders as I put mine around his waist. Letting him lean on me for support, we walked back up to the deck. I steadied Brad as he lowered himself onto one of the loungers and leaned back. I felt terrible. It was my fault this happened to him. I sat next to him and kept apologizing. I didn't know what else to say or do at that moment.

Looking sympathetically, I said, "I'm so sorry. Can I get you anything? Can I do anything for you?"

A smile slowly crept across his face that was dripping with sexiness when he said, "I can think of a few things I'd like you to do for me. Just let me sit here a little longer until the pain eases up."

I shook my head. "Do you ever stop flirting?"

"Not when there's somebody worth flirting with." He gave me a wink.

"Maybe I should listen to the warnings about you."

"I'm not going to lie. I have pictured you in various positions. All of which involve your legs wrapped around me. But that's not all I'm after."

I had goose bumps, on top of goose bumps, on top of goose bumps. After what felt like an eternity, I nervously asked, "What are you after?"

"All of you." And there it was again, that amazing, melt in your mouth sexy smile. What was it about this guy? One minute he says something highly inappropriate. The next minute he says something that makes me swoon a little more. God, I'm such a girl.

Brad and I sat out on the deck for an hour talking about school, plans for the summer, and what colleges we hoped to get into. We also did a fair amount of shameless flirting. Brad did most of it, of course. After all, he was quite skilled at it. I still wasn't completely comfortable around him, but I was getting there. His aggressive personality mixed with his sweetness kept me off balance. He was definitely a charmer and I was having a good time with him.

We had been at the party for a while and it was time for me to find a bathroom. “Would you excuse me for a minute? I need to find the bathroom,” I said shyly.

“Sure, but don’t be gone too long. I still need your healing hands on me where it hurts. By the way, a few other places have popped up that need your special touch.” He shot me a devilish grin and raised his eyebrows.

Smiling at him, I said, “You’re very pleased with yourself, aren’t you?”

He thought for a moment and replied, “Hmmm … I believe I am and I know you will be too.”

“Can you point me in the direction of a bathroom?”

He chuckled and then answered, “There’s one downstairs and two upstairs.”

“Thanks. I’ll be right back.”

I walked through the double French doors that led from the deck into the huge living room. The crowd hadn’t thinned out much, but it was a little quieter. I looked around for Noah. I felt it was best if I kept my distance from him right now. I hadn’t seen him since the fight. I still couldn’t get the look he gave me out of my head. I asked a couple of people if they had seen him. They both said he left right after the fight broke up. I was glad. Leaving was the best thing. He needed to go calm down. I could take care of myself.

I saw Jeremy on the makeshift dance floor grinding into, of all people, Beth. She must have gotten here while I was outside with Brad.

She and I still hadn’t spoken and by the look in her eyes, we weren’t going to any time soon. “So are you here to take Jeremy away from me too, Amanda?”

"No. And I didn't take anything or anyone away from you, Beth."

"Bullshit!"

"Ladies, don't fight. There's enough of me to go around," Jeremy slurred.

"Can you just tell me where the bathroom is down here?"

"Don't use the one downstairs. There's a line of people waiting. Go use one of the ones upstairs," Jeremy said.

I turned on my heels and headed to the stairs as the two got back to grinding each other into oblivion. It wasn't until I got to the top, that I realized I hadn't asked him where the bathroom was up here. I figured I would just start opening doors. I mean, there were only so many rooms up here. How hard could it be to find a bathroom?

The first door I opened was a closet. The next door I opened was a home office. Maybe finding the bathroom would be harder than I thought. Luckily, I spotted someone coming out of a door at the end of the hall. Bingo! The bathroom. I started to head that way when I heard a noise coming from behind the door I was in front of. It sounded like a thud, as if someone was being pushed up against it. Then I heard a female voice moan, "Oh baby. Yes. Fuck me hard."

I stood there unable to make my legs move. I knew I should get the hell away, but it was like I couldn't help myself. After a couple of more thuds and moans, the girl whined, "Kiss my lips. Why won't you kiss me on the lips? I want you to." An angry muffled guy's voice grunted at her. Gasping for air the girl said, "I can't talk now, either? Fine, then finish fucking me." A few more moans escaped and then it was silent.

When it dawned on me that the noises had stopped, I moved as quickly as possible to the bathroom, hoping no one was in there. Thankfully it was empty. I did what I needed to do, washed my hands, and did a quick check of my makeup in the mirror. I knew I was stalling. I wanted enough time to pass, so there wouldn't be any chance of running into The Thuds. It was unbelievable to me that people would have sex in someone else's house during a huge party. I wasn't a prude, but it seemed sleazy. There were people all over downstairs and upstairs, anyone could have heard them.

I cracked the bathroom door open enough to make sure the coast was clear. It was. I took three steps down the hall and then I heard it. The door to the sex room was creaking open. I froze. I should have run when I first heard the door. I knew it was stupid to stand there, but frankly I was a little curious to see who The Thuds were. The door slowly cracked open. Whoever it was, they wanted to make sure no one saw them coming out of that room. The guy stepped out first.

Amanda Marie Kelly, why didn't you run before that damn door opened?

Noah had his head down as he stepped through the door into the hall. I guess he sensed someone standing there because he immediately looked up in my direction. The blood drained completely from his face. I was numb from head to toe. All my systems were shutting down. The ability to think, speak and move had all left me. When I thought this situation couldn't get any worse, she walked out behind him and peered over his shoulder at me.

"Well, hello Amanda. What are you doing here?" Brittani said with the most self-satisfied smug look across her face. What I wouldn't give to punch that look right off her face.

I remained silent. How could I have been at the party this long and not have seen her until now? She was pretty easy to spot, at least her big ass was. Her arms crept around Noah's waist. He quickly stepped away from her. She looked pissed, but recovered quickly.

In a syrupy sweet voice, she said to Noah, "Baby that was amazing, as usual. No one fucks me like you. The way you suck my …"

"Shut up, Brittani," Noah said, cutting her off. Anger laced his voice while sadness overtook his eyes as they stayed fixated on me. She raised her hand to run her fingers through his hair, but he shrugged away from her.

Placing her hands on her hips, she huffed, and said in a whiney tone, "What's wrong?"

With his jaw clenched, Noah spat out, "Get out of here."

She looked over at me with her signature Cheshire cat smile plastered across her face. God, I hated that damn smile and face.

She purred at him, "I'll be downstairs when you're ready for round two, baby." Giving me one last shit eating grin, she headed downstairs.

Noah and I never broke eye contact the entire time we were standing in the hall. Suddenly, the feeling started to come back into my body. I felt like I was going to throw up. I turned and ran back to the bathroom. I hovered over the toilet for a few seconds before emptying the contents of my stomach into it. The last time I had eaten was nine hours ago, so there wasn't much to bring up. The dry heaves made my entire body convulse. My head was pounding and the ache in my chest was so intense, it felt as if my heart just shattered.

After I was sure all I had in me was gone, I sat on the floor, leaning back against the bathtub. The sobs started coming at a rapid pace. I had no control over myself. There was a soft knock on the door. I stayed quiet. There was another soft knock. Then I heard Noah ask, "Tweet, are you alright? Can I come in, please?"

Was he kidding me? I had gone from hurt, to devastated, to angry, to enraged in less than three minutes.

Trying to control my sobs I screamed at the door, "NO AND NO!"

The door behind me slowly opened. Trying to get to the bathroom as fast as I could, I forgot to lock it. I could not believe he was actually coming in here. I screamed, "STAY THE FUCK AWAY FROM ME, NOAH!"

I scrambled to my feet as the door swung wide open. I caught my reflection in the mirror. I looked like hell. My eyes were blood red, my face was blotchy, and streaked with tears. Noah stepped in, closing the door behind him.

"I know you don't want to hear this right now." His voice sounded so small and strained. "I am so, so, *so sorry.*"

"For what? I'm not anything to you," I said in as flat a voice as I could.

"It doesn't mean anything. She's just a fuck."

"Wow! What a romantic you are."

He rubbed his hands up and down his face. "I was so angry with you for choosing him."

"You're not going to blame me for what *you* just did with *her*. How could you with *her*?" I stormed toward the door, but he grabbed my arm.

"I don't know. When I saw you kneeling by that Smurffucker helping him … It pissed me off."

"So you fucked Brittani to get back at me?"

"No! I wasn't trying to get back at you. I just wanted to be numb." Tears continued to fall down my face as we looked at one another.

I shrugged out of his grip, took a step back, and said, "Why with *her*? You didn't see the look on her face when she came out of that room after the two of you … and saw me standing there. She looked so goddamn smug. Like she knew she had something that I never would." Sobs were pouring out of me.

"You *do* have me. Every part of me. You always have. You just don't want me." His words slapped me in the face. He had to know that wasn't the case. Why didn't he understand? It's never been about not *wanting* him. It's always been about not *losing* him. I explained all of this to him. I was beginning to suffocate. I had to get out of there. I shoved Noah as hard as I could. This time he let me move him out of my way.

Once I reached the hall, I took off running. I ran down the stairs, through the living room, across the deck, passing Brad who was still waiting for me. I had no clue how long I had been gone. It could have been minutes or hours. When I got to the bottom of the deck steps, I kicked off my flip flops, and ran full speed down the beach. I had no idea where I was going. I just knew I had to get away.

I ran as fast and as far as my legs allowed before I collapsed from exhaustion on the sand. My breathing was so fast and heavy I was lightheaded. I heard my name being called in the distance. I didn't care who it was. I didn't care about anything except forgetting this night. As the voice got louder I didn't look up, I knew who it was. Brad ran up and collapsed beside me, completely out of breath. I brought my knees to my chest and hugged my legs. I continued to stare out toward the ocean, hoping the crashing waves would calm me and help me forget what just happened.

When his breathing recovered, Brad turned to me and asked, "What can I do?"

My voice was flat. I didn't look at him when I answered, "Nothing."

We sat there in silence for several minutes before he spoke again. "I'm sorry you saw that."

I slowly turned my head to him and asked, "How did you know?"

"Brit likes to brag," he said sheepishly.

Looking back towards the ocean, I mumbled, "I want to completely forget the last hour ever happened." Turning to Brad, I whispered, "Help me forget." He leaned toward me and softly touched my cheek with his hand before brushing my lips lightly with his.

Brad stood up and offered me his hand, helping me to my feet. He kept his arm around my shoulders the entire walk back to the beach house. Once we got to the steps, I hesitated. I didn't know if Noah was still inside, but I knew I didn't want to see him.

Brad sensed my apprehension and said, "It's going to be fine. I'll make sure he doesn't come anywhere near you. I promise." He touched my chin, tilting my head back slightly. His look penetrated through me. "Trust me?" His eyes were filled with sincerity and were smoldering.

Breathlessly I answered, "Yes."

He tried to lighten the mood and make me smile. "Great. Stay here. I'll be back in a minute. Then we'll start *Operation Fo Getta Bout It*," he said, doing his best New York accent. He winked at me then looked at one another.

I shrugged out of his grip, took a step back, and said, "Why with *her*? You didn't see the look on her face when she came out of that room after the two of you … and saw me standing there. She looked so goddamn smug. Like she knew she had something that I never would." Sobs were pouring out of me.

"You *do* have me. Every part of me. You always have. You just don't want me." His words slapped me in the face. He had to know that wasn't the case. Why didn't he understand? It's never been about not *wanting* him. It's always been about not *losing* him. I explained all of this to him. I was beginning to suffocate. I had to get out of there. I shoved Noah as hard as I could. This time he let me move him out of my way.

Once I reached the hall, I took off running. I ran down the stairs, through the living room, across the deck, passing Brad who was still waiting for me. I had no clue how long I had been gone. It could have been minutes or hours. When I got to the bottom of the deck steps, I kicked off my flip flops, and ran full speed down the beach. I had no idea where I was going. I just knew I had to get away.

I ran as fast and as far as my legs allowed before I collapsed from exhaustion on the sand. My breathing was so fast and heavy I was lightheaded. I heard my name being called in the distance. I didn't care who it was. I didn't care about anything except forgetting this night. As the voice got louder I didn't look up, I knew who it was. Brad ran up and collapsed beside me, completely out of breath. I brought my knees to my chest and hugged my legs. I continued to stare out toward the ocean, hoping the crashing waves would calm me and help me forget what just happened.

When his breathing recovered, Brad turned to me and asked, "What can I do?"

My voice was flat. I didn't look at him when I answered, "Nothing."

We sat there in silence for several minutes before he spoke again. "I'm sorry you saw that."

I slowly turned my head to him and asked, "How did you know?"

"Brit likes to brag," he said sheepishly.

Looking back towards the ocean, I mumbled, "I want to completely forget the last hour ever happened." Turning to Brad, I whispered, "Help me forget." He leaned toward me and softly touched my cheek with his hand before brushing my lips lightly with his.

Brad stood up and offered me his hand, helping me to my feet. He kept his arm around my shoulders the entire walk back to the beach house. Once we got to the steps, I hesitated. I didn't know if Noah was still inside, but I knew I didn't want to see him.

Brad sensed my apprehension and said, "It's going to be fine. I'll make sure he doesn't come anywhere near you. I promise." He touched my chin, tilting my head back slightly. His look penetrated through me. "Trust me?" His eyes were filled with sincerity and were smoldering.

Breathlessly I answered, "Yes."

He tried to lighten the mood and make me smile. "Great. Stay here. I'll be back in a minute. Then we'll start *Operation Fo Getta Bout It,*" he said, doing his best New York accent. He winked at me then jogged up the stairs.

When Brad reappeared, he had a blanket under one arm, a plastic baggie full of lime wedges, a salt shaker, two shot glasses, and a bottle of tequila.

He pushed my elbow with his indicating he wanted me to

take the blanket. "Help a guy out." I grabbed the blanket from him.

"Follow me," he said walking past me.

We walked a few yards down the beach. There was enough light spilling over from the house, plus the moon was very bright, so we were able to see what we were doing. We were fairly well hidden from curious onlookers, though.

Turning to me, Brad said, "Please tell me if I'm wrong, but I'm assuming that you've never done tequila shots."

"You assume correctly, sir." Spreading the blanket out I glanced at all the stuff he was holding. "It looks complicated. There's a lot of stuff involved."

"Well, lucky for you, Beautiful, you're being taught by a master shots-man." His playfulness brought a slight smile to my face.

We sat facing each other with our legs crossed in front of us. Brad placed all the ingredients for the shots between us. He picked up a lime wedge and held it in his left hand. Looking up at me with his sapphire blue eyes, he licked the back of that hand, wetting it slightly, and then sprinkled a small amount of salt on it. Tilting his chin towards the tequila he said, "Pour some booze in one of those glasses for me."

Smiling, I did as I was told. He took the glass from me. Looking very serious, he said, "Pay close attention. There will be a quiz afterwards." I actually giggled. Brad was doing a great job of lifting my mood.

He quickly sucked the lime, then licked the salt, and downed the shot. He shook his head and growled, "Oh baby, that's tasty," making me laugh out loud/

Brad watched me intensely as I set up my first ever shot. I had the lime and salt all ready.

He handed me the shot of tequila he had poured. He instructed me, "It's best to go as quickly as possible and know the sequence. Remember SLS."

I looked at him confused and asked, "SLS?"

A sly grin appeared. "Suck. Lick. Swallow." I felt a deep red blush cross my cheeks. Leaning in closer, he said in a low voice, "SLS can also be applied in other situations." He gave me a devilish look and wink.

Sitting up tall, I squared my shoulders, and repeated SLS in my head. I sucked the lime, licked the salt, and swallowed the shot as quickly as I could. The minute the tequila hit the back of my throat, I began to choke and cough.

Brad crawled over to my side and patted me on the back until I calmed down. While he patted and rubbed my back, he admitted, "Probably should have mentioned that if you've never done shots before, the first two are a bitch."

"Thanks for that bit of info now," I choked out.

Brad was right. After my second shot, the others went down smooth as silk.

We continued *Operation Fo Getta Bout It* until our supplies had dwindled. I had lost track of time. But, I was feeling fantastic, without a care in the world. It didn't even hurt when I thought of what's his name. "Wow, the bottle is almost empaty … empatty … empty," I slurred.

"How do you feel?"

I cocked my head to one side and answered, "Buzzed and breezy." We both laughed.

"God, you're adorable and great at shots."

"I had a good teacher," I said, looking up at him through my eyelashes.

At this point, liquid courage was flowing steadily through my body and mind. I had never flirted before, so I was completely out of my element. I just hoped Brad wouldn't laugh in my face.

Leaning into me, he ran his nose up and down mine and whispered, "I'd like to teach you a few more things."

He moved in closer and started nibbling behind my ear. It tickled and sent chills throughout my body. I giggled. What was happening to me? I pulled away from him a little. The spot behind my ear was on fire.

Giving him a sideways glance, I grinned and asked, 'Like what?"

Brad propped himself up on his right arm. He returned to the spot behind my ear, running his lips gently over my skin. He whispered, "Come here."

Reaching over, he grabbed my hips, and pulled me on to his lap, so I was straddling him. The move was so quick it took me by surprise. He began to lick and suck a trail from my jaw down my neck. I tilted my head to the side to give him an obstacle free path. I like to help my fellow mankind whenever possible. It felt amazing. I was on fire and had chills all at the same time. His hands traveled down my hips. Palming my ass, he pulled me closer to his chest. The feel of his large hands holding and squeezing me made every part of my body tingle.

"Heyyy!" I looked back at Brad's fingers digging into me, and then I started to giggle. "You're touching my ass." I could feel him smiling against my neck. "No one has ever done that before."

"Ever?" he muttered, surprised, as he continued working his lips and tongue up and down my neck.

"Not on purpose," I giggled.

He brought his lips to mine. He sucked and lightly nipped my bottom lip. Every part of my body was responding to him. He pulled me in close and squeezed my ass again, causing a little moan to escape me.

He whispered against my lips, "That surprises me. It's such a cute little ass."

I could feel the heat and wetness spreading between my legs. He thrust his tongue deep and explored every inch of my mouth before pulling away. Again he nibbled a trail from my jaw to my neck. His hot breath washed over my neck as his hands started to travel up my back underneath my shirt.

Sounding out of breath, he said, "There are a lot more places on your body I want to touch on purpose." His tongue moved to behind my ear. I heard him mumble, "So sweet. I want to lick every inch of you." I thought I was going to explode. His words had my body feeling things I didn't know existed. They drove me crazy.

My hands moved from behind his neck up to his soft dirty-blonde hair. Brad let out a groan as I laced my fingers through it, slightly tugging. Our breathing was so fast and heavy, we had a hard time slowing it down.

He let out a low growl, and then whispered, "If I haven't made it perfectly clear, I *really* like you."

"I like you too," I said while laughing. I don't know if it was

Brad, the tequila, or a combination of both, but I was feeling very happy.

He held me tightly against him. "Can you feel *how* hard you make me?"

"Mmmhmm ..." My answer came out as a moan.

"Let's go somewhere less sandy."

"Ok," I smiled and then giggled. My head was swimming so fast, I wasn't exactly sure what I was agreeing to. All I knew was I felt warm, tingly, and turned on.

I crawled off Brad's lap. He struggled to stand up, taking a minute to regain his balance. Holding his hands out to me, I put mine in his, and he pulled me up off the blanket.

I started to gather our stuff when he said, "Don't worry about it."

"We shouldn't be litterbugs," I told him with my best pouty face. He burst out laughing. Yanking on my arms slightly, I fell into his chest, laughing.

"We'll deal with it later. Right now there are more important matters that need my attention." He gave me a quick kiss on the lips, grabbed my hand, and dragged me up the steps to the house.

The party had settled down quite a bit from earlier. Brad held my hand tightly as he maneuvered us through the large living room heading towards the upstairs. We made it up a couple of steps when I felt a strong warm hand grab my wrist, stopping me mid step. I stumbled back against the banister. I was so drunk from the tequila that it took me a few seconds before it registered who grabbed me.

"NOAH!!" I must have been crazy drunk, because I was thrilled to see him.

I twisted my hand out of Brad's. I fell towards Noah, draping my arms around his neck. He looked shocked at how affectionate I was towards him.

"Look Brad! It's Noah! *My* Noah! He's so sweet and sexy. He's *swexy.* He licked my thigh under my parent's dinner table. You remember licking me Noah?" I said in a loud high pitched voice.

Placing his hands on my shoulders, Noah helped me stand up straight. He said in a low voice, "I'm taking you home."

Looking up at his beautiful face, I replied, "But Brad was going to do *some things* to me on purpose. I don't know what, but I'm having fun. Hey! You want to come with us?" I asked.

I looked up towards Brad, who was standing there glaring at Noah, his hands balled into fist, and his jaw clenched tight. Noah snaked his arm around my waist and started leading me down the steps. Brad was right behind us. He grabbed my elbow, yanking me backwards out of Noah's arms.

In a low menacing voice, Brad growled at Noah, "Haven't you done enough to her tonight? She's having a great time with me, so get your fucking hands off of her."

I smiled up at Brad then turned to Noah and said, "I really am having fun. He's not a Smurffucker at all."

Noah tugged on my other arm, breaking me free of Brad's grip. We started towards the front door when once again I felt my arm being pulled by Brad. I was getting tired of them jerking me back and forth. Not to mention a little queasy with all the moving around. Not saying a word, Noah dropped my hand, walked over to Brad, and punched him directly in the stomach. My hand fell from Brad's as he doubled over and dropped to the floor. Noah then turned around and put me over his shoulder.

As we started towards the door, I grabbed the waistband of his pants, lifting my head, and yelled, "BYE BYE, BRAD! THANKS!

MAYBE *YOU* CAN LICK MY THIGH NEXT TIME! BYE, BYE!" He was still crumpled on the floor as we made it out the door.

Entry 14

You find out the true character of a person when they don't take advantage of a sure thing.

I must have fallen asleep in the car, because the next thing I knew I was at Noah's house in his bedroom, sitting on his bed. He was standing at his dresser with his back to me. My head was spinning and so was the room causing me to fall back on to the bed.

"Noah, you're room is like a ride at Disney World." I heard a slight chuckle coming from overhead. Barely lifting my head up off the bed, I slowly opened one eye, and saw him standing in front of me, holding a pair of green and white plaid boxer shorts and a white t-shirt. His anger had disappeared, replaced by sadness and guilt.

My face twisted in confusion. "You wear plaid underwear?" I asked, letting my head fall back and my eye close.

"Sometimes. Why?"

"I never pictured you wearing plaid boxers."

I felt the material of the t-shirt and boxers brush across my arm as he sat them down on the bed beside me.

His voice was gravely and hoarse when he said, "Change into this. I'm going to get you some water and aspirin."

"What am I going to do about my parents? I can't go home like this," I said.

"Both our parents went to Myrtle Beach this weekend. Remember?"

I heard his footsteps as he crossed the room, stopping when I whined, "Noah! I can't sit up. Help me!" I shot both arms up in the air, pointing them straight towards the ceiling. I felt his warm hands glide over mine as he pulled me up to a sitting position. My head was swimming as I swayed from side to side a few times before steadying myself.

Fumbling, I tried to unbutton my jeans, but the button kept eluding my grasp. If memory served me correctly, there was only one button on my jeans before the party, but apparently it had babies, because now I saw four.

I looked up at him helplessly, batting my eyes a couple of times, and said, "I seem to be having difficulty locating the actual boot-ton and zip-pah," I giggled and smiled at him.

Kneeling down in front of me, he smiled, and then whispered, "I'll help you."

Noah slipped my flip flops off and placed them to the side. Bringing his hands up, he unbuttoned and unzipped my jeans. A shiver ran through me when his fingers grazed my skin.

He looked into my eyes, gulped and said, "I'll go get your water and aspirin while you change." He stood and turned away, heading toward the door.

I made one attempt to stand up. When I leaned forward

slightly, the room started spinning rapidly. I flopped back on to the bed. "Noah, I can't stand up. I need you."

I heard him approach. "Tweet, are you okay?"

"Yes, but I need you. Don't leave me," I whispered.

He knelt back down in front of me and said, "I won't ever leave you. Just hold on to my shoulders to steady yourself."

Noah helped me sit back up. I placed my hands on his shoulders and leaned forward. As I stood my breasts came in direct contact with Noah's face. A prickly sensation covered my skin when I felt his face lightly graze my torso as I stood. My head began to swim, but I was able to remain standing as long as I held on to his strong shoulders.

Noah placed his hands on either side of my hips, his fingers hooked around the top of my jeans, and he slid them down to my mid-thigh. I glanced down and noticed him trying not to look at my naked thighs or my lacy purple boy shorts. I could feel his hot breath over the front of my panties. We stilled for a few seconds before I heard him swallow a big gulp of air. He helped me sit back down, and then pulled my jeans off the rest of the way. It was so cute how uncomfortable he was.

Holding out his boxers, I put one leg followed by the other into them. I stood up, again steadying myself with his shoulders while he pulled the boxers up my legs. Clearing his throat Noah said in a low voice, "I'm sure you'll be able to handle the rest on your own. I'll go get the water and aspirin."

The tequila was making me bold, forgetful, and horny. Memories of what happened between us just a few hours ago weren't hurting as much now. I wanted to know what it felt like to have Noah's hands on me. I wanted his lips on my skin. I wanted to know what it felt like to be Brittani.

While he was still kneeling in front of me, I grabbed the hem of my shirt and pulled it up over my head, tossing it to the side. Noah froze, gazing at me.

Grinning, I asked, "What are you looking at? I never struck you as a lacey bra kind of girl?" I sucked in my lower lip then slowly released it. "I have a black one, a red one, a white one, a pink one, a yellow one, and of course, you can see the purple one. They all have matching lace panties too." I gave him a little smile.

Damn, what had gotten into me? I was no longer average and plain Amanda Kelly. I had become some type of tequila slut. I was a Sluquila. I'm telling Noah all about my underwear. Oh! My! God! I'm telling Noah all about my underwear! Rather, Senorita Sluquila is.

Noah never took his eyes off of me or my bra, as he reached for the t-shirt and handed it to me. He exhaled a shaky deep sigh and then said, "Put this on. Now!"

I took the t-shirt and pulled it over my head. Noah was trying hard not to look in my direction. I turned off my brain and let Senorita Sluquila take over. Raising my leg, I slowly rubbed my inner calf up and down Noah's hip.

"You want to see how talented I am?" I asked looking at him through my eyelashes.

"What are you talking about?" he said.

I could tell he was still slightly dazed from my underwear soliloquy.

"Watch and learn, buddy boy." Keeping eye contact, Noah sat back on his heels ready for the show.

Moving one arm around to my back, I played with my bra hook for a few seconds, trying to unclasp it. Once it was undone I reached up into the sleeve of the shirt and pulled one strap down and out. I repeated the exact same move on the other side, this time I pulled the entire bra out from the sleeve, held it over my head, and loudly said, “Ta-dah!”

Noah started shaking his head and laughing, some of his nervousness disappearing. “You’re nuts.”

“And talented.” I gave him a wink.

“Yes, very talented,” he said, smiling at me.

The room got very quiet for a few seconds as we continued to maintain eye contact. I leaned back on the bed, propping myself up on my elbows. I tilted my head slightly to one side and shook it, letting my hair fall over my shoulder.

I’m not sure if I wanted him to be jealous or feel guilty because of Brittani, when I asked, “Do you want to know what Brad did to me?” I didn’t wait for him to answer. “He ran his hands up and down my bare back, over my hips, and grabbed my ass.”

I could see the anger build up in Noah’s eyes. His face was becoming strained, his hands were already formed into fists, and his breaths were coming out deep, and heavy. I rubbed his hip again with my leg. Suddenly, I felt his hands behind my knees, pulling me to the edge of the bed, and against his chest. I gasped. My hands gripped the edge of the bed while his remained behind my knees. We were nose-to-nose. Our chests rising and falling quickly, as our breaths became heavy.

Gazing into his beautiful hypnotic light blue eyes, I whispered, “Do *you* want to touch me?”

Closing his eyes, he tilted his head back and sighed, “Fuck, yes,” he whispered.

“Then do it,” I challenged.

He moved in closer. I felt his hands run over my hips and under my shirt. The sensation of them on my bare skin caused heat to radiate between my legs.

Our lips were almost touching when I whispered, "Touch me, Noah."

He stared at me for several seconds. The look in his eyes was a combination of desire and conflict. I felt his hands start to travel down my back and out from under my shirt. He pulled away from me and sat back on his heels.

"Fuck. Fuck. Fuck," he said under his breath.

I didn't understand what had just happened. I felt embarrassed and confused. I had obviously done something wrong. Noah didn't want me.

Somehow building up the courage, I asked, "What's wrong with me?"

"There's absolutely nothing wrong with you. It's just you've been drinking a lot and I don't want anything to happen between us while you're drunk."

I could feel my tears getting ready to spill over my cheeks. He didn't want me. I felt an all-consuming humiliation wash over me.

Looking down at my lap, I whispered, "I want to go home now."

Wiping away my tears, he said in a low voice, "Don't cry, Tweet. Talk to me."

I couldn't look at him. "It's just that I could tell Brittani was drunk and you still …" I trailed off. "Please let me go home now."

God, I was pathetic. If this was how I act when I'm drunk then I am never going to drink again.

Noah wrapped his arms around me and pulled me into his chest, and softly said, "I'm so sorry about tonight. I hate myself for hurting you," he pulled back, resting his forehead on mine. "It didn't matter if *she* was drunk. I don't care about her and she knows that. She doesn't care about me either. We were both using each other. You're not just a warm body that a guy screws when he's trying to numb himself. You mean everything to me." He kissed my forehead gently, and then whispered against it, "Don't go. Stay with me." I nodded. I wanted to stay. He then left to get me water and aspirin.

When the door closed, I laid back on the bed, staring up at the ceiling. I felt completely drained. My head began to throb from the events of the night running around in it. I scooted up the bed and crawled under the covers, lying on my side.

I heard the door open and close quietly. Noah walked around to my side of the bed. Sitting up, I took the water and aspirin he brought me. Noah had already changed into a pair of pajama pants and a t-shirt. I placed the glass on the nightstand and laid my head back down. The lights went out. I felt the bed dipped as he slipped under the covers behind me. Pressing his chest against my back, he let his arm drape around my waist and held me tight. I felt his warm breath flowing over the back of my neck. He calmed me.

I was ready for this night to be over, so it surprised me when I opened my big mouth and said, "Noah, can I ask you something?"

"You can ask me anything, Tweet," he whispered against my neck.

"Even if it's about Brittani?"

I felt his chest expand and contract as he took in a deep breath and then slowly let it out. "Yes."

"Why didn't you want to kiss her or hear her talk?"

The room fell quiet. Noah hugged me tight against him, and whispered, "Because she's not you."

That was all I needed to hear at that moment before drifting off to sleep with a smile of contentment on my face.

Entry 15

The invisible force occupies every part of my brain and permeates my body. There has never been a time in my life that it didn't hold me hostage. By the time I was able to fuse coherent thoughts together, it was too late and I didn't know where the exit was.

If I could see it, touch it, reason with it, maybe I would have a chance to survive it. Instead I only feel it and hear it. Its message is a constant in my life. Where did it come from? Why did it pick me? It seeped into my life so slowly I didn't notice it taking over before it consumed me.

(And that my friend is what they call fucked up thinking.)

When I first woke up, it took me several minutes to figure out where the hell I was. My head felt like a chainsaw was slicing into it.

My hair even hurt. I was barely able to lift my throbbing head off the pillow. Slowly, images of last night came back to me.

I remember I was at the party. Noah and Brad got into a fight. I got uber-drunk. Brad had his hands all over me. Noah brought me home. I threw myself at him. I still had this weird feeling that some other horrible thing had happened. I kept running last night through my head, trying to put things in some sort of sequence. Brad kissed me, and then the guys fought. I vaguely remember going up the stairs. Then my fuzzy brain started to clear and all the pieces fell into place. HOLY SHIT! I caught Noah and Brittani having sex!

I felt a cold shiver run up my entire body. My throat started to burn and a bitter taste invaded my mouth. I slapped my hand over my mouth and slid from Noah's bed, trying not to wake him. I made a mad quiet dash to the bathroom, getting there in the nick of time. I was astonished at how much *whatever* was coming out of me. It was like the freaking Exorcist.

I laid on the floor of the bathroom, pressing my cheek to the cool tile. It felt incredible. I could stay there all day. I was pretty sure I woke Noah up. I knew any minute there would be a knock on the door wanting to know if I was okay. I dreaded it. I knew the tequila shots Brad and I did were mostly to blame for my breakfast of acid chowder, but the memory of seeing Noah coming out of that room with *her* right behind him definitely helped push the contents of my stomach up and out.

I needed to get up. If I laid there any longer, I would have fallen asleep. I placed my arm on the side of the bathtub to steady myself as I tried to get up off the floor. It took three attempts, but I finally made it up and over to the sink. I rinsed my mouth out several times. God, I was so thirsty I felt like I could suck down an ocean of water. I washed my face and ran my fingers through my hair, gently, before heading back to Noah's room to grab my clothes. I just wanted to get my stuff and get out of there. I couldn't face him right now. I was ashamed, embarrassed, and humiliated.

I hadn't heard any noise in his room, so by some miracle he was either still asleep or possibly in his parent's bathroom taking a shower. The thought of a naked wet Noah flashed across my mind. I had to get out of there.

I opened the door to his bedroom as quietly as possible. By some miracle, he was still asleep. I could hear the pounding of my heart in my ears as I crept into the room. My shirt and jeans were on the floor at the foot of the bed where they had been tossed the night before. Slowly, I walked over, bent down, and picked them up. I scanned the room for the rest of my things. My flip-flops were on Noah's side of the bed. I decided to leave them and get them later. I wanted to make as quick a retreat as possible.

I scanned the room one more time. A wave of panic swept over me. The tingling started in the center of my chest and quickly spread to the rest of my body. My heart and lungs were working at warped speed. My eyes doubled in size. I closed them for a second trying to calm myself. Maybe I didn't see what I thought I saw. Opening my eyes slowly, I looked in the same direction and cringed. Yep, I saw it. My purple lace bra had been tossed on the lamp that sat on Noah's dresser. It was just hanging there, taunting me.

I tiptoed over to the dresser, and studied the bra for a moment, trying to figure out how best to free it. Somehow it had gotten tangled around the lamp. One of the straps had fallen, so half the bra was draped over the inside of the shade, wrapped around the base, and hooked around the switch. How the hell did that happen? I thought about leaving it, but this situation was humiliating enough without me having to ask for my underwear back.

I unhooked the strap from the switch with no problem. I carefully started untangling the bra and pulling it up. I thought I was in the clear, so to speed things up, I yanked on it. Somehow a piece of the lace snagged on something, causing the lamp to tip over. I caught it just before it hit the floor, but it still made a loud scraping sound. I held my breath and looked over my shoulder to check on Noah. I knew there was no way he slept through that. I watched him for a few seconds. His breathing was still even and he didn't move.

I started to unsnag the lace when a deep throaty voice startled me. I froze. "Leave it. I like having your pretty little lacey things scattered around my room." I inhaled a big gulp of air. "And how is my Tweet feeling this morning?"

I knew he was smirking at me. He was enjoying my discomfort from the tequila and standing there with my underwear in hand. The bastard. I didn't turn around. I didn't want him to see the humiliation on my face. Plus, there was a little bit of my vomit on his t-shirt that I was wearing. Looking at myself in the mirror, it dawned on me that he had a clear, unobstructed view of my face and had seen my humiliation.

I started to talk, but the words caught in my throat at first. Trying to sound chipper, I said, "Great. I'm going home to shower and wash my hair." My voice sounded as if I were a four pack a day smoker.

Noah got out of bed and walked up behind me, placing his hands on my hips. We looked at each other in the mirror. Damn, he looked hot standing there in his low hung pajama pants and well- worn grey t-shirt that covered his amazing toned and chiseled torso.

He lowered his mouth to my ear and said in a husky voice, "Don't go. You can shower here."

He took a small step back and pulled his shirt over his head, tossing it back onto the bed. There it was, that gorgeous chest I wanted to crawl up and down on. Noah continued, snapping me back to the present. "I'm going to go jump in the shower and then I'll make you some toast. It will help your stomach." He kissed the top of my head. Glancing down at his shirt I was wearing, splattered with the contents of my stomach, he said, "You can keep the shirt." I shifted my gaze down as the blush crept over my face. He then smiled at me, followed by a smack on my ass before leaving the room.

HE SMACKED MY ASS AND I LIKED IT!

I definitely had to get out of there.

I waited until I heard the shower turn on before I made my escape. I knew I was going to have to deal with this, but I couldn't right now. My head was swimming, my stomach was queasy, and my thoughts were all over the place. Not to mention, I felt icky and needed a shower. I quickly put my jeans on over Noah's boxers, slipped on my shoes, and made a beeline for the door.

I breathed a sigh of relief when I got home. Not only did I make it back here before Noah got out of the shower, but when I checked my phone, I saw I had a voicemail from Mom. They were staying in Myrtle Beach one more night and would be back late tomorrow. I'd have today and tomorrow to fully recover.

Just enough time had passed for me to take a shower before I heard him. Noah was in the house yelling my name. "TWEET!" He sounded beyond pissed at me for leaving.

I quickly stepped out of the shower and wrapped a big towel around me. I had started towel drying my hair when the bathroom door swung open. I spun around to see Noah glaring at me, supporting himself with one hand on the doorframe and the other gripping the doorknob tightly.

He leaned in and growled, "You and me are talking. Now!"

"Can I at least put some clothes on?"

"No. You have about ten seconds to get your sweet little ass out here." He abruptly turned and stomped away, leaving the door wide open.

I dried my hair as best I could and left it loose. Butterflies had taken over my stomach. I lowered my gaze with each step I took as I timidly walked down the hall to the family room. I had no idea what either of us was going to say. I reached the family room. Biting my lip, I looked up, but didn't see Noah. A sense of relief hit me. Maybe he had changed his mind and left to calm down before we talked. Then I heard him clear his throat. He was in the kitchen leaning up against the counter with his arms crossed over his chest. He was wearing a pair of dark blue basketball shorts, a sleeveless orange t-shirt, and he was barefoot. His hair was still slightly damp from his shower. Even with the scowl across his face, he was the most gorgeous guy I had ever seen. It took every ounce of strength I had to keep me from running and wrapping my arms and legs around him.

I walked into the room and stood on the other side of the kitchen island. I thought keeping a little distance between us was a good idea.

Neither one of us said anything at first. When he looked up at me, his eyes softened a little. I clutched the towel tightly around me. Noah's gaze started slowly gliding down the length of my body as his tongue darted out slightly, licking his lower lips. My breath started to quicken. The warm tingling sensation that I got whenever I was near him started to take over. I finally broke our eye contact, looking away, and nervously started biting my thumbnail. When I glanced back, the intensity had returned to his eyes and the scowl back to his face. His tone was strong and determined when he said, "Talk."

"About what?" I looked up at him with innocent eyes, as I continued to gnaw on my nail.

He let out a low deep growl as he shook his head. "How many times do I have to tell you not to play dumb? You're no good at it."

I released my thumb from its torture and said, "I'm not playing this time. I really don't know what you want me to say."

"Okay. How about we start with, why did you leave this morning?"

"I felt icky and needed a shower," I said.

"You could've showered at my house."

"I didn't want to."

"Why?"

"Because, my shampoo is over here and I like my shampoo."

Noah's breathing became deeper and picked up speed. The muscles in his arm tensed and relaxed each time he flexed his hands. He was losing patience. "You're a piece of work."

His arms unwrapped from around his chest. He took one step forward, placing his palms down on the kitchen island, and leaned in my direction. He had a look in his eye that I had only seen one other time. It was the same look he gave me last night after I ran to Brad's side. In a steady low-pitched voice, he slowly said, "Why did you run out this morning? Don't give me any shampoo bullshit."

I held eye contact and softly said, "I was having a hard time remembering what went on last night. I knew we needed to talk, but I needed to clear my head first," I paused. "I don't remember anything that happened after the tequila."

"You don't remember a thing after you got drunk?"

I shook my head. "No. Not a thing."

"You don't remember me carrying you out of the party and taking you to my house?" I shook my head. "You don't remember me undressing you? You don't remember my hands sliding up under your shirt, touching your back? And you don't remember asking me if I wanted to touch you and then telling me to touch you?" I took another huge gulp of air and shook my head. "None of that rings a bell?" he asked, his voice was low and gruff.

Every nerve ending in my body exploded and he hadn't even touched me. The hair on my arms and legs bristled. My lips slightly parted, sucking in as much oxygen as possible before I passed out. Warmth started at the top of my head and the tip of my toes, flowing over my body, and meeting smack-dab between my legs. I was feeling woozy and it wasn't from the aftermath of the tequila.

I stood there, immobile. I couldn't look away from him. I knew I needed to say something. He wasn't going anywhere until I did. I couldn't think of any words long enough to be able to string them together to form a sentence. The only word that came out of my mouth was, "No."

"That is such bullshit and you know it!" Noah looked down, concentrating on a spot on the countertop. He blew out a big breath and growl of frustration before looking back at me. He sounded so deflated when he said, "Last night, when I saw you standing in the hall … The way you looked at me … Broke me. You looked so hurt and disappointed. I thought I'd lost you for good. I couldn't think straight after I saw him kiss you. Then you ran to his side. I've never felt that out of control before. I wanted to be numb and forget, so I grabbed a lot of beer and the easiest piece of ass around, and fuck her."

"Noah …," I whispered. I understood him. Our actions echoed each other's last night.

"I always tell her not to talk, so I can pretend it's you. It's pathetic, I know. I don't want to pretend anymore, Tweet. I'm trying my damnedest to stay in the friend zone. It's just hard and I thought after last night in my room … The way you were acting... I knew you had been drinking. I just thought things would be different for us now."

"Always?" I said, the hurt evident in my voice.

He just opened himself up to me. Why did I zero in on that word? Why did I think last night was a one-time thing, a mistake? Apparently the rumors were true. The butterflies were gone, replaced by a huge boulder sitting in the pit of my stomach.

"A few times," he whispered, lowering his gaze.

"Was she your first?"

Tears I had been holding back started to seep out and fall. My mind was whirling. I hated that *she* had been his first. I hated that he had shared that part of himself with anyone, besides me. We would have been each other's first and he would be with me, if I didn't keep pushing him away. My head was so screwed up that

Freud would have thrown his hands up and retired.

Noah looked up at me through his long dark eyelashes. He didn't need to say anything. My eyes started stinging from the tears. I felt exhausted and drained.

I didn't look at him when I said, "I'm sorry I can't be with you like that." I choked back a sob that was trying to escape.

Looking back up, my gaze was met with piercing light blue eyes. Noah pushed off the counter and rounded the kitchen island, headed directly towards me. He was in front of me in two strides. Cupping one side of my face in his hand, he tilted my head back, forcing me to look straight into his eyes. His warm breath swept across my lips sending a shiver through my body. His nose skimmed across my cheek up to my temple as he whispered, "Stop pushing me away."

His lips started moving across my skin again, traveling down my cheek, over my jaw, landing on my neck.

I closed my eyes and let the sensations of his touch wash over me. It would be so easy to get lost in him, but I couldn't.

"Noah, you promised you'd stay in the zone," I whispered as he continued to nuzzle my neck.

"That was before last night."

As his lips made their way down and across my naked shoulder, I tightened my face, swallowed hard, and pulled away from him. His hands dropped and landed on his hips. His head was down.

"I can't do this with you. Don't you understand that? Please Noah, stop pushing me," I pleaded.

He straightened up, turned, and walked out the door, not saying another word or looking back.

It took me all afternoon to recover from the events of last night and this morning. After taking a nice long nap, eating a little something, and getting dressed I started feeling like my old average self again. I needed to talk with Noah. I needed to get us back on the friendship track. I had just gotten him back. I wasn't willing to give him up again.

I knocked on the Stewart's back door instead of just walking in as I usually did. I stood beside the door, so when he opened it the only thing he saw was my hand holding a plate with a big piece of chocolate cake on it. I could feel the smile he had across his face.

Grabbing the cake, he said, "Thanks. I wanted something sweet." Then he shut the door before I could walk in. He was playing with me, which was a good sign.

As I entered the house, I saw Noah in the kitchen, leaning against the counter, eating cake. I walked towards him. He looked at me, with his mouth full, and asked, "Did you want some?"

I narrowed my eyes. "Not if it's going to make you cry."

He held the fork out to me. Grabbing it, I plunged into the side of the cake that had the most frosting. Noah always left me that part because he knew how much I loved it. I handed the fork back to him and lifted myself up to sit on the counter next to where he was leaning. We continued to pass the fork between us until it was gone. Noah sat the empty plate behind him on the counter.

He dragged his hands up his face and through his hair. He blew out a breath, then asked, "What are we going to do, Tweet?"

"I need you in my life."

"I need you in mine, too."

"Be my friend," I said.

"Always."

I knew it was up to me to fix this. If we were going to remain in each other's lives, I had to be honest with him.

Clearing my throat, I struggled to find the right words. "Noah, next to my dad, you are the finest man I know. I can't bear the thought of you not being in my life."

"Tweet..."

He started to turn to face me, but I stopped him. This was going to be hard enough not looking at him. He shifted back in place against the counter, looking down. I heard him sigh deeply.

"You deserve better than me. If we were together, eventually I would screw it up. Then I wouldn't have you, any part of you." I felt tears forming and my throat tightening up. "I'm scared to death of losing you. Those four months that we were apart was the loneliest time of my life."

Noah crossed his arms over his chest. I could see the muscles in his arms tense up. I had to get this all out. I had to make him understand.

"I'm surprised I haven't screwed our friendship up yet. Of course, I might be doing that now. I just want the best for you and I'm not the best. I wish I were. You have no idea how I wish I could let you pull me across that line, but there's something that's got such a hold on me and I don't know how to let it go. It's nobody's fault. It's just the way I am. I've tried to think better of myself, I really have. Please stay my friend. Things are safer if we keep our relationship as friends. You're the only one I have and the only one I need. We have to move past this."

His voice was shaky and deep in his throat. "I don't know how or where you ever got it in your head that you're not good enough. You're beautiful, smart, funny, and kind. You're perfect for me and always have been. I wish you believed it."

"Me, too," I whispered.

He tried to make his voice steady and strong before he asked, "What does Brad mean to you?"

"Nothing." My answer came out quick. "He asked me to the party and we had fun, until you punched him in the stomach, of course."

Both of us chuckled, breaking the tension a little.

Noah turned to me. The look of concern and sadness on his face overwhelmed me. "He's not close to being good enough for you." He raised one hand to my face and cupped my jaw, running his thumb across my cheek. "If he does anything to hurt you, I swear to god, I'll kill him."

"Thank you for caring about me," I said quietly.

Noah and I leaned forward slightly, resting our foreheads against each other.

"I don't just care about you, Tweet."

A sob escaped me as the tears trickled down my face. I wrapped my arms around Noah's neck as his arms made their way around my waist. We held on to each other, neither of us making any attempt to pull away. We both knew once we let go, things would change. It would no longer be just the two of us. Life was going to start taking us in different directions, to new experiences, challenges, and people. While we continued to hold each other, I silently prayed that maybe one day I would be good enough, that I would find my way back into his arms and they would still be empty and waiting for me to fill them perfectly.

Entry 16

You should always listen to your gut. You may not know why you feel a certain way about something or someone, but that feeling you get in the pit of your stomach that causes you to hesitate is there for a reason.

Unfortunately, we tend to think with either our heads or our hearts, and ignore our gut. Ignore it one too many times and you end up paying the price.

Several months had passed since Noah and I had our talk about staying in the friend zone. We managed to keep the friendship intact for the most part. We both made sure we spent time together, even though it was limited by how busy we were. Our senior year was coming to an end and getting ready for college.

He started dating a girl name Brooke and they've been together for about two months. She was tall, pretty, lean, with blonde hair, and blue eyes. She was also smart and seemingly understanding about Noah's relationship with me. She didn't act threatened or jealous in any way. This kind of pissed me off, though. I interpreted it as an underhanded way of communicating to me and the world that she knew I wasn't good enough for Noah. It wasn't that I disliked her. I just had a weird feeling that I couldn't identify. I was suspicious that Brooke wasn't as shiny and bright on the inside as she appeared on the outside.

Fortunately, I didn't come in contact with her very often. She didn't go to our school. She was the cousin of one of Noah's teammates. They met after one of his games. She quickly glommed on to Noah. After he and I went back into the *friend* zone, he obviously felt a need to move on, and he moved on with Brooke. It killed me to see them together. Brooke apparently had some sort of disorder which prevented her from standing on her own whenever she was around Noah. Every time I saw them together, she was hanging off of him. Noah never flaunted his relationship with Brooke in my face. He didn't talk to me about her very much.

Brad and I continued to hang out. Technically, we weren't dating, but I had fond feelings for him. You can't spend as much time as we did together, doing the things we did together, and not develop some affection for the other person. He was simply a distraction, though, an extremely hot distraction, but a distraction nonetheless. He was fun and helped me get my mind off of Noah and Brooke, kind of. Even though I cared a lot for him, I knew I would never feel for Brad what I felt for Noah. I don't think I'll ever feel that way about another guy.

Brad and I were at his house one afternoon studying. He never talked much about his family, but I always got the impression that he was pretty much on his own. He and his mom were the only two living in this huge house. His parents had gotten a divorce when he was 10 years old and his older brother, Peyton, was off attending law school.

Brad's parents were both lawyers. The few times I had been over at his house, his mom was never there. There always seemed to be a big case she was working on. And there were several times when Brad called me to hang out on the weekend because plans with his dad had suddenly fallen through.

I tried to talk to him about serious subjects a few times, but he always made a joke of it and changed the topic. Our relationship was fun and breezy, nothing serious.

We had been studying for about an hour when Brad leaned over to me on the sofa and started nuzzling my neck, trailing soft kisses up and down. It made me shudder.

Against my neck he said, "I've exercised my brain enough today. It's time to exercise the rest of me."

He pulled the book I had resting on my lap away and tossed it on the coffee table. My eyes closed as I tilted my head to the side. Even though Brad and I didn't have a very deep relationship, my body always responded to his touch.

Breathlessly I said, "We really should be studying. We have that big exam we need to get ready for."

Grabbing my waist he pulled me over on to his lap. "I got something big you need to get ready for."

I burst out laughing as he showered my neck with quick little bites as his arm snaked around my waist.

"You have got to be the cheesiest high school senior ever."

Removing his lips from my neck, he looked at me with a suggestive smirk. Leaning in, he nipped at my bottom lip between each clipped sentence. "Admit it. You crave it. Ache for it. Lust after it. Have a thirst for it that can't be quenched."

"Alright, already, I do find you charming, but only a smidge," I said, my laughter dying down as a warm sensation took over my body.

Sapphire eyes pierced mine, holding a different more intense look. Brad's gaze went from my eyes to my lips, and then back. The air in the room shifted. Suddenly it felt very hot in there.

Sliding his hand behind my neck, he pulled me to him. Our lips touched and slowly began moving against each other. His tongue thrust into my mouth and caressed mine. I got lost in the all-consuming feeling of his movements.

Suddenly, the front door flew open and Brad's mom came barreling through the room.

Mrs. Johnson was a striking looking woman with the same dirty-blond hair and piercing sapphire eyes as Brad. I had only been around her briefly a few times, but she had this incredible presence that demanded you pay attention when she entered a room.

I quickly scooted off of Brad's lap, smoothed my hair, and adjusted my clothes before his mom had a chance to figure out what we were doing.

Brad looked annoyed. He ran his hand through his hair. "Mom, what are you doing here?"

Never looking up, she sorted through the mail while talking a mile a minute. "I was bombarded with calls at the office. I have a huge case coming up and couldn't get anything done with the constant interruptions. You two go ahead and finish whatever you were doing. I'm going to lock myself in my office."

Tossing the mail on the small entryway table, she started walking away, saying over her shoulder. "Bradley, remember I'm not to be disturbed for any reason. Pretend I'm not here," she said as she exited the room.

"That'll be easy," Brad muttered.

He stood, extending his hand to me. "Come on."

"Where are we going?" I asked.

"My room," he said as he flashed his megawatt smile. "I want to be alone with you."

I was a little hesitant because of how intense things seemed to get earlier. It wasn't that I didn't trust Brad. I didn't trust myself. I'd be lying if I said I hadn't thought about having sex with him. Plus, he had a way of getting me to do things I didn't normally do. I had done more physically with him than anyone else. He made me smile and laugh a lot. He was always sweet to me and I loved making out with him. I had a strange uneasy feeling in my gut because his mom was here.

Brad held my hand, pulling me behind him as we climbed the stairs. When we got to his room he opened the door and stepped aside to allow me to enter first. It was a typical high school baseball player's room. Trophies lined a big bookshelf and baseball pendants lined the wall. On his desk sat his laptop. He had a huge TV, a dresser, and bed.

He came up behind me and wrapped his arms around my waist, giving me a gentle kiss on my cheek. "You know what?" he asked playfully.

"What?"

"I gotta *girl* in my room." I felt his smile against my cheek.

"Somehow I don't think that's a rare occurrence."

"I've never had a girl in my room, unless you count my mom

and Miss Sally, and trust me, neither one of them have seen girldom in a long, long time."

Turning round in his arms to face him, I asked, "Who's Miss Sally?"

"The maid, she comes a few times a week. But today is her day off," he said winking at me.

Narrowing my eyes, I asked suspiciously, "So, I'm really the first girl you've *ever* had in your room?"

"The one and only."

"Why have I been granted this honor?"

"Because, you're special to me," he said as he gave me a sweet smile.

There was sincerity and warmth in his eyes. I could tell he meant what he said. In that moment, he wasn't a smooth talking high school Casanova. He wasn't the spoiled brat everyone at school thought he was. He was a sweet boy who made me happy and thought I was special.

"Make yourself comfortable. I'm going to check my email real quick."

Kicking off my flats, I scooted up the bed and leaned against the headboard. My gaze roamed around the room taking everything in before it landed on Brad sitting at his desk. He was even hot checking email. When he finished, he turned his chair around to face me.

"So, what do you want to do now?" I asked.

He slid off the chair on to his knees, crawling on all fours across the floor and up the bed to me. "Oh, there are several things I want to do now." He waggled his eyebrows. And just like that, the Casanova was back.

I started laughing. "I left myself wide open for that one."

"Oh Beautiful, I have about ten responses to that running through my head. All dirty. You're killing me." I slapped his arm and laughed. "Let's listen to some music," he said, kissing the tip of my nose before jumping off the bed and walking over to his impressive sound system. To my surprise, the awesome voice of Tracy Chapman filled the air. I always pegged Brad as a pop music kind of guy. That's usually what was playing in his car. I was impressed with his choice today.

"I love this CD," I said.

"Yeah, she's awesome."

Shaking my head, I looked up at him. "You surprise me."

He smirked as he walked back to his desk and sat. He playfully said, "Why, because I like music with soul and meaning? I'm not just a pretty face with an amazing body, Beautiful."

"I know that," I said, smiling slightly.

We listened to the music in silence for a while. I had decided to try and talk to Brad about something important. I didn't know if it was because I wanted to finally get to know another side of him or because I wanted to keep us busy talking, so things wouldn't get as hot and heavy as they were getting downstairs.

"What are you going to be when you grow up?"

Brad tilted the chair back, looking up like he was contemplating this question with great thought. "A fireman and a clown. No, wait a minute. I don't want to be a clown. They're scary as hell. Maybe a …"

"I'm serious. Why do you always do that?"

"Do what?" he asked while twisting his chair from side to side.

"Whenever I've tried to talk to you about anything serious, you always make a joke, and we drop it."

"I have my entire adult life to be serious. Why start now?"

We stared at each other. I couldn't pinpoint what was different about today, but when I looked at Brad I wanted more than a physical connection with him. Maybe this is what '*moving on*' felt like.

The air changed in the room, just like it had before while we were downstairs. I was extremely aware of the increasing pace of my heartbeat as I saw Brad's eyes run up and down my body. Just his look made the butterflies in my stomach wake up. I took in a big gulp of air when the tip of his tongue slid across his bottom lip. Clearing my throat, I broke the silence, and returned to my questioning.

"Answer the question."

"I guess a lawyer." He sounded very dispassionate.

"You don't sound very happy about it."

"Both my parents are lawyers. My granddad on my father's side was a lawyer. My brother will be a lawyer. I've always been told I was going to be a lawyer too." A sense of hopelessness clouded his words and the tone of his voice. It was as if he had no say in his future, whatsoever. He turned his attention back to his laptop, ending our conversation.

I closed my eyes and laid my head against the headboard, concentrating on the music. I could feel his gaze on me. My eyes shot open when I heard the creek of the chair as Brad got up. He walked over to the dresser and began to empty his pockets, placing the items on top.

I felt bad about the questions I asked earlier. When I saw the sadness in Brad's eyes I should have been a friend and asked him if he wanted to talk about it. Instead, I just let it go. I looked up at him still standing at the dresser, his back to me.

"So you don't sound like you really want to be a lawyer. What *do* you want to be?" There was some trepidation in my voice.

Spinning around, he held his hands up, palms facing out, and said, "A dancer!" In the blink of an eye fun Brad was back.

I did a full blown belly laugh. "You're crazy."

"Damn straight, Beautiful. Crazy for the dance." He began gyrating his hips as he walked toward me. "I got the music in me and its gotsta get out!"

He grabbed the hem of his shirt and slowly peeled it off, tossing it to the side, a la striptease. Wow, his body was insane. His chest was smooth and toned. His abs and V were not as prominent as Noah's, but they were there, and they were very nice.

I was laughing so hard my sides started hurting. I couldn't think straight. He continued to gyrate all the way to the foot of the bed. Leaning over, he grabbed my ankles, pulling me down towards him. Crawling up the bed and over my body, Brad hovered just above me, his hands on either side of my head. He leaned towards me slightly, as if he were doing a pushup, and asked in all seriousness, "Why are you laughing at my dream?"

"I'm not laughing at your dream. It's a very nice dream. I just never pictured you as Lord of the Dance," I said, trying hard to contain my laughter. His sapphire stare caused me to heat up.

"Oh yeah. The sequins, the jazz hands, the tights. It's what I live for."

"I apologize for mocking your dream," I said, a smile playing across my lips.

"I am very hurt and offended. But, I can think of twenty-five ways you can make it up to me," he looked up as if something had just dawned on him. "Wait, twenty-five and a half ways." He shot me a wink.

I rolled my eyes and continued to smile up at him. He really was fun, besides being terribly cute, sexy, and half naked.

He lowered his body a little closer and began running his nose along mine. Teasing me, he dipped his lips close to mine, but didn't touch them. He wanted me to come to him. I raised my head up capturing his lips with mine. We broke contact for a split second as he adjusted his position, laying beside me, using his elbow to prop himself up.

As our lips reconnected, I ran my hands over his ripped abdomen and up his chest, until they found their way into his hair. He let out several moans. Pressing on the back of his head, I pushed him closer to me as our tongues took turns going in and out of each other's mouths. It was like we couldn't taste each other fast enough. This was one reason why I didn't think it was a good idea for us to be in his bedroom. Whenever Brad touched me, my brain shut off. This scared me because I felt overwhelmed with sensations and out of control.

The music stopped, replaced by heavy breathing and moans.

"I really like you, Amanda," he said between kisses.

"I really like you too," I said between moans.

We both gasped between kisses, drawing in as much oxygen as we could, trying to catch our breath. Brad brought his left hand up and cupped the side of my face. He pulled his lips from mine, tugging my bottom lip as he broke away.

He looked down at me and whispered, "You're special to me." Sincerity spilled from his eyes.

I could feel the warmth cross over every part of my body. Returning his gaze, I trailed my hand down the side of his face to his strong jaw. "There's more to you than what you let people see," I whispered.

He leaned down and brushed my lips with his. His gaze was

smoldering and hot. "God, I want you so bad," he whispered against my lips.

"You have me. I think of us as close friends."

Chuckling, he said, "You're so damn adorable," he paused for a moment. "I want to be with you."

He started placing light kisses along my jaw, stating in between, "Amanda, you're so beautiful and sweet." His lips headed toward my neck. "… and hot." He moved to below my ear. "I'm going to explode if I don't get inside of you soon." He nipped at my earlobe, and then returned to my lips, keeping me from saying anything. I couldn't think straight or talk. All I could do was feel and react. Every part of my body was throbbing.

His hand slid down to my breast. As he massaged it, his thumb ran over my hard covered nipple. My nipples were standing at attention. He started nibbling across my jaw, again. Now was my chance to say something. This was getting out of hand fast and I needed to stop it from going farther. But no words came out of my mouth, only moans. I didn't want him to stop.

Using a low gravelly voice, he said, "Take your shirt and bra off. I need to get my mouth on your gorgeous tits."

It was as if my body had been taken over by aliens. I didn't seem to have any control over what I was doing. I continued to struggle with my thoughts and my gut feeling, but my body ignored them and succumbed to the sensations. It felt amazing. He felt amazing. He watched as I began to unbutton my shirt, his eyes eager and hungry.

Once my torso was exposed, he ran his hand up the middle of it. As I lifted up slightly he slip the shirt over my shoulders and down my arms, tossing it to the floor. His hands ran over my breasts, then my shoulders, finally landing on my back, and unclasped my bra. I had never been completely naked in front of a boy before. Even with the heavy make out sessions we had done, I always had enough control to keep my clothes on.

Brad slid the straps down my arm and threw my bra to the side. He looked down at me as if he wanted to devour every inch of my body. His chest heaved up and down as his breaths were coming out shallow and quick. "Fuck, you're gorgeous," he panted, just before his mouth descended on my nipple.

I laced my fingers through his soft hair as he wrapped his lips securely around my nipple, sucking on it hard at the same time he ran his tongue over it roughly. Waves of electricity ran through my body. I arched my back and put pressure on the back of his head, pushing myself farther into his mouth. I was so wet at this point, I was afraid it was going to seep through my jeans.

I felt Brad's hand begin to trail down my stomach, landing on the button of my jeans. I wanted him to take them off and keep going. I cared for him a lot and was incredibly attracted to him. He freed the button and slowly pulled the zipper down. Involuntarily, my hand flew to the top of his. He stopped and looked at me with smoldering eyes. I gave him a slight smile and moved my hand away from his.

He began to nibble, suck, and lick his way down my body. I closed my eyes, my body absorbing every sensation caused by his hands and mouth. Just as I was about to get completely lost in the feel of Brad's body and touch, the fact that his mother was downstairs flashed across my mind.

"Maybe we should stop. I mean your … um … we're not alone," I said, my voice raspy.

"It's okay. No one will bother us." A shiver ran through me, giving him all the permission he needed to continue.

I couldn't believe this was happening. I still had thoughts of stopping it from going farther, but the words wouldn't come out of my mouth. My eyes began to flutter shut when I felt tears running down my temples. Noah invaded my mind. I was thinking how much I wanted this to be him. How it should be him. But it's not and won't ever be. I felt cool air hit my legs as my jeans slid down and off. I was completely naked except for my panties.

Brad was sitting between my legs, resting back on his heels. His fingers slip under the top of my panties and then pulled them off. He performed one continuous lick the entire way up my body. His tongue stopped at one of my nipples, circling it before his lips sucked it into his mouth, all while pinching my other nipple. He pulled away slightly before plunging toward me, devouring my lips while he began to grind between my legs. I couldn't get over how hard he was. My hands found the button of his jeans. I struggled to undo it. Brad pulled away from me and stood up.

He quickly removed his jeans and boxers. I rose up on my elbows and looked at him. I had never seen a completely naked guy before. It was mesmerizing. A huge smile crossed his face when he saw how large my eyes had gotten at the sight of him. He opened the drawer of his bedside table and grabbed a condom, put it on, and was back on top of me in a flash.

He buried his head in the crook of my neck and slowly pushed into me. At first it felt weird, but as he moved in more and more I got used to it. Then with one forceful thrust a stabbing pain ran through my body causing me to cry out. I felt tears run down the sides of my face. Brad didn't react to my obvious pain and began to move faster and faster. The pain started to disappear and pleasure took its place.

I wrapped my arms around his neck as Brad bounced me up

and down on the bed. The area between my hips to the top of my thighs began to heat up. My body tightened and I felt a pressure inside of me build. My body got tighter and tighter as the pressure and heat increased. Then what felt like a giant contraction took over my body. My toes clenched, my nipples got even harder, and I was throbbing and convulsing inside. I was soaking wet. His thrusts got faster as he slid deeper into me. My legs started shaking and wave after wave of contractions went through me as I cried out Brad's name. I heard one muffled grunt and then his body stiffened before collapsing on top of me. We stayed that way for several minutes, both trying to slow our breaths down. Brad lifted his head to look at me, but never said a word. He smiled just before climbing off, causing me to wince a little as he slid out of me. I watched as he removed the condom and threw it into the trashcan.

I was startled by a noise I heard out in the hall. I looked up at Brad and asked in a low voice, "You locked the door, didn't you?"

"I'm pretty sure I did." He threw on his jeans and slipped his shirt over his head as he walked to the door. I saw him place his hand on the doorknob jiggling it to make sure it was locked. I was leaning over the side of the bed looking for where my clothes and underwear had landed when the door suddenly swung open.

My head shot up and it felt as if all the blood had drained from my vital organs. Standing in front of me were Brad's two friends, Jeremy and Spencer. I scrambled to grab the comforter and covered myself.

Jeremy took one step toward me then said to Brad, "Shit! I don't believe it. You won again." Brad and Spencer burst out laughing.

I was so shocked I wasn't able to comprehend what was happening. I watched as Spencer reached in his front pocket, pulled out a wad of cash, and slapped it into Brad's palm.

Looking up at Brad I asked, "What's going on?" My voice was so shaky and weak, I didn't recognize it.

Brad stepped forward, trying to stifle a laugh, and answered, "It's just a little friendly bet between some of us on the team."

"This is the third time in a row that this son of a bitch has won," Jeremy said.

Brad shrugged his shoulders. "What can I say? I'm a natural."

"Yeah, well, we almost didn't get to see it with our own eyes, so this fuck was almost disqualified. Your mom locked the front door. You better be glad we knew where the extra house key was hidden."

My body started to shake uncontrollably as tears spilled down my cheeks. They were carrying on a conversation like I wasn't even there, like I was a thing, not a person.

"Sorry about that. I wasn't expecting her to come home," Brad said.

"So on the cherry scale, how high does the sweet Amanda rate?" Spencer asked.

All three guys stood there watching me have a nervous breakdown, completely unaffected by what they had done to me.

A huge smile crossed Brad's face. "Sweet Amanda was fucktastic. I'd give her a nine point seven five out of ten."

"Bravo!" Jeremy and Spencer said in unison. All three started to slowly clap their hands.

The look on Brad's face was disgusting. He looked as if he had done me a favor, like I should be honored that he rated me so high on his sleazy scale.

"We'll give you some privacy so you can get dressed and leave," he said.

Jeremy and Spencer left the room followed by Brad. He turned to face me, lingering in the doorway. I was trembling and tears drenched my cheeks, but no sounds of sobs came out of me. This felt like an out of body experience. Physically I knew what had happened to me, but my mind wasn't ready to process it.

Looking up at Brad, I asked, "Why? I liked you. I thought we were friends." My voice was weak, almost inaudible.

"It's just sex, Amanda. It's no big deal," his voice was flat.

"It was to me," I said, my voice gaining strength. "I don't understand. Where's the boy I've been spending so much time with who was sweet?"

Looking into his eyes I thought I saw a hint of remorse flash through them, but then he said, "Me and the guys want to go grab something to eat, so if you could hurry up, that'd be great." Then he shut the door, ignoring my question completely.

The only sensation I felt now was the churning of my stomach. I slowly climbed out from under the comforter and looked for my clothes. When I looked down, I saw blood all over my legs and I got lightheaded. I didn't care about wiping it off. I needed to get out of there. I put my clothes on and slipped on my shoes. I was such an idiot. How could I let something like this happen? I should have known he had ulterior motives. Noah warned me. I had a weird feeling the entire climb up the stairs and while we were in here, but I thought I was just being silly because his mom was home.

My god, his mom is still downstairs.

I never imagined anyone being capable of doing something this cruel. All the time we spent together was nothing more than him setting me up for the big payoff of winning a sick bet.

Thinking how much I needed Noah right now to put his arms

around me and protect me, caused my sobs to escape.

I turned to leave and my stomach flipped. I grabbed the trashcan and held it for a minute. Maybe I could hold it together long enough to get home. My stomach started to settle down a bit. As I went to put the trashcan back I glanced down, spotted the used condom, and emptied my stomach all over it.

I crept downstairs as quietly as possible. The guys were in the kitchen talking and laughing. My body felt like it was starting to cave in on itself, ready to collapse at any minute. I grabbed my things and almost made it out the door when Brad's words stopped me. I didn't turn around.

"I don't kiss and tell, so you don't need to worry. Stewart won't find out."

I hugged my backpack tighter to my chest, flew out the door, and into my car.

I don't know how long I aimlessly drove around town in a daze. I didn't want to go home. I didn't want to be around anyone. My first time being with a boy was nothing more than a sick contest, something to be joked about by Brad and his friends. How could I have wasted this first experience? It should have been with someone who cared about me. Why didn't I say something to those three douchebags? Why did I just slink out of there without uttering one word? Why didn't I listen to my gut? I should have stopped things before they got so out of hand. I didn't even love Brad. If Noah ever found out what happened I wouldn't be able to look him in the eye again. He'd be completely disappointed and disgusted by me. I felt empty. I couldn't think anymore. I just wanted to disappear.

Entry 17

By the age of 10, I wished I was an adult. I couldn't wait to make my own decisions, go where I wanted to go, live where I wanted to live, dress the way I wanted to dress, and eat whatever I wanted, whenever I wanted. I dreamed of the day when it would be my decision to eat cake and ice cream for breakfast, lunch, and dinner.

Be careful what you wish for.

Growing up means that situations and people change, problems are bigger, and the hurt runs deeper.

Also, you really can't eat cake and ice cream for all three meals. The fat content alone puts you at risk for heart disease, diabetes, and an enormous ass. Yeah, growing-up sucks.

High school was done and I made it through, graduating with honors. I didn't finish first in my class like Emily had when she graduated. I landed in the number six spot. As usual, falling short of the big prize, but I wasn't surprised. Vincent was Valedictorian. He earned it.

My senior year had been a mixture of extreme highs and lows. I learned two important things, though. One, Brad was a sleazy Smurffucker, who kept his word. Noah never did find out about what happened. Two, I was very good at compartmentalizing. I let the Brad incident affect me for a few days. I stayed to myself as much as possible during that time, then I tucked what happened away into its own dark compartment, left it there, and moved on.

To celebrate all the graduates from my neighborhood, the parents put together a party at the neighborhood park. Younger brothers and sisters ran around playing as moms and dads congratulated each other on their graduate's achievement. Sitting in our spot, looking out toward the pond, I couldn't help but think about all the memories I had of this spot, both good and bad.

Remembering my dad pushing me and Emily on the swings, and him being at the bottom of the slide ready to catch me because he knew I was scared of falling off at the bottom. Of course, most of my memories were of Noah. Of how much fun we had on the playground and feeding the ducks as kids when my mom brought us here. I remember feeling so grown-up the first time we were allowed to walk here by ourselves, it was the first time Noah and I held hands. We had our first date and kiss here. I experienced my first heartbreak and healing here. Over the years, this became our spot to be alone with each other, to share dreams, talk about problems, to listen to each other, and on more than one occasion, eat cake.

"Earth to Tweet." Noah waved his hand in front of my face bringing me back to the present.

"Sorry."

He sat next to me. Both of us looked out over the pond.

"What do you have rattling around in that beautiful head?"

"Nothing much, I was just thinking about all the time we've spent here."

"You're not getting all sentimental and mushy on me, are you?"

"Maybe just a little." I gave him a slight smile.

"It's going be hard not having you around." There was an undercurrent of sadness in his voice.

"It's going to be hard not having *you* around. You'll come visit me, right? USC isn't far, only about an hour and a half."

There was only one university in South Carolina that offered a degree in journalism, USC. Since receiving my acceptance letter, I had asked Noah everyday if he would come visit me while I was there.

"Nothing could keep me away from my girl. I'll be up there so often you'll get sick of me," he said.

"Impossible."

He picked up my hand and placed a sweet gentle kiss on the back of it. We sat, quietly enjoying our spot before the silence was cracked by the shrill sound of his name being called.

"Noah!"

He dropped my hand and stood as Brooke walked up to us. I was still on the fence about how I felt in regards to her. She had always been pleasant to me in a fake kind of way. I wanted Noah to move on and find someone, but that didn't mean I had to like it or the person. Let's face it, Brooke could have been Santa Claus, the Tooth Fairy, and the Easter Bunny all rolled into one and I still wouldn't like her dating my Noah. I tried not to show my petty ugly side when she was around. Noah seemed to like her and as long as he was happy, so was I.

"Hey, baby. I've been looking for you," she said, wrapping her scrawny arms around Noah's neck and giving him a kiss right on the lips. The kiss lasted an abnormally long amount of time, I thought. We were after all in a public place with impressionable children running around. I cleared my throat reminding them that I was still sitting there.

Brooke released Noah's neck. My eyes followed as she slid her arms down around his waist. "Sorry Amanda. I love kissing my fella. I just never want to stop." I looked away to hide my eye roll. "Congrats on graduation," she said.

Brooke had also graduated this year. She and Noah were staying in town and attending the College of Charleston for their undergraduate degrees. Noah would then attend the Medical University of South Carolina for his doctor's degree in Sports Medicine. I didn't know what Brooke's educational plans were and I didn't give a shit.

"Thanks. Back at ya." I was monosyllabic when it came to Brooke. I couldn't think of anything to say to her other than, "*Get your slimy hands off my Noah*". She probably wouldn't want to hear that, so I kept it short and sweet.

"You hungry?" Noah asked Brooke.

She looked adoringly up at him and waggled her eyebrows. "I'm *always* hungry when you're around, No-No."

"Oh my god!! That's your nickname?" It was out of my mouth before my brain had time to stop it. The laughter burst out of me with such force it caused me to jump back a little. "Oh man, that is rich." I couldn't seem to help myself. This was the most I had ever said to Brooke and it was all snarky.

She narrowed her eyes at me, her lips forming into a flat line. "I think it's cute and Noah loves it when I call him that, especially followed by a moan."

A cough flew out of Noah as if a bug had just flown into his mouth and down his throat. He rubbed the back of his neck and glanced over at me with a slight smile. Brooke giggled as she hugged his arm tighter.

"Did I give you the impression that I didn't think it was cute? I'm sorry. It's as cute as a Smurffucking button," I said.

Now would be a good time to SHUT UP, Amanda.

An awkward pause fell over us. Somebody needed to leave. Noah glanced at me, as he put his arm around Brooke's shoulder and said, "Well, let's get you fed. See ya later, Tweet."

As they started to walk away Brooke said over her shoulder, "See ya, Tweet." Her sarcasm was evident. What a bitch.

Several yards away, they stopped. Noah whispered something into Brooke's ear then jogged back to me. I couldn't tell if he was mad or amused. Once he reached me, he leaned in close to my face.

"You will be severely punished later tonight." An adorable devilish grin slowly appeared that sent shivers through me. He took a few steps back before turning and jogging back to Brooke's side. She looked back at me with a smug expression that clearly said, "*He's mine*".

I watched them slide their hands down deep into each other's back pocket. I was shocked. I couldn't believe they were fornicating right in front of God and everybody. A burning sensation radiated throughout my chest and stomach. I turned my gaze back to the pond. I tried to get the picture of them groping each other out of my head. Looking down I started kicking the gravel with my heel. I felt someone walk up behind me. I turned and saw Emily holding two plates of food. I swung my legs over the bench to face her. She sat across the table and placed a plate in front of me.

"Thanks," I said.

"What are you doing hiding over here?" she asked.

"I'm not hiding." I fingered a potato chip before tossing it in my mouth.

"Brooke seems nice."

"Yeah, she *seems* nice."

"You don't like her?"

"I don't dislike her. I'm indifferent about her," I proclaimed.

"Hmmm …"

"What?"

"Nothing, it's just when it comes to Noah I've never known you to be indifferent. You're usually black and white. There's no gray area with you when it comes to him."

"I'm a dark gray about her. Happy?"

"Ecstatic. Can I ask you something?"

"Sure."

"Why isn't that you?" Emily tilted her chin in the direction of Noah and Brooke. We watched as they sat beside each other several tables away eating. Brooke giggled or kissed Noah between almost every bite of her food.

"It's not like that. We're best friends." My response sounded automatic as I continued to stare. Emily snorted slightly. "What was that for?" I asked.

"Whatever is between you and Noah is more than friendship."

"Emily, don't."

"What? It's pretty obvious."

"What are you talking about?"

"Amanda, anyone with half a brain can tell how much you care about each other."

"Of course we care about each other. Friends do that, you know."

"Why don't you want to be with Noah?"

"Why are you asking me this stuff right now?"

"Because I saw the look on your face when you and him were sitting here talking. Then I saw the look on your face when Brooke walked up."

"I'm going to be honest with you. It's a little creepy that you watch me that closely," I said.

Emily shook her head. "Typical Amanda."

"What's that supposed to mean?" She was beginning to annoy me.

"Whenever you get uncomfortable, you make a joke of things."

"Well, there's not enough laughter in the world." I gave her a smug look. My previous annoyance started to shift to anger. I could feel my body start to tense and stiffen.

"Why are you and Noah not together, Amanda?"

"I'm not his type, obviously. Besides, I would screw it up in a heartbeat. I won't risk losing him. There, now you know. I have felt like a failure and worthless for as long as I can remember."

I just stared at her. When the last word left my mouth, I regretted it. I was already in a bad mood because of the PDA between Noah and Brooke, then Emily just kept pushing, I snapped and said more than I should have.

She took in a deep breath. "I know it hasn't been easy being my sister. Growing up always being compared to me had to be a pain in the ass. Amanda, you're beautiful, intelligent, kind, and talented. You're perfect the way you are." Glancing in Noah's direction, she said, "You are so beyond good enough for Noah. I wish you believed it."

"I wish I did too, but I don't know any other way to be. Noah is with Brooke and he's happy. That's all that's important to me. I've just been emotional today reminiscing about things. I'm sorry I snapped at you like that."

Emily reached across the table and put her hand on the top of mine. "I'm here to listen, Manda, if you need me."

"I know. Thanks."

I knew Emily was trying to help, but both Noah and I had moved on. He had Brooke now and I was headed off to start my college career in a couple of months. He and I understood what our relationship was and we were good with it. It wasn't perfect, but nothing ever is.

I spent the rest of the night talking with friends and family. I tried not to pay any attention to Noah and Brooke. It was a challenge with Brooke's high pitched squeals of laughter piercing my ears. At times, my curiosity got the better of me and I glanced over at them. They were either kissing or hugging. Brooke always seemed to be sitting in his lap. Always. Like he was friggin' Santa Claus. I was done. I was tired from the party, the reminiscing and especially watching Romeo and Juliet. I went around and said my goodbyes to some friends. Before I was able to make my escape, I heard one more blood curdling squeal from Brooke coming from the fire pit area. People were standing around the pit roasting marshmallows. When I glanced over, I saw Noah standing behind Brooke with his arms wrapped around her waist, kissing her neck. Yep, it was definitely time to call it a night.

I had been home for a couple of hours, hanging out on the sofa, channel surfing. Nothing held my attention except the thoughts of Noah and Brooke together. I couldn't even get him alone long enough to give him his gift.

After getting my fill of the *Saved By The Bell* marathon, I turned the TV off and headed to my room. As I got closer, I heard my phone chime indicating I had a text. I grabbed it and looked to see who it was. I couldn't help but smile at the picture. It was of me and Noah in one of those photo booths with our faces scrunched up, making a fish face.

Noah: Our spot. Now. Come alone.
I want u all 2 myself. ;)

I loved and hated when he sent flirty texts to me. They brought into focus what I couldn't have with him. I typed out a quick reply.

Me: You're not the boss of me.
I'll come when I'm good & ready.
C u in a sec. ;)

Smiling as I hit send, I felt a rush of excitement. I couldn't wait to be alone with Noah and give him his gift.

I sprinted to the park, slowing down as I got closer. I didn't want to appear like the desperate loser I was, sitting home watching hours of old TV shows. I walked up to our spot. Noah was facing the pond. I stood there a second thinking about the time when I came here to help him practice kissing. Remembering how he had set up dinner for two as a surprise made me smile. I was such a sentimental fool tonight.

Without turning around, Noah said, "Are you going to come and sit down or look at my back the entire night?" I wouldn't mind looking at his back the entire night. He had a really nice back.

"Quit your bitchin," I said as I walked around the table and sat beside him.

I placed his gift down next to me, so he wouldn't see it just yet. Noah took my hand and laced our fingers together. I snuggled close to his side and laid my head on his shoulder.

"Where'd you run off to earlier?" he asked.

"I didn't run off. The party was winding down, I was tired, so I went home."

"You left without saying anything to me. I thought you were mad at me," he said.

"Why would I be mad at you?" I was curious of his answer.

"I don't know. I was just disappointed when I realized you'd left." He squeezed my hand slightly.

"Well, you seemed to have had your hands full." I didn't have to look to know he was smirking. "By the way, you guys were a bit much, don't you think? I mean, jeez, get a room."

"We did." I couldn't believe he just said that to me. I lifted my head off his shoulder, jerked my hand back, and leaned away from him.

"Don't joke about something like that with me." I bit down on my bottom lip and stared at him.

"Are you jealous?" he asked, as if he were challenging me.

I had already had my serious gut spilling talk for the day with Emily. I wasn't having this one with Noah.

"Brooke's nickname for you is stupid," I sneered at him.

A smirk slowly took over his face. "I know. And, you are so damn cute when you're jealous."

"It's lame. In fact, after I got through being embarrassed for you, I felt sorry for you, and then I threw up." I kept unwavering eye contact with him.

He placed his hand over his heart and said, "Oh baby, you've just gone from damn cute to smokin' hot."

"Bastard."

"I love when you talk dirty to me. Say something else."

"Asshole."

He started moaning, "Oooh yeah. That's the ticket."

"You're ridiculous," I said.

"And you are beautiful." Shaking my head I glanced away with a smirk on my face.

"Now that all that's out of the way, it's gift time." He clapped his hands and rubbed his palms together. "Me first."

He held out a heart shaped dark blue velvet gift box with a white ribbon tied around it. I looked at him, stunned. I thought it was beautiful and it was just the box. I thought he must have made a mistake and picked up Brooke's gift. It looked like a girlfriend's gift.

"Um, I think you brought me Brooke's gift by mistake."

"I brought the right gift to the right girl. Take it." I did and looked back up at him. "Open it, Tweet. It won't bite you." He gave me a sweet shy smile.

I untied the ribbon and slowly lifted the top of the hinged box. As I looked down and saw what was inside, tears started to gather behind my eyes. It was the most beautiful gold feather charm necklace. It was so delicate. I looked up at him with tears just starting to roll down my face. I was speechless.

Noah looked deep into my eyes. "I can take it back if you don't like it," he said with a smirk.

"It's the most beautiful thing I've ever seen. You're not going to touch it except to put it on me." I turned away from him slightly and moved my hair to one side.

As Noah clasped my necklace he whispered in my ear, "You'll always be my number one girl. Congratulations Tweet."

I closed my eyes. I was so overwhelmed with emotion I took a few seconds before turning back around. I finally was able to squeak out, "Thank you, Noah. I'm never going to take it off."

I looked at him for a few more seconds before handing him his gift. He tore through the wrapping like a little kid. "I hope you like it," I said anxiously.

My gift to Noah was a ballpark pendant and chain. The pendant was shaped like army dog tags and it was made from part of the original seats from Fenway Park.

His face lit up when he realized what it was. "Fenway, isn't it?" he asked with awe evident in his voice.

The biggest smile appeared across my face as I nodded. "It has it written on the back." I was beaming.

He flipped it over to read the words. He was completely

speechless. He pulled the chain and pendant over his head then wrapped his arms around me as I laid my head against his chest.

"I love it. Thank you, Tweet. I can't believe you remembered Fenway was my favorite." He squeezed me tighter. "It's the best gift I've ever gotten," he said, kissing the top of my head.

We sat there for a long time quietly holding each other and for the first time in a long time, things felt perfect.

Entry 18

I READ SOMEWHERE THAT THERE'S NO WORSE PAIN THAN EXPERIENCING THE DEATH OF A LOVED ONE. I THINK THERE IS ONE PAIN THAT'S WORSE, THOUGH: THE PAIN OF NOT BEING ABLE TO SAY GOODBYE.

YOU DON'T GET TO TELL HIM HOW MUCH HE'S INFLUENCED YOU. YOU DON'T GET TO TELL HIM HOW MUCH YOU APPRECIATE WHAT HE'S DONE FOR YOU. YOU DON'T GET TO TELL HIM HOW MUCH YOU LOVE HIM AND WILL MISS HIM.

WHEN YOU DON'T GET THE CHANCE TO SAY GOODBYE, YOU DON'T GET THE CHANCE TO SAY THANK YOU. EVERYONE DESERVES A THANK YOU AND GOODBYE.

I lightly knocked on his door and said, "Noah, it's me."

I heard his raspy deep voice answer, "Come in."

I entered and closed the door behind me. Noah was lying on

his back in bed with the heel of his palms covering his eyes. He brought his hands down, sat up, and looked at me. I almost crumbled to the floor. Sorrow and devastation poured off of him.

We looked into each other's eyes for a moment, and then Noah said, "He had a heart attack at work. He was gone before the paramedics had a chance to get there." He tried to compose himself enough to continue. "I just saw him this morning and he looked fine. We were going to Fenway next month, Tweet." He choked on every word, unable to contain his sobs any longer.

My eyes were full of tears. My heart had never ached so completely for anyone. I wanted desperately to take all his pain away. Not saying a word, I crossed the room to him. I kicked off my shoes, crawled up on his bed, and sat behind him. Noah rested back against my chest. Wrapping my arms and legs around him, I buried my head in the crook of his neck, and held him tight while he sobbed and cried out in pain.

I whispered into his neck, "You're dad was a great man and he was so proud of you."

Our sobs began to subside. We remained in the same position, sitting quietly. After a while there was a soft knock on the door.

A female voice said, "Noah, it' Brooke. Can I come in?"

Before he could answer, the door creaked open and Brooke walked in. Seeing us sitting on the bed in that position caused anger to flash across her face. Noah remained in my arms with his eyes closed. Brooke kept her glare on me while her voiced remained steady.

"What's going on?" she asked.

Rubbing his face, Noah replied, "Brooke, I really don't want to be around anyone right now. I'm sorry. I'll call you tomorrow."

Brooke narrowed her eyes at me, her glare becoming more

intense. I could see her body stiffen and become rigid. Her lips pursed together as her expression tightened. She was angry and hurt. I knew Brooke was his girlfriend and should be the one consoling him. I started to pull away from Noah so she could take my place, but he clamped onto my arm like a vise and wouldn't let me go.

I turned my head to her. My eyes asking her to understand how much pain he was in. He probably didn't realize how what he said sounded. Without saying another word, she turned and left.

"Maybe I should go and let her stay," I said.

Noah turned over on to his stomach, wrapped his arms tightly around my waist and rested his cheek on my chest.

He mumbled, "Don't leave me. I need you, just you. I don't want to be around anyone else, but you, Tweet." His body began to tremble. I could feel my shirt getting wet from his tears.

I squeezed him tighter and whispered, "I'm here. I'm not going anywhere." We never left Noah's bed that night. We fell asleep holding each other.

The next morning, Noah and his mom were scheduled to go to the funeral home to finalize his dad's arrangements. He asked me to go and I did. I never left his side. Noah kept physical contact with me constantly during the day. He was either holding my hand, sitting close, or wrapping his arms around my shoulders or waist. It was as if touching me calmed him and gave him some peace.

I didn't see Brooke the entire day. I wasn't sure if that was her decision or Noah's. It seemed odd to me that she wouldn't be here for him. I knew last night was awkward and she was hurt, but his father just died and he was devastated. I still hadn't formed a strong opinion one way or the other about Brooke, but I certainly didn't think she'd be so petty and be mad at Noah.

The Stewart's home was filled with a buzz of activity. People were stopping by constantly, bringing food and giving Noah and his mom condolences. My entire family was trying to help wherever we were needed. The Stewarts were our family. My dad and Mr. Stewart were like brothers. His death hit my dad extremely hard. The two men were the same age and Mr. Stewart appeared to be in as good shape as my dad. They ran together a few times a week and even played basketball often. The fact that Mr. Stewart could apparently be in good shape and this still happened, scared my dad.

I had done some laundry that afternoon. I was walking down the hallway headed to the linen closet to put up sheets and towels. I started to pass Mr. Stewart's home office. I stopped, remembering when we were kids that there was always candy in there. Noah's dad would bribe us with Skittles if we would go out in the backyard to play while he was working.

I heard Noah on his cellphone. "I can't do this right now." He paused to let whomever was on the other end talk. "Christ, Brooke, my dad just died and my mom is a basket case. I need her with me." There was another pause. "I've told you a thousand times she's my best friend." The next pause was a lot longer than the others. "I know what it must have looked like, but she's not going anywhere. She's a huge part of my life, so you'll have to get used to it, if we're together." There was one more quick pause. "That's up to you. I need to go. I'll see you tomorrow at the funeral." He hung up without saying goodbye.

Noah came out of the office and caught me eavesdropping.

"I guess you heard that." His hand went immediately to my shoulder. He noticed I glanced at it. "You think it's weird?" he asked.

"What?"

"That I can't seem to go more than two seconds without touching you."

"It's a good weird." I gave him a slight smile.

"I'll quit if you want." I shook my head. "It's just I feel like if I let go of you for too long, I'll lose you."

"I'm here as long as you need me. You don't have to let go until you're ready. But, I don't want to cause trouble for you with Brooke. She wasn't happy last night when she saw us in your room."

"She'll be fine … eventually." He let the corners of his mouth curl up slightly. "Brooke is pissed. Can you believe that? My dad just died and she's pissed because I need you."

"She just wants to help, Noah."

"She needs to understand that what I need right now is you. Nobody can take your place in my life, Tweet."

I couldn't help the slight blush that scattered across my cheeks. I liked the feeling of being needed by him.

I was having a hard time getting to sleep that night. The past two days had been so busy that I hadn't had time alone to write in my journal. There were so many thoughts and feelings running around in my head and I needed to get them down on paper. Usually that helped to clear my mind and I was able to fall asleep. My phone chimed and startled me.

Noah: Look out your window.

I got up, walked over to my window, and opened it. He was standing below. His eyes were glassy and red. I assumed from crying.

My voice was low and quiet. "Hey, what are you doing out here this late? Are you okay?" I knew that was a stupid question.

"No. I'm not okay. Can I come in?"

"Of course you can. Go around to the front door and I'll let you in."

"I don't need the front door."

He started climbing in my window. He seemed a little unsteady, so I helped pull him in the rest of the way. Once he was inside, I could smell the alcohol. I thought he had sounded a little strange outside. I couldn't blame him for being drunk after what he's been going through. He stumbled some on his way to my bed, so I followed behind him, helping him sit down. The look in his eyes broke my heart. He looked so lost and alone.

He reached out and grabbed my hips, pulling me into a hug. My bed was pretty high up. Standing in front of Noah while he sat brought my chest to his eye level. Without saying anything, I wrapped my arms around his neck and pulled him close to me. I let my fingers run through his silky hair. Even with the distinctive smell of alcohol, he smelled wonderful, fresh and citrusy.

"I wish I could take your pain away," I whispered into his hair. He hugged me tighter.

We stayed like this for a while, then I felt Noah's fingers start to slowly move underneath my shirt as he nuzzled my chest. It was late and I was dressed for bed in a pair of long pajama pants and a baby doll t-shirt. My nipples were rock hard as he nestled his face deeper. I was so embarrassed. I was trying to comfort my best friend and was getting turned on.

I tried to take a step back, but Noah held me tight, not letting me move. He looked up at me through his long dark lashes. His beautiful light blue eyes were dim with pain. The look shattered me. I wanted to make it disappear.

Our breathing became heavier. Noah never broke eye contact as he began to kiss my breasts over the t-shirt. His lips felt incredible even through the material. My skin was on fire while wave after wave of shivers ran up and down my body.

His lips moved down until he found the small spot of exposed skin right above my hip bone. My fingers curled around his hair and a slight gasp escaped me when I felt his tongue circle around my navel then dip deep into it. His hands slid down my back, landing on my ass. His lips traveled slowly up my torso, gently sucking and licking my blazing skin. He was drunk, in an enormous amount of pain, and had a girlfriend. Noah had stopped us from making a huge mistake the first time I was drunk, I needed to do the same. We had to stop. This had gotten completely out of control.

"Noah ..." My voice was so breathless and quiet, I wasn't sure he heard me.

"Your skin is so soft and sweet," he mumbled against my stomach.

"We can't do this," I whispered.

My fingers disentangled from his hair. My hands slid down his muscular arms and landed on top of his hands that were glued to my ass. I tried to remove them, but he had such a strong grip and wouldn't let go. He brushed his lips along my collarbone then nibbled his way to the spot right beneath my ear.

He whispered, "I need you. You're the only one I want. Every time I'm with *her*, I think of you. I need to be inside of you so bad. Please don't make me leave."

It took every ounce of strength not to give into him. I wanted him just as much as he wanted me. "Noah, you've been drinking and you're hurting. You're not able to think straight. Plus, you have a girlfriend. You're not that guy. You don't cheat."

Noah released his grip on me, curling his arms around my waist as I slid mine around his neck. We hugged each other so tight, it was hard to catch a deep breath. His body began to tremble slightly and I felt tears drip down my neck.

"Please don't leave me," he begged against my neck.

"I'm not going anywhere except where you go."

"Thank you," he whispered.

"Stay here tonight. You're aunts are at your house with your mom, right?" He simply nodded his head.

I took Noah's shoes off and helped him empty the pockets of his jeans. He was steady enough to manage taking them off himself. I pulled back the covers of my bed and he climbed in dressed in his boxers and t-shirt.

"I'm going to get you some water and aspirin," I said as I covered him up.

Noah grabbed my hand before it left the covers. He looked up at me, his beautiful eyes still glistening. "I couldn't get through this without you. I love you so much, Tweet."

I swallowed hard when I heard him say he loved me. This was the second time he had told me and I still never said it back to him, at least not so he could hear it. But, it didn't seem to matter whether I said it to him, he wanted me to know how I affected his heart. I hoped he could feel how much I loved him, even though I couldn't tell him.

"You're not going to have to get through anything without me." I gave him a small smile.

Relief spread across his face. I kissed him on his forehead before going to get his water and aspirin. By the time I returned to my room, he had already fallen asleep. I knew he hadn't gotten any sleep the past couple of nights, so I didn't bother to wake him up. I stared down at him for a long time. He looked so peaceful. Saying goodbye to his dad tomorrow was going to be the hardest thing Noah has ever had to do. At least he'll be able to have a few hours of peace while he sleeps.

I walked to the door and shut off the small lamp that was on my dresser. Before leaving, I turned to look at him one more time. The moonlight was shining through the window illuminating his beautiful peaceful face.

"I love you too, Noah," I said before shutting the door and heading to the guestroom for the night.

Entry 19

Sticks and stones may break my bones, but names will never hurt me. That's not true, really. Words have immense power.

We may not care what everyone thinks of us, but there's always that one person, who with a few words, holds the power to make us or break us.

The funeral was as heartbreaking as I expected, but Noah was a pillar of strength for his mom. Afterwards, Mrs. Stewart invited close friends and family back to her house. Noah was staying close to his mom's side, helping her greet and receive condolences. Brooke stayed close by Noah's side, keeping her arm securely linked with his whenever possible. I tried to keep a little distance. The situation was stressful enough. I noticed every now and then Noah would scan the room looking for me. Once Brooke noticed, she started shooting me hostile looks whenever Noah's attention was elsewhere. After about forty minutes of Brooke's glares, I needed to get some air. I got Noah's attention from across the room, letting him know where I would be.

I walked outside to the backyard and made my way over to the small vegetable garden at the far end. Mr. Stewart had planted it just a little over a month ago. There were already sprouts coming up from the ground. Even though it was the beginning of summer here, it felt cooler outside than it did in the house with all the people packed inside. Mr. Stewart was loved by many. That was evident today from all the people who attended the funeral. He was a good man. Noah is just like his father. I started thinking about all the vacations our two families took together. I felt tears prick my eyes. The sound of footsteps behind me caught my attention. Running my fingers under my eyes, I wiped away my tears.

"Can we talk?"

I turned around and came face-to-face with Brooke. Her expression was an exact duplicate of the way she looked at me the other night.

"I just came out here for a second to get some air. I'm heading back in," I said.

My shoulder muscles tensed up and I could hear the grinding of my teeth. I had no idea what Brooke would want to talk about, I didn't want this conversation to take place, especially not today and not here.

"I'll make it quick." She was determined this was going to happen.

"Okay," I answered hesitantly.

"What are you doing?" Her tone was accusatory.

"I'm not following you, Brooke."

"What are you doing with Noah?"

"Instead of playing twenty questions, just say what you want to say to me."

I wasn't interested in talking or listening to her right then. I started feeling anxious. This wasn't going to be pretty.

"I realize we don't know each other at all, really. Noah doesn't appear to want to share the details of his relationship with you. I asked my cousin about the two of you. He was under the impression that you had been together."

I started to interrupt and correct her, but I knew that would just prolong this and I wanted to get this over with.

She continued, "I didn't say anything the other night when I caught the two of you. Obviously, it wasn't the time or the place."

"Wait a second. When you *caught* us? You make it sound like we were doing something we shouldn't."

"You had your arms and legs wrapped around my boyfriend."

"Yeah, I was comforting my best friend."

"It looked like you were doing more than comforting him." She paused for a moment. She glanced around making sure we were alone and out of earshot of anyone. "Look, I don't want to fight with you and since I'm trying to be brief, I'll get to the point. Whatever you and Noah have is more than a friendship, even though he keeps telling me otherwise. I see the way he looks at you and how he always turns to you. That should have been me the other night with my arms around him. I'm asking you to give me and him some time without having you around. Noah can't seem to move on with me if you're still in the picture. His kneejerk reaction is to always turn to you. I don't know why you and he aren't together. I'm really not interested in that story." She paused, taking in a deep breath. "If you care about Noah and want him to be happy, then walk away. Let him see you're not the one he needs to turn to. I'm the one that's here for him now, not you."

I wasn't sure if I was more shocked or pissed at her request. I stared her straight in the eye keeping my face neutral.

"You'll get your wish in a couple of months when I leave for college."

"I was hoping you would walk away from him now."

"You expect me to abandon Noah now when he's just lost his father? That would break him. He'd hate me," I said.

"You're being a bit overdramatic with the, *it would break him*, don't you think?"

"Of all times to be thinking of yourself … You're an A-list selfish bitch, you know that?" I felt the veins in my neck throb. I involuntarily balled my hands into fists. She completely ignored my comment.

"And hate's a very strong word, but I think it's needed to finally make the break from you. I'm sure eventually Noah will want to talk to you again. By that time he and I will have a more solid relationship," she said.

I'm not a violent person, but I wanted to have a smack down right there in the Stewart's backyard.

"Why would I do this for you?" I asked.

"It wouldn't be for me. I know you love Noah. It's written all over your face. We both know you're not the right woman for him. Don't be selfish, Amanda. Let him move on and have a happy life. He has me now to give him that. He doesn't need to be attached to you anymore."

I was glued to my spot. I couldn't get my legs to move to get the hell away from her. I wanted to argue with her. Tell her she was out of line and completely insane if she thought I would walk away from Noah. I wanted to, but I couldn't. Deep down I knew she was right, not about her being what he needs, but everything else. If I were being honest with myself, I hadn't even considered going on a date with anyone since the Brad incident. I wasn't sure what I was waiting on. I guess maybe I wasn't able to move on while Noah was such a daily presence in my life.

I had enough of Brooke and her caring/jealous girlfriend bit. It was time to end our little chat.

"I'll think about it." I started to walk past her when her words stopped me.

"Whether you do it this week, next week, or whenever, it's going to hurt him. If you do it sooner rather than later, he'll at least have the summer to get over it. That way he'll be able to start his first semester at college with no distractions. Maybe I'm not the one here being so selfish." She gave me one last icy look, before I turned and walk away.

It had been a week since Brooke and I had our little talk. Well, she talked. I mainly listened. I officially hated Brooke now, no gray area at all. I knew she was right, though. It's pretty impossible to get past wanting someone you love when they are always in front of you, causing the love to only get stronger.

The night before Mr. Stewart's funeral proved that neither Noah nor I had much control over our feelings for one another. His happiness was the most important thing to me. I didn't know if Brooke would be the one to make him happy, but they deserved a shot at it. Noah deserved a shot at it. I knew he'd be furious with me, but I was sure after some time apart we will have both moved on and gotten over the pull that our attraction has on each of us, then we can be in each other's lives again as friends.

It felt like I was walking in quicksand as we made our way to our spot. I dreaded what I had to do. I kept telling myself I was doing it for Noah. I had spent every possible minute I could with him this week, because I knew this day was coming. I had gone over and over in my head what I was going to say. On the way to our spot, my mind went completely blank.

Once we got to our table, he started to help me up to sit, but I shook my head. He leaned against the end of the table, looking at me standing in front of him.

Confusion and concern were in his eyes when he asked, "What's going on? You've been so quiet this past week."

The tears that had started forming during our walk here began to run down my face. It felt like I stood there forever with the words stuck in my throat. The person who meant everything to me just buried his father and I was about to break my promise and leave him. Noah misread my tears as the emotions of the week catching up with me. Mr. Stewart was like my second dad.

He reached, pulling me into a hug. I put my arms around his neck and held on. I knew this was the last time I would feel his strong arms around me, touch his soft hair, and smell his wonderful citrusy scent. As he held me, I tried to get my sobs under control. I needed to do this quick before I chickened out.

I pulled back from him, his arms remained around my waist. "Noah, I need to say something."

"Okay."

Stepping away from him I still wasn't sure I could go through with this. Every part of me began to quiver, the inside as well as the outside. "Promise me you'll listen before you say anything."

"What's going on, Tweet?"

"Promise me."

"Okay. I promise," he said.

I swallowed my sobs. "You are the most important person in my life. Your happiness is my number one priority. Don't ever doubt that, because it will never change."

"You're scaring me." His voice was cracking with emotion. His beautiful light blue eyes that were filled with deep sadness started to glisten.

I knew this was it, my life would never be the same, and I was scared to death.

"I need to step away from us for a while. Seeing you with Brooke is harder than I thought it would be," I swallowed hard. I still couldn't believe I was doing this.

"I'll break up with her." His response was quick and said with such assurance. It caught me off guard.

"Brooke is who you should turn to now, not me. She's your girlfriend." My stomach churned when the words came out of my mouth. "She's good for you, Noah."

"You're a liar. You can't stand her," he said.

I could feel my sobs pushing against my chest wanting to get out, but I held them in. I had to stay strong.

"You need to stop being so attached to me."

My legs were barely holding me up they were so weak. The ache in my chest exploded with every word I said to him.

"Stop being so attached to you?" He pushed off of the table and took a step towards me.

"We're not kids anymore. I'm getting ready to go off to school …"

"Don't do this. I won't touch you again, I swear, not even a hug. You can't do this. I can't lose you, too." He stepped closer to me. "I love you."

Every part of me wanted to grab him and tell him how much I loved him, but I couldn't bring myself to do it. He wasn't going to make this easy on me. I had to say something that would cut right into him.

"Well, you shouldn't. I told you over and over that I couldn't be with you. But you kept pushing more and more each time. I *can't* be with you, Noah, and I don't want to be. I don't feel the same way about you."

I saw in his eyes when the shift from hurt to anger occurred. "So this is my fault? You always said the reason we couldn't be a couple was because you'd do something to mess it up and we'd lose our friendship. Now you're blaming me."

"No one is to blame." My voice sounded so small.

"Oh yeah? I blame you." I could feel the heat from his anger radiating off his body. "You don't give a shit about me or my happiness. All you care about is keeping things in the same little compartment, so you can control everything."

The look in his eyes shifted again, only this time it was from anger to hate. He was starting to hate me.

I stepped back and started to turn my head away when Noah grabbed my chin forcing me to look at him. "Don't you dare look away from me. You're not going to run away this time." I remained quiet, letting him say everything he needed to. "I've tried to stay away from you, to not touch you, and I've tried so fucking hard not to fall in love with you."

He moved in closer to me. Our chest pushed together with each heavy breath we took. Our eyes locked.

Noah's voice became low and raspy. "I know you want me. I

could tell the last time in your room how wet you were through your pajamas. You were so ready for me to slide into you. All I did was kiss your stomach and you almost came right in my arms … didn't you?"

I startled when he yelled demanding an answer. "DIDN'T YOU?!"

I simply nodded. He stepped back away from me. He shook his head and chuckled humorlessly. "You always said I deserved better than you. Maybe you really thought it was you who deserved better than me, because I'm not perfect and you always have to have everything so fucking perfect."

"That's not true. You are perfect, but I'm not. You deserve perfect."

"And you think Brooke is perfect for me?"

"I don't know. I just know that I'm not."

"SHUT THE FUCK UP! I'm tired of hearing you say that. All these years I hated what you thought about yourself. I know you think Emily's perfect. And I know you are constantly being compared to her. I put up with you pushing me away because I knew that. I was convinced you actually believed you weren't good enough for me. I figured if I kept telling you how incredible you were and how much I loved you that one day you'd believe it and stop all this bullshit. You're not a loser, Tweet. You're a coward, because you just threw away the chance to be with someone who wanted to spend the rest of his life loving you."

"Please don't hate me. Once you calm down and have a chance to think clearly you'll see this is for the best, right now." My voice kept quivering, I barely got the words out.

He stood there for a moment, silent, with his hands on his hips, looking down at the ground. His voice was low and strained when he said, "Get the fuck away from me."

"Noah …"

He looked up at me. I gasped. The look on his face was broken and devastated and I was the cause of it.

Looking me directly in the eye he slowly said, "Get. The. Fuck. Away. From. Me. Now."

As I walked away from him I felt the life drain from my body. I hadn't gotten very far when I heard repeated pounding and grunting. I turned and the last small piece of my heart died. Noah kicked and punched at our table before flipping it over, screaming, "MOTHER FUCKING … SELFISH … GODDAMN HER!"

I began to shake uncontrollably, bracing myself on a nearby tree. I raised a trembling hand to cover my mouth. I felt like I was about to be sick. I didn't turn away from him, though. I deserved every bit of pain and hurt that came my way for what I had just done to the only boy who will ever have my heart. What I worried about the most happening between us had just come true … and it didn't happen at all in the way my fears had imagined it. This was even worse. There's no going back now. He hates me and I can't blame him. I hate me, too.

Entry 20

We set limits for ourselves all the time. An imaginary line that we're positive we won't ever cross. Until we do.

A mother or father wouldn't hesitate about harming or even killing someone who is about to do the same to their child.

The line gets moved.

A girl who is so consumed by the empty ache of loneliness is driven to do anything, no matter how degrading, because she wants to numb the chronic pain.

The line gets moved.

The line keeps moving and moving until one day you realize you're limitless.

My body, mind, and soul stopped functioning when I saw Noah flip our table over and kick the legs until they broke. The sight of him as he dropped to his knees was hard enough to watch, but when he picked up one of the broken wooden legs, and threw it full throttle into the air, I couldn't take watching any longer, and turned my head away. I hated myself. How could I have done that to him? Glancing toward him one last time, I saw his shoulders begin to shake from sobbing and I was completely shattered.

Breaking up our friendship was only supposed to be temporary, but this didn't feel temporary. This didn't feel like the *break* we had last year. This felt permanent. He was done with all my excuses, all my insecurities, and all the times I gave into my desires only to pull away, again and again. Tonight was the last straw for him. Not only had I achieved my goal, I surpassed it. I didn't just break up our friendship, I completely destroyed it. I had to hold on to the belief that this was the right thing to do for him otherwise I wouldn't be able to live with myself.

I turned and started walking away from the park. I had no idea where I was going. My body felt numb and my mind was blank. I was unconscious of how long I had been walking or the direction I had been going in.

When I finally stopped and looked up, it took several minutes for my mind to clear and recognize where I was. I saw my hand move toward the doorbell and push it. When the door opened, the light from the inside ran across my face causing me to squint. He stood there, wide-eyed, and in shock. I wasn't positive, but I thought I saw a slight smile on his lips when he realized it was me.

"Amanda? What are you doing here?"

I didn't know how to answer him. I wasn't exactly sure what drew me here. I certainly didn't make a conscious choice to come here.

I hadn't talked to Brad since the day he humiliated me. By the look on his face, I could tell I had been standing there a while without answering his question.

"Are you alone?" My voice was weak and small. He eagerly looked back over his shoulder then back at me.

Quirking an eyebrow up and smiling he said, "No, but I can be. Just give me a second."

Stepping back, he motioned for me to come in. My legs didn't hesitate. I knew where I was and who I was with. This boy was responsible for my complete humiliation a few months ago. Maybe, subconsciously I knew Brad was what I deserved. I sure as hell didn't deserve anything better than this douchebag.

I could hear the sound of muffled music coming from down the hall where the game room was located. Brad ushered me quickly into the kitchen.

"Wait here while I get rid of my … um … company."

He walked out of the kitchen and disappeared down the hallway. The music stopped and muffled voices filled the air.

At one end of the kitchen there was a breakfast nook. I pushed myself in the corner of the nook as much as possible so I wouldn't be seen. The feeling in my numb body started to return. The voices got louder and clearer the closer they came. As the numbness continued to wear off I could feel a heaviness in my chest that was making it hard to breathe. My fingers were cold while my palms started to get moist. I could feel the trickle of sweat rolling down my forehead. I was burning up. My body wasn't the only thing coming back to life. I couldn't stop the pictures of Noah's pain from flashing across my mind. This wasn't the time or the place to have my nervous breakdown. I had to get numb again. I needed an escape from my heartache.

When I thought this night couldn't get any worse, I heard the syrupy sweet drawl that made me cringe.

"Where are we going? I thought you wanted to bend me over the pool table and …"

"Not tonight Brit. Something very important just came up." Brad sounded eager and in a hurry to get her out the door.

"I bet I can make something important come up," she said, laughing at herself.

Their voices got louder as if they were headed into the kitchen. I used the sleeve of my shirt to wipe the sweat away from my face and tried to calm my breathing down.

"Brittani, your cab will be here any second. You need to go wait for it outside," Brad told her.

"I just want to get a bottle of water."

Brittani stumbled into the kitchen and over to the refrigerator. Her back stayed facing me. She grabbed a bottle of water then leaned against the counter while she tilted her head back and drank. If either of us moved just a half an inch she'd discover me.

There were two ways into the kitchen, one from the hallway and the other from the dining room. The dining room was next to the living room and the living room was next to the front door. If she went through the dining room then she would walk straight out of here and not spot me.

She started toward the dining room. I let out a slow sigh of relief, and then suddenly she said, "I forgot my purse."

She whipped around and saw me. It took her a few seconds to focus her eyes before realizing it was me standing in front of her.

"What the fuck is she doing here? Is *this* the something *important* that just came up?" she snapped.

Brad simply shrugged his shoulders and gave her a cocky grin. "Brit, come on, your cab just drove up."

Reaching into his pocket, he pulled out a large wad of cash, and shoved it at her. I couldn't help but think this scene was a foreshadowing of her future career.

She grabbed the cash and took a few steps in my direction, all the while glaring at me.

"I don't get it," she said as she pointed her finger at me, making a zigzag motion in the air up and down my body. "Noah always wanted to get his dick in you and now you got Brad's twitchin'." She stumbled back slightly and chuckled. Looking at Brad she asked, "What is it about her? Does she have a magic vagina or something?"

"Okay Brit, it's time for you to go." Brad stepped toward her, taking her elbow.

"I need my purse," she said, shrugging out of his grasp.

"You have it already." He pointed to the purse dangling at her hip. He then grabbed her arm a little more forcefully and tugged her out the door to the awaiting cab.

I knew I should get out of there, but I didn't. I stayed right there in the kitchen, waiting for the douchebag to come back. How did I become this pathetic? I kept telling myself I just needed to be somewhere no one would find me.

Brad came back into the kitchen and landed right in front of me. His usual cocky expression covered his face.

"Your mom's not home?" I asked.

"Nope. She has a new beau, so every second she's not working on a case, she spends over at his place. I do believe the Mother of the Year Award will elude her again." He paused for a moment. His eyes scanning my body like some wild animal sizing up his prey. "Are you okay?"

I took in a deep breath and simply nodded. He took another step, bringing him so close to me I could smell the scent of cinnamon coming off of him.

"Why are you here, Amanda?" he asked, in a low sultry voice.

Sheepishly looking up at him, I answered, "I didn't have anywhere else to go. Can I stay here for a little while, please?"

"Sure. You want anything?" He had a look in his eye like he was ready to pounce on me.

"A drink would be good. Thanks."

"What's your pleasure? Besides my face between your legs, that is?"

I wanted to slap the smugness off his face. It was as if he knew why I had shown up on his doorstep. I still wasn't completely sure why I came here. Before, if he had said something like that I would have laughed because I'd know he was teasing me, but now everything out of his mouth had slime all over it.

Amanda, have an ounce of self-respect and leave.

"Something strong would be great," I said.

"I think I can give you something strong."

He stood back allowing me to go first. I knew they kept all the alcohol in the game room. I entered the room and immediately noticed the bar crowded with various bottles of liquor, enough for an entire party. It must have all been for Brittani. Brad didn't appear the slightest bit drunk. He sauntered behind the bar.

"What can I get you?" he asked.

"Anything. You choose."

"Those are dangerous words, Beautiful."

"Don't call me that," I snarled.

Climbing up on the barstool, I watched as he pulled a clean pitcher from behind the bar. Eyeing the measurements, he poured alcohol from several different bottles into it, occasionally glancing up at me. He threw some ice in a glass, poured a generous amount of the drink, and handed it to me. He then poured himself a glass and walked over to me.

"What is this?" I asked, glancing up at him.

"Long Island Iced Tea," he said peering at me over the rim of his glass. "You want to go sit on the sofa?"

"Not really. This is fine." I paused for a moment. "I'm sorry I ruined your evening." I put as much sarcasm in my statement as possible.

He shook his head. "Don't worry about it. Brit was only a three point five." He was such an arrogant bastard.

"You're disgusting."

Smiling, he leaned in close to me and said, "But in a good way." I rolled my eyes and took a gulp of my drink. "Amanda, are you going to tell me why you're here? You look like you just lost your best friend. Speaking of best friends … Stewart won't be looking for me tomorrow ready to kick my ass, will he?"

"You don't have to worry about Noah anymore."

I swiveled the chair around to the bar and poured myself another drink. I had downed the first one in record time. I wanted a buzz as soon as possible. I needed to feel numb again.

"Oh, is there trouble with Mr. Perfect?"

"Don't talk about him." Brad wasn't good enough to even have Noah's name cross his lips.

I downed drink two just as fast as the first. I was feeling pretty buzzed, but my mind wouldn't shut up.

I'm a horrible person and don't deserve anything good and decent in my life. I deserve this disgusting human being in front of me.

"You might want to slow down with those. I don't want to find another surprise in my trashcan like before," he said.

I started laughing. "I was so busy having a nervous breakdown, I forgot to enjoy the thought of you finding my puke in your room. Tell me, do the girls usually throw up after you've fucked them? Because if they do that doesn't bode well for you, buddy roe." I turned and poured myself another drink.

I hated Brad for what he had done to me, but somehow I was still attracted to him, drunk or not.

I was such a pathetic idiot.

He had on a pair of worn jeans that hung low on his narrow hips. They were ripped mid-thigh on both legs and just below his right knee. His t-shirt fit him like a glove. I had no trouble making out the details of his well-defined chest. He must have upped his workouts because he looked more chiseled than I remembered. The sleeves hugged the muscles of his toned arms, showing off how cut they were. The color was a deep coral which made his golden skin and hair stand out even more. Most guys wouldn't be able to pull off that color, but Brad could. We stared at each other as I drained my third glass dry. The pain I felt when I first got here had subsided. Long Island Iced Tea was a miracle elixir. I went to pour another glass, but Brad grabbed my elbow. "I think you need to take a breather."

"What a boy scout you are." I swiveled back and forth a few times in the chair, glancing around the room. Brad's eyes remained glued on me. "Sooo … you and Brit-ta-neee? You hit a dry spell or something, buddy?"

"What do you mean?" I could tell he was finding me amusing.

I leaned forward and loudly whispered, "She's kind of a skank. Besides, you said she was only a three and a halfer." I leaned back in my chair, laughing. "Even though you're a vetter birgin. No wait, a better virgin. That's not it either. You're not a virgin. Oh well, whatever, you're a Smurffucker. What was I talking about? Hey! Why did you let me in if you and Skankzilla were just about to play *pool*?"

"I've missed you." As if on cue, his trademark megawatt smile crept across his sexy face.

Yep, I had to admit it, Brad was a stack of hotcakes covered in sexy syrup and I wanted to fork him.

Brad is slime, but that's what I deserve after what I did to Noah.

"Well, a three point five sure thing is better than the memory of a nine point seven five. And that's all it will ever be with me, just a memory, Smurf fuc-kah." I raised my hand in front of his face and snapped my fingers, showing him I meant business.

"I'm charming as hell, though. I'm sure I can persuade you to sit on my face for a while."

"You make my skin crawl."

"I'd like to crawl all over your skin."

"Are you serious? Do you actually believe a girl would find that charming?"

Completely ignoring my question, he said, "Amanda, why did you come here?"

"I don't know why."

"Yes you do."

"Enlighten me then," I sneered at him.

"You and I aren't that different, you know. Yeah, I used you to win a bet, but you used me too."

"How the hell did I use you?"

"Who were you thinking of every time we hooked up and who are you trying to forget tonight?"

I stared at him, keeping my expression as neutral as I could. I didn't want to give him the satisfaction of knowing he was right.

"You used me as a stand-in for Mr. Perfect. I used you to make some cash and now you're back for more. When I fuck you tonight, I won't be making a dime off of it. When you close your eyes as I'm sliding into you, whose face will you see? So, you tell me, which one of us is more disgusting?"

Brad leaned into me, sitting his glass down on the bar. He was so close I could feel the heat radiate off his body. He looked down at me. Reaching up, he tucked some of my stray hair behind my ear then his fingers slowly moved down, tracing the outline of my jaw and continued down my neck, stopping just short of my breasts. Lifting my lids, I was hypnotized by sapphire blue eyes.

His touch sent shivers down my body. How could I be so attracted to someone I despised, someone who was responsible for one of the worst days of my life?

Because he's right, you're no better than he is, Amanda.

I couldn't take my eyes off of him. I just wanted to feel numb and forget the overwhelming pain I was in and caused.

"So now that we've cleared the air. Why are you really here, Amanda?" Brad asked.

"I want you to make me forget," I whispered. We were so close my lips brushed against his with each word.

"That wasn't so hard to admit, was it? In fact, I'll be happy to call you Tweet if it'll help." The sound of him saying my nickname made me sick.

Before Brad had a chance to say another word, I grabbed the back of his neck, pulled his lips to mine, sucking them in. I clawed at his shirt, silently begging him to take it off. He did. His hands wasted no time slipping underneath my skirt and finding my hips. Fingers dug into my skin as I wrapped my legs around his waist pulling him closer to me. Lifting me up, he carried me to the pool table and laid me on my back. I heard the sound of a zipper and then foil ripping. Grabbing behind my knees, Brad jerked me forward so that my hips sat right at the edge of the table. I felt his cold hands run up my legs. Before I knew it he had ripped my panties off and was pounding into me.

My head was fuzzy from the drinks, but I was extremely focused on what I was doing. I didn't think about the past or the future. The only thing that mattered was this moment in time. There was relief in this moment. There was no guilt, heartbreak, or loneliness. I was able to escape all of that with a few drinks and a willing guy. I'll deal with how ashamed I was about myself later.

I spent the summer trying to forget Noah with Brad. Sex with Brad was like a drug. It allowed me to shut down and shut out. It provided momentary relief, an escape from the pain that I woke up to every morning. Escaping became very addictive, but as with any drug, once you come down from the high the pain and loneliness return, accompanied by self-hate and disappointment.

Being with Brad also released me from my need to be perfect. I didn't care what Brad thought of me, expected of me, or did to me. He was irrelevant. Any guy could help me achieve the same results. Brad was just convenient and familiar.

When I wasn't with Brad, I tried to stay busy, but Noah always lingered in my thoughts. I plodded through my days as best I could. The one thing that would completely derail me was seeing Noah. That would send me straight to my room and under the covers until the next day. I did everything in my power to make sure that didn't happen. But there were days when I couldn't keep myself from peering out the window, hoping to catch a glimpse of him.

A week before I was to leave for school, I found myself glued to the window above the kitchen sink where I could get a clear view of the Stewart's backyard. Since I only had a week left before moving, I didn't think it would do any harm to stop fighting the pull that window had on me. Once I was at USC, Noah would be completely out of reach and sight.

Mom had already passed through the kitchen once and saw me standing there. Fifteen minutes later I was in the same spot and her curiosity got the best of her. Standing beside me, she followed my gaze out the window.

"Do you mind me asking what is so interesting in our backyard?"

"Nothing, I guess I just spaced out. I have a lot on my mind with getting ready for school," I lied.

What had me glued to that spot was Noah and Brooke hanging out at his pool. I had seen them out there before. What I hadn't seen before, in fact all summer, was a smile on Noah's face. The smile that I loved and missed had resurfaced. He was happy with Brooke. The ache that started in my stomach invaded the rest of my body. My heart broke because I knew I was the one who took that smile from him and Brooke was the one who gave it back.

Mom draped her arm around my shoulders and pressed her cheek to the side of my head, squeezing me slightly. "He's still seeing Brooke? Is that why he hasn't been around this summer?" I nodded.

"There wasn't enough room for Brooke and me both in his life." I felt my tears building up. "*She* makes him happy. Look at his smile."

I swallowed the lump in my throat. You could hear the shakiness in my voice.

Mom hugged me one more time and said, "Looks can be deceiving. You can't always tell what's going on inside a person from the outside. People put on a brave face when they're trying to get over heartbreak, but that doesn't mean they have. You and Noah have a rare bond and always will. There's no one out there who can break that."

"Thanks Mom."

I pried my eyes from the window, hugged my mom, and went to my room. I grabbed my phone and did what I had been doing all summer, especially when I saw Noah. I texted my dealer.

Me: U home alone & want some company?

His response was immediate.

Brad: It depends. What are you wearing? Forget it, doesn't matter. I'm just going to rip it off you. Come now! ;)

I felt my stomach churn as I read his words. He really was a Smurffucker. But none of that mattered. I knew in twenty minutes my thoughts would be focused somewhere else and I would have my escape.

ENTRY 21

I'VE GOT NOTHING FOR MY JOURNAL ENTRY TODAY. HOLY SHIT! I'M ATTENDING AN ACCLAIMED UNIVERSITY AND MAJORING IN JOURNALISM. HOW THE HELL CAN I NOT HAVE ANYTHING TO WRITE ABOUT? I ALWAYS HAVE SOMETHING TO SAY, AN OPINION, A STUPID IDEA, BUT NOT TODAY.

WHAT IF THIS CONTINUES WHEN I GET TO SCHOOL? I'LL BE A LAUGHING STOCK. OTHER STUDENTS WILL POINT, STARE, AND LAUGH UNCONTROLLABLY AT ME. I MEAN, A JOURNALIST WITHOUT WORDS IS ... SHIT! I DON'T EVEN HAVE THE RIGHT WORDS TO FINISH THAT SENTENCE. I'M GOING TO HAVE TO MOVE BACK HOME. I'LL BE WHISPERED ABOUT BEHIND MY BACK. THE ONLY JOB I'LL BE ABLE TO GET WILL BE MEASURING OLD LADIES FOR THEIR CORRECT BRA SIZE. NOBODY WANTS THAT JOB. THIS IS KARMA AND SHE'S BITCH SLAPPING ME ALL THE WAY INTO NEXT WEEK.

It took me about a month and a half to adjust, but college life suited me. The hardest part had been getting used to being away from home. I had no idea how good I had it at home. At school, I actually had to do laundry and was put on a schedule to clean the bathroom. It took moving away from my mom to really appreciate her.

My roommate, Lisa, was a no nonsense country girl from Missouri. She was beautiful with wavy copper colored hair that hit right at her shoulders, huge bright green eyes, and curves exactly where they should be. She was smart, funny, and a great roommate. It was nice to have a friend, again, and I did consider her my friend, even though we had only known each other for a short time.

My course schedule was fairly ambitious for a freshman. I was taking five classes, one of which was for my major. The campus was huge and spread out, but I was finding my way around pretty good now. All of this added up to some very long days. There were times when I was so tired at the end of the day I would just eat a couple of big spoonfuls of frosting I had stashed in the mini-fridge or I didn't eat at all. The upside to my new, *too busy to eat diet*, was that I avoided the freshmen fifteen, so far I hadn't gained an ounce. I had actually lost a little weight.

I hadn't been home for a visit yet because I knew going back too soon would cause me to backslide, and so far I was doing okay with getting over Noah. I was too busy most of the time during the week to focus that much on him. And I had been filling the weekends up with frat parties and meeting people. But nights were the hard. I studied in my room most of the time, and it was easy for me to let my mind drift to thoughts of him.

Five months had passed since I had any contact with Noah. When I thought of him, I still felt pain and loneliness. It was even stronger than on that day when I destroyed our friendship. If I allowed my thoughts to linger too long the tears would start and I'd spend most of the night in the bathroom hiding, so Lisa wouldn't see me and start asking a bunch of questions.

One night while studying for a psychology test, Lisa noticed that I hadn't turned a page in twenty minutes. Hopping off her bed, she grabbed two red cups and a bottle of wine she had smuggled in.

"Alright, space cadet, it's wine time," Lisa said plopping down in the chair across from me.

I looked up, surprised to see her sitting there. I was so lost in my thoughts, I didn't notice her until she shoved a red cup of wine at me.

Sitting back in the chair, her feet propped up on the desk, she asked, "Are you going to tell me who you were spacing out about?"

"I was concentrating," I said just before I took a sip of wine.

"Yeah, you were concentrating. What's his name?"

"Who's name?"

She shook her head. "The guy you cry about at night in the bathroom."

Her words caught me off guard. "I didn't know you heard me. I went in there so I wouldn't bother you. Sorry."

"So spill."

"Nobody, really." I was ashamed of myself for saying those words. Noah won't ever be a nobody to me, even if I never see him again. "I mean, he was someone very special, but isn't in my life anymore."

"I've got to call bullshit on that one. We've been here over a month and I've heard you crying at least once a week and … um … what's with the sleeping around?"

I choked on my wine when I heard the words come out of her

mouth. "Excuse me?"

"I just didn't peg you as being a sausage biscuit."

"A what?"

"A sausage biscuit. You seem to open your biscuit for every sausage you meet."

"No, I don't!" I wasn't really offended by her. I was more shocked that I gave out that impression. I wondered if other people thought that.

"You and I have gone to four parties since we've been here and you've already hooked up with three different guys that I know of. You're either trying to forget someone, get even with someone, or you're just a good old fashion sausage biscuit. I add the crying into the mix and I figure you're trying to forget someone."

I took a long sip of wine and tried to decide whether I wanted to share all that was Noah with her. I've always had a hard time opening up to people. Noah was the only person I did that with. Maybe if I talked to Lisa, got it out in the open, the pain would lessen.

"His name was Noah, we grew up together as best friends, and now we're not." I took a gulp of wine. It felt good to open up.

She sat up and pointed her finger in my direction. "You listen to me, beotch. I did *not* open this five dollar bottle of wine for the abridged version of your high school heartache. Details. Now."

We stayed up late that night, drinking wine and talking. I told her most of the details of my life with Noah. It was a relief to talk about it. Lisa was great. She listened, but never judged.

Lisa was a sophomore, so she already knew a good many students here. The weekend before classes started, she invited me to a party one of her friends was throwing. I went only because I thought it would be good bonding time for us. Besides, I needed a Brad replacement. I still craved the momentary relief he provided.

These college parties were pretty overwhelming and I didn't know anyone besides Lisa. A few drinks helped loosen me up, so drinking had become a weekly ritual. It didn't interfere with my grades, so no harm, no foul. I had no problem approaching guys after a drink or two. I didn't just pick random guys though. I had to be somewhat attracted to them and feel reasonably safe.

I met Matt at the first party I went to on my first weekend. He was cute. Black hair, dark brown eyes, tall, fairly good body. He didn't have muscles and wasn't toned like Noah or Brad, but that didn't really matter. He was kind of funny, at least he thought he was. We met, got drunk, and hooked up. There was no awkwardness in the morning because I was out of his room before he woke up. Matt was a junior theater major, so we rarely, if ever, crossed paths during the week.

The next weekend I met Jacob. Again, he was cute and we hooked up, but the next morning Jacob was under the impression we were in a relationship. Bye, bye, Jacob.

Then there was Thomas. He was a little creepy, so I just made out with him all night at one of the parties. I went back to Matt. He was tolerable, uncomplicated, and would do for the time being.

Matt and I started hanging out more than for just a weekend hook up. I suppose you could say we were dating. I liked him, alright. I would never love anyone except Noah. He was the love of my life, my soul mate. No one would ever replace him.

Lisa was not happy with my choice in boyfriends. To say she hated Matt would be an understatement. She tried at least once a week to convince me to breakup with him.

"Where are you off to?" Lisa asked.

I hesitated for a minute and threw on my jacket. "Matt is picking me up and we're going for a bite to eat. You want to go?"

I knew exactly what she would do. She'd roll her eyes, shake her head, and try to get me to come to my senses.

"Hell no, I don't want to go eat with that asshat with his asshattery ways. Anything I ingested would come right back up if I sat across the table from him."

"I don't understand why you hate Matt so much. You said you didn't know him before we met and he's always been nice to you."

"I don't give a shit if he's nice to me. What I don't like is how he treats you."

"He treats me okay."

My stomach started to quiver. There had been a few times that Matt had been mean to me in front of Lisa, but he was under a good bit of pressure with classes and a theater production he was in.

"Amanda, he treats you like shit. The way he talks to you, calls you to go out then never shows up, flirts with other girls in front of you. God only knows what he's doing behind your back."

"Do you know something?"

"No." Lisa walked over to me. "I don't mean to hurt your feelings. It's just, you deserve better than that asshat."

I gave her a slight smile as she drew me into a hug.

Pulling back from her, I said, "Thanks, but I really don't."

There was a knock on the door. Lisa crossed the room and opened it.

Over her shoulder she said, "Amanda, the asshat's here."

"It's always such a pleasure to see you too, Lisa," Matt said sarcastically. "Hey Stick."

That was his nickname for me. He thought I was stick thin. He gave it to me one night after we had slept together.

Rolling off of me he said, *"Fucking you is like fucking a stick. Hey, I just stuck my stick into a stick. That's your nickname, Stick."*

He thought it was hilarious. I hated it. In fact, I cringed every time he said it.

"Is that what you're wearing?" he asked.

"Yeah. Why?" I had on jeans, a blue sweater, and my black and gray peacoat.

"It would be nice if you fixed yourself up sometimes. Danielle always looks hot even when we're just at rehearsal."

Danielle was the female lead in the play Matt was in.

"I think I look nice," I said.

"Nice is stretching it a bit. You look okay."

Out of the corner of my eye, I could see Lisa gearing up to let him have it. I quickly grabbed his elbow and rushed out the door before there was a bloodbath.

ENTRY 22

LIKE MOST YOUNG GIRLS, I BOUGHT INTO THE FANTASY OF FINDING PRINCE CHARMING, MY KNIGHT IN SHINING OR PLASTIC ARMOR, MY HERO.

WHAT I NEVER STOPPED TO THINK ABOUT WAS THE ACTUAL DEFINITION OF "FANTASY." I KISSED FROG AFTER FROG WAITING FOR HIM TO TURN INTO A PRINCE, BUT A FROG ONLY KNOWS HOW TO BE A FROG.

It was the weekend before Thanksgiving break. One of the fraternities, I never knew which one threw the parties I went to, had one final big blowout before we all left for the holiday. As usual, the people were packed in the house like sardines, the music was loud, and the beer was flowing freely.

Matt and I had been there for about an hour and we were already pretty drunk. We made our way around the house, stopping to chat with some friends. Actually, Matt chatted with his friends. I was so happy when I finally found Lisa in the crowd. She was as drunk as I was.

"A-MAN-DAAAA!!" she yelled, wobbling towards me.

We hugged each other like old friends who hadn't seen one another in years.

"I love this girl! She's my girl! Not in a lesbionic way. Fellas, I'm still up for grabs and grabbin'!" she slurred.

"You're so drunk."

"Damn straight, baby. I'm seeing three of you right now. Hey, where's asshat?"

"He's right behind me." I turned to grab Matt's hand, but he wasn't there. "He must be getting us another drink or talking with someone," I said.

Just then a strong muscular tattooed arm snaked around Lisa's waist, pulling her back against a chiseled naked chest. The guy buried his head in the crook of her neck and started kissing it. She let her head fall back on to his tatted shoulder.

"Who is that?" I asked in a loud voice.

"I have no idea, but I'm about to find out."

She turned and faced him. He picked her up, her legs wrapped around him, and they disappeared into the crowd.

Two more beers and forty-five minutes later, I was still looking for Matt with no luck. I passed Lisa and her tattooed mystery man twice. I didn't know if she ever found out his name, but from the looks of it, she was getting to know him very well.

I was tired and ready to leave with or without Matt. I would just walk back to my dorm. I staggered through the crowd heading for the door when I felt a hand grab my arm and jerk me back. I fell into Matt's arms.

"Where have you been?" I asked.

"Right here."

His eyes were glazed over and he had a permanent grin painted on his face. He backed me up into a corner and started feeling his way up and down my body while kissing my neck.

"Matt, are you high?"

"Just a little," he said against my skin. I could smell it on him now that we weren't in the middle of the crowd. I pulled away slightly. "That's why you left me, to go get high?"

"No. I left you because I saw Danielle. She looked awesomely hot. I needed to ask her something."

"For almost an hour?" I asked, getting more annoyed.

He took a handful of my hair and studied it. "Have you ever thought about getting those highlighty thingys in your hair like Danielle? They might make you look hot." I shoved on his chest, but he didn't budge. "… *er*, hotter. I forgot the *er.*" He started laughing as he leaned into me, taking my lower lip into his mouth. Then I heard it.

"*Everything*" by Lifehouse floated through the room and hit my ears. I jerked my head away from Matt. I had to get out of there. I hadn't listened to that song in over five months.

"Matt, stop it. I want to go."

"Well, I don't. I want to take you in the bedroom and fuck your brains out. Come on."

He grabbed my wrist and started tugging me through the crowd towards the back of the house. I struggled to pull my arm free.

"Matt, I don't want to!" I yelled.

"Come on Stick. Don't be mad because I hooked up with Danielle a little bit. She primed me up. All you got to do is lay there." The grip he had on me had gotten so tight my arm started to burn. "You want me to get rough with you like before? You liked that. I know you did."

He yanked on my arm one last time, causing me to fall against him. He pinned my hands behind me and started kissing my neck again. I kept struggling, but he had a strong hold on me. We didn't draw attention from anyone around us. They were either drunk, high, or hooking up.

All of a sudden my hands were freed, dropping to my side, and I saw Matt stumbling backwards away from me.

"Shit! What are you doing, dude?!" Matt yelled.

I looked up and saw Noah standing there with a handful of Matt's shirt.

"She doesn't want to go with you, dickhead."

Noah's eyes were concentrated on me. They were warm and caring while his entire body was tense with anger.

Matt shrugged out of Noah's grip. "I'm her boyfriend."

"I don't give a fuck who you are. She's not going anywhere with you," Noah snarled.

"Fuck you, dude. Come on, Stick."

Matt reached for my arm. I stepped aside at the same time Noah grabbed his shirt, spun him around, landing blows to his stomach and jaw. Matt stumbled and fell into the crowd of people behind him. Quickly grabbing my arm, Noah weaved us through the house and out the door.

Once we reached the front yard, I jerked my arm free and stopped walking. "Noah? What are you doing here?"

When I first saw him, I wasn't sure he was real. Between the song playing and being drunk, I thought I was hallucinating.

He turned to face me. "Are you okay? Are you hurt anywhere?" I shook my head. "It's cold, put this on."

He slipped off his jacket and held it open for me. I slipped my arms through the sleeves and he wrapped it around me. I felt warm and comforted. It smelled like Noah, like an orange.

"I'll go back and get your coat later," he said.

"How did you know where I was?" I was in a daze. What were the chances of Noah showing up when I needed him, while our song blasted through the speakers?

"I didn't. I had just walked in and saw you. Brooke came up here for a bachelorette party with some of her girlfriends."

Oh my god, he asked Brooke to marry him.

I couldn't say anything. I hadn't been in contact with him for six months. You would think news like that wouldn't impact me that much now, but it did. Our time apart hadn't lessened my feelings for him in the slightest. Tears started falling from my eyes. Immediately I brushed passed him, walking quickly in the direction of my dorm.

Noah yelled after me. "Tweet!"

I continuously wiped tears away. I hadn't heard him call me that in so long. I started picking up speed until I was jogging across campus but I could hear Noah behind me. I picked up more speed until I had broken out into an all-out run. I made a sharp right to cut across the grass in the courtyard and got half way across when my left foot landed wrong, twisted, and caused me to crash to the ground.

I rolled over and sat up. As I rubbed my ankle, I started to cry harder, partly because of the pain in my ankle and partly because of the pain in my heart. Noah jogged up and fell to his knees next to me.

"Are you okay?" he said, trying to catch his breath.

"Just leave me alone, Noah."

"I'm not leaving you alone out here. Why did you run from me?"

I struggled to stand up as best I could and tried to take a few steps. I winced in pain as I put the slightest pressure on my ankle. Noah got up and reached for my arm, but I jerked it away. I tried to take another step before falling into a heap on the ground.

"Would you let me help you?" He knelt down beside me.

"Noah, just go back to your *fiancé*." The word caught in my throat like a cotton ball.

"Is that why you ran from me?" I didn't answer. I just continued to rub my ankle and cry. "Tweet, she's here for a friend. It's not Brooke's bachelorette party. I haven't asked anyone to marry me."

I wasn't looking at him, but I could feel his smile. The bastard.

"Then why are you here?"

"Travis goes here and has been asking me to come up. Brooke didn't want to drive all this way alone. I figured it would be safer for her if I came, and …"

"How boyfriendy of you." I couldn't help how snide that sounded.

"… and I was hoping to see you."

I lifted my gaze up and looked into his beautiful light blue eyes that I have missed so much that they made me ache. He examined my face for a long moment. "God, I've missed you. You have no idea how much," he whispered.

Moving in closer, he cupped my face in his hands, running his thumbs along my cheeks and wiped away my tears. "I hate when you cry, Tweet." I gave him a shy smile. "Let me take care of you."

He stood and extended his hand to me. When I placed my hand in his an electric jolt sped through my body. Not one thing had changed in six months. He still affected me just as much as he always did. Noah pulled me to a standing position. When I put a little weight on the ankle, there was pain.

"Can you walk?" he asked.

Biting down on my bottom lip, I just shook my head. The next thing I knew Noah picked me up, cradling me in his arms. My breathing started to accelerate and warmth traveled to every inch of my body. I had missed the feeling of his protective arms around me.

"Won't Brooke be mad if she finds out you carried me all the way back to my dorm?"

He twisted from side to side looking around, swinging me back and forth. We both started laughing.

"I don't see her around. Besides, she wouldn't want me to leave you out here. She's not like that, Tweet."

I didn't respond. I knew Brooke was his girlfriend and he was supposed to stick up for her like any good boyfriend would, but I didn't want to hear him do it.

We headed toward my dorm. "Oh, by the way, I live on the fourth floor."

"Ok." He was starting to breathe heavier.

"And there's no elevator." I smiled at him. The look on his face was priceless.

Entry 23

We wake up one day surprised to find ourselves in a less desirable situation that we don't remember consenting to, but we stay in it because for some reason we feel obligated. As time passes, we convince, fool, and talk ourselves into believing things are normal.

It's not until we see the dream we lost that we realize what a nightmare we're in.

When we got to my dorm, Noah was relieved when he found out I actually lived on the second floor. I loved being in his arms again as he carried me all the way back to my room. I wished I lived further across campus so I could have stayed wrapped in them longer. After dropping me off he went to the convenience store across the street from my dorm to get ice for my swollen ankle, and I was sitting on my bed waiting for him.

There was a soft knock on the door as it slowly opened. Noah carried in two bags, one was a shopping bag and the other was a huge bag of ice.

"Dude, that's a lot of ice," I teased.

"I know, but you have ginormous ankles." I laughed out loud. "It's nice to hear that again."

"What?"

"Your laugh."

He tossed the shopping bag onto Lisa's bed then walked in the bathroom with the bag of ice. He returned with a towel wrapped around some of it. I moved over, giving him room to sit.

He held the ice to my ankle. "Does that feel alright?" he asked.

I nodded. "Thank you, Noah. Sorry you had to carry me all the way here."

"No problem. You aren't as heavy as you use to be."

I grabbed the pillow from behind me and hit him with it. He started laughing. I missed his laugh too.

"Are you saying I was fat before?"

"No!" He paused for a moment. "You have some awesome curves in all the right places, though." I felt tingles as piercing blue eyes scanned my body and the corners of his mouth curled up.

We sat in silence as Noah glanced around my room. He took a deep breath before his beautiful light blue eyes landed on me. Those eyes could always make me melt.

Clearing his throat he said, "Um … Tweet?"

"Yeah," I said.

He took a big gulp of air. He was so cute when he was nervous. "I've missed you." He looked down and shook his head slightly. "No, I've more than missed you. It's like when my dad died." I felt a surge of pain run through me remembering what I had done to him during that time. "I couldn't imagine a life without him in it. I couldn't bring him back, so I had to adjust. Even though I've started to adjust there's an emptiness that I can't fill. You and my parents have always been the three most important people in my life."

His eyes started turning liquid blue. They conveyed such intense pain and to know that I was partly to blame for it made me ashamed.

"Not having two of the three most important people in my life anymore … I've just been going through the motions each day, mainly for my mom's sake. Being here with you, smiling and laughing, it's the first time I've done that since you left that it wasn't fake. I need you back in my life."

I knew my answer should have been a definite *no*, but I had spent six months without him and all it did was make me miss him more. I love having his arms wrapped around me, being here together. This is the first time in months that I haven't hurt and felt lonely.

"What about Brooke? How do you think she would react to me being around again?"

"I think she'd be fine with it … eventually. Besides, Brooke doesn't dictate who my friends are."

Brooke has had six months with him without me being around. If she hasn't managed to establish a solid relationship with Noah by now then certainly my presence won't make a difference. Plus, I'm an hour and a half away, so I won't be seeing them every day. It would be wonderful just to be able to talk to him again.

"You don't hate me for what I did?" I asked, glancing down at my lap.

Noah placed his finger under my chin, lifting my gaze to meet his. "I could never hate you, Tweet. I severely disliked you for a while." He winked at me.

"I'm sorry I hurt you like that. I was just wanting …" My voice cracked with emotion. I remembered that horrible day when I left him in the park.

"I think I understand why you did it. I promise I will stay completely in the friend zone. I will not tempt you at all with my body."

I shook my head and laughed. "Okay."

"Really?" I nodded my head. "Don't take this the wrong way, but I'm so glad you fell."

"Yeah, me too." Two of the biggest Kool-Aid smiles ever appeared across both our faces.

Noah glanced over at the bag he had thrown on Lisa's bed. "Hold this on your ankle for a second. I got you something."

He walked over to grab the bag. I had no idea what he would have gotten me. He came back and sat on my bed, keeping the item hidden behind his back.

"Well, what is it?" I wasn't a very patient person.

"Close your eyes," he said. I did as I was told. "Don't open them until I say so."

"I won't."

"Promise?"

"Mmmhmm."

"Say it."

I couldn't stop my laughter. "I promise I won't open my eyes."

"Good." There was silence for a few seconds. "Okay, open your eyes."

The first thing I saw was the beautiful boy sitting in front of me with a shy smile on his lips. I followed his gaze as he glanced down. He was holding a box of chocolate snack cakes, a container of chocolate frosting, and a plastic spoon.

"Hey bestie. It's great to have you back," he said.

"It's great to be back."

We ate cake and frosting, well I ate frosting, while we caught each other up on our lives. Noah loved school. Although he loved baseball, he opted not to play this season even though the coach begged and offered him a scholarship. Noah's parents had been saving for college since the day he was born. Scholarship or not, his tuition was paid for.

He didn't want to play was because he felt he needed to concentrate on his classes. Although he didn't say it, I think the main reason was because of his dad not being here. I don't think his heart had healed enough for him to be able to go out on the field knowing his dad wasn't in the stands cheering him on.

I told him Emily had moved back to Charleston, was a lawyer at a law firm downtown, specializing in corporate law, and had bought a condo in the in the historic Radcliffborough section of town. I talked about adjusting to life away from home, but how much I loved my classes. I filled him in on Lisa and he was anxious to meet her. It was as if the six months apart had never happened. We talked just like we always had. Both of us avoided the subject of Brooke and Matt as long as we could. We were enjoying being together.

Noah was leaning back against the wall massaging my hurt ankle that rested in his lap when his phone chirped with a text. He looked at it and smirked.

"Brooke?" I asked.

"Yeah. She sent me a picture. Looks like they're having a good time." He typed a quick reply then tossed the phone on the bed.

"You can go if you want. I'm fine. Thanks for taking care of me . . ."

"Would you stop it. I'm not going anywhere."

"I don't want to cause any problems for you, Noah," I said.

"You're not."

"Are you in love with her?" The words flew out of my mouth before I knew it.

A knot immediately formed in my stomach and twisted tighter and tighter with the passing of each second of silence. My teeth started to grind together and my body tensed.

He slowly let out a deep sigh. "Honestly? Between my dad passing away, taking care of my mom, and missing you, I haven't thought about my feelings for Brooke. I know I sound like a dick."

"You're just being honest. You've had a lot to deal with this year."

"She tells me she loves me all the time. I never say anything back. I just smile and change the subject. I care about her."

"I shouldn't have asked you that."

He had a genuine look in his eyes and said, "You can ask me anything, Tweet. I just don't know how to answer you right now."

"Fair enough."

"So who was that Smurffucker you were with at the party?" he asked in a calm, controlled voice.

He started working his jaw and the veins in his neck began popping out slightly. He was trying hard not to show his anger or jealousy. He was trying to stay in the friend zone.

"His name is Matt. And you know I don't refer to Brooke as

Princess Bitchella." I smiled at him.

"You've been thinking on that one for a while, haven't you?"

"Nope. Actually, it just came to me."

"Matt ..." He said the name like it left a bad taste in his mouth. "Is he your boyfriend?"

"Yes." This was the first time I admitted to anyone, even myself, that Matt was my boyfriend. I wanted Noah to know I had moved on.

"I heard what he said to you, Tweet."

"How long had you been at the party? I walked all over that place and never saw you."

"I had just walked in when I saw you and Matt." I could see a slight cringe cross his face. "Has he forced you to do anything you didn't want to do?" he asked.

I shook my head. "No," I said with a hint of defensiveness in my voice.

I shifted my gaze down. It was sort of a lie. There had been two times when Matt pushed me to have sex with him when I told him I didn't want to. He didn't hurt me, but I did have a bruise for a week on my upper arm where he grabbed me.

"He's not usually like that. He was drunk. He's a theater major and is under a lot of pressure with this upcoming production...plus with classes ..." I was rambling and fidgeting with the hem of my shirt. Noah placed his hand on top of mine, stopping my fidgeting.

"Does he treat you right, Tweet?" I didn't look up at him. I just nodded. "If he does anything to hurt you, I'll break every fucking bone in his body."

I knew Noah meant what he said and I couldn't stop the small smile from forming on my face. I felt safe now that my hero was back in my life.

At 2 am, the door slowly creaked open and Lisa stuck her head in cautiously.

"You can come in," I told her.

She staggered toward me, still feeling the effects of the alcohol, but more subdued. She walked straight over to her bed, her eyes half closed, never once glancing in our direction, and plopped down.

"Lisa?" I asked.

"Mmmhmm?"

"This is Noah."

Her eyes shot open, she sat straight up, and turned toward us. "*The* Noah?" She smiled.

Noah glanced over at me looking curious to know what I had told her.

"Yes."

Noah slid to the edge of the bed and held his hand out to her. "Hey, it's great to meet you, Lisa."

She reached and grabbed his hand. "Well, hellooo *The* Noah. It's really great to see you … here … with Amanda." She looked back and forth between us, grinning like a cat that had just caught a canary.

"I guess I should be going." Noah stood and started collecting the trash from our snack.

Lisa stood and intercepted him. "I'll take that for you, so you can say toodles to each other."

She walked to the other side of the room pretending to give us some privacy.

"I'm not sure what time I'm heading back tomorrow. I want to see you before I go, but I don't know if I'll be able to. You know?" A look of disappointment crossed his face.

"I know," I said.

"I'll definitely talk to you tomorrow."

"And I'll be home for Thanksgiving in a few days," I said.

I guess we stared at each for an abnormal amount of time because Lisa felt it necessary to clear her throat, loudly. Noah leaned down to give me a kiss on my forehead. I couldn't help closing my eyes and savoring the feel of his lips on me again.

"Goodnight, Tweet," he whispered.

"Goodnight, Noah."

He turned to Lisa. "Goodnight, Lisa."

"Goodnight, *The* Noah."

He smiled as he glanced over at me. He grabbed his jacket and headed out the door.

Lisa watched Noah until the door closed behind him and then plopped back down on her bed. "Well, well, well ... *The* Noah is licktastic," she said, cocking one eyebrow up.

"We're going to try and do the friend thing."

"That's good. Start off slow."

"What do you mean *start* off slow? We're friends. That's it. Nothing else is going to happen between us. Noah's with Brooke and I'm with Matt."

She made sure I saw her roll her eyes.

"Sweetheart, there was so much eye fucking going on between the two of you, it was like an ophthalmologist's wet dream. And I saw how you reacted when he kissed you."

"How?"

"You didn't just *breathe* him in. You inhaled him deeply. You didn't soak him in. You ab-sorb-ed him in." She laid back down.

"You're still drunk."

"Mmmhmm. INHALED DEEPLY!"

The next morning I woke up to the sound of my phone chiming with a text.

Noah: Mornin Tweet. How's your ankle?

Me: A little better. Thx.

Noah: Not able to stop by. Sorry.

Me: That's ok. Have a safe trip home.

Noah: Last night was amazing. See you in a few days. Look outside your door.

Me: Ok. Just a sec.

I got up as quietly as possible so I wouldn't wake up Lisa. It took me a few minutes to get to the door. My ankle was stiff and still hurt. I cracked the door open slightly. The hallway was empty. I opened it the rest of the way, looked in both directions down the hall, but still didn't see anything. My phone chimed.

Noah: Look down.

I looked down. Sitting on the floor was a bag with my coat in it. He remembered to go get it from the frat house. Butterflies swarmed inside my stomach. I hadn't felt them in months. Then I saw it. My cheeks started hurting because I was unable to wipe the ridiculous smile off my face. Sitting in front of the bag, looking up at me, was a windup yellow bird Koosh toy. I picked it up and texted him immediately.

Me: Thx for getting my coat back and for my tweet. I love it. ;)

Noah: ;)

I picked up the bag and headed back into my room. I shut the door and leaned back on it as I looked over at Lisa who was wide awake, sitting up in bed. "Noah brought my coat back."

"That was nice of him. What else you got there?"

"It's a little windup Koosh bird." Her eyebrows scrunched together not understanding. "His nickname for me is Tweet. It's a little tweet."

"Well, dammit all to hell. If that isn't the sweetest fucking thing I've ever heard of. I think I just had a little orgasm."

"You're crazy." I put the bag on my bed, tweet on my dresser, and headed to take my shower.

As I closed the bathroom door, I heard Lisa yell, "INHALED DEEPLY!"

The smile never left my face for the rest of the day. I knew I looked like an idiot, but I didn't care. I wanted to enjoy this. I didn't even see Matt that day because I knew he would try and ruin my good mood. I had been miserable for six months and deserved a little happiness. It was going to be a great holiday because I had my Noah back.

ENTRY 24

THE CAPACITY TO FORGIVE IS ENDLESS,

BUT HOW MANY OF US TAKE ADVANTAGE AND TAP INTO IT?

YOUR TRUE SOUL MATE WILL ALWAYS FORGIVE, LOVE, AND SUPPORT YOU UNCONDITIONALLY. IF YOU LET HIM SLIP THROUGH YOUR FINGERS ONCE, SHAME ON YOU. IF YOU LET HIM SLIP THROUGH YOUR FINGERS AGAIN, THEN YOU DON'T DESERVE HIM.

I excused myself from the table so I could go text Noah. Standing in the stall of the ladies room, I sent for backups.

Me: 911! I'VE HAD 3 COSMOS ALREADY & HE'S STILL PUTTING ME TO SLEEP. HEADED BACK TO TABLE. CALL ME WITH A TRAGIC EMERGENCY THAT NEEDS MY ATTENTION. ;)

I couldn't believe I let Lisa talk me into this blind date with her cousin. And, to make matters worse, she chose to tell me about it while I was packing for my trip home for Thanksgiving break.

She was sitting back on her bed drinking Diet Coke and eating her second Pop-Tart while I shoved clothes into my suitcase without even ironing them first.

"Lisa, how could you go and set me up on a date? I know you don't like Matt, but I *am* dating him."

I was so agitated. I hated when I didn't feel in control of a situation and her going behind my back was inexcusable.

"I know you're pissed at me, but it's just one date. I know you're with asshat, and you and *The* Noah are satisfied with eye fucking each other. I just wanted you to see there are other options in the world. Think of it as a favor to sweet lovable me."

I stopped packing and narrowed my eyes at her. It was hard to stay angry with Lisa. I knew her heart was in the right place.

"One date and Matt doesn't need to know about it."

"Agreed," she said.

"What's your cousin like?"

"I have no idea. I've never met him."

"What?"

She popped the last piece of chemically laced cardboard pastry in her mouth as she raised her index finger to me indicating she needed a second.

"I've actually never met the dude. All I know is he just moved to Charleston, he's 25, and is loaded. Even if he's not for you, you'll get a good meal out of it."

I jumped up and down clapping my hands and sarcastically said, "Oh boy! A gourmet meal really does make this less humiliating."

"Smartass. The guy has got to be pretty great. I mean, he is related to me and you know how awesome I am. Everybody loves me." She cocked her head to one side and flashed me a huge toothy grin.

So here I am, spending part of my precious school break in one of the finest restaurants in Charleston, Cypress, with a guy I don't even know and don't want to know.

I waited a few more seconds in hopes that Noah would reply. These past few days have been incredible. After we reunited last weekend, Noah and I have talked at least twice a day. Thank god for unlimited minutes. I waited another moment for a text. Nothing.

I slowly headed back to the table and my blind date, Joshua McPherson. Awesomeness does not run in Lisa's family. He's smug, arrogant, and boring. I tried, but couldn't walk any slower back to the table. As I approached, Joshua was berating the waiter for something stupid and pointless. I had determined that Joshua must have a tiny dick and is overcompensating by being an asshole to the wait staff.

Sitting down, I made eye contact with our waiter, trying to convey my apologies for Joshua and to signal him to bring Cosmo number three STAT. The one upside to this evening is that I have been able to drink, even though I'm two years from being legal. I guess when you have money like Joshua, you get away with a lot of things.

Twenty minutes passed and I was beyond bored and pissed. Noah had still not replied to my 911. Brooke had gone out of town for the holiday so I knew she wasn't the reason for the no reply. I looked across the table at Joshua as he rambled on about the blah, blah and its blah, blah, when I heard someone beside me clear his throat. I looked up and there he was, my knight in plastic armor.

He was dressed in a gray suit, a light blue shirt that made his eyes look even bluer, and a gray and silver pinstripe tie. He looked gorgeous.

"Excuse me, but don't I know you?" I just sat there stunned, wondering what he was up to. "Noah Stewart," he said, pointing at himself.

"Oh, yeah Noah Stewart from..."

"Middle school."

"That's right, middle school." I turned to Joshua. "Joshua McPherson, this is Noah Stewart from middle school."

Joshua stood extending his hand. Noah grabbed it and shook it rapidly. "Nice to meet you, Josh."

"It's nice meeting you, too. It's Joshua, by the way."

"Huh?"

"My name is Joshua, not Josh, Joshua." Noah just stared at him as Joshua sat back down.

My Cosmo haze was nice and thick at this point. I just smiled, looking back and forth between the two guys. I knew things were about to get fun now that my knight was here to rescue me.

"So …" Noah looked at me confused, like he had forgotten my name. Since Halloween 1996, Noah has called me Tweet. I have not heard him say my actual name since the age of six.

"A-man-da," I said, trying to help him out.

"Yeah, that's right. It's great to see you," Noah said.

"It's great to see you, too. What are you doing here?" I asked.

"Well, I was supposed to meet some friends here for drinks and dinner. I just got a call, something came up and they can't make it."

"I'm sorry your plans got cancelled."

"Yeah, me too. I hate to eat alone and being that I don't live in town anymore, I really don't know too many people. Lost track of friends. You know how it is. Well, it was great running into you." Noah turned to Joshua and reached out to shake his hand. "Great meeting you, Joshua."

I gave Joshua a pitiful look and then turn to Noah. "Noah, why don't you join us? Joshua wouldn't mind." I glanced over at him. "Would you?"

Joshua looked stunned as he stammered out, "Uh … no, not at all. Please, join us." He snapped his fingers at a passing waiter. "Get us another chair. The gentleman will be joining us."

"Thanks man. I really appreciate it," Noah said, excitedly.

The waiter returned with the extra chair. Noah positioned himself between Joshua and me. There was an awkward silence for a moment. I had no idea where Noah was going with this little charade, but he had a mischievous twinkle in his eye. I was buzzed and along for the ride.

Grinning like a fool, Noah looked back and forth between me and Joshua. Finally, he landed his eyes back on me. "So, how do you two know each other?" Noah asked.

Glancing over at Joshua, I answered, "We're actually on a blind date."

"Oh hell, this is a date?! You two are on a romantic date and I'm crashing it. I'm an idiot. I'm sorry. Look, I'm going to leave and..."

I grabbed his arm as he started to get up. "NO! I mean, please stay. We really want you to stay. Don't we, Joshua?"

"Sure. Stay. Please."

"Well, if you insist."

He settled back into his chair, grabbed a breadstick from the basket in the middle of the table, and took a big bite. There was another minute of awkward silence.

I took a sip of my Cosmo and got the party started. "So, Noah, where are you living now?"

"Saskatchewan."

It took every bit of strength I had to contain my laughter, which caused me to choke on my drink.

"Saskatchewan, you say?" I looked over at him and smirked, still trying to control myself.

Noah returned my smirk "Yep, Sas … kat … che … waaan."

I looked over at Joshua, who still appeared dazed and confused that our date had been hijacked.

"Saskatchewan," I said.

From the look in his eyes, I could tell Joshua's fog was starting to lift. "What do you do in Saskatchewan, Noah?" Joshua asked.

"I work on portfolios." Our waiter came over to fill our water glasses and I motioned to him to bring me another Cosmo.

Joshua perked up at the mention of portfolios and appeared genuinely interested. "Oh, great. I'm an investment banker at Smith, Barney & Kline. What type of portfolios do you specialize in? Aggressive? Defensive? E-Commerce?"

The waiter arrived with my drink, placed it in front of me, and stood there while I drained the last drop of my previous Cosmo before taking my glass away.

"Pleather," Noah answered.

"Excuse me?"

"Pleather."

"I'm sorry. I don't understand," Joshua said, confusion plastered across his face.

At this point I'm trying desperately to hold back tears and a mouthful of liquor.

"I make portfolios out of pleather. You know, fake leather. I used to work in vinyl but nowadays everyone wants to look so sophisticated."

"The fuck you say!" I blurted out. "Noah makes pleather portfolios in Saskatchewan. Isn't that fan-fucking-tastic, Josh?"

Noah sat back in his chair, grinning from ear to ear.

Our dinner arrived and we ate while Noah enlightened us about the history of Saskatchewan and pleather. I had no idea if what he was telling us was true or not, but it sounded convincing.

Afterward, the three of us walked out of the restaurant together. I was feeling pretty happy by then. I held on to Noah's arm as Joshua handed his ticket to the valet. Noah turned to Joshua, extending his hand.

"Thank you for dinner. I wish you had let me pay for at least half."

"Don't worry about it. It was my pleasure."

"Just so you know, I'm not the kind of guy who puts out just because you bought me a meal." I almost lost it. Joshua looked at Noah with confusion, again. "I'm just screwing with ya, dude."

Joshua laughed a fake laugh.

Looking at me, Noah asked, "Do you still live on Sycamore Drive?"

"I believe I do," I said, proudly.

"Joshua, where do you live?"

"Beechwood Street on the Isle of Palms."

"That's in the opposite direction of Sycamore. It will take you about an hour and some change to get back home. Listen, I'm headed that way. Let me take her home for you."

Stammering, Joshua said, "Uh … that's okay. I'm fine taking her back home. I thought we might take a carriage ride down by the water at the Battery before we end the evening."

"Oh that's not necessary, Joshie. I've had my fair share of looking at a horse's ass tonight," I giggled, swaying into Noah's side. I felt his chest rumble trying to hold in his laughter.

"No, let me do it as a thank you for picking up the check. I insist. I won't take no for an answer," Noah said.

Looking at me Joshua asked, "Uh … are you fine with that?"

"Fine by me, puddin' pop," I slurred, slightly.

"Okay, if you're fine." Joshua stared at me as the valet pulled up in his BMW.

"Your ride up, Josh," Noah said.

"It was nice meeting you, Amanda. I'll call you."

"Okie dokie."

Joshua leaned in, giving me a quick kiss on my cheek. There was one more moment of awkward silence before he got in his car and drove away.

Once the BMW was out of sight, Noah snaked one of his arms around my waist and pulled me abruptly against his chest. I place both hands on his muscular biceps to brace myself. My body aligned with his perfectly. Our lips were close, and I couldn't take my eyes off of his. If I were to stick my tongue out just a little bit, I would be able to graze his bottom lip.

A low sultry voice interrupted my fantasy when Noah said, "Tweet."

"Mmmhmm?"

He stared at my lips for a moment. Between the Cosmos and the feel of his body pressed against mine, I was feeling all kinds of tingles in all kinds of places.

"Do you think Joshua will call us for a second date?" I watched as his lips slowly turned into a sensual smirk.

I burst out laughing. "I doubt it since you wouldn't put out." I smiled at him.

"Bastard! Men are such pigs," he said as he spanked my ass, causing me to jump and yelp a little.

The valet pulled up in the car. Taking my hand, Noah led me towards the passenger's side and helped me in. He rounded the front of the car and slid into the driver's seat. Holy moly, his ass looked incredible sliding into that seat. Before he started the car, I placed my hand on top of his thigh and squeezed slightly.

"Thank you for tonight. It was the best blind date in the history of blind dates." I shyly smiled.

He picked up my hand, brought it to his lips, and placed a soft kiss on my palm, maintaining constant eye contact with me. It made me shudder. I had to squeeze my legs together tightly as the tingles quickly turned into vibrations.

He placed my hand back on his thigh and smirked. "Pleather portfolio making Noah from Saskatchewan knows how to show his number one girl a good time," he said and winked at me.

I wanted to jumped across the seat, straddle him, and suck on his tongue and other body parts. I wouldn't do it, of course. Nope, we were in the friend zone and I wouldn't jeopardize that. Besides, he was with Brooke and I was with … what's his name. This was the way it was supposed to be all along. Noah and I dating other people while remaining best friends, even though I still wanted to suck on his bottom lip.

Entry 25

In the immortal words of Sally Brown (Charlie's sister), "All I want is my fair share. All I want is what's coming to me." Words to live by.

I knew it was cold from the cloud of smoke that escaped my mouth whenever I exhaled. But I certainly couldn't feel the cold. I couldn't feel anything. I sat in our spot staring out across the pond thinking of nothing and everything. Somehow my life had changed, turned upside down in a matter of minutes and I never saw it coming.

I heard the crunch of the gravel behind me. My phone had been blowing up with calls and texts from my family. None of them knew where I had run off to. If they knew I was literally three blocks away from them, they'd be furious. I wasn't surprised that he knew exactly where to find me. I heard more gravel crunching as he rounded the picnic table. They replaced the one Noah demolished several months ago. He moved closer to me, but neither one of us said a word. I continued to stare across the pond.

"Tweet," he said. His voice was low and shaky.

He moved in closer, getting ready to wrap his arms around me. I leaned away from him and held my hand up, palm out, signaling him to stop.

"Don't touch me."

"Why?"

"Because, if you touch me, I'll fall apart. I've already pulled myself back together once today. I don't think I could do it again."

I could see out of the corner of my eye that he was texting someone, probably my family to let them know he found me. I knew he wouldn't tell them where I was, so I didn't protest.

He sat down next to me, but kept a safe distance so we wouldn't be touching. We sat in silence. Noah knew I would talk when I was ready.

I let my thoughts drift back through the last few months. I started with the beginning of school. It was a good semester. I made the Dean's list, I was getting used to being away from home, I loved my roommate, and I got Noah back.

Two days ago when I got home for Christmas break I could no longer ignore the signs. In fact, my mom insisted something be done immediately. If she hadn't forced my hand, I would still be blissfully ignorant, with my life intact. Interesting how a little knowledge and two short words can demolish your entire world.

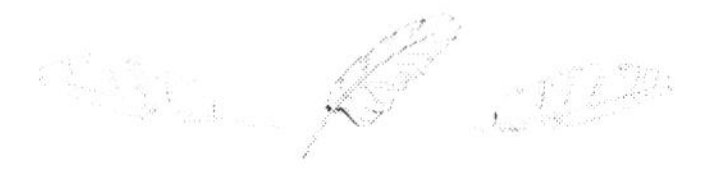

"Bone cancer." Everything the doctor said after that was muffled.

I felt like I was under water, drowning. I was so confused. I came here because of a sprained ankle and the pain in my calf that had persisted for a month. I thought the doctor made a mistake, mixed up my x-rays with someone else's. I looked over at my mom, who was sitting in the corner with tears rolling down her face. Why was she crying? It was just a sprained ankle.

"Amanda, did you hear me?" Dr. Thompson asked.

"What?"

"I'm sorry. The x-ray shows a tumor with irregular borders. That along with your weight loss, fatigue, and the leg pain you described, leads me to believe that that's what we're dealing with. I'm going to send you over to Dr. Lang. He's an excellent oncologist."

His mouth moved and I heard noise coming out of it, but he must have been speaking a foreign language because I couldn't comprehend what he was saying.

My mom walked over to me, and wrapped her arm around my shoulders securely. She placed her hand on top of mine as the doctor continued.

"It's fairly rare that bone cancer develops as the primary cancer. It usually is a result having metastasized from another site, so we'll test for that."

"What are you testing me for?" I asked.

I didn't understand what was going on. Why did the doctor look so serious and why was my mom getting more upset the longer he talked? Didn't they realize it's just a sprained ankle?

"We need to find out if the cancer has invaded any other organs," he said.

"It's just a sprained ankle," I insisted. I looked up at my mom, my eyes pleading with hers to make him understand. "Mom, tell him it's just a sprained ankle."

She pulled me into her and held me while stroking my hair. "Sweetie, we're going to get through this."

I abruptly jerked away from her and got up from the exam table. The anger was evident in my voice.

"Why won't you tell him?!" I insisted.

I backed away as she took a step toward me. "TELL HIM IT'S JUST A SPRAINED ANKLE, MOM!"

My body started to convulse with sobs as I sunk down into one of the chairs. I felt like I was in one of those dreams where you feel like you're falling. You try to grasp onto something to stop the fall, then suddenly you wake up. It takes a second before you realize that it was only a dream. That's how I felt—but without the waking up part.

Mom's arms encircled me as tears poured out of me. "It's a lot for us to take in all at once," she said to the doctor.

"I understand. Why don't you go home and adjust. I'll have my nurse call you about scheduling the MRI and an appointment with Dr. Lang. If you have any questions, it's a good idea to write them down. I wish you had come in earlier when you first noticed the symptoms."

I looked up at him. My face was drenched in tears. "I didn't know I had symptoms. I was so busy and didn't always have time to eat. I thought my leg hurt because of shin splints. I overslept a few times and my parking space was pretty far from my dorm, so I'd run down the stairs cause there's no elevator in my dorm. I couldn't be late for class. I just couldn't. I had to make the Dean's List and I did. I made the Dean's List. Didn't I, Mom?" I knew I was rambling, but I couldn't stop myself. I was trying to make sense of the senseless. I needed an answer to why this was happening.

I looked at them both, hoping one could explain this to me, but neither could. The only thing I heard over my sobs was the doctor bombarding my mom with information about tests that would need to be performed.

"What's the treatment for this?" Mom asked.

"Well, I'm not an oncologist, but usually surgery, chemo, and sometimes radiation."

"What kind of surgery?"

"If the cancer is localized, they would try and remove the entire tumor. If its spread throughout the tissue the best course of treatment would be a below knee amputation."

I bolted from my seat and dashed out the door as fast as I could. My limp had become pretty pronounced since Thanksgiving because of the pain. I had heard enough. I couldn't handle anymore. I didn't stop moving until I reached my mom's car. I stood there facing the car, my hand poised on the door handle. I heard the lock click, I swung the door open, and got inside, slamming it shut. I heard the driver's side door open and felt a slight movement as Mom slid onto her seat.

"Sweetheart …"

"Don't. I can't talk right now. I just want to go home."

We drove the entire way home in silence. Occasionally, I caught a glimpse out of the corner of my eye of Mom wiping a tear away from her cheek. When we pulled into our driveway, I immediately got out of the car and headed to the backyard to get my bike. I got on it and rode away without saying a word about where I was headed because I didn't know. I just needed to be alone. I could hear my mom call my name through her choked cries. I don't know how long I rode around. I stopped when I got tired and found myself at my and Noah's spot.

Noah's presence always and gave me peace, but when I heard his footsteps behind me, I didn't feel the same sense of relief that I usually did. For the first time in my life, my knight in plastic armor couldn't save me.

"You talked to my mom?"

He cleared his throat. "Yeah. She called in a panic. She didn't know where you were and you wouldn't answer your phone." He scooted a little closer to me. "It's cold out here, Tweet. Let's go somewhere warm."

"I've been trying to figure out what I did," I said.

"What do you mean?"

"What I am being punished for?"

I could feel the tears starting to build behind my eyes. I desperately wanted to hold them back. When I let them spill over, it opened me up too much and the feelings were overwhelming. I wanted to stay numb just a little longer.

"You're not being punished."

Glancing over at Noah, I could see he was getting antsy. His fingers twitched as if he couldn't keep himself from touching me for much longer. I finally looked at him. He looked devastated. We stared at each other for a moment before he finally gave in and threw his arms around me. As we made contact, tears started gushing out of me.

Noah pulled me onto his lap. I buried my head in the crook of his neck and let all the emotions of the day spill out. He held me so tight, it was almost hard to breathe.

"You're frozen, baby. Let me take you home," he said.

I held on to him more securely. I didn't want to go home yet. I had convinced myself that as long as I stayed out here, none of what was happening was real. If I set foot in my house, the reality would set in and I wouldn't be able to hide from it any longer. I knew I would have to go back soon, but in this moment I needed to pretend everything was fine and savor being wrapped up in Noah's arms.

Entry 26

Cancer is a game changer, a dictator, and the great and powerful Oz all rolled up into one all-consuming beast.

I had lived two days with the diagnosis. It still didn't feel real to me, but I knew it was real every time I saw the faces of Emily or my parents. I was scheduled for an MRI the next morning, and then I had an appointment with the doctor in the afternoon.

Mom contacted the university and explained the situation. Obviously, I wouldn't be going back to school next semester. I was angry about that. I hated that something out of my control was dictating every decision I made. We needed to go pack up my things now because once treatment started, I wouldn't be going anywhere for a while.

I also needed to tell Matt face-to-face while I was in town. He was staying with some friends until Christmas Eve when he would fly home. Noah was coming with us to help. The plan was for my parents to drive up with the SUV, and Noah and I would drive up in his truck.

We had been spending every possible minute with each other. I didn't know how Noah was handling this with Brooke. We never discussed it. In fact, he and I hadn't even talked about my diagnosis. Whenever the subject came up, he'd remain quiet. But he's been by my side, helping me with anything I needed.

We were all quiet as we packed everything up from my extremely short college career. Lisa, of course, was home in Missouri for the holidays. We had a tear filled conversation yesterday. She promised to come see me when she got back next semester. Whether Lisa and I were roommates or not, I knew she would always be in my life. Sometimes you meet people and know immediately that they were meant to be your friend. Lisa was that for me.

Once my parent's car was packed up, they headed back home. I told them Noah and I would be along after I talked to Matt. Noah drove me over and waited in his truck while I went inside to break the news. I had texted Matt that I was in town and was headed over.

I felt nervous for some reason as I walked up the stairs to his place. I knocked and the door immediately swung open. Matt scooped me up in his arms like he hadn't seen me in years.

"God, it's good to see you," he said.

"You okay? You just saw me a few days ago."

"I know, but I've missed you. Can't a guy miss his woman?" He started kissing my neck.

"Matt, we need to talk. I need to tell you something." He pulled back and looked at me with concern in his eyes.

"Are you breaking up with me, Stick? Because in my defense, I was completely wasted and didn't know what was going on," he rambled on.

"What are you talking about?" I stepped away from him.

"Usually when someone says *we need to talk*, they're planning to break up with you."

"You slept with Danielle, didn't you?"

"I thought about you the entire time. She wasn't as good as I thought she would be. With her being so hot, I thought she'd be better than …"

"Me?!"

He wrapped his arms around my waist, and whispered in my ear, "Don't be mad, Stick. I told you she wasn't any good." He started to nuzzle my neck.

"I have bone cancer, will probably have to have my leg amputated and go through chemo," I said, flatly.

He stepped back. When he looked at me, his face was void of any emotion. I assumed he was waiting for me to finish, so I did.

"I just packed up my room. I'm not coming back next semester."

He didn't say anything for several minutes as he ran his hand through his hair.

He let out a deep sigh and said, "I got the lead in next semester's production."

I thought I heard him wrong for a second. When I played this conversation over in my head, this was not even a possible option of what I imagined he would say to me.

I headed to the door. I heard Matt's footsteps behind me.

"Stick! Wait! You caught me off guard!" He grabbed my upper arm and spun me around to face him. "I didn't know what to say to you. I thought you were coming to break up with me because you were mad about Danielle."

"I don't care about you enough to be mad about Danielle. I have to go. Noah's waiting downstairs to drive me home."

"Are you fucking him?"

He still hadn't let go of me. In fact, his grip had gotten tighter.

"What?" I tried to yank my arm away, but his hold was too strong. "Matt, let me go. You're hurting me."

"I'm not an idiot, Amanda. I see how you react whenever he calls. And he calls a lot. How long have you been fucking him?"

"He's my friend." I yank again, harder, but still couldn't free my arm.

The next few seconds happened so fast, it was a complete blur. I looked at Matt and saw a hand clamp around his neck and shove him up against the wall. He released his hold on my arm causing me to stumble backwards. When I looked up, I saw Noah's hand tighten around Matt's neck. Matt was gasping for air with each squeeze.

"A tight grip doesn't feel so good when you're the grippee, does it, Smurffucker?" Noah put more pressure on Matt's neck, completely cutting off any air flow. Matt's eyes began to protrude and he was starting to turn blue. "Tweet, go get in the car."

"Noah, he can't breathe. Don't kill him."

"Go get in the goddamn car. Now!"

I turned and rushed out the door. Once in the hallway, I heard some loud thuds, grunts, and the sound of furniture breaking. Within minutes the noises ceased, and Noah walked out, grabbed my hand, and led me back to the truck.

He flung open the passenger door and I got in. I watched as he paced back and forth in front of his truck, trying to calm himself down. He walked over to the driver's side. There were a couple of loud blows to the side of the truck just before he got in. I thought something had been thrown and hit the truck. He was clenching and unclenching his hand. I could see his knuckles were red from hitting something and someone.

"Noah, are you okay?"

"Has he hurt you before?" he asked through gritted teeth.

I wasn't exactly sure how to answer him. Technically, Matt had never hit me. He almost did one time, but he claimed he was just playing.

"He's never hit me."

"Has he ever *hurt* you?"

"Just grabbing my arm a few times too tight, but he was drunk and …"

His chest was rising and falling faster, pumping oxygen in and out of him in short spurts. "Has he ever forced himself on you? Don't lie to me."

I hesitated for several seconds before answering. "Yes," I whispered.

Noah began pounding relentlessly on the steering wheel. Seconds later, he shoved his door open and jumped out. I heard and felt the pounding of metal as he yelled, "Fuck!!" over and over.

He got back in the truck, turned the ignition, and sped out of the parking lot. Beads of sweat were dripping down his forehead.

"Noah …"

He raised his index finger and said in a low growl, "I can't talk right now." The entire hour and a half drive home, he wouldn't talk to me.

When we arrived at my house, he walked me to the front door. I desperately tried to think of something to say while I fumbled for my keys.

"Thank you for everything and I'm sorry about …"

"What time is your appointment tomorrow?"

"The MRI is at 10 o'clock and I see the doctor at 3 o'clock."

"I'll be over at 8 to unload your stuff. We'll have plenty of time to get to your appointment."

"You don't have to go. Both my parents will be with me."

"I know I don't have to go. I want to go. Get some sleep. I'll see you in the morning." He gave me a kiss on the forehead and headed down the steps.

Tomorrow my life will start to change. It will be filled with doctor appointments, diagnostic tests, and hospitals instead of classes and frat parties. I will no longer be Amanda Kelly, journalism major. I will be Amanda Kelly, cancer patient.

Entry 27

When you're diagnosed with a life altering illness, the first few days you walk around shell shocked, not quite believing it.

After that, you live in a state of limbo. You still feel like your old self, still see the same image in the mirror, and you, occasionally, forget that you are sick.

Once the doctor visits and tests become more frequent you turn into a patient with a life altering illness. You start to forget what you felt like before the diagnosis. Your pre-diagnosis persona disappears and is replaced by a stranger who is sad, scared, tired, and at times wants to give up the fight.

The MRI was a giant colossal suck-tacular, mother sucking, suck fest. The machine looked like an enormous white penis and balls. Well, one ball actually. No doubt an inadequately endowed male invented this machine.

I laid down on the enormous white penis and the tech slid me up into the ball, where I had to lay perfectly still for one hour. When I felt the tech sliding me out, I breathed a sigh of relief. I had never been so happy to get off a penis in my life.

After the MRI, we decided to go to lunch. My parents, Noah, and I either sat in silence or talked about everything except what was going on. We were all in a state of confusion, not quite knowing what our roles were or how to act in this new world.

After lunch we headed to my oncologist appointment. We sat in the waiting room for forty-five minutes before being ushered back into his office.

Dr. Lang was a middle-aged man, which I liked. I didn't want some young doctor holding his textbook over me while he figured out where my parts were. He was a straight talking, no nonsense kind of guy. I wasn't a patient person, so I liked that. Noah stood in the back of the room, while I sat in front of the doctor's desk, flanked on either side by my parents.

"Well, I have some good news," Dr. Lang said while he looked down at my records and results. "There doesn't seem to be any evidence of cancer elsewhere. Your left leg appears to be the only area affected now." Four audible deep sighs filled the office. "But there does appear to be infiltration into the surrounding soft tissue. Because of this, I recommend a below knee amputation."

He looked up right at me, I guess trying to gauge my reaction. I sat there staring back at him. It wasn't a surprise that this was the recommendation. But before it was a possibility. Now it was a reality. It took me a moment to adjust. The doctor glanced back down at my records, breaking eye contact with me.

In the short moment that we looked at each other, I could tell he was thinking of his own daughter. I saw a picture of his family on the table as I walked into his office. She looked to be almost my age.

"They have come a long way in prosthetic limbs. I've seen some that look so real, you wouldn't even know they weren't," he said.

I guess this was *the making lemonade out of lemons* speech.

I heard my dad clear his throat and ask, "So if it's just in her left leg, once the …" His voice cracked. He paused for a moment trying to compose himself before he continued. "Once the surgery is done, she'll be cancer free, right?"

Dr. Lang kept his eyes focused on my file when he answered my dad. "Technically, yes. She'll still have to go through chemo, though."

"But if it's just in her leg, why does she need to go through chemo?" Mom asked.

Dr. Lang looked up and said, "Mr. and Mrs. Kelly, Amanda, and young man."

"That's my best friend, Noah," I said. The doctor nodded in Noah's direction.

"Amanda has osteosarcoma. It's a very aggressive form of bone cancer. From what I know about your case, I'd say aggressive is an understatement. Your symptoms came on very quickly. We need to make sure we kill any stray cells that could potentially metastasize to your lungs. The chemo will give us the best chance of stopping that from occurring. I know this is extremely overwhelming. Let's take it a little at a time. My nurse will talk to you about scheduling the surgery and information on amputations and give you a few names of prosthetists in the area."

"A prosthetist?" I asked.

"They're the ones who fit you for your new leg," he explained. "It will be a few weeks before you'll get fitted and start chemo. We want you to heal from the surgery first. Do you have any questions?"

There was too much information coming at us and none of us could think clearly enough to ask anything. I was still trying to process that I was going to have my leg sawed off.

"I'm sure I'll have a million questions as soon as I walk out the door." I smiled weakly.

He looked at me with warm brown eyes. "I have a daughter a couple of years younger than Amanda. I'd be beside myself if she got sick. We're going to do everything we can for you, Amanda."

"I know."

He hesitated before continuing. "I don't usually talk to patients about this. I'm saying this because of the type of cancer you have, the type of chemo that you'll have, and your young age. Most young people don't think about this type of thing, but Amanda, you may want to go ahead and talk to your parents about what type of arrangements you want, just in case."

I heard my mom let out a slight gasp.

"I'm going to be staying with my sister, Emily," I told him. "She has a ground floor condo in Radcliffborourgh close to the hospital. My parent's house has steps going into it. We figured Emily's would be a good place to stay."

As I talked, I noticed the expression on the doctor's face. I looked over at my mom and then my dad. Their expressions matched the doctor's.

"He's not talking about living arrangements, sweetheart," Dad said.

Then it suddenly dawned on me. He was telling me to start planning my funeral. What's weird is that it never crossed my mind that I might die.

We filed out of the office with a stack of information to read on the type of cancer I had, what to expect from the surgery, and names of local leg people. Calling them prosthetists sounded too much like prostitute for my liking.

I wasn't in the mood to go home then. My parents hugged and kissed me goodbye, got in their car and drove home. I had never seen them so visibly shaken before. I think we all needed our alone time now.

Noah and I sat in his truck, processing the appointment. Out of the corner of my eye, I could see he was fidgeting, tapping his fingers on the steering wheel. It looked like he was about to say something.

"Noah, don't. I need a little time think about what was said in there."

"I know. What do you want to do?"

I continued staring straight ahead and said, "Runaway."

He didn't respond. He simply started the truck and pulled out of the parking lot.

We drove further into downtown, past Colonial Lake and the College of Charleston, pulling into Emily's tree lined neighborhood and up to a very nice three story pale green Charleston home with white trim, a huge wrap around porch on the first level and screened in porches on the two upper levels.

Noah cut the engine, turned to me, and said, "I'm staying here for a few weeks. The house has been divided into three condo units."

"It's really nice. Why are you staying here?"

"It's Carter Perry's place. I hang out here all the time. It's within walking distance of school. He asked me to stay while he was out of town for Christmas. He won't be back until after New Year's. It's great having some privacy," he said.

"Emily's place is only a couple of blocks away. You'll be so close by."

"I know, funny how it worked out that way." He smiled at me before getting out of the car. I had a feeling that his staying at this condo wasn't just a coincidence.

I watched as he walked around to my side of the car and opened the passenger door. I placed my hand in his and we walked inside.

It was a very nice two bedroom condo. It was a typical guy's place, sparsely furnished with a huge sofa and flat screen TV. We shrugged out of our coats, tossing them on the sofa.

"Do you want anything to drink or eat?" Noah asked.

"No, I'm fine. Thanks."

"Make yourself comfortable. I'll be right back," he said.

"Ok."

I walked over to the large floor to ceiling window and looked out. My mind drifted to planning my funeral. What music would I like? What kind of coffin would I want to be in? I wonder if they make yellow coffins. Do they even make different color coffins? I was so engrossed in my thoughts I didn't hear Noah come back into the room.

"Tweet, are you sure you don't want anything?"

I continued staring out the window. "I don't want to die." My voice was so soft and low, like I said it more to myself than to Noah.

There was a slight pause before Noah said, "You're not going to die."

He was standing by the kitchen counter, drinking a bottle of water when I turned to face him.

"How do you know?"

"I don't want to talk about this right now," he said, just before taking another drink of water.

"But, I do. I need to talk about it with my best friend. I know it's not easy. We haven't talked about it at all. Things are going to get bad, and I need you to understand that."

Lowering his head, he inhaled a deep breath. I saw his shoulders start to tremble. The next thing I knew a plastic bottle of water was flying through the air, smashing into the wall. He looked up and I saw pain and helplessness in his beautiful blue eyes as they filled with tears. "You don't think I understand how bad things are? I'm going to be a fucking orthopedic surgeon one day. You don't think I know, that if the cancer doesn't eat you up that, the meds they're going to pump into your body might? You don't think I've read that you have a sixty-five percent chance of surviving five years? For most people, that would be pretty good odds, but not for you. You deserve one hundred percent guaranteed survival." Tears were now gushing from our eyes.

He was standing in front of me in three quick strides. He pinned me to the window as he placed his hands on either side of my face. Our eyes locked. Our lips were barely touching when he whispered, "I can't lose you. You're my everything. Not having you in my life wrecked me before, but not having you in my world would completely destroy me. My purpose is to take care of you and protect you, but there's nothing I can do to take this away from you. I don't know how to help you.

"Noah …," I said breathlessly.

"Please, don't push me away, Tweet," he begged.

"I'm not pushing," I whispered.

My fingers ran through his hair. Noah's hands slid down my body and landed behind the top of my thighs. As he lifted me up, I wrapped my legs securely around his waist. My back was pushed harder against the window with every grind of his hips. I wanted him to take my pain away. I wanted to feel safe and protected like I always did when I was with him. I wanted to feel normal one last time. I've never told Noah how much I loved him and I needed to before it was too late.

My chest pressed against his with each rapid breath. We looked into each other's eyes.

"Noah, I …" Before I could get another word out we heard the front door open and his name being called.

Quickly, I disentangled my hands from his hair and slid down his body, until my feet hit the floor. Running his hands through his hair a few times, Noah stepped away from me a second before Brooke rounded the corner. Seeing me, stopped her in her tracks.

"I didn't know we were having company." I found her choice of words odd. This wasn't even Noah's place. I didn't understand how she even got in.

Never taking his eyes off me, Noah said, "Brooke, can you give us a minute, please."

"No, I can't," she said, annoyed.

"Please."

"Noah, we were supposed to have this place all to ourselves through New Year's Eve."

Noah turned on his heels and headed toward Brooke, grabbing

her arm, they disappeared into what I assumed was a bedroom.

I was frozen in place. I didn't know what to do. I could hear them through the door arguing.

"Noah, I'm sorry she's dying, but she's not going to use that to come between us and ruin our time here. The world does not revolve around Amanda Kelly."

"Don't you ever talk about her like that."

"I'm not trying to be a bitch. It's just, this was supposed to be our time. We wouldn't have to worry about roommates or your mom catching us. That's what this time was supposed to be …"

Oh my god, they were playing house together over Christmas break. The privacy he was talking about was so he and Brooke could screw each other as much as they wanted.

I hurried out the door as I texted Emily to come pick me up. I walked as quickly and as far away as I could tolerate. I was starting to limp a lot more. I didn't think I could handle anymore walking, or Noah, at the moment.

What was he thinking taking me there? He had to know she would be coming back. I was a second away from telling him how much I loved him and being in his bed. What I heard of their argument about my impending death kept playing on a continuous loop in my head.

Suddenly, a realization hit me. Noah felt sorry for me. He wanted to make me feel better and the only thing he could do was have pity sex with me. Wrapping my arms around myself, I tried to keep my sobs trapped in my throat. I could feel the tremors start to course through my body as I continued to walk until I spotted Emily who drove me home.

It was time to crawl into my bed, throw the covers over my head, and block out Noah, Brooke, and cancer for now. I knew I would have to deal with each of them soon enough, but right now I needed to shut down.

Entry 28

IF ANYONE LOOKED ON MY COMPUTER AT MY RECENT SEARCHES...LET'S JUST SAY I'D HAVE SOME SPLAININ' TO DO.

MY LEG WILL BE SAWED OFF. SINCE THERE'S CANCER, THE TISSUE WILL BE STUDIED, AND THEN THE LEG WILL BE INCINERATED. UP IN FLAMES. I ASKED THE DOCTOR WHAT WOULD HAPPEN TO MY LEG AFTER THE SURGERY. HE WOULDN'T TELL ME. I DON'T KNOW WHY. IT WASN'T LIKE I WAS GOING TO ASK THEM TO WRAP IT UP TO GO SO I COULD TAKE IT TO SHOW AND TELL.

I'M NOT SURE WHY I WANTED TO KNOW THE GORY DETAILS OF MY LEG'S FUTURE. I GUESS BECAUSE IT HAD BEEN WITH ME FOREVER AND TO JUST LET IT GO, WITHOUT EVEN KNOWING WHAT WOULD BECOME OF IT, SEEMED WRONG TO ME.

My surgery was scheduled to take place a week before Christmas. My parents asked if it could be done after the holidays, but Dr.

Lang said it was too risky to wait.

I was sitting in my room. It was the last night my leg and I would spend together. I didn't know what bone cancer looked like, but I imagined it to be black in color and gooey. It was hard to believe that between my knee and ankle this black goo was eating away a part of my body.

I tucked my left leg beneath me. I wanted to prepare myself for how my body would look after surgery. I looked online at some pictures of amputees. In the photos, the people were surfing, skiing, and hiking mountains. I did none of those things now and hoped that I wouldn't be peer pressured into becoming a shining example of how full a life without limbs could be.

I took a deep breath then quickly looked. When I saw only my right leg out in front of me, reality set in. Things had been so hectic the past few weeks that I hardly had time to think. All my focus had been on the actual surgery date, the chemo schedule, and learning about the cancer. What was life going to *be* like as an amputee? After everyone goes back to their normal lives, what was my life going to be like. At this time tomorrow, a part of me would be gone.

I straightened my leg back out, rubbed it with some strawberry scented body lotion, dressed it up in my cute red patent leather heels, and took a few pictures of it with my phone. My leg was getting the royal treatment on its last night. After all, it had been with me almost twenty years and had served me well. Giving it a proper sendoff was the right thing to do. After the fifteenth picture I took of my leg, my phone chimed with a text.

Noah: I'm at your window. Park?

Noah and I agreed not to discuss what happened at the condo the other day. I had too many things on my mind that took priority. We'd deal with it, just not now.

Me: I don't think I can make it there. My leg is hurting.

Noah: Put your coat on. I have a surprise for you.

Me: What is it?

Noah: A surprise. I'm headed to your front door. :)

Noah carried me the entire three blocks to the park. There was no other place I wanted to be tonight than in his arms. Instead of taking me over to our spot, he headed to the fire pit area. He placed me in a chair, and draped a big fleece blanket over me that he had already brought here. I watched as he built a fire. He was wearing his high school letterman jacket and a College of Charleston baseball cap twisted backwards. He looked so cute. It was sweet the way he was trying to get my mind off of tomorrow.

Sitting beside me, he poured two cups of hot chocolate from the thermos that was sitting by his chair. I lifted the blanket up as he scooted his chair closer and joined me underneath. I snuggled into his side as his arm draped over my shoulders and he pulled me closer to him. Through my coat I could feel his hand running slowly back and forth over my shoulder. We were quiet for a while drinking our hot chocolate. My eyes shifted between looking at the fire and the beautiful clear sky filled with stars. It was as if Noah had ordered those stars just for tonight.

"This is perfect." The words drifted from my mouth as a whisper.

"Yeah, it is," he said.

"Thank you for this, Noah." His arm squeezed my shoulders slightly.

"Tweet?"

"Mmmhmm?"

"I'm sorry."

I shifted, looking up at him. "For what?"

He focused straight ahead. The light from the fire caused the tears running down his face to glisten.

"That night you sprained your ankle … I should have taken you to the ER. If I had done that … maybe they would have caught the cancer sooner and could have saved your leg."

I sat my cup of hot chocolate down. Twisting my body completely toward him, I threw my arms around his neck and squeezed.

"Don't do that to yourself. It's no one's fault," I whispered, choking back my tears. I was completely overwhelmed by how deeply he cared for me.

"We're going to get through this. I'm going to be with you every step of the way," he said.

"Are you trying to be funny?" I asked teasingly. He broke from our hug and look into my eyes.

"Sorry about that." There was complete determination in his face when he said, "We are going to get through this."

I wanted to believe it and in that moment I did. In that moment, snuggling under a blanket watching the fire with Noah was perfect. I didn't feel like I had cancer and that I was going to have surgery in the morning.

We drank hot chocolate and watched the flames until they turned into glowing embers. We didn't say much more to each other. We didn't need to. I took a break from thoughts of cancer, surgery, chemo, and my future. I wasn't going to let anything ruin this moment for me. The present was perfect and I was going to stay in it for as long as possible.

When I heard I had to be at the hospital at 5 am for a 7 am surgery, I thought they were screwing with me. Wasn't it enough that I was getting my leg sawed off? Now I had to get up early too? This being a cancer patient thing sucked.

The hospital was fairly quiet at that ungodly hour. When I walked into the waiting area, I could feel the nervous energy surrounding the patients waiting to be called back for their surgery. In attendance with me this morning was Mom, Dad, and Emily. It had been a while since we had all done something together. I may be saying goodbye to my leg today, but we got a family trip out of it. Lemonade! I'm trying like hell to make lemonade out of all this.

Mom sat staring at nothing. Dad paced back and forth between where we sat and the free coffee that was set up in the corner of the room. Emily spent her time trying to engage us in conversation. She talks *a lot* when she's nervous. I may have looked calm on the outside, but my nerves were in overdrive. My stomach alternated between feeling nauseous and sinking into the ground.

All I wanted to do was stop time from moving forward. I

wanted to run. I wasn't strong enough to get through this—the amputation, the chemo, or the cancer. Once I walked through that door, there was no turning back. If I was going to bolt out of there, I needed to do it now. I started to lean forward in my chair, when the door swung open.

The face of each patient flinched as a nurse stepped out. She scanned the room, and said, "Amanda Kelly?"

Shit, I was up. I didn't react. I hadn't had enough time to adjust. I needed more time. The nurse called my name again. I felt the eyes of my parents and sister on me.

Mom leaned over and whispered, "Sweetheart, it's time." My dad walked back to us as Mom, Emily and I stood.

The nurse approached our little group. "Amanda Kelly?"

"Yes." That one little word had me almost in tears.

"You can come with me." All four of us started to follow her, when she abruptly stopped, looked at my parents and said, "You'll be able to come back once we have Amanda all set up. I'll come get you."

I lifted my head up to my mom's with pleading eyes. I didn't want to go alone. Her eyes overflowed with sorrow. I knew it was killing her that she was powerless to make this all go away for me. "Amanda, we will be back there the minute they say we can." I just nodded my head and desperately tried to hold back my tears.

I was led down a long sterile hallway. I tried to stay focused on my nurse as she walked ahead of me. I was afraid to pay too much attention to the sights and sounds around me, like a doctor possibly running past me laughing in a demonic way as he revved up a chainsaw.

Her shirt was covered with cartoon puppies and her shoes squeaked across the sterile floor. She opened the door to a small holding room with a stretcher, a couple of chairs and an IV pole. I stood there waiting for instructions.

"My name is Sarah and I'll be your nurse today. You can sit up on the stretcher." She flipped through some papers and then asked. "Can you tell me your name and your date of birth?"

"Amanda Kelly. March 23, 1990." She snapped an ID bracelet on my wrist.

"And what type of surgery are we having today?"

"I don't know about you, but I'm having my left leg amputated."

She glanced up from her papers and gave me a slight smirk. Placing the papers at the end of the stretcher, she pulled a flimsy gown, and plastic bag from the built in cabinet behind me.

"You can go ahead and get undressed and put this gown on. Here's a bag to put your things in. Make sure you take off all jewelry. The anesthesiologist will be in soon and I'll be back to start your IV." She left and closed the door behind her.

I dressed in the fashionable gown and placed my clothes in the bag. As soon as I had crawled under the covers, the door swung open. A happy smiling man dressed in scrubs came in, followed by another nurse and then Nurse Sarah.

The nurses took positions on either side of the stretcher as Dr. Smiles extended his hand to me. "Amanda Kelly?" I nodded. "Hi, I'm Dr. McFadden, anesthesiology."

"Hi."

He sat down in one of the chairs and flipped through a folder. "Can you tell me your date of birth and what type of surgery you're having done?"

"March 23, 1990 and left leg amputation." I felt like I was on a demented game show, *The Wheel of Misfortune*."

As Dr. Smiles was rattling off how he was going to knock me out, the nurse to the left of me took my blood pressure as Nurse Sarah tapped my right arm in various places.

"What are you doing?" I asked.

"I'm looking for a vein to start your IV." She tapped the top of my right hand a couple of times and uttered, "That one looks nice and plump."

The doctor was still rattling on, the other nurse was shoving a thermometer in my mouth, and I saw a huge needle headed towards my hand. There was too much happening at one time. I couldn't focus on any one thing. I had never felt this helpless and unsure of what was going on. I winced as the needle pierced my skin. A few tears began to trickle down my cheek.

Nurse Sarah looked up, her expression apologetic. "I'm sorry. I didn't mean to hurt you." I wondered if she thought it would feel great as she shoved a sharp pointy object into my skin.

Things were being done without anyone asking me first. Before leaving, the doctor said, "I'll be back in a bit to give you some happy juice." I didn't know what he was talking about. I was too focused on the mound of tape Nurse Sarah was wrapping around my IV.

She finished torturing me and then said, "I'll go get your family. Dr. Lang will be in to check on you before we take you back."

"Thanks."

"Can I get you anything?"

"Out of here." I smirked.

Both nurses gathered all their things and headed out of the room. Before closing the door, Nurse Sarah leaned in and said, "I know it's pretty scary. Dr. Lang is one of the best in the country." She gave me a small smile. "I'll go tell your family they can come back."

Minutes later Mom, Dad, and Emily filed into the tiny room. Mom and Emily sat while Dad remained standing. He looked like a caged animal. Sitting and waiting were not his forte. He was more comfortable doing something than sitting and staring at the four walls. This whole situation was hard on both my parents, but I think Dad was slightly more affected than Mom. He was used to being my protector and he couldn't be that now.

At 6:30 Dr. Lang came in to check on me and reassure me that he thought I'd do fine during the surgery. After he left, Nurse Sarah came in and told me and my family that I was about to be taken back, so we needed to say our goodbyes.

Emily got up first and gave me a long hug. I couldn't hold my tears back any longer. I clutched onto her tightly, knowing that when I let go, I was one second closer to the operating room. "Don't cry, Manda. We're going to get you through this. I love you." I nodded my head, which was glued to the crook of her neck. Emily left the room in tears.

When Mom and Dad stepped up, Mom's arms immediately wrapped around me. "I love you, Amanda, and I'm so proud of you." she said, repeatedly.

I looked up at my dad, who was standing on the other side. He was quietly crying. I had never seen Daddy cry before. It broke my heart knowing that I was the cause of his tears. "I'm sorry, Daddy," was the only thing I could think to say. He bent down and kissed the top of my head.

"You have nothing to be sorry about, Princess. I just wish it was me instead of you getting ready to go through this."

The door opened and Dr. Smiles poked his head in, signaling to my parents it was time for them to leave. "We'll take good care of her," he said as they passed by, before directing his attention on me. "So you ready to feel happy?" I nodded as I wiped my face dry.

He had a syringe of something and shot it through the IV tube. Within seconds, I felt the medication and it was awesome. While I was on a fast train to Loopyville, I heard a commotion outside my door. Dr. Smiles opened it to see what was going on.

I heard a female voice that sounded like my nurse say, "Young man, you can't go in there now. She's about to go back to surgery."

"I got caught in traffic. I'll only stay a second. Please. I'm her brother."

I thought it was so nice of my brother to come see me, and then I remembered I didn't have a brother. Did I?

"He can come in for a few minutes," Dr. Smiles said to the female voice.

I turned my head towards the door. A huge smile spread across my face, partly because of the happy juice, but mostly because my knight in plastic armor was here to save me. "I just gave her some medicine, so she's pretty loopy right now."

"Thanks," Noah said, walking over and sitting by me on the stretcher. I felt his hand glide down the side of my face. "Hey Tweet. How are you feeling?"

"Gooood." He chuckled.

"I'm sorry I didn't get here sooner. There was an accident and I was stuck in traffic."

"That's alright, my brother. It's all good. You're here now. Grab my clothes and let's go." I sat up bringing us face-to-face.

"Tweet, you can't leave right now."

I narrowed my eyes at him and grinned. "You want to hook up? This gown has easy access and I got nothing on underneath it."

We stared at each other for a few seconds before the door was opened, startling both of us, and Nurse Sarah walked in. I kept my eyes on Noah for another second. Even in my foggy state, I could see all the love he had for me in his eyes. I hoped he could see the love I had for him in mine.

He stood allowing Nurse Sarah to come around the back of the stretcher and start pushing me out the door. "Nurse Sarah, has anyone ever told you, you were a buzz kill?" I heard her laugh behind me.

"I've been called worse."

"This is my Noah. Isn't he hot?"

"He's very handsome," she said.

"He's an awesome kisser too. His tongue tastes like thin mints. He's even touched my boobs and …"

"Tweet, I don't think the nurse cares about any of that," Noah interrupted.

Stepping around to my side, Nurse Sarah asked, "I thought you were her brother?" She looked at me and then at Noah, giving us both a knowing smile.

"We're a very close family." I heard Noah say, as I was pushed out the door and down the hall.

The operating room was freezing and extremely bright. Once I was on the table, the nurses got to work. They reminded me of a NASCAR pit crew. Everyone had their specific job. One nurse made sure my IV had the right medicine. One nurse covered me in warm blankets. One nurse attached electrodes to various parts of my body. Then I saw Dr. Smiles hovering over me.

"Amanda, I'm going to put this mask on you and give you a little oxygen. Just breathe deeply." I did as I was told. It was unnerving not being able to look up at what people were doing to me. Turning my head slightly, I could see a tray covered with a blue cloth. I assumed those were the surgical instruments. Me being the masochist I am, I looked up what type of saw was used to amputate legs. The thirteen-inch stainless steel bone saw sold for $17.99 and had a five star rating on Amazon. Customers who bought this also bought a $39.90 chef's knife.

I turned my gaze back up and saw Dr. Smiles hovering over me again. "Amanda, we're almost ready. I'm going to give you some medicine that will put you to sleep." I looked up at him. I could feel the tears, falling down the side of my face. This was it. There was no turning back now. The time had come and things were completely out of my control. The medicine took over and my eyelids closed as I left my old life behind.

Entry 29

YOUR STRENGTH AND CHARACTER GROW STRONGER AND DEEPER WHILE YOU WAIT FOR HOPE TO RETURN.

I was at Emily's place, sitting in an almost exact replica of my bedroom at home. My parents had basically moved my bedroom from our house over to here. They wanted me to feel comfortable and thought being surrounded by familiar things would achieve that.

My hospital stay lasted four days. The first two days, I was so drugged up with morphine, I didn't know what was happening. Day three, my head was clearer and physical therapy started. They got me out of bed and had me using a walker to walk to the recliner in the corner of the room. Little by little I inched my way to it, my arms straining from bearing my weight. It was probably six steps away from my bed. I was exhausted by the time I got to the chair.

I had only glanced down once, very quickly, at my residual limb. I was informed that it's not politically correct to call it a stump anymore. I figured that if I wanted to call it a stump though, I would. It was my stump, after all. I still hadn't built up the courage to look at the stump side-by-side with my right leg.

Mom stayed with me all day and Dad and Emily visited at night after work. I don't know how he did it, but somehow Noah managed to sneak in my room and stay with me all night. No doubt, he flashed his sexy smile, winked his bright light blues a few times, and completely charmed the panties off of the night nurse.

Day four, I was discharged and would do physical therapy three times a week. In two weeks, if my surgical site was healed well enough I would start the process of being fitted for a temporary prosthesis and start chemo. Good times.

The two things that I was most afraid of right were starting chemo and having phantom pain. It felt like the lower portion of my left leg was still there. It was a mind fuck when I looked down and saw no leg. Dr. Lang said not every amputee experiences phantom pain. I was hoping that would be the case for me.

Before the official physical therapy started, the doctor had given me instructions on activities to do at home. I was to walk around the apartment using the walker, do some stretching exercises, and that was it. I was resting on the bed, leaning against the headboard, with my legs stretched out in front of me, when my eyes trailed down and froze. This was the first time I had allowed myself to look at my legs side-by-side. I stared for a long time feeling very detached from my lower limbs, as if they didn't belong to me.

Slowly the realization washed over me that this half leg was mine. Quiet tears started flowing out of me. It was gone. A part of me that had always been there, wasn't coming back. All I could do was adjust.

I told myself that I hadn't ever given much thought to that portion of my leg in the past. I told myself, that that part of my leg would have definitely killed me if I had kept it. I told myself that once I was fitted with a prosthesis I'd be able to walk again. I tried to convince myself that I shouldn't be upset. I should be grateful.

The problem is you can't reason with loss, you can only feel it. In that moment, all I felt was how much I missed my leg, and that maybe I had made a huge mistake.

I wasn't sure what to do. Talking about it with someone wasn't going to bring my leg back, nothing would. I don't get a do over or a second chance.

Six days had passed since the surgery. Emily, Noah, and I had ordered pizza for dinner and we were now watching a movie. I wasn't feeling well. I didn't have a headache or stomachache. I just felt uncomfortable in my skin. My mind and nerve endings were still telling me that the amputated part of my leg was still there. The sensation started to change into feeling like I was wearing a tight shoe. It wasn't painful, just annoying.

"I'm going to go to bed," I said.

"You alright?" Emily asked.

"Yeah, I think I'm just tired." I started rolling away in my wheelchair.

"You need any help, Tweet?"

"No, I'll be fine. Goodnight."

I entered my room, threw on my pajama pants, t-shirt, and got into bed. The tight shoe sensation kept getting worse and worse until it felt more like a vice had been clamped onto my leg. Then out of nowhere, a jolt of pain shot through the lower part of my leg that wasn't there. I let out a blood curdling scream.

Noah was the first to burst through my door, followed quickly by Emily. I was screaming and sobbing uncontrollably, I couldn't tell them what was happening. Noah sat on the side of the bed and scooped me into his arms. The pain was relentless. Someone needed to take the vice off my leg, but there was no visible vice to remove.

I kept screaming into Noah's chest as the pain grew more intense. My body convulsed with every jolt of electricity that shot through me. Emily stood at the end of my bed looking helpless, tears running down her cheeks. There was nothing anyone could do because there was nothing there. Noah started rubbing my back trying to calm me down.

One hour turned into two, turned into three. By the time we were headed into the fourth hour, I thought I was going to lose my mind. The pain started to ebb and flow. I got some relief for fifteen or twenty minutes and then the vice would start to twist and tighten again, and the shockwaves would return, surprising me every time.

As the sun started to come up, the pain subsided. Noah still had his arms wrapped around me, rubbing my back. My head rested on his chest, my eyes were closed, but I wasn't sleeping yet. I was completely drained. I had never experienced anything like it in my life.

I heard the door open and Emily come in. "Noah, I think she's asleep now. Why don't you go home and try to do the same. You look exhausted," she whispered.

"I'm fine. I'm not leaving her." Emily didn't force the issue. The next sound I heard was the click of the door closing.

On Christmas day my parents, Mrs. Stewart, and Noah came over to Emily's to exchange gifts and have dinner. I wondered what was going on with Noah and Brooke. He had been with me almost constantly since my surgery. He never brought it up and I never asked. I was afraid if I did, he would feel guilty about being away from Brooke and disappear.

Wine was poured and gifts were exchanged before dinner. I felt bad. The past few weeks had been such a whirlwind, I hadn't been able to get anyone a gift. All the ladies retreated to the kitchen to get the food ready while Dad went to open another bottle of wine, leaving Noah and me alone.

"There's one more gift." He handed me a small black velvet jewelry box. "Merry Christmas, Tweet."

"Noah, you and your mom already gave me a gift. The cashmere sweaters were from both of you," I said.

"Yeah, my mom picked those out. Today was the first time I had seen them."

"I'm sorry I wasn't able to get you anything."

"Would you shut up and open the box?" He smiled at me.

I lifted the top of the hinged lid. Inside was the most beautiful pair of yellow diamond stud earrings. My mouth literally dropped open. I was speechless. I looked up at him, stunned.

"I take it you like them?" he asked, smirking.

"I don't know what to say. This is too much."

"Do you like them?"

"I love them." I smiled at him.

"Seeing that smile, made them totally worth it."

I bit my bottom lip, trying to hold the tears back. I didn't think it was possible to love him more than I already did, but I was wrong.

I wanted to tell him how much I loved him. I wanted him to know he is my first and only love. I wanted to say all of that, but I didn't. I wish I hadn't wasted all this time trying not to love him, but I did, and now it's too late. I won't saddle him with me, not with the way I am now. He needs to live his life and not spend it being a nurse to me. I kept my mouth shut and looked down at the beautiful gift.

"Dinner's ready," we heard my mom say from the kitchen.

"Listen, I have to get going," Noah said.

"You're not staying to eat?"

"I'm going to go eat with Brooke's family." He looked away from me, as if he were embarrassed. I guess I just got my answer about what was going on with them. They're still together.

A wave of self-pity and disappointment flowed through me. I had spent the past few weeks being with Noah almost constantly, and it still wasn't enough time with him. I was used to him being by my side and I didn't want him to go. I would have to face the phantom pain by myself tonight. I already felt alone and he was sitting right in front of me.

I looked up with tears streaming down my face. "Why are you crying?" he asked.

I shook my head and lied. "I'm just tired and the holidays make me sentimental." I forced a smile.

Cupping my face, he ran his thumbs over my cheeks, wiping away my tears. "You want me to push you to the table?"

"No. I'll do it in a minute."

Standing he said, "You call me if you need me." I nodded. "Merry Christmas, Tweet."

"Merry Christmas, Noah."

He said his goodbyes to the others and walked out the door.

"You need some help, princess?" my dad asked as he entered the room.

I shook my head. "I'll be right there, Daddy."

I rolled into my bedroom as quickly as possible and closed the door. Grabbing a pillow off my bed, I hugged it to my chest, and cried into it. There was a gnawing ache in the pit of my stomach. I felt all alone. I was glad Noah was spending Christmas with his girlfriend. That's how it should be. He was going back to his normal life. Soon everyone would be going back to their normal lives, except me. I'll be adjusting to a new normal.

ENTRY 30

QUALITY VERSUS QUANTITY? MOST PEOPLE WOULD PICK QUALITY. I'D RATHER HAVE ONE REALLY NICE CAR THAN FIVE CRAPPY CARS. ALTHOUGH, M&Ms ARE TASTY, A PIECE OF GODIVA CHOCOLATE IS MORE DELICIOUS AND DECADENT.

WHAT'S MORE IMPORTANT WHEN YOU'RE DEALING WITH A POTENTIALLY FATAL ILLNESS? SHOULD YOU LIVE OUT YOUR LIFE, DOING WHAT YOU WANT, FEELING GOOD UNTIL YOU'RE CLOSE TO THE END OR SHOULD YOU TAKE ADVANTAGE OF EVERY MEDICAL ADVANCEMENT AVAILABLE?

CANCEROUS LIMBS CAN BE SAWED OFF, CANCEROUS SKIN CAN BE SCOOPED OUT, ORGANS REMOVED, AND TOXIC CHEMICALS CAN BE PUMPED INTO YOUR BODY. BUT IS IT WORTH IT? IS THE FEAR OF DEATH GREATER THAN THE FEAR OF LIVING WITH AND FIGHTING CANCER?

TODAY, MY ANSWER IS YES.

Chemo was going to start right after the New Year. I had to go through ten cycles, alternating chemo weeks and off weeks. This would be a part of my life for at least four months, longer if needed. Of all the things I had to do to battle cancer, I was most afraid of chemo. I didn't know if I would lose my hair, throw up all the time, or have ulcers in my mouth. Chemo doesn't only attack the cancer cells, it also hinders your body from making good cells so the probability of infection is high. I had to be extremely careful around other people. A common cold could put me in the hospital for weeks or kill me.

Mom and I pulled into the parking lot of the hospital. I was confused because I was supposed to have the chemo at the clinic. Mom parked the car. Before getting out to get my wheelchair she turned to me, guilt written across her face.

"Amanda, you're not having chemo today. You're having a portacath put in today."

"I don't understand. What is that?"

"It's a catheter that they're going to put right here in your chest." She pointed to the area just below her shoulder. "You'll be asleep while they put it in. It's so when you do get chemo or they need to draw blood, they won't have to stick you. They'll just put the medicine through the catheter," she explained.

"So I'm going to have this thing sticking out of my chest all the time?" I felt the tears prick my eyes. God, I was so done with crying.

"For a little while."

"Why didn't you tell me?"

"Sweetheart, I didn't want you to worry about it over the holidays and have it ruin your Christmas."

"Cause the cancer and amputation made Christmas just a little more special and fun."

Mom looked away from me and out the windshield. Her chin started to quiver and a tear trickled down her face. "I'm sorry, Amanda. I just thought it would be one less thing you needed to deal with over the holidays."

"I know. I'm sorry I was being a smartass."

"I would do anything to take this away from you."

Mom grabbed my hand and brought it to her cheek. I felt her warm tears fall onto it. We sat there crying for as long as possible before heading inside for the procedure.

The next day I had an appointment with my leg guy. As Mom rolled me back into the exam room we passed a wall lined with legs of all different shapes, sizes, and skin tones. When we reached the room we were greeted by David. He was a big guy with a booming voice, but had a sweet way about him. He made me feel comfortable right from the start.

David explained the entire process of creating my new leg and getting me walking again. He would cast my stump today for the test socket. Once it was made, I would come back and if everything fit, he would then make my temporary socket. It was temporary because my stump was still swollen and when the swelling went down I would have to get a new socket. He then explained how the prosthetic would stay on. I'd have to wear a silicone liner which I would roll onto my stump and over my knee. A pin attached to the end of the liner would fit into a hole at the bottom of the socket which would hold the prosthesis in place. He then showed me the prosthetic foot and titanium rod that would be my limb.

David set up his supplies. As he began unwrapping my stump, his hand grazed it. My body became tense and my breathing shallow. No one had touched my stump before, not even me. When I took my bath each day Mom would unwrap it for me and I simply swished it around in the water, never looking down. Tears started building in my eyes. I knew my leg was gone. Everything I did was a constant reminder of that fact: getting in and out of the bathtub, getting on and off the toilet, planning how early I needed to wake up to get dressed for an appointment because it took me three times as long as it used to. Every time I wanted to get out of my wheelchair, I had to consider whether my tired arms could withstand my weight. Everything I did reminded me of this fucking amputation and how much I missed my leg and my old life. I don't want this new life that was forced on me. And this prosthetic is one more thing that makes this awful new reality, all too real.

My first session of chemo was a few days after they placed the catheter in me. I hated having something sticking out of me. I couldn't look at it.

Mom and I entered a room with recliners lining the walls. Each had its own IV pole. There were only a couple of chairs open. This cancer was trying to mow down everybody. I picked one of the two recliners available and sat. Once the nurse came in she wiped the end of my catheter with an alcohol swab before she drew my blood from it. She wiped it again with another alcohol swab, hung a couple of bags filled with saline and steroids, and told me they were waiting for the chemo drugs to come from the pharmacy.

Mom read a magazine while I snuck glances at the faces surrounding me. There were two grandmother age ladies, a granddaddy age man, a guy that looked to be my age, who was pretty cute, and a young girl, who couldn't have been more than 10 years old.

My nurse returned carrying bright green baggies that I soon found out contained the chemo drugs. I put in my ear buds, closed my eyes and turned Lifehouse up as high as I could without disturbing the other people, while the toxic concoction was pumped into my bloodstream.

Forty-five minutes into chemo, I still felt okay. Maybe it wouldn't be as bad as I thought. I opened my eyes and removed my ear buds when Mom tapped me on the shoulder. "Sweetheart, will you be okay if I go get a cup of coffee?"

"Sure."

"Do you want anything?" she asked.

"No thanks."

As she walked out the room, I noticed that most of the chairs were empty. The patients who had been there when Mom and I arrived had all gone, except for the cute guy. I placed the ear buds back in and closed my eyes.

Soon after, I felt a tap on my arm. I turned my head and opened my eyes thinking Mom had forgotten something. I was met by the deepest dark blue eyes I had ever seen. It was the cute guy from across the room, only up close he was more than just cute. His hair was light brown, cut short and looked like he had just gotten out of bed. His chiseled jawline was speckled with a light beard and I would kill for his cheekbones and nose. Both were perfect. He was leaning over the arm of the chair slightly, staring and smiling at me. He was a hottie.

"Can I help you?" I asked removing my ear buds.

"Nah, I'm good." He stayed like that for a few more seconds. Oddly enough, it didn't bother me to have a cute sexy stranger this close.

Then he grabbed my iPod, sat back in his chair, and started flipping through it. "Let's see what we have here. Lifehouse," he said, nodding his approval. "Snow Patrol, nice. Green Day, awesome. Tracey Chapman, cool. Coldplay and Linkin Park, excellent taste. Oh, oh, oh … wait a sec … what's this?" Shaking his head he said, "I thought for a minute, you were the love of my life."

"Really? What changed your mind?"

"N'Sync. Breaks my heart."

"There's nothing wrong with them. They gave us JT."

Arching one eyebrow, he said, "True. They also gave us Joey Fatone." I returned the smile he flashed at me. "Dalton Connor." We shook hands.

"Amanda Kelly."

"It's nice to meet you, Amanda Kelly. I wish we could have worked something out."

"It was fun while it lasted," I said, as he handed my iPod back.

I noticed he had picked his up. I snatched it from him and started flipping through songs.

"Let's see what we have here. The Police … hmmm. The Stones, Eric Clapton, You're an old schooler." I flipped through a few more songs. "Now what do we have here? *The Bodyguard* soundtrack, *Whitney Houston-The Ultimate Collection, Just Whitney*, and of course, no collection would be complete without *I'm Your Baby Tonight*." Smirking with satisfaction, I glanced over at him. "What do you have to say for yourself?"

"I'm a romantic." I tossed his iPod back to him.

"So, what's a hot girl with one leg doing in a place like this?"

"Um ... I have the cancer."

"That's pretty obvious, smartass. What kind?" he asked.

"Osteosarcoma."

"Stage?" I looked at him in obvious confusion. "What stage is your cancer? One through four, four being the worst or the best depending on your perspective."

"I have no idea."

"You're such a newb. I have stage four brain cancer. It's full throttle for me, baby." I didn't know what to say to that, so I just stared at him. "Don't worry, though. I will guide you through the treacherous waters of the cancer ocean and teach you my ways, young grasshopper."

"I appreciate that Mr. Miyagi."

He shook his head. "Not only are you mixing TV with movie characters, but Kung Fu and The Karate Kid are like a decade apart."

"Your point?"

Slowly the corners of his mouth curled up into a mischievous grin. He leaned in close to me like he had a secret. "Amanda Kelly, are you legal?"

"What?"

"Are you legal age?"

"Why?"

"Because when you finally give into your desires, rip my clothes off, and have your way with me, I don't want to be arrested, and end up the girlfriend of inmate 25043."

"I thought you didn't want me to be your girl because of my

poor choice in music."

"True, but you're hot and I'd still fuck you."

If anyone else, on our first meeting, had said that to me, I would have been completely offended, but coming from this boy, it made me smile.

"You're disgusting," I teased.

"I'm also adorable as hell. All the girls think so," he said, winking at me.

"Apparently, they're not the only ones who think that."

"I like you, Amanda Kelly, and I want you to be my friend."

"I like you too, Dalton Connor, and I'd be proud to be your friend." We shook hands sealing our new found friendship.

"So, the lady with you is your mom?"

"Yeah. Who's here with you?" I asked.

"I'm ridin' solo."

"Where's your mom?"

"Let's see, today is Wednesday … she's probably on her third margarita while she sits with my dad on the cruise ship."

"They're on a trip while you're sick?"

"I've been sick for so long I don't remember a time when I wasn't. Other people can't stop living their lives just because mine is coming to an end."

I felt my heart completely break for this boy.

He interrupted my train of thought, saying, "Don't look at me like that."

"Like what?"

"With pity."

"I'm sorry. It's just … you shouldn't have to go through this alone."

"I won't now that I have you."

Dalton sat with me for the rest of my chemo that day, even though his was done an hour before mine. He met Mom and charmed her, just as much as he had me. He had been diagnosed when he was fifteen and just turned twenty in December. He told me his doctors were shocked that he had survived this long. He had one brother who lived in New York, but other than his parents, he didn't have any other family here.

There was something about this boy that I immediately connected with, besides the common denominator of cancer. I had only had that feeling before with Noah. Dalton was sweet, funny, smart, brave, and alone. I wanted him to come home with us, so I could take care of him. I had only known him for one afternoon and I felt like I had a new best friend.

Entry 31

Today is the first time I haven't felt like writing since I learned how to write. There have been days when I didn't know what to write about, but the desire to write was always there.

Writing is such a part of who I am. My identity. Cancer is not only eating away at my body, it's eating away at what I love. I don't consider myself a very strong person. I don't know how much I can take before I break. I just know I feel the crack becoming longer and wider each time the cancer devours another part of me.

The side effects of chemo are worse than the symptoms of cancer. A person could live for years with cancer growing inside them and never know it until a doctor tells them so. Cancer is a quiet bastard that sneaks in and consumes you before you realize what's happened.

Chemo, on the other hand, is loud and proud. It won't let you forget about it. Not only does it let you know that it's invading your body at the clinic, it follows you home and moves in. I started feeling the effects shortly after I had gotten home from treatment number one.

At first, I thought all the stress and anxiety I had during the day was crashing in on me. As the day went on, I felt progressively worse. The first visible sign of the cancer killing chemicals flowing through my body was the first time I went to the bathroom. My pee was red and freaked me out. I really should have read all the info Dr. Lang gave me.

The second side effect was the sensation of heat building up inside me. It started in my chest and then radiated throughout my entire body. That, coupled with the phantom pain I was still experiencing, made me want to blow my brains out.

The next day I woke up, after only an hour's worth of sleep, flushed red all over my body and my face was hot and puffy. Later that day, I started getting very intense indigestion and some hiccups. The hiccups were not of the normal variety. They were so forceful that they shook my body and lasted for an hour or so at a time.

The nausea started settling in, a couple of hours after the indigestion started. The nausea was also not of the normal variety. Chemo nausea was a sharp pain that continuously stabbed at my stomach. It reminded me of the phantom pain I had. The pain shocks me because it came out of nowhere. Each time I threw up, my throat burned a little more until it was completely raw. The nausea was relentless. I had thrown up all the contents of my stomach after three episodes. From then on, I had dry heaves that left my stomach and back in unbearable pain.

I always thought chemo took your appetite away. Maybe for some it did but for me, my appetite skyrocketed. I was starving. I wanted to eat and I tried to, but I had developed a couple of ulcers in my mouth and the pain I felt when any food or drink washed over them wasn't worth it.

By day three post first chemo I was completely exhausted. I don't mean a little tired. I mean I could barely lift my head up off the pillow exhausted. I had lived on milkshakes and apple juice for three days before the diarrhea started and it burned as if someone had taken a hot poker and shoved it up my ass and left it there.

I felt depression setting in. I was still mourning the loss of my leg and the effects of the chemo were causing me to fall deeper into despair. I couldn't do this. I wasn't strong enough. I considered calling Dr. Lang and telling him I wanted to stop the chemo and just take my chances.

Noah called me several times a day wanting to come over, but I just couldn't let him see me this way. Besides, his second semester had started and there was Brooke. He didn't need to spend time watching me throw up. I also decided that I needed to pull away from him some. After the way I felt watching him walk out the door Christmas day, I knew I was becoming more dependent on him and at some point, I wouldn't be able to let him go. I made a promise to myself that I was not going to burden Noah with any of this. I wanted him to have a happy normal life, not one being a nurse to me.

I was sitting in my wheelchair, my new leg attached, waiting on my first official physical therapy session to begin. I was scheduled to be here at least an hour, so Mom went to do some shopping while I learned how to carry this ten ton piece of titanium around. Looking around the room I saw an elderly man who had obviously suffered a stroke, a child's puzzle toy in front of him. He was desperately trying to match the shapes to the correct opening in the red and blue plastic holder. A middle-aged woman moaned every now and again as her therapist helped her with stretching exercises on an elevated padded mat. Then I saw him. He was leaning up against the doorframe, arms crossed in front of him, super dark sunglasses hiding his deep blue eyes. A sexy grin plastered on his face. I felt a tickle of excitement through my body. Finally a friendly face.

"Hey, baby." He pushed his glasses back on this head and sauntered over to me.

"Hey Dalton. What are you doing here?"

Placing his hands on the armrests of my chair, he leaned in, bringing us face-to-face, and said, "You're going to stand up and walk today, right?"

"That's what they tell me."

"Well, that's why I'm here. There was no way in hell I was going to miss being introduced to your sweet little round ass as it swayed back and forth between those parallel bars." He gave me a wink.

"Is everything sexual to you?" I asked.

"I'm a 20-year-old, heterosexual male, with stage four cancer … Um … Yeah."

I felt my throat begin to close up as I choked back tears. I was scared about what the future held for this smart, funny, sweet, sexy boy in front of me. "Don't do that," I said in a low voice.

"Do what?"

"Make jokes about being sick. It's not funny."

"I know," he said as he pushed away from me and took a seat against the wall.

Dalton and I sat staring at each other in silence until my therapist walked up.

"Hi, I'm Jane," she said extending her hand to me.

"Hi, Amanda."

Turning to Dalton, Jane said, "Hello Mr. Connor. What trouble are you up to today?"

"I had a little extra time on my hands and thought I'd come and do a little ass watchin' and gropin'."

I looked between the two and asked, "Ya'll know each other?"

"Jane is single handedly responsible for the breathtaking beautiful male figure you see before you."

Jane smiled and said, "After Dalton's first brain surgery he needed to work a little on his motor skills."

"How many brain surgeries have you had?"

His expression turned from flirty to serious. "Enough to last me a lifetime."

The next hour was spent trying to stand and walk. It's odd how something I did without thinking about all my life suddenly took so much focus and concentration. The prosthesis didn't hurt. I just felt pressure on the sides of my leg and at the bottom. I couldn't get past my fear that the rod would break the minute I put all my weight on it. I managed to take a few steps and that was all. I was exhausted before the hour was even up. It wasn't that I thought I would be walking like my old self immediately, but I didn't think it was going to be this hard to do something that was once so simple and natural.

My second round of chemo was even worse, if that was possible. I was in the bathroom puking my guts out when I heard voices in the hallway. It was Noah. He and Emily were arguing. "Noah, she's having a bad day."

"I need to see her, Emily."

"Now is not a good time. She's very sick today. The chemo hit her harder this week."

"I want to take care of her."

"Noah, please go …"

"No. She's pushed me away since Christmas and I don't understand why. I promised her we'd get through this together. I haven't seen her in two weeks. I need to see her. Please, Emily."

I heard a soft knock on the door and Emily asked, "Manda, are you okay? Can I come in?"

I sat back on the tile floor, my back resting against the tub. "Yes." My voice sounded so weak. The exhaustion had set in earlier this week than before. I was barely able to sit up.

The door slowly opened and Emily stepped in, closing it behind her. She got a rag, ran warm water over it, and pressed it against my forehead. "Noah's here and he wants to see you."

"Emily …"

"I told him you were sick, but … Manda, if you could see the look on his face. It broke my heart. He looks so sad and lost. He wants to be here for you."

"He doesn't need to spend his life taking care of me," I whispered.

"But I think he wants to."

"I want to go back to bed now."

Emily started helping me up. I was still getting used to my *new* leg. The leg guy said eventually it would feel like an extension of me. But right now, it felt like it weighed a ton and was awkward as hell to maneuver.

Once I was up on my feet, my knees felt weak and collapsed underneath me. My knee caps hit the tile floor hard and sent a piercing pain up my legs. I started to cry uncontrollably. Then I felt the warm protective arms of Noah scoop me up and carry me into my bedroom, all the while he whispered into my hair, "I've got you, Tweet. I'll take care of you."

I couldn't stop crying. I felt so physically and mentally defeated, I couldn't pull myself together. Emily was standing in the doorway with tears running down her face. Sitting in front of me on the bed, Noah brought his hands up to my face, and wiped my tears away with this thumbs.

I looked at him through blurred vision and said, "I'm so ashamed."

"Why?" he asked.

"Because I can't do anything for myself anymore. Every part of my body feels sick. I just want to die." I looked up at him with pleading eyes. "Noah, tell them to let me go." My sobs became so heavy, I was having a hard time catching my breath. I heard Emily crying louder.

Noah shifted to sit behind me and enveloped me in his arms, my back pressed securely to his chest. He buried his face in my neck. I felt it get wet with his tears as he whispered, "I can't do that. I need you too much. Don't leave me."

I fell asleep and slept soundly the entire night for the first time in over a week. When I woke up the next morning, he still had his arms around me.

Dalton helped get me through my bad days as much as possible. He called every day to check on me and came over to hang out when he was having a good day. He even went to the hospital with me when they removed my portacath. It got infected. Since all these chemo drugs were in me, my immune system was shot to hell, so the catheter needed to be removed immediately. I told Dr. Lang I didn't want another one. I hated the idea and look of something under my skin, always sticking out of my body. I would just suck it up and deal with the IV sticks for chemo.

I don't know how I would have gotten through everything without Dalton. My family and Noah were a tremendous help, but they could only empathize. Dalton knew what my body was feeling and how my mind was trying to process it all. I didn't have to explain anything to him. He read me just as well as Noah.

I had become very attached to Dalton, in a relatively short period of time. And I could tell my parents and Emily were concerned that I was becoming too attached by the looks on their faces whenever they saw us together or when I talked about him. I didn't know what my feelings were toward him. I just knew I needed him in my life. I always thought there was one soul mate out there for each person. Dalton made me think twice about that. Maybe some people are lucky enough to have two.

The *on* weeks of chemo made me feel like I was living in that movie *Groundhog's Day*. I've had four cycles so far and they were almost identical, same nausea, vomiting, exhaustion, etc. The only good thing about *on* weeks was that Dalton and I spent a lot of time together. We started spending time together during our *off* weeks too, but it was during our chemo weeks that we really bonded. We were both stuck in that room for at least four hours, so there wasn't much else to do, but talk.

I felt like I had known Dalton all my life and it had just been two months. There was a comfort I felt with him that I didn't feel with other people right now, including my family and even Noah. Ever since this whole cancer thing started, I just wanted to feel normal and Dalton made me feel that way, even when we were both being pumped full of chemicals. Everyone else talked to me about cancer or the amputation.

"Favorite movie?" he asked.

"I have four actually."

"You can't have four," he protested.

"Why not?"

"*Favorite, a person or thing regarded with favor or preference.* You can have a favorite drama and a favorite comedy, but you can't have multiple favorites in the same category." I looked at him with my eyebrows furrowed together. Him and his crazy rules.

"I have four …" I held up four fingers and wiggled them in front of his face. "… favorite comedies." He just huffed and shook his head at me.

"*The Breakfast Club*, *Ferris Bueller*, *The Jerk*, and *Forest Gump*."

"Aw, I see you are a fan of the classics."

"Oh, and anything with George Clooney in it." He shook his head at me again. "What is your favorite?"

"Die Hard."

"Which one?" I asked.

"All of them."

"You just berated me for having four favorites. There are five Die Hard movies."

"They're installments of the same movie."

"Your logic is convoluted."

"A little too intellectual for you to comprehend?"

"Bite me."

"Hot damn! I've been waiting two months for you to let me do that." I laughed out loud startling Estelle, one of the elderly ladies who had her chemo on the same day as Dalton and I.

"Favorite line from a movie?" I asked.

"Are you serious? *Yippee ki-yay, motherfucker*." I made no attempt at hiding my eye roll.

Dalton closed his eyes and rested his head back against the chair. We sat in relaxed silence. Looking around the room I noticed that Dalton, Estelle, and I were the only ones left. "Hey, Dalton?"

"Mmmhmm?"

"Ashley isn't here today and she wasn't here the last chemo day." Ashley was a little girl I had seen the first day of chemo. She was quiet and kept to herself, but very sweet. "I wonder why."

"Dead." His words shocked me.

"What?" He turned his head toward me and opened his eyes.

"I said she's dead."

"Dalton, that's a terrible thing to say. You don't know."

"Yes I do. I went to her funeral last week."

"Why didn't you tell me? I would have gone."

"I didn't think your first cancer funeral should be that of a 10-year-old's. They're pretty rough."

I stared straight ahead, not knowing what to say. I felt a warm hand cover mine and lightly squeeze, causing me to look over at him. "Hey, are you okay?" he asked.

"Yeah. I thought maybe she had gotten better and didn't need to come here anymore. Stupid, right?"

"Not stupid, just naive."

"Are you afraid of dying?" I asked.

He turned his head and looked toward the ceiling, contemplating his answer. "Yes, I'm afraid of dying, but I'm not afraid of being dead."

"What's the difference?"

"Dying is a process. Dead means you've already arrived at your destination." He turned to me, his dark blue eyes pierced mine as if they could see all the way into my soul. "What about you? Are you afraid of dying?"

"Lately, I feel like I'm afraid of everything, dying, living, Tuesdays."

I noticed that we were still holding hands. It felt really nice and really right. I was becoming confused about the feelings I was developing for this boy. They weren't as strong as my feelings for Noah, but given time I was afraid they could be. I needed to change the subject.

Pulling my hand away from his and using it to tuck some of my hair behind my ear, I said, "My friend, Lisa is coming for a visit next weekend. It's the beginning of her spring break and she's going to spend a couple of days here before heading to Florida."

"This is the cute little redhead you showed me a picture of?"

"Yep."

"You think she'd let me bang her?"

"You're a pig."

"What?! I'm just asking. A cute little redhead, ready to blow off some steam during spring break … she might as well start by blowing me." I narrowed my eyes at him.

I had texted a picture of Dalton to Lisa when I first met him and she thought he was hot.

"She probably would. She thinks you're hot."

He slid across the back of the chair in my direction. A huge grin plastered across his face. "And how does she know what I look like?"

"I may have texted her a picture of you a few weeks ago."

"Sweet. Do you have a pen and some paper?"

"I think so." I searched through my bag and came up with a pen and scrap of paper. "Here."

He straightened up in his chair and flipped his hand toward me. "Take this down," he said.

"When did I become your secretary?"

"Gatorade, vitamins, protein drink, double A batteries, pancake syrup, Vaseline, a paint brush-soft bristles, rope, duct tape, and a pack of pens. I'm out of pens. Oh, and …" He slid back across the back of the chair in my direction, smiling, and in a low voice said, "Trojan Magnum, box of 36, the pleasure pack sampler." He leaned away, grinning at me. I just stared at him, speechless and tossed the pen and paper in his lap.

Entry 32

When I was a kid, it felt like it took forever for things like Christmas and my birthday to come around. Soon was never soon enough. In ten seconds, the length of time it takes for a doctor to tell you your diagnosis, you go from thinking the world is full of an infinite amount of time to realizing nothing in this world is infinite.

Everything has a beginning, middle, and end. Before cancer, I didn't give much thought to the end. It's a cruel joke that when you realize there is an end, time starts to move faster, speeding towards it. Life moves pretty fast. Soon can take it's time getting here now.

This entry was inspired by the great philosopher Ferris Bueller... Bueller... Bueller...

I was walking back to our table from the bathroom. As I slipped into the booth beside Dalton I could not believe the conversation my two friends were having.

"So you want to fuck me?"

"Yes, if you're agreeable."

"I'm only staying for a couple of days before heading to Florida. I won't be here much longer."

"Neither will I." My head whipped back and forth between them so fast that I almost got whiplash.

Lisa, Dalton, and I were downtown near the college having lunch at the Hungry Lion, a hole in the wall, with the best burgers around. Lisa had gotten into town early that morning and we met Dalton for lunch. They hit it off immediately, which I knew they would, but I had no idea this would be the topic of their first conversation.

"I can't believe the two of you are sitting here discussing this at lunch, in front of me."

"Time is of the essence, grasshopper," Dalton said, holding up a French fry before tossing in his mouth.

"Dalton speaks the truth." Lisa leaned into the table slightly toward Dalton as if she were about to tell him a secret. "Just so you know upfront … that's the only point of entry I'll allow you. I don't do any back door partying."

Diet Pepsi came flying out of my mouth and I inadvertently snorted it up my nose. Lisa and Dalton burst into a fit of laughter.

Once he stopped laughing and recovered the ability to breathe, Dalton said, "Young grasshopper, the only thing getting fucked this weekend is your mind."

"We were just messing with you," Lisa said. She and Dalton shook hands. "Bravo to you, sir, for your exquisite portrayal of a horny pig bastard."

"Why, thank you. And I must say you play quite a convincing skank."

"You two are hi-lar-i-ous." I said sarcastically.

It was nice having Lisa and Dalton meet. It was also weird having two of my worlds collide. It's like they each knew a completely different aspect of me, but not all of me.

"So what's the plan for tonight?" Lisa asked.

"I thought we would come back downtown and walk around. There's always something going on, especially now that the tourists are starting to come around. Dalton, is that good for you?" I asked.

"Do with me what you will. I'm all yours."

I spotted him as soon as he walked in the door. I hadn't told Noah about Dalton and vice versa. The subject just never came up. Besides, I wasn't with either one of them like *that,* but it didn't stop me from feeling as if I had just gotten caught doing something I shouldn't, especially since I was sitting next to Dalton.

"Tweet?"

"Noah, hey." His eyes immediately zeroed in on Dalton. "Noah, you remember Lisa?"

"Yeah, hey. How are you?"

"Hello, *The* Noah. I'm good," she answered. He smiled at her nickname.

"And this is Dalton," I said.

"Hi. You and Lisa are together?" Noah asked.

"No, actually …"

Oh shit! Dalton loves to mess with people no matter the consequences.

Draping his arm around my shoulders, he pulled me into his chest. "… my young grasshopper and I hook up every Monday." He followed this bit of info with a smirk aimed right at Noah. Noah looked like he was about to lift Dalton right out of his chair.

"Yep, we've been at it for about two months, right?" He looked over at me. "Our time together wears me completely out."

Noah started working his jaw and clenching and unclenching his fists.

"He's talking about chemo. We have chemo together on Mondays. Dalton, tell him it's chemo," I begged.

"Is that what the kids are calling it these days?" Lisa was trying to hold in her laughter while I panicked. Noah looked like he was ready to beat Dalton to a pulp. "I'm just messing with you, dude. We have chemo together. That's all. Unless you consider the blow job in the supply closet a relationship."

"Tweet, can I talk to you for a minute? Outside." Just then Noah's name was called. It was Brooke.

She walked up to our table, not acknowledging any of us. "Our table is ready."

"I'll be right there."

She looked at the faces around our table and then focused on me. "Hey Amanda, how's the leg?"

"Still lost."

Brooke liked to bring up my amputated leg a lot. She wanted to appear as if she had a caring heart while at the same time reminding Noah that I was damaged goods.

She wrapped her scrawny hands around Noah's muscular arm and said, "Come on before somebody else steals our table."

"Go sit down. I'll be there in a minute." She huffed and puffed, and stomped off. "Tweet, outside." He turned and walked away, not waiting for me.

Once outside, I found Noah running his hand through his hair. "Who is that asshole?"

"He's not an asshole. He was just joking around. He does that."

“He likes joking around about fucking you?” His voice was harsh and angry. I wasn’t sure where this was coming from. “Is he?”

“Is he what?”

“Fucking you?”

“Where the hell is this coming from? Dalton and I are friends. He was joking around. What’s wrong with you?”

“I don’t like guys talking about you like that. I don’t like him.”

“Well, I do like him and he’s helping me get through all the shit I’m dealing with right now. I need him.” It wasn’t my intention, but I could tell my words were like a punch to his stomach.

“You used to need me.” The hurt in his eyes crushed me.

“Noah, I always need you. It’s just... Dalton understands exactly what I’m going through. This is ridiculous. I’ve watched Brooke climb all over you every chance she gets and she loves to constantly remind me that I have a limb chopped off. Now I have someone in my life to take …”

“My place?”

“No. No one will ever take your place. Why can you have someone and I can’t?”

He leaned in so close, our noses were touching. “May I remind you, sweetheart, I never wanted someone else. That was your call.” He pushed passed me and headed back into the café.

The rest of the weekend went a lot better. Lisa and I went shopping Saturday and we met up with Dalton for dinner and a movie that night. It was great having Lisa around. I missed her. Even though we texted and talked on the phone every few days it wasn't the same as being together.

It was Sunday night before Monday chemo. Dalton and I were hanging out at the apartment, eating pizza and listening to music. We had started spending the Sunday before our *on* weeks together. Chemo was bad enough, but the night before was a close second. That's when the dread set in because we knew the next week was going to be hell. Dalton and I helped each other focus on other things.

"You're right, grasshopper. Lifehouse is a hell of a group."

"Ah, the student becomes the master and the master becomes the student." Dalton picked up a pillow from the sofa and popped me with it.

I started gathering up our leftover pizza to put in the kitchen. "So why aren't you and Mr. Perfect together?" My head snapped involuntarily in his direction.

"Wow! Not into subtle transitions, are you?"

"I don't have time for that shit. Answer the question."

"Um ..." I sat back down on the sofa.

"Small dick? Is that what it is?" He tilted his head to the side with mock sympathy across his face.

"No," I said.

"Dick too big? You know a lot of people think it's size that matters, but that's not true. You could be hung the size of a baseball bat, but if you don't know how to swing it, then it's just a dried up piece of wood. If you know what I mean," he said, raising his eyebrows and tilting his head again. I just stared at him. The things that came out of his mouth sometimes were truly amazing, and not in a good way.

"It's complicated."

"What's so complicated? He gets nekkid. You get nekkid and …" He suddenly stopped talking in mid-sentence. I looked over, concerned. He was staring straight ahead, not moving. I knew he had had seizures before and thought he might be having one now.

"Dalton? Are you okay?"

Keeping his gaze still and focus ahead, he held up his index finger and said, "Hold on … I'm still picturing you nekkid."

Slapping his upper arm, I yelled, "Dammit Dalton! That's not funny."

"So where was I? Oh yes. You both get nekkid and get bizzzaaay." He paused for a moment, looking at me with sincerity. Seriously, what's the deal?"

I let out a deep sigh and debated whether or not to answer his question.

"Noah and I have always been best friends. I need him in my life. If we were to cross that line and something happened to break us up, I wouldn't be able to survive it. I would rather keep him in my life as a friend, than risk losing him completely. And I would lose him because I would do something to ruin things. I always do."

Dalton studied my face for a few seconds. I saw his eyebrows slowly scrunch together, his eyes narrowed at me as his lips formed in to a straight line. "Amanda, that is the stupidest and lamest shit I have ever heard."

"It's true. My sister and her friend dated and it ended badly.

They hate each other now. Emily is perfect at everything. If she couldn't make it work then I sure as hell can't. Noah deserves better than that."

He twisted his entire body around to face me. "Ah young grasshopper...perfection is an illusion nurtured by insecurities." I looked at him as if he had gone insane. "Emily's not perfect."

"You don't have to say that to make me feel better."

"I'm not. She's got a crazy left eye."

"What are you talking about?"

"I noticed it the first time I met her. I looked her in the eye. Her right eye looked at me, but that left eye was all over the place. It freaked me out." He made a goofy face and rolled his eyes all around, causing me to laugh out loud.

"I've never noticed that before."

"Maybe the guy she was dating got freaked out by the crazy eye."

"I don't know. She never said what happened."

"Now that we have established that Emily is a circus freak and not perfect, you can't use her as an excuse. So, answer the question."

We sat there several minutes before I was able to answer. I wasn't comfortable talking to Dalton about Noah, but once he started a conversation, he wouldn't let it go.

"I've never measured up to be what I feel he deserves and now with the amputation and cancer … I don't want to be a burden."

"Stop making excuses because you're scared. Why don't you let him decide the type of life he wants and who he wants in it?"

"What are you talking about?"

"Amanda, you can't do anything about the past and people like us, don't know if we have a future. The past doesn't exist anymore.

All we have is the present. The present's perfect, young grasshopper, because we're breathing, moving, laughing, crying, and are surprised when we finally meet someone we connect with. Stop living in the past and wasting your present. You need to tell Noah how you feel."

"What if it's too late and Brooke is the one who makes him happy?"

"It doesn't matter. He deserves to know how he impacted your life. He gave you a gift. You know what it feels like to love someone. That doesn't come along every day, at least not the real kind. You need to go thank him for that before you have to say goodbye. Everyone deserves a thank you and goodbye."

The recognition I felt when he said those last few words ran like a shockwave through me. I wrote that exact same thing in my journal when Noah's dad died.

"*Come Away With Me*" by Nora Jones started flowing out of the speakers. Dalton stood, holding his hand out to me. "Let's try out that new leg. Dance with me," he said.

I slid my hand into his. He led me to the middle of the room. As I stepped into his chest, we wrapped our arms around each other. I laid my head on his shoulder as he lowered his and rested it between my neck and shoulder.

As the sultry voice of Nora Jones swirled around the room, we began to sway. The movement was so slight, it was almost imperceptible. I closed my eyes and let the feel of the music and his body against mine take me over. Present perfect.

As the song came to an end, Dalton whispered in my ear, "I'm so glad I was here long enough to meet you. Thank you for giving me someone to miss."

We pulled apart slightly, but kept our arms wrapped around

each other.

"I wouldn't be able to get through this without you. The one good thing about all of this has been that you were brought into my life." He leaned his forehead against mine and we stayed this way for several minutes after the song ended.

Dalton lifted his head, kissed my forehead and whispered, "I better go."

He walked toward the door. Before opening it, he turned and looked at me. "Always remember present perfect, grasshopper." A beautiful smile appeared on his face before he turned away and left.

It had been a week since Dalton and I had danced together at the apartment. Something changed that night between us or maybe I just finally realized it that night. Dalton was my soul mate. I was supposed to meet him when I did. Dalton and cancer had forced me to think differently, see the world differently, and see myself differently.

No, I wasn't perfect and never would be, but that's fine. There are more important things in life than chasing after this myth of perfection. Perfect is in the eye of the beholder. I had wasted enough time trying to control things in my life and it was exhausting. The only thing I could control was myself. If I put myself out there and got hurt, then I got hurt. At least I won't be living with regret.

So, here I am standing in front of his door, ready to put myself out there. I wasn't sure what I was going to say, hopefully something would come to me. I had just texted him, letting him know I was standing at his door. I raised my hand and knocked. When he opened the door, a long breath escaped my body. He stood there shirtless, in worn jeans, and his hair tousled. We stared at each other. Even though I had texted him, he looked surprised, he had no idea why I was there. I took in a deep breath. The time had come, no regrets.

"I love you. I've loved you from the first moment we met. I love you deeper every time I see you. And, I know the timing is awful, but there's never a perfect time. So, no matter what happens, I needed you to know how I feel." I finally exhaled.

He looked completely stunned. My instinct was to get the hell out of there, but I stayed and waited for his response.

It felt like we stood there for hours before he whispered, "Tweet ..."

No sooner had Noah said my name than I heard his name being yelled. I looked around him and saw Brooke wrapped in a sheet, stomping into the room.

"Oh my god! I thought you were alone. I only saw your car out front." I turned to leave when I felt him grab my arm.

"Tweet, don't leave. Just give me some time. Brooke, let's go in the other room."

"YOU READ HER TEXT WHILE YOU WERE FUCKING ME!!!" Brooke screamed.

"My phone was on the bedside table. I just glanced over at it."

"Then, you almost broke your fucking neck jumping off of me to get to the door."

I couldn't stand there any longer. I turned, ran to my car, and peeled out of the driveway. My head was spinning and adrenalin was pumping through my body. That went worse than I could have ever imagined. By far, that was the most embarrassing and humiliating thing I've ever experienced, and that includes being a part of Brad's *bag a virgin* bet. Wow, the first time I open up and tell a guy I love him, it had to be seconds after he was on top of his girlfriend.

ENTRY 33

SOME DAYS ARE WORTH A DO OVER, IN A GOOD WAY.

Idiot! I should have known he was busy when he didn't text me back. I went straight home, changed into my lounge pants and t-shirt, crawled into bed, and pulled the covers over my head.

I opened my eyes to moonlight shining through my window. I must have fallen asleep because I woke up to the sound of my phone blowing up. I reached over, grabbed it, and tried to focus on the screen. It was full of voicemails and texts from Noah. I needed some time before listening to and reading them. I fell back in the bed and tried to clear the sleep out of my head.

Finally, I got up, grabbed a diet soda, and tore into a bag of chocolate Sweet Sixteen doughnuts. I needed caffeine and sugar. As I sat there running the last few hours over in my head, it dawned on me that I wasn't sorry for telling Noah I loved him. What I hated was seeing Brooke with a sheet wrapped around her, coming out of his room, a room that I had grown up in and had fallen in love with him in. I'm not stupid. I knew they had been having sex since the first month they started dating, but as long as I didn't see evidence of it, I could pretend it wasn't happening. A loud rapid knock jolted me from my thoughts.

When I opened the door, he was leaning against the doorframe, wearing jeans and a soft gray t-shirt. It was simple, but there was something about Noah in jeans and that shirt that left me breathless.

"Hi," he said. His expression wasn't giving anything away, it stayed neutral.

"Hi," I whispered. Blood was pulsating through my body so rapidly it made me lightheaded.

"Brooke broke up with me," he said, bluntly.

"Oh god, Noah, I'm sorry. I should have waited until you texted me back before barging over there. What did you say to her?"

"Goodbye." His eyes were smoldering and his lips had just the hint of a grin. He pushed off of the doorframe, revealing a plate with a huge piece of chocolate cake on it that he had been hiding.

Once inside, he kicked his leg back to close the door, never once breaking eye contact. I walked backwards as he confidently strode toward me. "Where's Emily?" he asked.

"She went to Hilton Head for a girl's weekend."

He backed me up against the counter that separated the living room from the kitchen. He sat the cake down and placed both hands on either side of me, as he leaned in close. "Did you mean everything you said to me?"

"Every word of it," I said breathlessly. My heart was pounding so hard and fast it caused my body to vibrate.

"I can't believe it. You're finally mine," he said, astonishment in his voice.

"I was always yours."

"I know, but now we can touch and do *things* to each other and you won't stop … You won't stop, right?"

"I'm done stopping. It's full throttle from here on out. What kind of *things* were you thinking about doing?"

"The first thing involves you naked and that chocolate cake." A wicked smile crept across his beautiful face. "What changed?" he asked.

"Do you really want to talk right now?"

"I figured I'd better get the talking out of the way because once my lips are on your body, they aren't leaving it for quite a while."

"Oh my," I sighed, breathlessly.

We stared for a few moments, taking each other in. I don't think either of us could believe what was about to happen.

"Fuck it. I don't care what it changed," he said.

Noah's tongue plunged into my mouth. He grabbed my hips and held them securely while grinding into me. I was already wet and we still had several layers of clothes between us. My fingers twisted their way into his soft dark hair as our loud breaths and moans filled the room. Dipping down slightly, Noah's hands slid up my thighs, over my hips, and then to my ass.

Against my lips, he said, "Wrap your legs around me, baby." I opened my legs as he lifted me up and wrapped them tightly around his waist. I needed him closer. Now.

We headed straight to my bedroom and over to my bed.

I slid down his body until my feet touched the floor. Our lips stayed connected the entire time. It amazed me how lost in him I could get in a matter of seconds. Leaving his hair, my hands traveled down his back. I grabbed the hem of his shirt and started pulling it up. Noah broke from my lips long enough to raise his arms and help me peel his shirt off. I could feel the shiver run through his body as my hands ran over his bare skin. It caused me to shudder. Noah looked at me and smiled at the way our bodies affected each other.

His tongue slipped between my lips and into my mouth, slowly and deeply before his lips started the journey across my jaw and down my neck. He ran his nose up and down my neck a few times whispering, "You're beautiful. I love you more than anything else in this world."

I was so overwhelmed with joy and desire at hearing his words that I almost started crying. I couldn't believe this incredible man was mine and he loved me. He smoothly moved down between my breasts and came to rest on my stomach. Lifting my shirt slightly, he nuzzled into me. His tongue started to circle my naval as he placed soft kisses over my stomach.

My fingers clenched his hair as I moaned, "Oh god, Noah." I swear, I almost came right then and there. I could feel his lips smiling against me. His hands ran up and down my ass, lightly squeezing as his tongue continued swirling around. I looked down at him enjoying the taste of me. Heat and moisture spread between my legs with such intensity, I wasn't sure how much more I could take before coming undone.

I felt his fingers slide under my waistband. Noah's lips followed the path of my pants as they slid down my legs. He ran the tip of his tongue along the top of my thighs and then lightly kissed between my legs. My knees buckled and I landed on the bed. My body felt like jelly. He slid my pants the rest of the way down and off, leaving me in my t-shirt and panties.

His hands stroked up and down my legs slowly. I noticed him staring at my prosthesis. I took in a big gulp of air causing him to look up.

"Are you okay with me taking this off? I won't if you don't want me to." Concern and love flowed from his eyes.

"It's pretty cumbersome, so I guess off would be best," I said, my voice shaky.

He pushed the button on the side of the leg to release the pin that held it securely on to the liner and then began to peel the liner off of me.

Pulling back slightly, I said in a timid voice, "Noah, I should go in the bathroom and take care of the liner."

"I can do it. I want to." A few tears escaped and trickled down my face. "What's wrong, baby? You look so scared. Breathe, Tweet. It's me."

My voice began to crack. "The liner is made of silicone and it gets hot when I wear it. It makes me sweat." I tried to swallow back my sobs as much as possible, but I was so embarrassed. No one wants sweaty body parts before making love, during, sure, but not before. "Please, let me go and take care of it."

"What do you usually do?"

"I wash it with soap and warm water."

He got up, bent down, kissed me, and then whispered, "I want to take care of you in every way."

He walked into the bathroom and came back with a warm soapy washcloth and a towel. Noah peeled the liner off and set it to one side. He took the warm washcloth and began wiping off my left leg. When done, he wrapped the fluffy towel around my leg, gently massaging as he dried it off. I kept my gaze down, not making eye contact with him. I felt completely vulnerable and exposed.

Noah took my chin between his fingers and tilted my gaze up to meet his. "We don't have to do this if you're not ready."

"I'm nervous."

"Why?"

"Because it's you and I want to be sexy and beautiful for you." He looked at me confused. "A prosthetic leg is not exactly hot, neither is an amputated leg."

His eyes slowly scanned up and down my body, then back up to meet my eyes. He stared at me for several seconds, then said, "I've been waiting years for this moment, do you really think something like that's going to stop me? You are and have always been the most beautiful and sexiest woman I've ever known. I love you. I love everything about you- not just your legs, or arms, or eyes, or heart, or humor, or intellect. I love all of it. I love all of you. That will never change." Tears were trickling down my face. Then with a flirtatious grin, he said, "Besides, I've never been much of a leg man. I'm more of a breasts kind of guy and yours are phenomenal." Laughter burst out of me while I wiped away my tears.

"I love you, Noah."

"Say it again." He moved closer to me.

"I love you, Noah." I looked up at him, smiling.

"One more time." He moved in until there was no space between us.

"I love you, Noah."

His lips crashed into mine and our tongues collided with such force that it pushed me back slightly. I wrapped my legs and arms around him, pulling him against me. I ran my teeth along his jaw to just under his ear. Grabbing his earlobe between them, I bit down lightly, and whispered, "I need you inside of me."

Standing, he slipped off his shoes while I worked on his jeans. I slid both my hands down over his perfect jean covered ass, and then moved toward his zipper. His jeans hung just slightly below the top of where his V started. I nibbled and licked across his abs down to his V as my hands worked on his zipper.

I was so focused that I was surprised when I felt him grab both my wrists and pull them away, halting my progress. Bending down, he kissed me. "I've wanted to get my lips on you for years. Let's take our time. I want to taste every inch of you, slowly."

Noah knelt in front of me on the floor, sitting back on his heels, our eyes staying connected the entire time. He raised my left leg up slightly and began placing soft feather light kisses over it. His lips traveled slowly up, alternating between my inner and outer leg, until they reached the top of my thigh. Then he gave my right leg the same attention.

He started at the tip of my toes, traveling up my ankle, my calf, and over my knee until he reached my upper thigh, placing the same feather light kisses along the way. I was completely breathless as I leaned back on to my elbows and watched him continue his ascent. His lips moved slowly and methodically from hip to hip. He showed my body complete love and reverence. I had never experienced anything like this before. I felt beautiful, sexy, loved, and protected. I felt worshiped.

As he moved up my stomach, my shirt slid up and over my breasts exposing my pale yellow lace bra. I felt vibrations emanating from his chest and then heard a low deep growl that made me shiver. My elbows slipped out to the side of me, causing me to land flat on my back. This was the second time I almost came undone and we still had a few items of clothing on. He really was taking this painstakingly slow and I loved it. I loved him. I raised my arms over my head as Noah slipped my shirt the rest of the way up and off.

Grabbing around my waist, he lifted me towards his chest, and placed me farther up on the bed. He hovered over me for several seconds, with a look of admiration, before leaning down to kiss the skin just above my breasts. He kissed his way over my shoulder as he slid my bra strap off, repeating the movement on the other side. I lifted up slightly so he could unclasp my bra. The feel of the material sliding across my hard nipples made me shudder. I laid there completely exposed except for my panties and didn't feel at all embarrassed or awkward.

Noah lowered his head and wrapped his lips around one nipple sucking on it hard while his thumb circled the other. He released my nipple and then looked at me. His beautiful light blue eyes were beginning to glisten, causing mine to do the same. I had never felt this all-consuming love before.

We stared at each other for several seconds before Noah whispered, "Thank you for finally letting me love you."

We devoured each other's mouths briefly then he worked his tongue back down my body. I felt his teeth skim over one hip, hooking my panties while on the other side his fingers did the work. As they slid down, Noah glanced up at me and said, "You won't be needing those for a while."

Sitting back on his heels, he grabbed my right leg, raising it up towards his lips. His hands moved smoothly up my outer legs as he kissed his way up to my inner thigh. I could feel my body tense up with anticipation. The throbbing between my legs was almost unbearable. He lowered my leg and positioned himself between them. My back arched up off the bed as my hands began fisting the sheets. Noah's lips and tongue flicked and sucked me as my body writhed uncontrollably. The only verbal communication between us was moans of satisfaction. The more my body tossed back and forth, the faster his tongue moved until he plunged it deep inside of me.

"NOAH!" I screamed as wave after wave of sensation had my body convulsing. He pulled back slightly and I could feel the puff of air against the area as he chuckled.

His lips traveled up my body, slowly, finally landing on my lips. Looking down at me, he said, "You're my favorite taste in the world."

"You didn't get those moves from Wal-Mart," I said, my breaths coming out heavy as if I had run a ten mile race.

"I had to up my game for my number one girl." The look in Noah's eyes was heart stopping. It was the perfect combination of hunger and love.

He climbed off the bed and quickly stepped out of his jeans and boxers. My breath hitched when I first saw him. I had never seen completely naked Noah before. His body was as perfect as his heart and I was mesmerized. Sucking in my bottom lip, my eyes ran up and down his body.

Noah caught me staring and asked, "What are you looking at, Tweet?"

"What?" I looked up and saw the biggest sexiest grin I had ever seen. The blush ran across my cheeks and I shifted my gaze away from him.

Crawling back on top of me, he said, "I like looking at you too … and undressing you … and kissing you … and running my tongue all over you, tasting you."

Turning my head to the side, I closed my eyes, enjoying his words and how he felt between my legs.

His warm breath drifted over my neck. "Tweet, look at me." I opened my eyes gazing up at him. "I need to see you, hear you, and feel you, so I know this is real, and I don't have to pretend anymore."

I swallowed a big gulp of air. I had never made eye contact with the other guys I had been with. I kept my eyes closed when we had sex, because I always pictured Noah. Looking into the other person's eyes seemed too intimate to share with anyone, but him.

His hips began to rock as he slid into me, slow and gentle at first then faster and faster, as we held eye contact. "You feel incredible, baby. We fit perfectly," he panted against my lips.

"I love you so much, Noah."

We came together. It was the longest and most powerful climax I had ever experienced. By the look on Noah's face, it was the same for him. We laid there, still, our foreheads resting against each other, trying to calm our breathing. All of a sudden a wave of sadness crashed over me and tears started running down the side of my face. "I'm so sorry," I whispered.

"There's nothing to be sorry about." He kissed my tears. "Don't cry, Tweet."

"I wasted so much time and hurt you."

"Nothing has ever been a waste when it comes to you. Not my time, my thoughts, or my heart. I don't regret anything about my life with you, even the times we were apart. Those times showed me how much I belonged to you. I knew we would be together one day. I just had to be patient and wait. And you were so worth waiting for."

Noah and I *were* a perfect fit. In fact, we managed to fit together three more times before leaving the bed.

I still had cancer and a few more chemo treatments, but life was beautiful. By my side, I had the love of my life, my soul mate, my hero and what could be more perfect than that?

"I love your hair like that."

"It's just piled on top of my head and pinned. It's a mess."

"I like you all messy," he said, as his lips skimmed up and down the side of my neck.

It took some convincing, but I finally talked Noah into taking a bubble bath with me. He was all onboard with getting naked in the water with me. But he wasn't sure about the bubble part. My tub was a fairly large one, so he was able to stretch out in it. I was on his lap, facing him. Bubbles were splashing against us.

We were eating chocolate cake. I had just given him a forkful with lots of frosting. I noticed a little bit still on his lips. I leaned in and sucked his bottom lip into my mouth. "This is the best way to eat cake," I said as I continued to devour his lips. A deep moan escaped him. I could feel him getting hard underneath me. He brought his hands up to my cheeks and pulled his lips away.

"Is everything alright?" I asked.

"I'm with the woman who I love and adore, who also happens to be hot as hell. There's nakedness and cake involved. What could be better?" He paused for a few seconds. "You never got a chance to answer the question I asked earlier about what changed."

"My perceptions. I've wasted a lot of my *present* holding onto past perceptions and trying to second guess the future, so it wouldn't catch me off guard. It's like I grew up, but my perception of myself and other people never changed. I always felt everyone else was better than me, that they had all the answers, but wouldn't share them with me. Then I got sick and met a friend who shared his answers. The only thing perfect is our present because we're breathing, moving, loving, feeling. And we're able to let the people in our lives know how much they mean to us."

"Every time I'm around you, you touch my soul. I didn't think I could love you more, but when I found out you were …" He swallowed hard. I saw a tear trickle down his face. I raised my hand and touched his cheek, wiping away his tears.

"Noah …" My voice was shaky and tears began to pool in my eyes. "I don't want another day to go by without you knowing how much I love you. I've wasted my life up to this point not letting you know that I've loved you ever since March 23, 1990. I don't know what the future holds, but I'll never stop loving you. I don't know how."

"Tweet, put it down." The look in his eyes was determined and full of desire.

"Huh?"

"The cake, put it down. Now."

I sat the cake on the side of the tub. Noah reached behind my neck, pulling me against him. Our lips came together and our tongues knew exactly where to go and what to do. Grabbing his shoulders, I lifted myself up and then slowly sunk down onto him as his mouth and hands found my already hard nipples.

"This is the best bubble bath in the history of bubble baths," I moaned.

ENTRY 34

NOAH HAS 99.9% OF MY HEART. THE REST WILL ALWAYS BELONG TO A SPECIAL BOY WHO CHANGED MY LIFE FOREVER.

I still spent time with Dalton on the Sundays before chemo. It gave me comfort and strength to face another treatment.

"Dalton, I did it. I told Noah I loved him and he loves me. I wasn't too late."

I knelt, placing the flowers down and ran my hand over his name. Dalton Michael Connor.

The night I danced with Dalton was the last time I saw him. When I went to chemo the next morning, I found out he had died in his sleep, just a few hours after leaving me.

Dalton was the first cancer funeral I went to. He had planned it himself. There was a cover band that played The Stones, AC/DC, and of course, Whitney Houston. There wasn't a day that went by that I didn't miss him. I realize now that what I felt between us that night was Dalton giving me my thank you and goodbye. But most of all, he was giving me my life with Noah.

Entry 35

See ya, goodbye, adios, sayonara,
good riddance, ciao and good night to you.

My chemo finally came to an end just before summer. To say I was ecstatic would be an understatement. Other than my memories of being in treatment alongside Dalton, I wanted that part of my life to be over. I still believe that everything happens for a reason, even the bad stuff. And I'll always be grateful for the lessons cancer taught me, for the people it brought into my life and the bright light it cast on those already in my life, so that I could see how deeply their love for me was. I was ready to start back at school and make a life with Noah. Cancer had given me a second chance and I wasn't going to waste it.

Noah and I were inseparable. Other than when he was in class, we were together. I guess we were trying to make up for all the time we weren't a couple. We decided to move in together. His dad had left him enough money for a sizable down payment and then some, so he bought a condo in the same community as his friend Carter, which was great because we weren't far from Emily. And Emily and I were closer than ever. The support and strength she gave me during the worst of my treatment was incredible. I couldn't have survived it without her.

Noah and I moved into our place July 1, 2009 It was one of the happiest days of my life.

He was eager to graduate early and start medical school, so he took classes over the summer and worked a full time job as a transporter at MUSC, the medical school he would be attending.

I decided to take a couple of core classes when the fall semester started at the College of Charleston. I planned to find a school that offered a major in journalism through online courses. I wasn't going to leave Charleston, my family, and of course, Noah.

Over the summer, I did some freelance writing for a local magazine. It was great because I was gaining experience and making contacts. Life was good and busy. Busy is good because it means you're alive. That sounds like something Dalton aka Mr. Miyagi would say. That boy made quite an impression on me.

I reached my one year anniversary of being cancer free. I went in for monthly checkups at first, then it turned into every three months, and since I've hit the one year mark, I'll go every six months unless I have any trouble. I couldn't believe it had been a year and a half since the diagnosis and amputation. My artificial leg finally started to feel like a part of me.

I miss Dalton every day. Even though my chemo is over, I still go visit him on those Sundays before what would be our *on* week. I started volunteering once a week at the Hollings Cancer Center. I'd never be someone's Dalton because what he and I had was special and unique, but I can hold the hand of a scared child or listen to a teenager talk about her concerns about what lies ahead.

Noah graduated from the College of Charleston in three years with honors. I don't know who was more proud of him on his graduation day, me or his mom. Most likely, it was a tie. He was beyond excited to start medical school.

My second anniversary of being cancer free came and went without a lot of attention. I was glad. That meant I was no longer defined by cancer. Noah and I celebrated quietly with a dinner cruise around Charleston Harbor. It was nice spending an entire evening together. He'd been so busy with classes that he rarely had a free night. Medical school was more demanding than either of us thought it would be. But we would get through this together, piece of cake.

By my third anniversary cancer free I began to relax a little. I was more than halfway to the five year benchmark which I've been told is quite a mental turning point for cancer survivors. It feels like you can finally move on without being defined by the disease. I was sitting in Dr. Lang's office waiting for him. When Noah and I finally became an official couple, he went with me to the remaining chemo treatments and to every follow-up appointment, except for today.

He was up late last night studying. He didn't have classes until later, so I wanted him to catch up on his sleep. He'd be pissed when he woke up and discovered I snuck out of the condo and came here without him, but it wasn't necessary to always have someone by my side at every appointment. Everything had been going well and I felt great. Dr. Lang walked in and sat behind his desk.

"Noah didn't come with you today?"

"He was up late last night studying, so I let him sleep. He'll be mad, but he'll get over it."

"He's been with you at every other appointment. I assumed he would be with you today." He looked up at me.

I had gotten to know Dr. Lang pretty well over the past few years. I could tell in his eyes that he didn't have good news.

"Amanda, I think Noah needs to be here so we can talk. I'll have Gayle call him."

"No. Don't call him. He's sleeping."

"He'd want to be here." The door opened and his receptionist Gayle walked in. "Gayle would you call Noah Stewart and …"

I stood up abruptly and said, "Do not call him. He is sleeping." The tears stung my eyes.

That underwater feeling that I had almost forgotten about came rushing back. The doctor motioned to Gayle and she left us alone. I sat back down.

"Amanda, you're in no condition to drive yourself home. We need to discuss our plan of action. Noah needs to be here. We can call your parents too, if you like." I simply shook my head.

A half hour later Noah was sitting by my side, clutching my hand. "There were a couple of suspicious spots that showed up on your chest x-ray. The other tests show that the cancer is back. I'm sorry. I think another round of chemo is advisable," the doctor said.

Another round of chemo echoed in my head. Another round of chemo with the nausea and exhaustion. Another round of chemo, but without Dalton.

Even though I knew the stats and Dr. Lang never hid the fact that the cancer could come back, most likely in my lungs, I still fooled myself into believing I was free and clear at this point. My anxiety level had shot through the roof during the first year of checkups, but I had started to relax after the second anniversary.

"My recommendation is that we do what we did last time, ten cycles and …"

"I'm pregnant," I blurted out.

Dr. Lang looked up at me and Noah. He knew already.

"Yes, I realize that." He exhaled a deep breath. "I know that the recurrence comes as horrible and unexpected news. You're still early into the pregnancy." Noah and I glanced at each other. I think we were both still in shock because neither of us were understanding what he was suggesting. "You're both young and still have plenty of time to start a family."

"I'm having our baby."

"Amanda, you know how strong the chemo drugs are. The baby would be at an extremely high risk."

"Then I won't have the chemo until after the baby is born," I said

"Tweet …"

"I'm not going to kill our baby with chemo or any other way."

Dr. Lang stood and rounded his desk.

"I know this is a difficult decision. I'm going to step out for a bit, so you can have some privacy."

Once I heard the door click shut, sobs poured out of me. Noah rushed over and knelt in front of me. We wrapped our arms around each other, holding on tightly, I melted into him.

He kept repeating, "I love and adore you." His voice cracking as he held me and stroked my hair.

My only response was, "I'm sorry for getting sick again."

His arms tightened around me. I don't know how long we stayed like that. I was exhausted from the sobs, but I couldn't seem to stop.

"Tweet, you know I *want* our baby, but I *need* you. I want to have a life with *you.*"

"If I don't have our baby and I don't survive, then you'll be alone. I don't want you to be alone. I know it will be a lot, but my mom will help, and so will your mom, and Emily …"

"I could have the entire fucking city helping me, but if you're not with me I *will* be alone."

I looked into his beautiful light blue eyes with tears flowing from them nonstop, drenching his face. Those beautiful eyes were overflowing with love and fear.

Hours must have passed as we sat there, weighing all our options. When Noah and I left the office, we had made our decision. We knew it was going to be hard, but there really was no other option for us.

Entry 36

I love all the tools we now have to communicate.
Cell phones, texts, emails, Facetime, Skype, but there's
still nothing quite like a handwritten letter or note.
They're warm, cozy, and personal. Sure, it might take
longer for them to get to you,
but some things are worth the wait.

I was in the nursery curled up in the huge glider my parents had given us as a baby gift. I had two more months to go before I would meet this little one. I hoped that if my time here was coming to an end, that I would at least get to meet my child first, even if it was only for a brief moment.

Noah walked by and stopped in the doorway. "There you are. What are you up to?" he asked.

"I'm writing more notes."

"Why?" It was a knee jerk reaction. I smiled up at him. He

understood why I was doing this, but he wasn't comfortable talking about it.

"Don't do that," I said.

"Do what?"

"Play dumb. You're no good at it."

"Slapped in the face by my own words." He chuckled as he came over to me. Bending down, he kissed the top of my head. "Good. You can read them to her when she gets old enough to understand."

I looked up at him. It never ceased to amaze me how much I loved him. I've known him all my life and every day that passes, I love him more. And even if I'm not here, I will never stop loving my knight in plastic armor.

I knew Noah was terrified of the future. He didn't talk about it, but I could see it in his eyes every time someone brought it up. I wanted to still be a part of raising Halle even if I wasn't physically here. The day we walked out of Dr. Lang's office, we decided that I would wait to have chemo until immediately after Halle was born. It was risky since my cancer was so aggressive before, but it was a risk I had to take for our daughter.

I started writing notes to Halle that night. I needed to make sure I gave her, her thank you and goodbye, just in case I didn't get to meet her, and I knew that the present was the perfect time to make sure she would get that.

Notes to Halle

Halle,

I love you and I'm sorry I'm not able to be there to watch you grow into a beautiful intelligent woman. I'm writing you these notes for two reasons.

Reason one: Even though your daddy is a wonderful man, and you grandmothers and aunt Emily will be there to answer any questions, there are certain things that only a mother can teach her daughter. I will do my best to cover the most important topics.

Reason two: Even though your daddy has taken a ton of video of me for you to watch, I'm writing these notes because I want you to be able to take them with you wherever you go, so you can pull one out to read when you need me. My words will always be with you.

You have no idea how happy I was when I found out you were coming. I loved you from that second on. You were perfect because you were mine and your daddy's. I love him very much, Halle. I was blessed to have him in my life. When the doctor told me I was sick again, my first and only thought was to protect you. There was no way I would do anything to hurt you and keep you from meeting your daddy. I hope someday you understand my choice. I love you with my heart & soul.

Mommy

Halle,

Enjoy being a kid. There will be a lot of influences, like peer pressure and things you see on TV and in movies, pushing you to grow up. Don't feel pressured to do what they say. Have fun, laugh, make friends, and play. All the grownup stuff will still be there for you when you're ready for it. I love you.

Mommy

Halle,

I had my mother, your grandmother, sign a paper stating that she will in no way force you to wear a Halloween costume that is not of your choosing. Just to be on the safe side, your aunt Emily notarized it. When you're old enough, you will be able to go up to the doors, knock, and say trick or treat by yourself. There's no reason to be scared. There are no monsters behind any of those doors. I promise. I love you.

Mommy

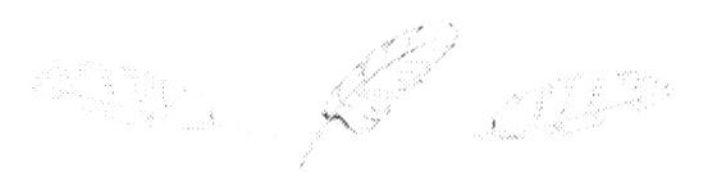

Halle,

Chocolate cake makes a lot of things in life better. Just don't eat too much. I love you.

Mommy

Halle,

Smart is cool and will never go out of style. Don't ever dumb yourself down for anyone. I love you.

Momma

Halle,

Friends: It's not the quantity, but the quality that matters. You will meet a lot of people throughout your life, not everyone will be your friend. That's ok. You'll know when you meet a true friend. True friends are trusting and loyal. They are there for you during good and bad times. They come in all shapes, sizes, and colors. It doesn't matter what they look like on the outside. The inside is where you find their true quality. I love you.

Momma

Halle,

Your daddy is a wonderful man. There's never been a time in my life that I didn't love him. We were pretty young when you arrived. What I'm trying to say is that one day, your daddy will probably find someone who makes him happy. He may even want to marry her. He deserves to be happy and in love. I want you to be happy for him. Don't be jealous. It doesn't mean he loves you any less. It just means his heart has healed. I love you.

Momma

Halle,

Don't let anything hold you back. Whether you have a passion for sports, art, or science, don't believe anyone who says you can't do it. If you want to play baseball, hockey, or football, don't let anyone tell you that you can't. If you want to play with Hot Wheel cars and Legos, then do it. Only you are the boss of you. (Technically, your daddy is the boss of you until you're 18, but you get my drift.) I love you.

Momma

Halle,

On the subject of fashion/makeup: With makeup, less is more is the general rule.

Fashion: Fewer, micro-mini, tight, lower are all words to avoid when looking for clothes.

Underwear is to be worn under your clothes. That's why it's called underwear and not outerwear.

Respect yourself and your body. Half shirts and short shorts are okay at the beach—if your daddy lets you out of the house dressed in them. I love you.

Momma

Halle,

Travel to other towns, states, and countries. Realize that your way is not the only way. Different doesn't equal bad or wrong. Be open minded and informed before making a decision. I love you.

Momma

Halle,

Expand your mind. Read something every day whether it's a book or an article. I love you.

Momma

Halle,

Go against the grain and be confident. You don't need to be a size 2, with blonde highlights, and big boobs. Being different and unique has gotten a bad rap. Different and unique equals original and rare. There is not another Halle

Marie Stewart in the world like you. No one else will see the world like you do. Nurture your originality, don't ever bury it away. I love you.

Mom

Halle,

Don't compare yourself to others and don't let others compare you. Believe in your abilities. Set your goals and work hard toward them. You won't always reach them and that's okay. If you did your best then you should be proud of that. You may not get the trophy, but the ribbon for participation is pretty cool. I love you.

Mom

Halle,

You may hear, on occasion, your daddy use a term that involves the word "Smurf." Don't repeat that word … especially to your grandmothers … or grandfather … or … just don't repeat it. I love you.

Mom

Halle,

Don't be afraid to love with all your heart. You risk getting hurt, but the benefits are worth the risks. Your daddy and granddaddy were the finest men I ever knew. Find a boy who you can say that about. When you find him, let him love you. We all have faults, parts of ourselves we don't like, but true love sees past all that and focuses on your heart. If you love someone, tell them. It doesn't matter if they say it back to you. Whoever makes you feel that deeply and that intensely, deserves to know how they've impacted you. I love you.

Mom

Halle,

You will have difficult times in your life, everyone does. I hope you have very few. Have a sense of humor. It will get you through those times. Don't run from difficulties. Getting through them builds strength and character. I love you.

Mom

Halle,

I'm proud of you. Whether you've decided to be a wife, mother, career woman or all three. (You most definitely can be all three.) I'm proud of the woman you've become. You're probably wondering how I could be proud of you when I'm not there to see how you turned out. I know you grew into a wonderful woman because I know the wonderful man who raised you. I love you.

Mom

Halle,

Find something/ someone that you'll miss. Because this means that your life was enhanced and that you cared. I miss you.

Mom

Halle,

People will tell you that there is one soul mate in the world for every person and when you find this person, you'll know and fall in romantic love. That's a load of crap. It's extremely rare to have more than one soul mate in your lifetime, but it's possible. And the soul mate doesn't have to be a romantic relationship. Sometimes in life, you meet people when you need them, and there is an immediate connection.I was lucky enough to have two soul mates in my life. Your daddy was the first, the love of my life. When I was 19, I met my second soul mate, a boy named Dalton. I never stopped loving your daddy. Dalton came into my life exactly when he was supposed to. He was only in my life for a short time, but he made an indelible impression on me.

I love you.

Mom

Halle,

Everyone deserves a thank you and goodbye. I love you.

Mom

Halle,

I wish I could have been there to wrap my arms around you when you were hurt and when you were happy. I wish I could have been there to wipe your tears away and to let you know things would get better while we ate a piece of chocolate cake. I wish I could have been there to share all your firsts with you. But where ever you go in life, I'll be with you through my words and in your heart and soul. You don't need to be perfect in your life, but always be present in it. The present is the most perfect gift you can have. I love you.

Mom

THE END

Epilogue

Five years later – Noah

I knew the exact day and time when I fell in love with her, March 23, 1990 at 10:59 pm. I have always loved her. As a kid, I didn't know that what I felt was love, I just knew that I got excited when I saw her and I wanted to see her all the time.

I also knew the exact date and time when I realized Tweet had turned into a girl and I turned into a horny bastard. May 27, 2004 at 7:03 pm.

Tweet and I were walking to our spot. She stopped suddenly. "See a penny, pick it up. All day long you'll have good luck," she said in a sing song voice.

I chuckled as she bent down to pick up the penny. When I looked down, I couldn't believe what I saw. The cutest, roundest, most beautiful ass in the world, that would fit perfectly in my hands.

She held the penny up proudly, like it was worth a million dollars. I couldn't help but stare at her smiling lips. Her pale pink, heart-shaped lips that I wanted to kiss. I stood there hypnotized as I thought of other parts that I wanted to kiss. Tweet was hot!

She wasn't skinny like a lot of girls at school. She had the right curves in just the right places. Her legs were great, but the best part of them was that they led to that beautiful ass. Her chocolate brown hair hit just below her creamy shoulders and was always so shiny. Her eyes were incredible. They were teal. I'd never seen anyone with eyes that color. When they looked at me, I swear they could see all the way into my soul. What the hell is wrong with me? I sound like a girl. Then I felt a twitching in my cargo shorts. Nope, I was definitely a red blooded, all American horny bastard.

I jolted from my fantasy when I heard her yell, "NOAH! ARE YOU COMING?"

"Yeah, I'm coming!" I walked several steps behind her. There was a lot more twitching going on in my shorts that she didn't need to see.

That entire summer, I spent a lot of time thinking about touching her, and trying my best to subtly touch her as much as possible.

Dear Noah,

I'm sitting here trying to figure out how to start this letter. I always hated that part of writing. The blank page is an ugly thing to stare at.

I was never sure about a lot of things in life except that I have always loved you. Every single minute of every single day that I have been on earth, my heart has belonged to you. It was never a question. Never a doubt. My love has taken on many forms over the years, but it was always constant. A gazillion books, articles, and poems have been written about love. We're led to believe it is complicated. It's not the love that's complicated. It's all the crap we attach to it, that makes it complicated. I'm sorry it took me so long to realize this.

Thank you for loving me. You've given me 1000 lifetimes of happiness. You showed me what it was like to be loved and to love. You are my strength, my hope, my peace, and my light. You are my everything.

Thank you for being my soul mate, the love of my life, and my friend.

Thank you for all the talks, the laughter, the music, and the quiet times in our spot.

Thank you for sharing your firsts with me.

Thank you for all the chocolate cake.

Thank you for all the tingles, vibrations, chills, shivers, and shudders you sent through me.

Thank you for holding my hand and for all the hugs. Thank you for my first kiss and thank you for my last kiss.

Thank you for being in my life. I'm sorry I had to say goodbye to you so soon. But you have Halle. She will give you strength and hope. You're going to be the best father.

Thank you for giving me something to miss.

I love you deeply and completely. Me not being there won't ever change that.

Goodbye, Noah.

I'll love you forever, Tweet

I was folding up the letter when Emily walked in the house. "Hey, Noah."

"Hey."

"What are you up to?"

"I was just reading this letter your sister wrote me."

Emily looked at me with sadness in her eyes. She had been incredible during Tweet's illness.

"So where's my sweet Halle?"

"She's in her room making sure she has just the right dolls for your girl's night."

"Well, that's very important." She paused, looking at me for a moment. "Hey, you okay?"

"Yeah, I'm just nervous for some reason," I said, chuckling slightly.

"It's going to be okay, you know. Why don't you let me keep Halle overnight? That way you can stay out as late as you want. It's been rough, Noah. You deserve a night not having to be somewhere at a certain time. Go and have fun."

"That'd be great, Emily. Thanks. I'll go pack a bag for Halle."

"I'll go do it."

Just then we heard small shoes pouncing down the hall. I loved to watch Halle do anything, but especially run. She did it with such purpose and determination.

"Emmie! Emmie! Emmie!" Halle yelled.

Halle was so excited to see her aunt. She loved spending time with Emily, doing girly things. She ran across the room crashing into Emily's open arms, which were waiting for a hug.

"Hey, chickadee. How would you like to spend the night at my place?"

"I would love it, but I have to pack more dolls."

"Of course, that goes without saying."

Halle turned her sweet little round face up to me. Concern etched all over it. "Daddy, what you doing tonight?"

"I have plans tonight. I'm going to meet a friend." Emily and I exchanged a knowing glance.

"I miss Mommy."

"I know, little bird. So do I. Listen, I need to get going. I'm meeting my friend and I want to get there a little early."

"Halle, let's go pack up more dolls and maybe even some pj's and a toothbrush," Emily said.

Halle put her small hand into Emily's and they started down the hallway to her room. I few seconds later Halle came barreling towards me. I picked her up and we wrapped our arms around one another. I squeezed her slightly and whispered into her hair, "I love you to pieces, little bird."

The most beautiful light blue eyes looked back at me. The corners of her tiny mouth curled into a bright smile and she said, "I love you to pieces too, Daddy."

I was so nervous on the ride over here that I had to wipe my palms on my pants a couple of times. I got out of the car and walked over to where we were meeting. I stood there trying to calm myself down. I stretched my neck from side to side, rolled my shoulders back and forth a few times, and took a few deep breaths. None of it really helped. Then I heard my name.

"Noah?"

I turned and stared at her. I swallowed the basketball size lump in my throat. My god, she was beautiful. "Hey," I said, smiling at her.

"Sorry I'm late. The traffic from the airport was pretty heavy." Standing there, she kept her smile on me, but her eyes took in the surroundings. "Um … what is all this?"

Keeping eye contact, I got to her in three quick strides, landing right in front of her. "Can't a guy do something special for his number one girl?"

Narrowing those incredible teal colored eyes at me, she said, "Yes, I believe he can."

"Welcome home, Tweet."

I placed one hand behind her neck while snaking my other arm around her waist, and pulled her against me as our lips crashed into each other. I loved kissing her. She was still my favorite taste in the world.

I pulled back and smiled when I heard her softly groan. We were both out of breath. Our lips were still touching when I said, "Did I ever tell you how much I hate it when you go out of town to work on an article?"

"Yeah, but the homecoming sex is pretty awesome." She winked at me.

I shook my head trying to clear the thought of her naked and lying underneath me. I had to get my head in the game. We were at our spot, so that would have to wait.

I had come out here earlier to scatter yellow rose petals around our table, and I tapped into the electricity wired over at the grill area and hung a few strands of small pale yellow lights in the trees above our table. The sun was beginning to set, so the lights were just now becoming visible. The table was set for two with white plates, silverware, a bottle of wine, two glasses, and a piece of chocolate frosted cake.

I grabbed her hand, turned, and pulled her behind me over to the table.

"Where's Halle?" She asked.

"Emily's"

I stopped in front of the table and reached over, turning the music on my iPhone on. I still had the same little speakers I used on our first date. I knew I'd use them again someday. I turned and pulled her into my chest as "*Everything*" began to play.

"She didn't want to come see me?"

"You know if I told her you were coming home today, she would have wanted to come with me and I wanted you all to myself for a while." She looked up at me and smiled, not saying a word. I placed a light kiss on her lips and whispered, "I've missed your lips."

"They've missed you too. All of you." She gave me a sexy grin.

We stayed that way for several minutes, barely swaying back and forth. I couldn't believe what I was getting ready to do, but it was time.

Swallowing hard, I hesitated for a moment. "Dr. Lang called today with the results of your tests." We stopped moving and stared at each other. "All clear again this year. That makes it four years cancer free." I almost choked on the words.

Even though the chemo after Halle's birth had worked and Tweet continued to be cancer free, these checkups were heart stopping and stressful. I thought I was going to lose her twice and those memories came flooding back with each follow-up.

She let out a deep sigh and said, "I hate this time of year. Even though my body has been clear, I guess I won't ever really be free from cancer."

I held her tighter. "I wish I could tell you that it will get better every year."

"Did you find your letter?" she asked.

"I did. Why did you finally decide to finally give it to me now?" She had left the letter on our bedroom dresser before leaving on her business trip.

"It felt like the right time. I was going to wait until I was five years clear, but why wait?" She looked up at me with piercing teal eyes that were now filling with tears.

I needed to turn this around. We should be celebrating, not thinking of the past.

"How do you want to celebrate your fifth anniversary?" I asked.

"We should do something special to celebrate. You know, go somewhere."

"How about a wedding?"

She looked at me with confusion. "A wedding? Whose wedding would we go to?"

"How about ours?"

I took a step back and got down on one knee. The look of pure shock on her face was priceless. I almost grabbed my phone to take a picture of her, but I wised up quickly enough to realize that probably wouldn't be a good idea.

"When I look into your eyes, I see everything I want and need. I wake up every day excited because I know I'm going to see you that day and be with you that night. And in between I get to spend time with you and our beautiful daughter.

Every second of every minute of every day, month, and year with you has been perfect. I love you. I adore you. And I want to spend the rest of my life making you happy." I paused for a moment as I slipped the yellow diamond ring out of my pocket. Looking up into her eyes I said, "Aman …"

"That's not what you call me. Don't try and change it now." Tears were streaming down her face.

"Tweet, will you do me the honor of being my wife?"

She couldn't get her words out, she was so choked up. She held out her trembling hand and I slowly slide the ring on her finger.

Standing, I grabbed her and gave her a slow deep kiss that left her breathless.

"I love you, Noah."

"Say it again."

"I love you, Noah."

"One more time."

"I love you, Noah." She paused for a few seconds. "I'm going to be Mrs. Tweet Stewart." She began to laugh at her own words. "I'm sorry for laughing. It just sounds so …"

"Perfect?" I said.

"As a matter of fact, it couldn't be any more perfect."

Turn the page for a preview of Brad's story:

Past Imperfect

Preview of Brad's story:

Past Imperfect

Prologue–Three Years Earlier

I was making a mental note of all the things I needed to get done this week. I had to stop by Jason's place and get the notes from Ethics class and then go get my car washed. I was supposed to meet Mom in thirty minutes for dinner. She was in town for business and must have been feeling guilty about something. When she thinks she's not being a good mother, which is a rare, she buys me something expensive. She'll ask a few inane questions, that I'll mindlessly answer, and then we will stare at each other for the next hour. This charade seems to soothe her guilt and at least I get a good meal out of it.

"Faster, Brad! I need it faster!" she moaned.

I'm going as fast as I can. I'm not a fucking hummingbird. She was the one who needed to hurry up. I liked Becca, okay, but she took forever to come. When we first started this "relationship," for lack of a better word, it was a challenge. I tried to beat my best time, but now I'm over it, and ready to move on. For the past three weeks I'd been dropping hints that things were coming to an end, but she didn't seem to be picking up on any of them. It wasn't that I didn't like having her around. She ran a lot of errands for me and did my laundry every week, which really freed up my time. But I could feel she was getting too attached and thinking we were something more than we were. So, this was it. One last goodbye fuck and I was out of her and here. That is, if she'd finish up already.

"I'm almost there," she yelled out.

"Becca, I have to meet my mom for dinner in like thirty minutes," I grunted.

I thrust into her hard one more time causing her to finally come unglued.

"Ooooh, Brad! I love you!" she screamed.

Shit, this was going to be awkward.

I started to climb off when her arms wrapped around my neck, stopping me.

"Don't move yet. Stay inside of me for a while." The grip she had on my neck was like a vise.

"I can't, Becca. I told you I have plans tonight."

I saw tears start to pool in her eyes as her grip loosened. I slid out and off of her as quickly as possible. I need to go ahead and let her know this was the end of the road for us. Tossing the condom in the trashcan, I quickly threw on my boxers and jeans. Glancing back, I saw her lying on her side, curled up in a ball, watching me. A few tears had managed to roll down her cheeks. I shrugged my shirt on and started to button it. I felt her eyes burning a hole in my back.

Regardless of what women think, it's difficult for a guy when he has to breakup with them. There were usually tears and either fury or begging. I'd rather deal with fury because it makes for a quick getaway and confirms that break-up was a good call.

The beggars were more difficult because I had to sit there and pretend to care while I listened to them whine—usually for a prolonged period of time. I'm always somewhat physically attracted to the girls I'm with, otherwise I wouldn't be fucking them. But things usually fell apart when they opened their mouths. I'd never been very interested in listening. The only exception had been Amanda Kelly. I really liked what came out of her mouth. I liked Becca, but I liked her more for her ability to get the wrinkles out of my shirts than anything else. I inhaled a deep breath before turning around. This was it, I couldn't put it off any longer.

As our eyes locked, I got a strange feeling that what I was about to do was going to hurt her more than it had the other girls.

I cleared my throat and said, "Becca, I think we're done."

"I know, you said you have plans and you're dressed already," she said quietly, struggling to hold her voice steady.

"I'm not talking about tonight. It's time we move on."

Slowly raising herself up onto her elbows, she blinked a couple of times in disbelief. "I don't understand."

Sweet Jesus, this girl's got a 4.0 average. Apparently, book smarts doesn't translate into real life comprehension.

"We should start seeing other people," I said as neutrally as possible. My intention was never to be mean, but if the chick pushed me, I had no problem laying it out there.

"I don't want to see other people. What did I do wrong?"

"Nothing. In fact, you do my laundry better than our maid."

"Is it because I said I loved you?" Panic was starting to surface in her tone. "You don't have to say it back right now, if you don't feel it yet."

The look in her eyes was pathetic. I don't understand why girls can't just let things go. Why do they need to dig and dig for an answer or an explanation until they force a guy to hurt them? I didn't have the time or patience to deal with a beggar today. I needed to turn her into a hater, so I wouldn't be late for dinner.

"Becca, the thing is I'm never going to feel it for you."

"Why?" Her voice cracked and tears were streaming down her face.

"Because, I'm just not." I glanced at my watch seeing the time ticking away as my impatience grew.

"But, I've always done everything you asked me to do and I don't think I've asked a lot of you. I don't need to hear you say the words, Brad. Just don't run because I said them."

"I'm not running because you said them," pausing for a moment, I knew what I was about to say would tear into her, but she left me no choice. "Becca, it was fun for a while, but now it's over. We were never anything more than fuck buddies, more emphasis on the fuck than buddies. I'm done and have been for a long time. Sorry, but I need to leave now or I'll be late for my dinner."

Not giving her a second to respond, I grabbed my jacket, turned, and was out the door in one fluid movement.

The next day I was pulling onto campus, headed to Jason's to pick up the notes he was lending me from class. I parked the car and started walking towards his dorm. As I rounded the corner I was met by a flurry of activity that made me stop. I recognized a lot of the faculty, staff, and students who were standing around talking. Suddenly, I felt a hand on my shoulder.

"Shit Brad, I've been trying to get in touch with you all morning," Jason said with relief in his voice.

"I've had my phone turned off since last night. I forgot to turn it back on." Mom outlawed cell phones at the dinner table. Or rather, she outlawed mine and my brother Peyton's cell phones, at the dinner table. She, on the other hand, needed hers close by for business. What a hypocrite.

"I'm really sorry, man. Are you doing okay?" Jason asked.

"Yeah, I'm fine. Why wouldn't I be?"

The look on his face morphed from concern, to confusion, to shocking realization.

"You don't know?"

"Know what?" I asked.

My gaze shifted away from him towards the crowd of people standing around the ambulance that I hadn't noticed before.

"It's Becca …"

Those were the last words I heard before seeing a white sheet covered stretcher, flanked by two paramedics coming out of the dorm across the parking lot. In one torrential downpour the sights and sounds flooded my senses. I heard crying, gasps, orders being yelled, car doors being slammed, and sirens.

Not looking at Jason, I asked, "What happened?"

"I'm sorry, Brad, I thought you knew. I mean I know you guys have been together for a while … I just assumed someone had already told you."

"Told me what?"

He placed his hand on my shoulder in comfort and said, "Becca killed herself last night."

"Fuck me."

DELETED SCENE FROM PRESENT PERFECT

FROSTING

I stretched my arm and reached out, but all I felt was air and a cool sheet. My eyes immediately shot open and I sat up, as if a nightmare had jolted me back to reality. The room was completely dark. I had no idea what time it was. While I tried to orient myself, my chest tightened as a sinking feeling took over my stomach. Please, don't let the past several hours have been a dream. Once my eyes adjusted to the darkness I saw a light coming from the other room. I got out of bed and quickly shrugged on my jeans. The feeling in my chest got heavier. I was afraid today had been a dream, that I was still in the dream, and it was about to turn into a nightmare. I left the room and walked in the direction of the light.

I stopped and turned, facing the kitchen. A deep breath of relief was released from my lungs. Today was real. She was here, right in front of me. She had on my t-shirt and boxers. Her dark hair was a tousled sexy mess hanging down over my shirt. Her back was facing me. I didn't say a word. I watched as the hem of the shirt shifted upwards slightly when she raised her hand to what I assumed was her mouth. The material skimmed over the top curve of her perfect ass. I tried to calm my rapidly accelerating breath as I watched this same movement a few more times.

I stood gazing at her, thinking how every part of my body and soul loved her. I knew if she didn't survive, neither would I. My throat began to tighten and burn as I tried not to let my emotions take over. Please, God, don't take her away from me, not now, when I just got all of her. I pushed away thoughts of losing Tweet. She froze when she heard the clearing of my throat. She didn't turn around immediately, though.

"What'cha up to, Tweet," I said, the smile obvious in my tone.

Slowly she turned in my direction. When she was completely facing me I felt a huge smirk take over my face. She was standing there, holding the rest of the cake we didn't finish earlier, with the fork sticking out of her mouth, looking like her secret had been discovered. Tweet standing there, looking like that, was either the most beautiful thing, the sexiest thing, or the most adorable thing I had ever seen. I decided it was all three.

She pulled the fork from her mouth. "I was just finishing up the cake. No sense in wasting a perfectly good piece of cake," she said with her mouth full.

I walked towards her. The look in her eyes shifted from "oh shit" I got caught to a smoldering "oh shit" I got caught. She was standing here in my shirt and boxers, wearing her prosthetic leg, and she felt sexy and beautiful. I could tell by the way she was looking up at me through her long dark lashes. I was so happy and proud of her for finally believing how much I wanted her, every part of her.

Holding her gaze, I took the cake and placed it on the counter, the same counter I backed her up against. Goose bumps were popping up all over her arms just as fast as her breaths were coming. Her eyes struggled a few times to stay locked on mine and not drop down to look at my chest. I grabbed her hips and lifted her up on to the counter. My palms fell to the marble as I leaned into her as close as possible without making contact. I ran my nose across her jaw and down her neck, breathing her in. Her scent was a cross between raspberry, vanilla, and chocolate. Neither of us had said another word since she turned around. Tweet and I didn't need a lot of words to communicate what each of us wanted right now.

I glanced down and watched as her chest rose and fell, her hard nipples strained against the material. I slipped my hands underneath her shirt. Raising her arms, she allowed me to peel it off. I stood back slightly and let my eyes roam up and down her body. I'd never get tired of looking at her. She began to squirm under my gaze. My eyes made their way back up to hers. There was a mischievous sparkle in them now along with a matching smirk across her pink well kissed lips.

She brought her chocolate covered index finger up to her lips. I swallowed hard several times as I watched and waited to see what she was going to do with all that frosting. The tip of her tongue slowly slipped between her lips and moved up her finger capturing some of the sweet. She closed her eyes and tilted her head back, letting out a long deep moan as the frosting disappeared into her mouth. *Fuck me.*

My palms were still flat on the counter, more for support than caging Tweet in. My dick was so hard pressing against my jeans, standing was becoming painful, but I wasn't about to move.

Opening her eyes, she looked at me and asked, "Do you want some?" She held her coated finger up while at the same time biting her bottom lip.

"Yes," I choked out in a hoarse voice.

I leaned in, but froze when she started to drag her finger across her chin and down her neck, leaving a trail of chocolate behind. *Fuck me twice.* My eyes, my heart, and my dick were all popping out. I didn't know how much longer I would be able to last before I grabbed her, ripped off those boxers, and buried myself deep inside her.

Her hand finally stopped moving, landing on one of her tits. My breaths were becoming shallow and leaving my lungs at a rapid pace. She ran her finger across the pointy hard nipple, coating it with chocolate. My hands had moved and were gripping the edge of the counter so tight my knuckles looked as if I had soaked them in bleach. My arms were shaking as I tried to hold back and wait for her to give me the go ahead. I watched as she gave the same treatment to the other nipple. I shut my eyes and bowed my head, trying my damnedest to stay in control. Not seeing her tits coated in chocolate didn't prevent me from thinking it or knowing it was right in front of me.

I snapped out of my fantasy when I heard her say, "Noah? I seem to have dropped some frosting on me. Could you help clean me off …?"

I didn't give her a chance to get the rest of her sentence out before I plunged my mouth on to her neck, taking her by surprise. Her gasps and giggles spurred me on. Taking hold of her hips, I slid her to the edge of the counter, her legs tightening around my waist, pulling me in close to her. After cleaning off her neck, my tongue moved to her chin, and then into her mouth. Our chests were pushed together and I could feel the frosting being smeared on mine. The thought of Tweet licking it off of me sent my motions into overdrive.

I pulled out of her mouth and headed to her chest, cleaning ever drop of frosting off of her body on the way. I swept my tongue across her nipple before my lips closed around it and I sucked it into my mouth. The moans coming from Tweet were like music to my ears. Her fingers were tangled in my hair, holding me firmly against her.

I pulled back slightly, gasping for air, and whispered against her skin, "Fuck, Tweet."

"Yeah, fuck me!" she moaned.

I lifted her up off the counter and yanked the boxers down her legs and off. When I stood back up, Tweet immediately grabbed the waistband of my jeans and pulled. I stumble forward, catching myself on the counter. As our tongues collided I felt my zipper open and her hand slip inside, stroking me. A deep growl caused my chest to vibrate against hers. I released her lips. Placing my hands at the back of her upper thighs, I lifted her up, bringing my mouth directly in line with her tits. Her arms encircled my head and her legs found their rightful place around my waist. I sucked off what frosting remained as I walked her over to the fridge, shoving her back against it.

I looked up as she gasped and jerk slightly. Big teal eyes gazed down at me. "It's cold," she said breathlessly causing me to chuckle.

I lowered her slowly on to me. Each time I slid inside her was better than the last and each time had been perfect.

Arching her back, she dropped her head back and said, "Faster, baby!"

I worked into her so fast and deep I thought my body was going to collapse. Sweat beaded up across both our bodies. I felt her body tense at the same time as mine and we came together yelling each other's name.

I rested my sweaty forehead against hers, both of us trying to calm our breathing down. I peered into her eyes and said, "We're definitely buying that kind of cake again."

"Definitely," she agreed, breathlessly.

About the Author

Alison G. Bailey

Alison was born and raised in Charleston, SC. As a child she used her imagination to write additional scenes to TV shows and movies that she watched. She attended Winthrop University and graduating with a BA in Theater. While at Winthrop she began writing one act plays which she later produced. Throughout the years she continued writing and producing several one act plays, but then life got in the way and she hung up her pen for a while. On the advice of a friend, she started writing again. In January 2013, Alison sat down at her computer and began writing her first novel, Present Perfect.

Alison lives in Charleston, South Carolina with her husband, Jef, and their two furry children (dogs). She's addicted to Diet Pepsi and anything with sugar.

Links:

-Facebook

https://www.facebook.com/pages/Alison-G-Bailey/223772144436171

-Goodreads

http://www.goodreads.com/author/show/7032185.Alison_G_Bailey

http://www.goodreads.com/book/show/17727279-present-perfect

-Twitter: @AlisonGBailey1

https://twitter.com/AlisonGBailey1

-Present Perfect Playlist

Present Perfect

http://open.spotify.com/user/1244737523/playlist/6n0dBZe7RKTbhXXmWcn1j1

-Pinterest:

http://pinterest.com/alisongbailey/present-perfect-by-alison-g-bailey/

-Blog

http://alisongbailey.blogspot.com/